It should have been perfect—Tristan and me and a remote log cabin with a crackling fireplace nestled on a west Arkansas mountain in December. No Clann or vampire council members nearby to bother us. No more rules or secrets to keep us apart. No more risk of accidentally killing Tristan with a [...]

Instead, it was all wrong.

* * *

PRAISE FOR THE CLANN SERIES

Covet

"*Covet* is a fresh take on the paranormal genre. Darnell made it interesting, giving strong voices to defined ch[...] Overall, I enjoyed *Covet,* and I think you will also."
—Michelle at *Dark Fairie Tales*

"Darnell has an excellent writing style that seamlessly brings the story together, allowing for the plot to develop at a natural pace, adding to the appeal of the story."
—Devin E., reviewer at *Kees2Create* (www.kees2create.com.au)

"The sheer depth of the raw emotion in *Covet* was absolutely staggering as I felt like I was being torn apart right along with the characters. This was an absolutely brilliant follow-up to *Crave,* and I highly recommend it."
—*A Book Obsession*

Crave

"An enticing mix of forbidden love, magic, betrayal, and heartache, this romance will leave you craving more."
—*Mundie Moms*

"Melissa Darnell has written a beautiful love story centered around the supernatural world. There is nothing sweeter than forbidden love…"
—*Realm of Fiction*

"A spellbinding, compelling, and completely enjoyable debut, *Crave* had me flipping pages until there were none left to flip."
—*Electrifying Reviews*

**Books by Melissa Darnell
from Harlequin TEEN**

The Clann series

(in reading order)

CRAVE
COVET
CONSUME

THE CLANN

CONSUME

Melissa Darnell

HARLEQUIN®TEEN

Recycling programs
for this product may
not exist in your area.

ISBN-13: 978-0-373-21087-9

CONSUME

Printed in U.S.A.

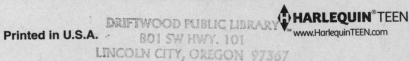

HARLEQUIN® TEEN
www.HarlequinTEEN.com

This one's dedicated to you, the readers of this series,
for all your awesome continued support and love for the world
and characters of The Clann series!

CHAPTER 1

SAVANNAH

I stared at the surrounding forest on Rich Mountain, one hand braced against the trunk of a leafless hardwood tree at my side, my too-quick breaths making puffs of fog in the afternoon air as the feeble sun edged beneath the winter-stripped branches of the tree line. The air was smoky, acrid with the false promise of comfort from the chimney of a cabin several yards behind me, which I was struggling to ignore during my few blessed minutes of solitude outside.

It should have been perfect.... Tristan and me and a remote log cabin with a crackling fireplace nestled on a west Arkansas mountain in December. No Clann or vampire council nearby to bother us. No more rules or secrets to keep us apart. No more risk of accidentally draining and killing Tristan with a kiss.

Instead, it was all wrong, and I was staggering under the weight of what we now faced.

We weren't alone here. My dad had come along, not for Tristan's safety or even my own, but for anyone else who might come too close and trigger the bloodlust within Tristan. If not for Dad's holding him back last night, Tristan might have slaughtered his own family in the Circle, the Clann's clearing and primary meeting place in our hometown woods where so much Clann and vamp blood had been shed only hours ago.

Just the memory of how Tristan had looked there—his once soft emerald eyes turned white-silver with need, his normally full lips stretched thin and baring newly formed fangs as he snarled with rage—forced a shudder to ripple through my body. Until that moment, I'd never seen a vampire lose control to the bloodlust. Now that I had, I would never forget it.

Coming to this isolated cabin hadn't been optional, and staying here promised to be anything but fun or peaceful. We'd had to load up Dad's car last night and come here immediately after the battle in the Circle just to get Tristan away from all humans before the bloodlust drove him crazy. Even stopping for gas had been a nightmare. Thank heavens Jacksonville, our East Texas hometown, was only a day's drive, so we hadn't been forced to stop often. Now that Tristan was a full vampire, his strength was far beyond my own thanks to his years of playing football and strength training before being turned. The one time we had stopped, I'd had to fill the gas tank so that Dad could hold Tristan inside the car and away from the humans in the gas station.

And afterward, the new mind connection had made it all so much worse, allowing Tristan to pick up my every thought while I silently struggled not to freak out.

Before I had turned Tristan, the ESP between us had been a one-way street and I hadn't had to worry about his hearing my every thought. Because vampires and Clann were natural-born enemies, mental blocks had evolved in both the vamp and Clann species so that neither side could read the others' minds. But because I was a dhampir—born from a human mother and a vampire father—I could read both sides' minds yet was shielded from their reading mine.

Unfortunately now that Tristan was half Clann and half vampire like me, we suddenly had zero trouble reading each other's every thought. This would have been great if there had been some sort of off switch to the ability. But for now, at least, there didn't seem to be one, turning the new ability into more of a curse. The only way we could block each other's thoughts was to be in separate rooms. Walls with closed doors and windows between us thankfully seemed to cut off our brain waves from each other.

It used to make me feel so alone, this ability to read but not be read by all the open minds around me. But now that Tristan had become the one person on this planet who could read my every thought as soon as it formed, I realized how spoiled I'd become by having the freedom to think anything I wanted. I had no idea how to discipline the panicked, guilty chaos inside my head while around him. And because of my lack of mental self-control, I was hurting him over and over.

Which was why, after Tristan had fallen asleep inside the cabin still hurt and confused by my reaction to him at the gas station, I'd snuck out here to the woods to catch a breath. And to finally give in to the thousand and one worries I had fought so hard not to think when he was awake.

What had I done to him? To us?

I wrapped an arm around a nearby tree and leaned against it, allowing it to hold me up. I was so tired, but my mind refused to shut off and let me rest.

The cabin door creaked out in warning, and another chunk of tree bark crumbled under my fingers as I twisted to look back over my shoulder.

Dad walked over to join me, and my shoulders sagged under a wave of relief. I'd almost forgotten that I wasn't alone in this. Thank God I had Dad to turn to for advice on how to train a fledgling, because I was completely clueless here.

"Come to get some fresh mountain air?" he said.

"No. Just…needing some space to worry about Tristan. He can hear my every thought now, whether I want him to or not. But he doesn't remember anything except the memories he got from my blood. He's so lost and confused, and he doesn't understand why I'm freaking out." My voice was rising. I took a breath and struggled to bring it down to a murmur so Tristan wouldn't hear us. "How are we going to tell him about everything?"

Dad had said the biggest danger for all fledglings was in the first few months after they'd turned, when the human mind struggled to adjust to the vampire DNA. During this phase, he said the brain tended to react as if after a concussion, shutting off the memory center and operating solely on the baser levels of senses and instincts. The memory would return in time, but it could take several months.

In the meantime, Tristan might be highly emotional and possibly even irrational sometimes, and it would be hard for him to concentrate for long periods of time. In addition, he would have the impulse to feed on humans with no understanding of why he felt such cravings, and he'd have the speed, strength and reflexes of a full vampire.

"We cannot attempt to hasten the recovery of his memories in any way," Dad said. "We must be patient and allow his memories to return to him on their own. Telling him what he has forgotten will only stress and confuse him still further. He will never truly believe what he does not remember himself, and right now he is in much too volatile a state to handle all the ramifications of our current situation. You will have to continue to protect him from your thoughts as much as you are able to."

Easier said than done.

"What if he never remembers it all? What if I'm not strong enough, or smart enough, or we don't train him right or fast enough...?"

Dad rested a hand on my shoulder. "Now you know all that I have gone through with you. Becoming responsible for another's continued existence is the heaviest responsibility there is. But it does grow easier with time."

Time. How much did we even have? "Will the council try to find us out here?"

He shook his head. "They trust me to be truthful in my reports to them by phone. The Clann, however..."

I frowned in confusion. "Tristan's mom is leading them now. Why would they be a problem?"

"We both know how she feels about our kind."

And Nancy Coleman blamed me for turning her only son into the very thing she feared the most in life.

"Okay, so she might hate my guts," I said. "But if she'd wanted to take me out, she could have done it last night in the Circle."

"With such a mixed audience of both Clann and vampire councilmen present?"

Hmm. I saw his point. A chill spread over my skin. "Still, she's Tristan's mom. She knows he needs me to help train him now."

"Unless she decides you and Tristan are too great a threat to the Clann after all. Especially now that you have proven your blood can turn descendants where no other vampire's has been able to before."

My stomach twisted. I took a slow and careful breath. "She wouldn't do that. Not to her own son. She adores Tristan, no matter what I've turned him into."

"For all our sakes, let us hope you are right. Let us also hope that she gains control over the Clann quickly before any descendants can decide to take matters into their own hands and seek retribution against you for turning their leader."

"Tristan was only their leader for about two minutes."

"Even still, he was their leader. And now he is cast out and all but dead to them. You turned him into that which they fear above all else in this world. It is not likely that they will forget that fact soon."

I stared at the seemingly endless miles of surrounding woods now turning to shades of gray in the fast growing dusk. "Even if the Clann comes after us, they can't find us out here. We didn't leave a trail, and no one knows about this place. Right?"

"They do not have to know about it. If the Clann is determined to find us, the odds are in their favor that they will. Do not forget, they have both spells and the Keepers to aid them."

Oh, lord. I had forgotten about the Clann's alliance with

the Keepers, a group of families also originally from Ireland who, in the old country, had agreed to have a shapeshifter spell placed upon them that spanned generations. Once they shifted into the form of giant black panthers, the Keepers could read both Clann and vampire minds, including mine and probably still Tristan's, too. My best friend's boyfriend, Ron Abernathy, was one of a long line of Keepers.

Could the Clann force Ron and his family to help them hunt us?

I swallowed against a growing knot in my throat. We were buried deep in the woods two states away from the Clann's Jacksonville headquarters. How would the Keepers scent us down—by following the smell of our car exhaust?

"I took every precaution possible during our trip," Dad said. "And we will stay away from the surrounding towns to lessen the humans' knowledge of our presence here. Nevertheless, we must remain cautious. If you sense any sort of magic being used, you must let me know at once. They may try to use a spell to track us down if they become truly determined."

Oh, great. I hadn't thought of that, either.

Like all Clann descendants, I had the ability to feel when magic was being used nearby. It would hit me as a sensation of pins and needles stabbing the back of my neck and arms. But I was still new to using my Clann abilities and, as an outcast of the Clann since before my birth, I was also completely self-taught. There was so much I didn't know about magic. How far away could it be used on someone? Would I feel that spell if the user was physically far away from me?

Then I remembered who I was talking to and froze.

Both the Clann and the vampire council had demanded

my mother and grandmother never teach me how to use magic. But I'd broken that rule and secretly learned how to anyway. Until last night, I'd worked especially hard to keep my growing Clann abilities a secret from my dad, because the vampire council could read his every thought.

This was the first time Dad had openly acknowledged he knew I could use magic.

He must have seen me throwing defensive spells last night in the Circle. The council members probably had seen it, too. During the heat of the battle while blocking and returning spells, hiding my new abilities had been the absolute last thing on my mind.

I didn't know whether to be relieved that my final secret was out, or even more worried. "Has the council said anything to you about my new...um, skills?"

He shook his head, his mouth set in a grim line. "I suspect they are waiting to see how Tristan's training turns out first. It would not be strategically wise of them to risk upsetting the only two vampires in the world who also have magical abilities, especially when one of them is currently so unstable and the treaty with the Clann is in question. But eventually I do expect them to call both of you in for...a discussion."

Great. The last time the council had summoned me to their headquarters in Paris, they'd kidnapped Tristan and used him to test my ability to resist the bloodlust for Clann blood, the most powerful temptation to any vamp alive. I'd passed the test, but barely.

I had zero desire to see how a ticked-off, newly turned Tristan would react to facing the council in their headquarters.

I pressed a shaky hand to my pounding temple. One crisis at a time. First we had to stabilize Tristan, make it safe for him to be around others again. Then we'd deal with the council.

"So about Tristan's training," I said. "You've got a plan, right?"

"Not exactly."

I turned to stare at him. "You're joking, right? You're over three hundred years old. You've probably trained tons of fledglings by now."

"You are my only fledgling still alive."

"What happened to the ones who came before me?"

"There was only one. In the first hundred years of my immortal life, Gowin was busy with his many other fledglings and I became lonely and disillusioned by my existence. I foolishly attempted to turn a dying friend so that I might have a companion, someone to speak with about our unique trials and tribulations."

My heartbeat raced. "What happened?"

"I failed to help him overcome the initial hurdle of the bloodlust."

"So the council...?"

"My fledgling was out of control despite my best efforts, and ultimately I could not argue with the council's decision to put him down."

Put him down?

Oh. He meant they'd *killed* his first fledgling.

And since I was a dhampir instead of a full vamp, my version of training probably didn't count toward Dad's true track record as a vamp sire. Which meant Dad didn't know what he was doing, either.

"Why do y'all have to call it that?" I whispered, trying

not to picture Tristan facing the council's wrath if Dad and I failed to teach him self-control. "They're not animals to be 'put down.' They're people."

"When the council decides to end a fledgling's existence, believe me, it is not because that fledgling is exhibiting any higher form of civilized traits. They *are* animals, driven by nothing other than the base need to feed. 'Putting them down' is the only apt way to describe it. It is an act of compassion made with the understanding that the person that fledgling once was can never be brought back in any shape or form, thus hopefully saving both the fledgling's soul along with all the souls of the lives they would otherwise take from this world."

I stared at my dad, sensing both the quick buzzing quality of his emotions in the air between us and hearing his thoughts. I'd never seen him so wound up like this, both afraid and desperate and ashamed all at the same time. Ashamed of his previous failure, fearful that we would fail again and this time it would be *my* fledgling who would face the council's ultimate punishment.

But my dad was a three-hundred-year-old vamp and a former member of the council. He was supposed to have all the answers.

"What about asking the council for advice?" I said.

"Even council members occasionally fail with their fledglings. You become a council member for your age and political skills, not because you know more than everyone else in the community. Besides, our situation with the council is already exceedingly tenuous, and I have no desire to further sway them toward making any hasty decisions. As it is, they are alarmed beyond measure at the thought of not one but two vamps with magical abilities who might one day rise up against them. If they believe we are incapable of training Tristan to control himself..."

He didn't have to finish that thought. My imagination could fill in the gap all too easily.

"What about asking for help from other vamps not on the council? Somebody out there's got to have this training stuff down by now."

He continued to stare off into the distance, letting silence answer for him.

"So we just have to figure this out on our own?" I couldn't breathe as the enormity of what we were facing crashed over me.

"I am sorry to disappoint you, Savannah, but there is no *Vampire Training for Dummies* guide to assist us, no vampire fledgling school to send him to. Every fledgling is a unique case, this one more so than ever. I can only try the methods my sire utilized with me during my initial days as a vamp while you attempt to keep Tristan calm and guide him to avoid using his Clann abilities. It is the best that we can do."

So we were alone in this. Pass or fail, it was all up to us and only us to figure out how to bring an irrational, moody amnesiac vamp with magic skills far beyond my own back from the proverbial ledge. And to do it, we would be using antiquated training methods that had already failed my dad once. Worse, those training methods had been passed down from the very same vampire councilman who had gone rogue, tried to rip out Tristan's heart and caused this entire mess in the first place.

The cabin door creaked open again, and my heartbeat pounded even harder in my chest and ears.

Tristan was awake.

I forced my mind to go blank and the air to fill and leave my lungs in a steadier rhythm.

A second later Tristan was at my other side. "I woke up and no one was around."

"Just out getting some fresh air," Dad murmured. "It is a lovely sunset, is it not?" A quick peek into his mind revealed he was thinking about nature.

But Tristan watched only me, frowning, his thoughts showing he was trying to read my emotions when he couldn't get anything from my thoughts. "Are you okay?" *Your heart is racing, and I can smell fear on you,* he added silently.

I made myself smile. "Everything's fine. How'd you sleep?"

He shrugged. "Okay, I guess. I woke up thirsty, though."

Dad's gaze darted sideways to meet mine. He turned toward us. "We should go inside and feed."

But Tristan wasn't listening. Frowning, he raised his chin several inches and sniffed the air. "What is that?"

"What?" I sniffed the air, too, but smelled only the chimney smoke, the dead leaves under our feet, the dirt.

And then Tristan was gone. He ran so fast that even my vamp eyes couldn't follow his movements.

Shocked, I looked at Dad. "What the…"

"Deer hunters," Dad growled.

Oh, God. Tristan had scented humans somewhere in the woods.

We took off after him with only the newly disturbed leaves to show where he had been.

CHAPTER 2

When we caught up to him minutes later, it was almost too late.

Trapped between Tristan and a tree, the lone human hunter gasped and struggled to breathe, Tristan's hand at the man's throat cutting off his airway, his rifle forgotten several yards away where he must have dropped it.

Tristan ducked his head, closing the distance between his fangs and the man's throat, smiling in anticipation.

"Tristan, stop!" Dad shouted, forgetting that neither Tristan nor I could be compelled by any older vampire's command due to our mix of Clann and vamp genes.

Tristan ignored him, his fangs burying themselves in the man's neck a half second later.

"Tristan, please," I begged, fear and horror making my own throat tighten up. If he killed this man, he would never forgive himself later. And I would never forgive myself for not stopping it. But how could I stop him? If I tried to yank them apart, Tristan's fangs would rip the man's throat open.

Either my words or the fear behind them made Tristan pause.

Why should I stop? Tristan thought, his fangs still deep within the man's skin. But at least he was no longer gulping down his victim's blood. *I'm thirsty, and he's food.*

There are other ways to feed, ways that won't hurt anyone. We have more than enough blood for all of us back at the cabin, I answered silently, not wanting to further scare Tristan's victim, who stood paralyzed beneath Tristan's grip. The poor man's eyes were already round with terror because Tristan didn't know how to gaze daze him first to calm him.

But why go all the way back there when this human is right here?

Tristan didn't care about scaring the human, yet he continued to speak to me silently. He hadn't responded to Dad's command to stop, yet he was willing to listen to me. Whether due to my blood, the few memories we now shared because of it, or because some lingering emotion of love had survived the change within him, it seemed our bond was the only thing stopping him from going over the edge.

I had to find a way to use that bond to save him from his instincts. But how?

Because this isn't who you really are, I thought.

But I'm thirsty, his mind snarled at me. *And this blood is fresh. How could it be bad?*

If only he had all his memories, this would be so much easier to explain. I struggled to find the right words, knowing this human's life depended on what I thought next.

Right now, it seems like what you want. But that's because you don't have all your memories back yet. You will, though, in a few months probably. And when that happens, you'll remember why you would never want to hurt this human or any other. Right now, biting him feels good. But later, the memory of that mistake will haunt you forever. And it's a mistake you can't ever take back once you make it.

That would have been enough of an explanation to make the old Tristan release his captive. But the new Tristan only raised his head a few inches and stared at me over one hunched shoulder, his red lips parted as if even this one small pause in feeding was excruciating to him. Gone was the boy I had loved for so long, replaced by a nearly mindless predator bent on ending someone's life for his own pleasure. He had become everything I feared I might turn into if I made the wrong decisions or lost control for even an instant.

Something rang deep and hollow through me, reverberating off the core of love for Tristan that had always seemed so rock solid inside me and leaving behind a single, long crack. The strange sensation left me shaken inside and out. But I didn't have time to figure it out right now. Something else to deal with some other day.

I had to find some way to convince Tristan not to kill this man. But what? He had no memories of his own to guide him, and obviously the few he'd gotten from my blood weren't helping, either. Neither was trying to reason with him. If not for whatever blood bond we shared, he would have already drained the guy dry. He still could.

And if he killed this human with my dad as a witness, the vampire council would eventually read my dad's memories of it. They would know we had been unable to prevent Tristan from losing control around a human.

I swallowed hard, my pulse beating at the base of my throat hard enough to rock my entire body. *Tristan, if you hurt this human, I'll—I'll leave you.* It was sheer desperation that made this thought pop into my head, and panic that had me latching on to it as the only threat that might get his attention.

His shoulders jerked up a couple of inches, his shock and hurt knifing through us both. *You'd leave me? Over a stranger? But you made me this way!*

I nodded and tried to ignore my own pain. This wasn't about me. This was about saving Tristan. *You're right, I did turn you. But just because we're different now doesn't mean we have to hurt others. We still have a choice. We don't have to be killers. And if you hurt this human, even if you get away with it, someday when you're back to your old self and remember this moment, it will destroy you. And maybe what we have together, too. You might start to blame me for not finding a way to stop you. You would want me to do whatever it took to keep you from making this mistake.*

I could see our future then, how his guilty conscience would tear him apart, how he would grow to hate himself. And me, too, even if he didn't want to, because not only had I turned him but I'd failed to stop him from killing someone.

This moment would destroy us one way or another if I didn't do whatever it took to stop him.

Curiosity kicked in within him. He cocked his head to the side, the human trapped beneath his grip all but forgotten. *How are we different now?*

You haven't been this way for long. Before last night, you would never have even thought about attacking an innocent person like this.

And before last night, before I became...like this...were we always together?

We were best friends first, years ago as little kids. But I've always loved you. Since the beginning of time, it felt like. I'd give anything to go back in time to when things were so much easier for us.

You're sad. You...don't like me now because I'm different. Different how?

I love you, I thought fiercely, taking a step closer to him. *I will always love you. But I do miss the way you used to be. The Tristan I fell in love with, my first best friend, would never hurt someone like this.* I purposely remembered the day he'd helped one of my best friends, Michelle, off the high school track at an eighth-grade track meet when shin splints made it nearly impossible for her to walk on her own to the stands after her long-distance run. He hadn't even known her, and it had happened before we'd started dating when his parents were still forbidding him from being friends with me. He hadn't helped Michelle for me. He'd done it because he'd seen a stranger hurting and no one else had stepped up and helped.

He frowned as he watched that memory replay in my mind and tried to adjust his faint concept of himself with that brief glimpse of who he once was. The seconds ticked by, his broad palm still firm beneath his prey's chin as he wrestled with his instincts.

I have no memory of this person you say I used to be, he finally thought. *All I remember are moments of the two of us sitting by a stream somewhere and in a mirrored room dancing together. And something about you in a white dress with...wings?*

A tear slid down my cheek. I wiped it away as one corner of my lips twitched with the urge to smile. He remembered our dancing together at the Charmers masq ball fundraiser two years ago when we'd first begun to secretly date.

It was a Halloween costume, I silently explained.

Why can't I remember much? His frown deepened as tinges of cold fear trickled from him. *I feel like I should be able to remember more, but when I try, it's like getting lost in a fog.*

It'll all come back. I promise. I'll help you remember. But until your memory comes back, can you please just trust me and let this man go?

You won't leave me?

I swallowed down the hard lump in my throat and shook my head. *We'll figure this out together.*

Taking a deep breath, Tristan stepped away from the human, releasing him and moving to my side in a blur even my own eyes struggled to follow. The human started to slump down the bare hardwood tree's trunk in shock. Dad darted forward and caught him before he hit the ground, pulling him to his feet then capturing the man's gaze with his own. Under the thrall of the vampire gaze daze, the man's eyes widened then went blank as Dad began to murmur instructions to him to alter his memory and send him safely home.

If only recovering Tristan's memory could be as easy as making this human forget part of his.

My own knees weak with relief, I slipped an arm around Tristan's waist and slowly led him through the woods back toward the cabin. And tried not to think about how much the sweet, delicious scent of blood on his lips made my stomach clench and my heart race with need.

We spent every waking moment of the next five months training Tristan to control the speed of his reflexes and movements using tai chi, because it had worked so well for both my dad and me. Dad's theory was that a lot of a fledgling's control issues came from the fact that our bodies moved even faster than our minds, so instinctual urges to feed kicked in and made us attack before we could even realize what we were doing and make a conscious decision to stop ourselves.

The longer Tristan practiced tai chi, the more I began to see hints of the Tristan I'd loved for so long. His movements became less like a bird's and more fluid, like the human athlete he used to be. As Tristan developed self-control, he also gained something other than his memory loss to focus on, which allowed him to relax and gradually become more independent.

When I wasn't helping Dad train Tristan, I was working on homework. And there was a lot of it. I'd figured Tristan and I could retake our junior year of high school someday after Tristan got his memory back. If we were both going to live forever, what was one year's delay in our education going to matter? But Dad insisted on signing us up for homeschooling via the internet and having me do both Tristan's and my homework so we wouldn't fall behind. Once Tristan's memory returned, the plan was to have him speed-read over everything he'd missed to get caught up.

I think Dad was just trying to keep me busy so I wouldn't worry all the time.

But how could I not? Especially with Tristan's sister, Emily, constantly texting requests for updates on Tristan's progress. At first I thought she was just concerned about her little brother. But lately I'd started to wonder if maybe she wasn't the only one in the Clann who was worried about Tristan.

One early April morning, my cell phone's beep woke me up with an alert for a new text message.

Still half-asleep, I rolled onto my side, grabbed my phone, and cracked one eyelid to read the message before the beeping could wake anyone else.

My mother wants to know when you two will be coming back to Jacksonville.

Why would we return? I texted back.

You have to, Emily's reply read. The Clann needs to be sure he's in control and not a danger to anyone.

I scowled at the screen. As far as I was concerned, we were never going back to Jacksonville. How could we, when Tristan was still more animal than man? I wasn't sure he could even control himself in a crowd full of humans, much less descendants.

Sighing, I propped up on one elbow, looked around and froze.

I was alone in the cabin.

Had Tristan run outside after another hunter? Maybe Dad had been in too much of a hurry chasing after him to wake me? If so, why hadn't I heard anything?

My pulse racing, I jumped to my feet and rushed toward the door. But movement outside the window stopped me. Tristan and Dad were practicing tai chi a few yards from the cabin.

Blowing out a long sigh of relief, I moved closer to the window to watch them, and a sigh of a different kind slipped from my lungs.

In the cold morning air, still predawn gray, Tristan's fiercely determined focus turned each motion into a thing of both beauty and danger, like a fighter in a martial arts movie preparing for a battle. I wrapped my arms around myself and watched him unseen and unheard for once, and in that moment remembered again why I loved him. It wasn't just the way he moved, or the beautiful lines formed by his sculpted body, honed by endless football practices over the years and perfected by vampire blood. It was the look in his eyes, the firm set to his mouth and jaw, that single-minded determination to succeed at whatever he attempted. Just like he always had.

It was a rare glimpse of the old Tristan I knew and loved and had missed every waking day of the past five months.

When he smoothly slid down into a low right lunge in Form 16, I actually shivered. A minute later, as he progressed to Form 18 and his left palm slowly pushed forward as if pressing open an invisible door, my shiver turned into full-on goose bumps down the back of my neck and arms. But this time it wasn't because of the beauty of the moment.

Tristan was about to use magic.

I had time to think *Oh, no* and rush for the door. By the time I opened it a half second later, a nearby tree had already gone up in a thunderous boom of flames. The morning's tai chi lesson was definitely over.

Tristan stared at the tree. He glanced down at his hands then up at me, his eyes wide as I ran over to him.

"I... Did I just..." he sputtered.

"It's okay," I said, taking his hands into mine. "You did it with your willpower and that bundle of energy inside you. Can you feel that energy?"

He frowned then slowly nodded.

"Good. Now focus on that energy. Think about keeping it as a tight ball inside you if you can."

"I didn't mean to set the tree on fire. I just...I was ticked off. I got distracted. I was thinking..."

I read his mind. He was thinking that he was tired of not knowing who and what he was. And then his anger had triggered his willpower to kick in and spit out a bit of magic in the form of a fireball.

A fireball that could have easily killed my dad or me if he'd aimed it in a different direction.

I pushed that thought away. "I know. It was an accident. That's why we do the tai chi. It gives you a way to physically get the emotions out without, well, blowing stuff up." I turned toward the tree, took a deep breath, held out my hands, and willed the tree to cool off. The flames died down then extinguished in a thick cloud of smoke.

"Savannah, the smoke..." Dad muttered. "Others will see it for miles. Can you do anything to disperse it?"

I thought for a moment, nibbling at the inner corner of my mouth. Then I raised my hands and imagined a strong breeze blowing out from my palms toward the smoke.

Tristan hissed and rubbed his arms as wind whispered to life, gathered the smoke, and shredded it into long gray ribbons that trailed off into nothing.

"There." I turned to Tristan with a forced smile. "See? All better. Just try to keep your willpower under control and you'll be okay."

But Tristan was frozen in place, staring with wide, unseeing eyes at the now blackened trees.

"Tristan?"

He didn't blink, didn't move, his mind a million miles

away in another place and time when he had last worked with someone to learn how to control his Clann powers.

TRISTAN

Images I didn't understand at first flashed through my mind, of myself and a big bear of a man with a thick silver beard standing in a yard at night.

Then I recognized him. The answers flowed to me without my having to struggle for them.

Dad. We were standing in the backyard behind our house.

Okay, Dad said. *So here's the basics of casting a spell. Every witch starts off at the beginner level of spell casting by saying a word and using a small hand gesture. This helps you focus and control when the spell is actually cast, until you learn how to discipline your mind. Someday, when you're ready, I'll teach you how to cast a spell even if you're tied up with your mouth taped shut, just by thinking the word and using your willpower. Eventually you'll learn to cast a spell without a word at all, just by thinking about the results you want to create. Like you do when you create fire or ground your energy.*

The brief memory was like the strong wind Savannah had just whispered into life, blowing away the mental fog that had filled my head for months now. I remembered. Everything that had been lost to me came back in wave after wave of memory. I remembered Dad training me how to use magic…the vamp council abducting me and handcuffing me to a chair in their underground Paris headquarters to test Savannah's self-control…Mom expecting me to follow in Dad's footsteps to become the next Clann leader and how desperately I had wanted to play pro football someday instead and our endless family arguments about it…Dad's death…Mom's heartache turning into happiness as I finally took the stone throne as Clann leader…the pain that exploded in my chest as Gowin tried to rip out my heart through my back…and then waking up in Savannah's arms with only the memory of her smile to anchor me as everything else faded beneath the fog that had filled my head.

I remembered it all. But it was too much too fast, a thousand different memories and emotions swirling around me like a tornado trying to rip me into pieces. I couldn't breathe, couldn't control it.

I had to get away, get some air, find a way to sort through it all one memory and emotion at a time before I went insane.

CHAPTER 3

SAVANNAH

Tristan staggered, and I reached out for him. But he turned away, a choking tidal wave of shock and horror swamping him as memory after memory slammed into him from every direction, each one tied to and triggering the next, each one robbing his lungs of air or the ability to draw another breath.

"Tristan!" I took a step after him. He was getting his memories back, but they were returning too fast. No one should be hit with seventeen years' worth of memories all at once.

"Dad, the memories…they're all coming back." What should I do? Should I try to hold him, let him feel me there beside him so he would know he wasn't alone?

I reached out for Tristan again, but he brushed my hand away and stumbled toward the nearby ledge where he liked to go sometimes to sit and watch the sun set. My heart missed a beat. He was getting too close to the edge. He would survive the fall, according to Dad. But I still didn't want to see him hurt.

"Let him go. He will need some time and space to work through them on his own."

I held my breath until Tristan found the large stone he usually sat on. His hands fumbled over its surface, guiding him as he sank down onto the rock.

"Are you sure he should be alone right now?"

"Yes, I am sure. Some things you cannot save him from."

I hated the idea of Tristan having to deal with the return of his memories alone. Especially the memory of his father's death, which had happened just a week before Tristan had nearly died and I'd had to turn him in order to keep him alive.

But I followed Dad's suggestion, staying when I wanted to follow, watching when I wanted to actively help in some way. After a moment of silence, I realized Dad was actually smiling.

"You can't possibly be happy about this," I snapped. "Tristan's hurting. I know you're not that callous."

"I do not enjoy his mental pain, no. But the return of his memories means he will quickly regain all his former self-control and discipline. The one advantage of his being who he was within the Clann is that he should have had plenty of previous training in these areas. Otherwise he never would have been able to keep his infamous Coleman Clann abilities contained in public. And if he could contain *those* abilities..."

"Then he can control his vamp instincts, too," I finished for him without looking away from the slump of Tristan's shoulders. He'd always had the best posture, holding his shoulders back, unashamed that his six-foot-plus height made him taller than most.

"Correct. Which means our days of training here on this mountain are at an end, and we must prepare to take him back to Jacksonville."

"Jacksonville?" I hissed, finally able to look at my dad. "Are you crazy? We can't go back there!"

"We must. The council demands it."

"The council…" I sputtered. "You've got to be kidding. They can't possibly want us to go back into Clann territory."

"But they do. They know you and Tristan can read the descendants' thoughts."

And then it sank in. I groaned. "No. No way. Tristan and I are not going to spy for the council."

Dad stared at me, his silver eyes darkening to a slate-gray. "You must. The council demands it."

I stared back at him with one eyebrow raised. We both knew how much I loved being told what to do by the council.

He sighed. "Let me rephrase. Caravass and the other council members would greatly appreciate it if you two would consider going back to Jacksonville and keeping us apprised of any alarming developments within the Clann. They only wish to maintain peace with the Clann, nothing more."

I leaned in closer. "Tristan is just now getting his memories back, including the ones about his family. And now the council wants him to go spy on them?"

"They cast him out of the Clann."

"Because they had to! He's a vampire now. They couldn't let a vamp be a member." Wasn't it in the Clann laws or something? They sure seemed to have some rule about descendants and vamps dating, considering they'd cast out my

mother for marrying my father, and then cast out my grandmother for failing to stop that union.

"I repeat, the council only seeks any information that will
help them maintain the peace treaty with the Clann. Nothing more."

I searched his thoughts. He was telling the truth.

The anger seeped out of me, leaving a horrible sinking
feeling behind. "I really don't want to go back there." I
tried to control my voice, but a slight tremble snuck into it
anyway. "You of all people have got to understand what it's
like…finally getting to be with the person you love, facing
all that hatred and judgment. The descendants are going to
want to kill me for turning Tristan! In fact, they probably
won't even want us back there."

It was Dad's turn to stare at me with one eyebrow arched.
"Do not think I have not read Emily's messages request-
ing Tristan's return to Jacksonville. I am well aware that his
mother and the rest of the Clann seek reassurance that he is
no longer a danger."

I turned away and crossed my arms.

"Savannah, do try to be mature about this. We must return to Jacksonville. It is the only way to reassure the Clann
that you and Tristan are no longer a threat to them. And the
council is relying upon us to provide them with accurate
warnings only the two of you can provide. Think of the
good that you can do, the lives that you can save, by helping
to prevent another war."

Great. Dad must have picked up a few of my mother's guilt
trip methods. He was doing a really great job of making me
feel like a selfish child.

I hung my head and closed my eyes. I had gone through

so much for years now because of the stupid hate and fear between the vamps and the Clann…I'd given up my dreams of being a dancer on my high school dance team so I wouldn't reveal my vamp abilities to the world. I'd risked everything, even losing my Nanna, by breaking the rules to date Tristan. I'd even given up being with Tristan for months just to make the vampire council and the Clann happy.

And now, when it finally seemed that Tristan and I could safely be together at last without breaking any rules, without having to sneak around…now when his memory had finally returned and I could have my Tristan back again…the council had the nerve to make yet *another* demand.

I was so tired of it all…of the hate and the fear and the whispers and judging stares, of having to do what everyone else wanted. When would it matter what *I* wanted? Or what Tristan wanted? Even now, after everything we'd gone through, we still weren't free.

Dad tried to rest a hand on my shoulder, but I took a step forward so his hand fell away.

He sighed. "Do you not miss your friends and your dance team?"

I shrugged one shoulder. "I assumed I would never see them again."

"Well, now you can."

I didn't want to, but I could hear my dad's thoughts as he struggled for some new and more compelling argument to try with me. As my dad, he hated having to push me on this issue. But as a representative of the vampire council, he was duty bound to. He would be forced to badger me endlessly until I gave in.

I gritted my teeth and held up a hand to stop him. "Fine.

We'll go back to Jacksonville. But only when Tristan is ready. Until then, until *he's* sure he's in control, we're staying right here. Okay?"

"Agreed."

Tristan stayed out at the ridge all day. By sunset, I couldn't take it anymore and had to join him.

"How are you feeling?" I asked, reaching out to him and then hesitating before dropping my hand at my own side again. Maybe he still wanted to be alone.

He continued to stare out at the sky, now slowly darkening beneath the early winter sunset. "I remember everything. Dad and Mom, Emily and Gowin. You and me. The Clann and the vampire council. The battle at the Circle, and Gowin's sucker punch through my back. You turning me."

I froze, fearing my nightmare was about to come true. Did he hate me for the selfish decision I'd made, for my inability to let him die?

He finally turned his head to look at me. "Thanks, by the way."

"Sorry about the amnesia. I didn't know about it till after I'd turned you, since I never had it. I didn't know it would be so complete or last this long."

He gave a half shrug and returned to staring at the sky. "It's over. That's all that matters."

I nodded in silence, not knowing what else to say. After spending so many days trying to adjust to the childlike and helpless Tristan, I had to readjust to the return of the old Tristan. Except he still wasn't quite himself.

For instance, he hadn't reached out to touch me in any way yet.

"Sorry. Guess I've been a little lost lately." Sighing, he reached out to take my hand and gently tug me closer.

As soon as his hand touched mine, warmth spread over my skin and the tension melted from my whole body. It was going to be okay now. We'd made it through the hardest part.

I sat down beside him before relief could make my legs give out beneath me, wrapped an arm across the small of his back and rested my cheek against the muscled curve of his shoulder. "I missed you. The real you, I mean."

"I missed me, too." He raised our joined hands to press a slow kiss to each of my fingers.

I raised my head, and he leaned over and kissed my lips. A heady mix of relief and love rose up through my body, stealing my breath and driving me to wrap both arms around him. The intensity of the emotions surprised both of us, and when we stopped to catch a breath, one corner of his mouth rose.

"Wow. You really did miss me, didn't you?"

"I was afraid... ." Too many emotions pounded through me to put them into words...the gut-wrenching fear of losing him when he nearly died, the horror of discovering I'd temporarily turned him into more animal than man, the responsibility of keeping him safe from his own actions and the fear of screwing up as his sire, being terrified for months that I'd only saved him physically but might never have the real Tristan back, the agonizing guilt and worry over whether I'd made the wrong decision after all by turning him. It was too much to describe out loud, so I simply let him see and feel all the emotions and memories inside my head.

"Hey, it's okay now," he murmured, cupping my face and using his thumbs to brush away my tears of relief. "I'm not going anywhere ever again. It's you and me till the end of time. Or at least until you decide you can't stand me any-more."

He pressed a slow, lingering kiss to my forehead, then each cheek, the tip of my nose and then my lips again.

And I was finally whole once more.

The moment Dad exited the cabin and got close enough to us for me to pick up his thoughts, though, I remembered my promise to him and the tension flowed right back into me.

I sighed and rested my forehead against Tristan's. "Did you hear what Dad said earlier about the council's newest request?"

"About our going back to Jacksonville?"

I nodded, my throat making a dry, sticky sound as I tried to swallow past the growing tightness within it.

"Yeah, I heard." He hesitated. "I also heard the part where my sister and mother want us to come back, too."

"Yeah. The Clann wants to be sure you're...you know, in control of everything."

"Okay. So we'll go back to Jacksonville."

I leaned back to frown at him. "You'd actually spy on your friends and family?"

"I'd never tell the council anything that could hurt the Clann. But if I were the council, I'd want to keep a close and constant eye on the Clann, too. You've got to under-stand, collectively sometimes the Clann acts like a bunch of scared cattle ready to stampede whether it makes sense to or not. Look at how they tried to keep us apart for so long."

"Yeah, well maybe they had a point there. Look at what ended up happening to you."

"Hey, I'm happy that you finally turned me. Now we can

be together without you worrying about draining me every time we kiss."

"True. But at what cost? You've lost your family."

"I didn't lose them. My mother made her choice. She sided with the Clann over me. Besides, you and your dad are my family now. Right?"

"Yeah, but, Tristan, your mother and sister still love you, too."

He didn't say anything for a long time, staring in silence as the sun disappeared beneath the curve of the earth and the sky deepened into dark shades of purple.

When he finally spoke again, his voice was quieter, deeper. "Your dad's right, Sav. We might be able to help prevent another war. If the peace treaty fails, it's not just the vamps and the Clann who would be hurt. It would be your friends—Anne and Carrie and Michelle—and any other humans who got caught in the cross fire. Not to mention Ron and all of the Keepers."

He draped an arm around my shoulders, and I nestled against him, resting my head in the hard curve where his shoulder and neck met. I wished I could burrow even deeper, somehow get away from his words and the entire world around us.

But there was no way to escape my own mind or the realization that Dad and Tristan were both right. Much as I hated it.

"Is it so wrong of me to just want to be with you without a panel of judges constantly weighing in on everything we say and do?" I whispered.

"No, it's not wrong." He slowly rubbed my back, his broad, strong hand soothing my nerves. It was every bit as comforting as a cup of Nanna's homegrown chamomile tea used to be.

Silence fell like a soft blanket over us. But its weight seemed to grow heavier on me with every passing second.

Finally I sighed. "Okay. We'll do the right thing and go back to Jacksonville."

CHAPTER 4

"Please?" Tristan murmured with big puppy-dog eyes. "I love you. I adore you. Don't tell me you're going to hold out on me now, after all we've been through."

"No, Tristan. The answer was no yesterday, and last night, and two hours ago, and it's still no now." Crossing my arms, I leaned against my silver Corvette Stingray. "And if you keep up the whining, I'm going to be late for Charmers practice. And we both know how much Mrs. Daniels loves people who show up late for practice."

"But, Sav, it's a Corvette! How can you refuse to let me drive it? Just this once? Pretty please?"

"Nuh-uh. You say it's just this once. But once you've driven a 'Vette, there's no going back. You'll be whining the same old tune every single day for the rest of our lives. Which means you'll literally be bugging me for all eternity about this. Let's just agree to drop it now and get on with our day, okay?"

He stuck out his lower lip in a pout.

"Nope. Not going to work." I made a point of looking at my watch then circling around the car to the driver's side. "Now would you please hurry up and get in?" Thank heavens we lived in town. If we'd had to drive the ten miles from Nanna's house, we would most definitely be late. I would have to push the speed limit as it was just to get us there on time.

Heaving a noisy sigh, he got into the car, and I had to hide a smile as I reached for my seat belt. "Put your seat belt on, please. I don't want to get pulled over for a belt violation again."

"Again? How often do you get pulled over?"

"Trust me, you don't want to get pulled over by a Clann cop even once when you're a vamp."

I slipped and let a memory flit through my mind of the one time I'd been pulled over. To this day, I still occasionally had nightmares of the hatred and barely restrained violence in that uniformed descendant's thoughts as he'd held me trapped there in my car for ten long minutes while he decided whether to be a good cop or an even better descendant.

Tristan grabbed my hand, his eyes furious. "Seriously? Did he do anything, or just think about doing it?"

Crap. I really needed to find a way to block this mind connection thing between us. I swallowed hard. "Don't worry, he was a good cop. That day. But I don't ever want to tempt him again. Which is why we can't speed this morning to make up time."

"I should—" he began in a growl.

"No, you shouldn't. Just use it as a lesson. We've got to be on our toes about this stuff. And I'm not just talking about following the traffic laws here. We can't do *anything* to give any of them a reason to go after us. Okay? No matter how much they may push us, we've got to keep it together. No mistakes, no losing control." I searched his eyes, needing to know he was hearing me loud and clear here.

He sighed, letting go of his anger for now. "Yeah, okay."

He put on his seat belt, and I put the key into the ignition. Then I caught his longing stare at the steering wheel.

He *really* wanted to drive my car.

I groaned. "Fine. Just this once, you can—"

But he was already out the door and around the car, opening the door for me like a chauffeur.

Laughing, I got out and let the spoiled brat have his way, as usual.

Ten minutes later we pulled into the parking lot with two whole minutes to spare, Tristan still grinning just like he had the whole way here. Shaking my head, I grabbed my trusty blue leather Charmers duffle bag, got out and circled the car so I could lean in through the driver's side window to say goodbye.

The plan was for him to stay in the car till the bell for first period rang in an hour and a half. Then he'd head for the office in the main hall, where he would once again be helping out as an office aide till second period.

So I was surprised when he got out of the car with me.

"Just wanted to say a proper goodbye now that we don't have to hide anymore," he murmured, leaning against the side of the car and pulling me against him for a kiss.

Realizing we were out in the open where anyone could

see us together sent a thrill skittering across my every nerve ending and made my lips curve into a huge grin against his. "Hmm. I could get used to this."

We kissed again, then he leaned his head back a few inches and grinned. "And just think, we've also got lunch together in the cafeteria to look forward to."

I pictured his sitting beside me at my friends' table. Just the idea seemed like a fantasy that couldn't possibly ever come true. And yet it would. *Today.* My heart skipped another beat in anticipation.

Then I remembered…all the Clann kids would be staring at us in the cafeteria. I could already imagine how much they would love seeing their former leader, now a vamp, sitting with the enemy instead of them. I sighed, my excitement deflating a bit. If only we were at some other school…

"They'll get over it," Tristan said. "Today might be rough, but eventually they'll get so used to seeing us together that they won't even think about it anymore."

"Promises, promises," I muttered. Then I checked my watch and hissed. "Ouch. I have really gotta go." I gave him one last kiss, turned away then hesitated. "Are you sure you'll be okay?"

"With sitting in the 'Vette till first period? Sure. What's the big deal?"

"No, I mean with…this." I waved a hand at the school campus. "You, me, being back here so soon. I know what Dad and the council and your mother want, but are *you* sure—"

The image of him pinning that nameless hunter to a tree in the Arkansas woods flashed through my mind. I pushed it away, but not fast enough.

Tristan's head rocked back as if I'd slapped him. After a long beat of silence, he muttered, "That won't happen again, Savannah."

Great. Now I'd done it.

"Right," I said too quickly with a smile that felt fake even to me. "I know that. You weren't yourself that day. Now you are."

Except now we would be facing a way bigger challenge than resisting regular human blood. Today we would be around members of the Clann, each one of them full of the most tempting blood any vamp could ever wish for, thanks to the powerful extra energy their magical abilities filled them with. Tristan was going to feel like a newly recovering alcoholic forced to spend eight hours trapped inside a bar.

A bar where just asking for a drink could risk starting a war, and would also probably send the vamp council after us, as well.

And there was nothing more I could do to help him resist that urge to drink.

He looked down at his feet, staring without seeing, his mind filling with images and memories…of the feel of that hunter's fragile neck trapped within his hand, the human's heartbeat pounding beneath his fingertips. The taste of the blood as it had rushed down Tristan's throat, warming him, filling him not just with energy and life but a rush of power and excitement, as well.

Just a short moment in time that had seemed so good yet now had become his worst mistake ever. A mistake that had haunted his nightmares yet again last night.

He hated himself for that mistake, for what he had done and nearly could have done to that innocent human. Thanks to his victim's blood memories, he knew that man, though divorced, still loved and missed his wife and the two little girls he only got to see at Christmas now that their mother had moved them three states away. He knew that man had been in those woods hunting only because this Christmas, he hadn't had enough money to see his girls, so he'd gone hunting alone to try to distract himself from his misery and loneliness. And he'd nearly died because Tristan had lost control.

"But he didn't die," I murmured, my heart hurting for Tristan so much it caused a physical ache within my chest. "He's still alive with no memory of what happened."

"Yeah, well, you and I sure remember."

Tristan wouldn't look at me now, his gaze rising only as high as my knees. But I could see the misery in his eyes.

All the joking around about who would drive us to school this morning had been an act, a distraction to keep him from thinking about what he would be facing today. He was worried, too, afraid he wouldn't be strong enough, and scared to admit that fear to me or even to himself.

And here I was with my stupid, wayward memories adding to his fear and making his first day back even harder on him.

"I'm sorry I remembered that." I laid a hand along one hard side of his face, waiting until he looked me in the eyes. "I wish I wasn't worried, or that at least I could turn off this mind connection thing sometimes so you wouldn't have to feel my worry. But just because I'm worried doesn't mean I don't have faith in you. I know you'll do your best to stay in control today. I just also know how hard it can be to fight the bloodlust, especially for Clann blood." I hesitated, then handed him a thin braid of red, brown and white.

"What's this?" he asked, his voice coming out rough.

CONSUME 47

"Remember that old tapestry blanket we always shared at the cabin? I pulled some threads from it before we left."

One corner of his mouth hitched as he stared down at the braid.

I gently took it back from him then tied it around his left wrist. "And then I added a little oomph to it to help block any vamp wards the descendants might be using today. It should last you through at least the morning, if not the whole day, and we can recharge it tonight if needed." I had a matching one tied around my left ankle under my sock, so I wouldn't have to answer any questions from my friends about it.

Now both sides of his mouth curved up. He lifted his head and looked at me, his eyes softer as some of the fear there was replaced with love. "Thanks, Sav."

I leaned in for one last kiss, resting my palms against his chest, his strong arms wrapped around my waist, feeling his heart beating beneath my fingertips.

I rested my forehead against his. "No matter what happens today, I'll still love you," I whispered, wishing there was some other spell I could do to somehow magically make this day easier for him.

We stood there in silence for a moment longer, both of us trying not to think or worry.

I wanted to stay with him in the parking lot. I'd gotten spoiled, used to being with him all the time. Maybe it was because he carried some of my blood within himself now, or maybe it was because I could read his thoughts as easily as my own. Whatever the reason, over the past five months, he had become like an extension of my own body, so much so that sometimes when we held hands I could no longer tell where his hand ended and mine began. All I knew was that when I was with him I felt warmer, almost human again. And when we were apart, I felt cold and every bit the inhuman hybrid I really was.

But it was time to return to reality, whether I was ready for it or not.

So I took a deep breath then forced myself to step away from him, hating the feel of his arms loosening around me and then their complete absence. The moment we no longer touched, I could already feel my body losing the tiny amount of heat it always managed to generate from direct contact between our skin, setting me up for a long day of hiding shivers I wasn't supposed to have in the humid, late, East Texas spring.

As I crossed the parking lot and headed for Charmers practice, trying to resist the urge to rub the growing chill from my arms, I looked back over my shoulder at Tristan and said, "See you for lunch? I've got chem class second period today. Maybe you could pick me up outside it?"

One corner of his mouth lifted in a half smile as he said, "It's a date."

The third floor of the sports and arts building—where the Charmers' dance room, storage closets and director's office were located—had a great second set of stairs that led down to the left side of the school theater's stage. This backstage access between the floors allowed the dancers and stage crew to easily run up and down the stairs during shows without having to be seen in the second floor foyer where audience members might be. It was also the most direct route for me this morning. Two weeks before a Spring Show usually meant the Charmers would still be working out the kinks in each show number's choreography and transitions, which meant frequent rewinding and fast-forwarding to specific parts in each song. The theater's built-in sound system was harder to do this kind of stuff on, so I figured we would probably still be using the portable sound system for a few more days.

The sophomore managers were running even later than I was, judging by the fact that the sound system and trainer's bag were still in the director's office. By the time I retrieved the equipment and brought it down the backstage stairs, most of the Charmers had already arrived and gathered to stretch in the two aisles that cut through the auditorium's seating, and the sophomore managers were just strolling in through the main auditorium doors.

The familiar dusty smells of paint and freshly sanded wooden props made me sigh and smile. Now here was a silver lining to having to come back to Jacksonville. While football season came in a close second, Spring Show season was my absolute favorite time of the Charmers performance year. I was lucky that we'd returned in time for me to help with it. Normally Spring Show happened a few weeks earlier in the year. But this year for some reason the director had pushed the show back, and we still had two more weeks of rehearsals left. Maybe there had been some scheduling conflict for use of the theater?

I slipped through the wing's shadows and along the side of the center stage, stopping at its front edge, or apron, to set down the sound system. Immediately several people gasped and whispered my name, and all conversation in the auditorium died.

I froze and looked up to find forty-plus dancers equally frozen in midstretch, their eyes blinking fast as they openly stared at me.

That's when I realized I was on stage, both literally and figuratively.

And though the theater was silent, their thoughts were anything but.

Oh. My. God. She actually had the nerve to come back?

Miss Savannah's back! Oh, thank God. If I had to listen to Mrs. Daniels rip the soph managers apart one more time...

Oh, boy. Miss Savannah's back. I wonder if Tristan's back, too. If he is, just wait till Miss Bethany sees him. That'll *be a show!*

I forced my suddenly stiff legs to carry me down the short flight of stairs off the side of the stage and into the audience area, then around to the front edge of the stage so I could finish setting up the sound system. This also gave me a reason to keep my back to everyone and hide my face so they wouldn't see me react to the thoughts that kept washing over me in wave after wave. After five blissful months of having to listen to only Dad's and Tristan's thoughts, I'd forgotten just how loud a bunch of humans thinking fast and furiously could be. I'd have to reschool my face not to show anything.

And still their thoughts kept coming.

Miss Savannah's back! Just in time, too, 'cuz I was totally considering quitting this team. Bad enough having to fetch crap constantly, much less get yelled at every single day. Just because I haven't had as much practice working the music like Miss Savannah has doesn't mean I deserve to be made to feel like crap about it...

Wow. Look at her...you can't even tell she was ever pregnant. I wonder who's watching the baby? Or maybe she gave it up for adoption? Maybe Tristan found out it was Ron Abernathy's and made her give it up?

Whoa. Gone away for five months to secretly have Ron's

baby? *That* was the rumor behind my disappearance? I didn't know whether to laugh or cry.

I pressed a shaky hand to my forehead as it started to pound. Normally I would have dreaded listening to the sniping thoughts of the Clann. But right now, I would have given anything to have a descendant's mind to listen to and drown out the humans' thoughts instead. At least the descendants all knew the real reason behind our absence. Unfortunately no descendant had made the dance team in the past couple of years. Maybe they preferred being on the cheer team. Or maybe they were just avoiding me.

I took a deep breath. *Focus, Sav. Just think about what you're here to do. The gossip will die down eventually.*

"Miss Savannah!"

I turned around just in time to be wrapped in a tight hug.

Mrs. Daniels leaned back, gripping my shoulders, her face lit up. "Oh, thank G—" She glanced sideways at a nearby sophomore manager. "I mean, I'm so happy you're back! You are back for good now, aren't you?" Her eyes turned a little panicky.

"Um, yes, ma'am." I blinked fast, trying to assimilate the fact that my usually frosty dance team director had just hugged me.

She let out the longest sigh. "That is the best news I've had all year. Welcome back, dear!"

We can finally get our practices back on track! Mrs. Daniels thought to herself as she turned and headed back up the aisle to take a seat toward the center back of the audience. *Too bad Savannah wasn't here for the first part of show season; maybe then we could have held the show when we were supposed to, instead of having to delay it because of these inept newbie managers. I swear, this has been the longest year of my life!*

I had to turn back to the stereo to hide a smile. At least someone on this team was happy I was back.

"Hey, Miss Savannah!" A voice behind me made me turn around yet again to find the entire team lining up to welcome me back with hugs as they followed their director's lead. They still weren't sure why I had missed five months of school. But if their director was okay with my return, then they would be, too.

I noticed Bethany Brookes, however, wasn't so eager to join the welcome wagon. She stopped to fiddle with her shoe, then took her time removing her warm-ups from over her dance outfit. By the time she managed to actually get in line, Mrs. Daniels was calling everyone to get ready for the start of practice. Bethany's shoulders seemed to sag a bit with relief as she took a seat with the dancers who weren't climbing the stage steps in preparation for the first number.

Bethany and I had always had a lot of awkward tension between us, though we both did our best to be polite to each other in spite of it. She was actually a really nice girl. It wasn't her fault that Mrs. Daniels had started to call out my number, then corrected herself and called out Bethany's instead, at Charmers tryouts our freshman year. Or that Bethany used to have a terrible crush on Tristan while he and I were secretly dating last year. Or that he accidentally and very stupidly led her on for months after the vamp council and Clann made me break up with him.

And now she probably knew, or was about to find out, that he and I were very publicly together again.

I just hoped she wouldn't hold it against me for too long.

Otherwise getting through Charmers practices was going to be extremely awkward.

By the end of first period, I was all too eager to escape to chemistry class, where Ron also surprised me with a huge hug as soon as I walked up to our lab table.

"It's about time!" he said with a grin as we settled onto our wobbly metal stools. "So? How's the...uh...new situation working out?"

"Well, we're both here today," I answered cautiously, trying and failing to ignore the fresh wave of whispers involving both my and Tristan's names that broke out behind us.

Ugh. First the Charmers. Then everyone on campus that I'd been forced to walk past on my way here. And now this. Was it going to be like this all day long? I honestly didn't know how much more of the JHS rumor mill I could take.

"Oh, yeah, she totally slept with both of them, so it's anybody's guess who the baby daddy really is," someone whispered.

That was it.

I twisted around to glare at my classmates, stopping just short of baring my fangs at them. The whispering stopped.

Hmm. Maybe being the only female vamp on campus did have some perks after all.

"And our golden boy?" Ron asked. "How's the...er, transition going?"

I faced forward again and shrugged one shoulder. "I haven't heard any screams or explosions yet, so I guess he's doing all right so far."

Ron laughed as he reached for a glass beaker to begin the day's lab experiment. Then he glanced at me and realized I was serious. "Jeez. You two must have had a fun five months away."

"Oh, yeah, and then some." I scowled at the lab table's black enamel surface, scarred by countless knicks and bored students' carvings. "Let's just say it's been a learning process for both of us."

Ron grunted. "I guess it's safe to assume you two won't be eating with us in the cafeteria then?"

I looked at him in surprise. "Why wouldn't we?"

"Uh, because of all the humans and descendants that'll be packed in there?"

"He thinks he can handle it. He's even looking forward to it now that we don't have to sneak around anymore."

Ron snickered. "Yeah? And is he also looking forward to getting grilled by all of your friends? Who, I should mention, all blame Tristan for your five-month absence from their lives."

Oh. I hadn't thought of that. I'd stayed in contact with my friends by way of the occasional text message. But life in that cabin in Arkansas had been pretty boring, and since Anne was the only one of my human friends who knew the truth about vampires and the Clann, I hadn't been able to say much to Carrie or Michelle.

So now, not only would Tristan be dealing with smelling and hearing all those humans and their stinky human food and the hateful descendants around us—plus feeling the Clann kids' constant scrutiny of his every little twitch and blink—but he would also be trying to earn my friends' approval as my boyfriend.

Not to mention we'd be sort of rubbing our relationship into poor Bethany Brookes's face.

What the heck was I thinking when I agreed to our eating together in the cafeteria?

Groaning, I propped my elbows on the table and buried my face in my hands. "This is going to be a disaster, isn't it?"

"Probably. But it'll sure be entertaining."

I stared down at the sheet of instructions, the letters blurring together into a meaningless jumble. Somehow I had to find a way to talk Tristan out of our going to the cafeteria today. Maybe I could convince him to delay tackling that challenge till later in the week when we both knew he could handle being around so many humans and descendants. Facing it all on his first day back, however, was practically suicidal.

The problem was finding a way to bring up this suggestion in a way that wouldn't further bruise his ego and make him think I had no faith in him.

I rubbed my pounding temples and tried to figure out the best arguments to use on him. Deep down inside, I had a hunch nothing I said was going to come out right. Especially since he could read every thought in my head whether I verbalized it or not.

Why wasn't there some kind of training manual for sires of teenaged vamps, like *How to Train Your Teen Fledgling?*

I glanced at the clock on the wall, which suddenly seemed to have sped up. All morning long, the seconds had eked by while I worried about Tristan losing control in class.

Now I wanted nothing more than for time to slow down again.

CHAPTER 5

TRISTAN

I was waiting for her at the door of her chemistry class before the bell rang. She didn't see me at first, her head bent as she slowly gathered her things, those too-kissable lips of hers turned down into a frown as she trudged across the room toward me.

Then she looked up. Our eyes met, and she smiled.

And just like that, getting through the long, boring, tense morning was worth it.

Ron Abernathy shot me a sympathetic grin as he exited the room. "Good luck at lunch," he muttered, not sticking around long enough for me to figure out what that was supposed to mean.

It didn't matter. All that mattered was Savannah and finally getting to be a real couple with her. No more secrets. No more lies or sneaking around.

God, he's gorgeous, she thought, forgetting yet again that I could hear her.

I swallowed down a laugh. She knew just what to think to make a guy feel like he could take on the whole world if needed.

"Hi," she murmured as she drew close to me. "How was your morning?"

"Fine. Ready for lunch?" It was an effort not to rub my hands together in pure anticipation. And it definitely wasn't the food I was looking forward to.

"Mmm." She stepped out of the room and off to the side a little, making way for others in the hall to pass us by. "You know, I've been thinking about that. Maybe it's not such a good idea. We don't have to go to the cafeteria. We could go to the library and hang out instead. Ron's mom is the librarian. She wouldn't mind—"

"And miss out on all the fun? No way!" I held out a bent elbow. It took her a few seconds to realize I wanted her to hold my arm.

She slipped a free hand between my elbow and my body, her fingers coming to rest in the bend of my arm as if made to nestle there. I squeezed my arm tight against my body so her hand wouldn't slip away, and we headed into the packed main hall.

I stumbled to a halt as a flood of strange sensations poured over me. Savannah grabbed my arm with both her hands.

What is it? she thought, her eyes darting side to side as she searched my face. *What's wrong? Talk to me. Is it the bloodlust? We should get out of here.*

No, it's not that, I thought, struggling to breathe as the sensations kept changing, throwing me continually off balance.

I tried to find a way to describe what I was feeling. *It's… something else. Like falling into one of those bouncy castles for kids, but this one's filled with giant cotton balls and knives and fire ants and stuff that's hitting me from all sides.*

Try to breathe through it, she thought, rubbing my upper arm. *You're just picking up their emotions. It'll take you a little while to learn how to match up their emotions with their thoughts so you can label them and recognize what you're sensing. If it starts to get too overwhelming, remember the key is to stay calm. The stronger your own emotions, the less you'll be able to control your abilities. And if all else fails, try to focus on a nearby descendant instead.*

A descendant? I couldn't help but scowl at her for a second. Then I went back to searching the hallway, my instincts screaming at me to stay alert though I didn't understand why. *Why would I want to sense anything from them?*

Because it's like tuning in to a different radio station. It makes the humans go quiet. Clann thoughts might be nastier, but at least they're quieter since there are fewer descendants than humans.

Huh. Okay, if it shut off the thousand and one voices inside my head…

I nodded and tried to follow her instructions, focusing on the few descendants who passed by till the hall began to clear as the students rushed off to the cafeteria or their next class.

She was right. Listening to the descendants' thoughts was like tuning in to a much quieter radio station. Too bad it was one playing the "I hate Tristan and Savannah" soundtrack 24/7.

When the hall was half-empty, I found it easier to start moving again.

"We can wait here till they're all gone," she murmured,

ignoring the curious glances shot our way. "I'm here. Just breathe."

"I'm okay. It was just…a surprise, is all." I took a deep breath, squeezed her hand at my elbow and started walking again. I could breathe easier again, too. "So this is what you had to deal with every day?"

She nodded. "I promise it gets easier."

We headed down the now mostly empty hall toward the main building's rear exit, her thoughts filling with a glow from the simple pleasure of our getting to walk together like this on campus around others for the first time ever. But it was hard for me to join in with a steady dose of guilt growing inside my chest.

I really owed her an apology.

"Sorry," I mumbled. "You know, for using this ESP thing against you all those times." It had been bad enough for me to have to deal with hearing and feeling all those thoughts and feelings from everyone else with Savannah there to guide me through it for the first time. I couldn't even imagine how frightening it must have been for her to go through it alone with no one there to hold her hand, reassure her that she wasn't going insane, tell her how to turn down the volume on it by listening to the descendants instead.

And I'd made it worse by teasing and tormenting her with my thoughts every chance I'd gotten, in a dumb campaign to make her jealous.

"You're forgiven." She said it so simply, as if it were no big deal.

Did she have any idea how much I loved her?

Sometimes I do, she thought, ducking her head to hide a knowing smile.

We walked in silence out of the building, along the cement catwalk with its metal awning roof, then down the cement steps to the sidewalk that wrapped around the cylinder-shaped brick cafeteria. At the doors, she tugged me to a stop.

"Are you *sure* you want to do this?" she asked.

I didn't even have to consider my answer. I nodded. "I want to rub their faces in it so hard they can't see straight for a week."

"But why? We don't have to prove anything to them or anyone else in there."

"Yes, we do."

She frowned. "Why? Why does it matter what they think?"

"It doesn't."

"Then why push it? And why do we have to do this today? We could always come back later in the week."

"I told you, I've dreamed about this moment for a really long time. And I'm not going to let them or what they think keep us from finally having this."

She sighed. "It's our first day back. It feels like we're pushing it too hard. Like if we get greedy, something's going to break. Isn't it hard enough to be in your classes without facing this many of them all at once?" She hesitated. "And then there's the small matter of my friends."

I searched her face. "Worried I won't pass judgment as your boyfriend?"

"No, of course not! I just don't feel you should have to try to earn their approval and deal with all those humans and the smells and sounds and the Clann's attitude on your very first day back."

I stared at her, everything inside me going still now. "Are you worried I can't handle it?"

She groaned. "All I'm saying is, why push so hard all at once when you could space out the challenges a little and make it easier on yourself?"

"You're forgetting I used to play football. I like a good challenge, and the bigger the better."

She groaned again. "Fine. But the second you look like you're stressing out, we're out of here. Okay?"

I nodded.

"Promise me."

I grinned and held up a pinky. "Pinky swear."

The flashback to our childhood got a grin out of her. She hooked her pinky with mine. "Deal."

Finally.

I grabbed the metal handles of both doors, threw them wide-open, and we made our grand entrance into the bee-hive that was JHS's cafeteria. Almost every head in the place turned to stare at us. You could practically hear crickets chirp.

SAVANNAH

He was all too happy to lead the way to my friends' table, which he didn't even have to search for.

I told you, I've spent hours over the years staring at you with your friends and wishing I could be there beside you, he explained silently. *I could map out this table's location in my head at home.*

Mmm, stalker much? I teased, trying to ignore the audience all around us.

"Sav!" Michelle squealed as soon as she saw us. All of my friends jumped up from our table.

"Finally!" Anne pushed past Ron so she could be the first

to give me a fierce hug. "I knew we should have ignored you and gone over to your house last night anyways."

As Carrie elbowed her out of the way so she could give me a hug next, I gave Anne a pointed look over Carrie's shoulder. "You know we had a lot of…unpacking to do."

Actually, I'd been too nervous about having all three of my human friends at my house with Tristan and my dad. The mere idea had seemed a disaster in the making, so I'd begged my friends to wait for lunchtime today for our group reunion.

Carrie stepped back, and I smiled at Michelle, expecting her to step up for a hug, as well.

But she seemed rooted to the linoleum floor, her already large eyes even bigger as she stared openmouthed at something over my left shoulder.

Oh. Of course, Tristan.

"Hey," he said by way of a greeting.

Time to ease Tristan into the group. "Everyone, you know Tristan Coleman, right?" Who didn't at our school? "He'll, um, be sitting with us from now on."

"I thought you were going to skip this?" Ron leaned over and muttered.

I shrugged and made a face. "I tried to, but somebody's a spoiled brat and insisted on it."

Tristan waited to see which chair I reached for so he could be sure none of us had switched the routine seating arrangement. Then he gently nudged my hands free of the plastic chair so he could pull it out and hold it for me. I rolled my eyes. He was taking this show way too far.

Carrie poked Michelle in the ribs, making her jump then remember to return to her seat on the opposite side of the table.

As everyone sat back down, Tristan took his sweet time helping me hang my Charmers bag's strap over my chair. Finally he flopped down in the chair beside me, turning sideways away from me to stretch out his long legs. Sighing loudly with satisfaction, he propped his hands behind his head then grinned at my friends.

Gradually the noise level around our table returned to normal as everyone lost interest. But then the hairs along the back of my neck stood up. I snuck a peek over my shoulder. Yep. We still had a small audience over at the Clann table, and they did not look happy. My hands yearned to rub away the mild prickly sensation caused by their staring, but I resisted the urge, knowing the movement would give them a tiny victory they didn't deserve.

Tristan caught that thought and made a big show of throwing an arm around my shoulders across the back of my chair. In the process, he tossed them a quick grin over his shoulder. I shook my head, glad at least he was able to enjoy this ordeal despite the noise of the cafeteria that had to be giving the inside of his head a beating by now.

Then he settled into his chair and turned to face my friends.

Our table was quiet. Too quiet, like they didn't know what to say to him. Not the reaction I'd hoped for. I had figured they would jabber on among themselves like they always did, and Tristan could either sit back in silence while getting used to everyone, or he could choose to jump into the group conversation when he was ready. Instead, everyone sat there staring at us with raised eyebrows as if they expected us to do all the talking. But what could we say about our long absence? Anne and Ron were the only ones at our table who even knew about the existence of vampires and magic.

As a Coleman and the former Clann golden boy, Tristan was known by everyone on our campus. But since my friends weren't descendants, none of them had spent much time hanging out with him. So what could they really talk about with him?

I looked at my friends, quickly considering each one's history with Tristan. Sitting at my right side, my best friend, Anne, was first on the list. She knew the truth, and she'd even helped out during the battle between the vamp and the Clann in the Circle last November. So she'd been there and actually seen me turn Tristan with her own eyes. She'd also teamed up with Tristan once or twice to secretly help fend off my first gaze-daze victims last year.

Not that we could talk about any of *that* as a group.

Next up was Ron, who sat at Anne's other side. As a shape-shifting Keeper and an ally of the Clann, he also knew all about vamps and the Clann and had seen me turn Tristan. He and Tristan had played for the JHS Fighting Indians football team, before Tristan's Clann abilities forced his parents to pull him from the team last year. Now Tristan's new vamp abilities would still keep him off the team.

That crossed football off the list of subjects to talk about.

Michelle sat on Ron's right. But she had a weird hero worship thing going on with Tristan, thanks to his helping her off the track at an eighth-grade track meet when she could hardly walk from shin splints. Even if she could actually find her voice before the end of our lunch break, they didn't have much in common to talk about. Neither of them had run track since junior high.

That left Carrie. But out of all of my friends, hers would be the toughest approval for Tristan to earn. Like Michelle, she knew only general rumors about the Clann and nothing about their true abilities or that vampires existed. And Tristan had never had an opportunity to help her or work with her on anything. A quick peek into her mind showed all she knew about him was his reputation as our school's biggest, richest player. She hated players. But worse than that was the money issue. She wanted to become a doctor, but her parents didn't earn a lot and were struggling to figure out how to finance her college dreams. Even my switch to expensive clothing, at my father's demand last summer when I'd moved in with him, had temporarily caused some tension between us. And we'd been friends for years.

Could she look past Tristan's last name and reputation?

Thankfully Michelle found her voice again and broke the silence to launch into her usual nonstop JHS gossip report, which brought the tension level down a few notches.

But while everyone else basically ignored Tristan, Carrie kept throwing quick little glances his way in between taking bites of her salad. I took another quick peek at Carrie's thoughts. She was trying to figure out what the attraction was between Tristan and me. Or more specifically, why I was attracted to Tristan beyond his good looks. She figured she understood why he was drawn to me…she thought of me as smart, nice, loyal to my friends almost to a fault, though occasionally a little weird and moody. But Tristan seemed the total opposite…a societal apex predator who went after anything in a skirt, cared more about money and image than what might lie underneath, and was about as deep as a dried-up creek.

Her words, not mine.

This wasn't going well.

Desperate to foster some sort of friendship between them, I reached for the first idea that came to my mind.

"Hey, Tristan, did you know Carrie's going to be a doctor someday?" I said, making my voice loud enough to carry across the table.

Carrie's eyebrows shot up then dipped into a frown as she wondered what I was up to.

"Oh, yeah?" Tristan turned to her with real interest. "That's cool. You know, I just learned some interesting stuff from Mrs. Horne today. She was talking about how there are companies out there now making synthetic blood using a process called blood pharming. Have you heard anything about it?"

Mrs. Horne the biology teacher? I silently asked him. *When did you talk to her?* We all took biology last year.

I ran into her in the hall on the way to your chem class and we got to talking, Tristan silently answered. Then he looked at Carrie again, waiting for her reply.

Carrie blinked several times in shock as she tried to assimilate her previous ideas of Tristan with this conversation starter.

Oh, of course, she thought. *He's just trying to sound smart to impress me. Well, let's see how long it takes to reveal his real lack of IQ.*

Out loud, she said, "Yes, I've read a few articles online about that. They're mainly creating the synthetic blood for use in the military in war zones."

Tristan nodded. "Because the regular donor blood doesn't last long enough on the shelf for use in areas far away from hospitals. By the time it reaches the soldiers, it's already too old and only lasts about a week. Plus there's that whole problem of getting enough of the more generally accepted O type blood donated."

"Too bad the synthetic blood requires the use of umbilical cords to make it." Carrie grimaced.

"How's that a problem?" Tristan said. "It's not like they're using the cells from the actual babies."

"Yeah, but it's an issue ripe for misuse," Carrie snapped. "Think about it. Who's got a big supply of umbilical cords they'd be too happy to sell off?"

"Hospitals?" Tristan said.

"And abortion clinics," Carrie said. "I'm all for a woman's right to choose, but I don't think anyone should be making money off of that. Abortion clinics would be only too happy to make some side profits by selling a bunch of umbilical cords to DARPA."

"DARPA?" Michelle asked, her eyebrows drawn in confusion.

"The Defense Advanced Research Projects Agency," Tristan and Carrie explained at the same time.

Carrie stared at him with round eyes, her shock deepening. "DARPA's funding the research behind the blood pharming. And they're the ones who'll probably end up using taxpayer dollars to buy the big old steaming piles of umbilical cords for all the blood pharming."

Anne made a choking sound and pushed away her chili cheese fries. "I'm not hungry anymore."

"Me neither," Ron muttered.

Oh, boy. What the heck had I started? "Um, guys, maybe we should talk about something else—"

But it was too late. Carrie and Tristan were deep into the debate now, and there was no stopping them.

"Why shouldn't we find a use for something that's going to be thrown away?" Tristan said.

"Because it comes from dead babies, that's why!" Carrie said, shaking her long blond bangs out of her furious eyes.

"Not only dead babies. And it's not like blood pharming is the cause of their deaths," Tristan said. "What about all the umbilical cords from babies delivered alive? Those get thrown out most of the time, too. Why not reduce the bio-waste and help save lives at the same time?"

Carrie rolled her eyes and sat back in her chair with her arms crossed. "If the cords were only obtained from live births, that would be okay. But who's going to regulate that, especially if demand for synthetic blood skyrockets? Besides, blood pharming costs too much to be worth it. They can only create twenty units of blood from each cord, and it costs something like five thousand dollars to do it. That's around two hundred and fifty bucks to make each unit, not includ-ing whatever fees they work out to pay for the cord itself. If the masses start thinking they don't need to donate blood anymore because we can all rely on synthetic blood instead, there goes all the donor blood that's already in short sup-ply. Then we really do end up having to rely solely or even mostly on expensive synthetic blood. Do you have any idea how much health-care costs would shoot through the roof then? A trauma victim can require up to fifty units of blood. And cancer patients make up twenty percent of all blood transfusions given. Can you imagine what their health-care costs would become?"

Of course you can't, she finished silently, not realizing Tristan and I could both hear her thoughts. *Because you've never had to worry about money in your entire life!*

Whoa. I sat back in my chair with a thump. I had never heard Carrie talk so much.

"The synthetic blood's only expensive right now because it's new and nobody's making it yet," Tristan said. "Once more companies learn how to create it and ramp up production to meet the demand, the costs will drop and make it more affordable."

"Oh, so you're going to rely on the free market's supply and demand to set the prices and help reduce health-care costs?" Carrie snorted. *Why am I not surprised? Typical rich boy, taking zero account for human greed because he's full of it himself.* "I guess you would be pretty excited, seeing how your family owns a biomedical supply company."

Tristan frowned. "What does that have to do with it?"

"Because obviously you're all set up to jump on the synthetic blood wagon and make a few billion more off others' misery for your family," Carrie said.

Tristan blinked at her in surprise. "To be honest, I didn't know my family's company could even do that sort of thing. I thought we only made sterilized containers for medical supplies."

One of Carrie's eyebrows arched as she thought, *Ha! I knew he was stupid after all.*

Out loud she said, "That's my point. Your company's facilities are already set up for creating stuff in sterile environments for the medical industry. I doubt it'd be all that hard to add some lab equipment and a few geneticists to start making synthetic blood for public use. Especially when the setup costs would earn out in no time."

"You really think so?" Tristan asked, his eyebrows raised.

Unable to read his thoughts, Carrie slowly nodded and watched him with narrowed eyes.

"Huh." He stared off into space for a minute. "It's an interesting idea. I wonder if Emily's heard about synthetic blood."

"Your sister? Why would she care?" Carrie asked. She'd always thought of Emily as a stereotypical dumb blonde cheerleader.

"Because she's the one destined to take over the family company as soon as she graduates from college," Tristan answered automatically. *She's the future brains of the family, not me,* he thought to himself, forgetting for a moment that I could hear him. "Em's always been the brains of my family."

He sounds sad about that, Carrie thought. *Like maybe he wished he was as smart as his sister.*

She cleared her throat, and when she spoke again, her tone was slightly softer. "You know, intelligence isn't set at birth. It can be improved with a little applied education. For instance, take a look around you at this table. Almost everyone here was practically flunking their science courses till I started tutoring them." She hesitated. "If you ever need any help in that area, by the way, you can always bring your homework here at lunch." She finished with an attempted half smile.

Surprised by the offer, Tristan smiled back. "Thanks. I may take you up on that. Emily used to help me with my homework, but now that she's gone off to college…"

"Hey, what am I, chopped liver?" I blurted out with a laugh.

Carrie snickered. "Do *not* get her help with science unless you really do want to flunk. English is Sav's forte."

Michelle nodded, making her short honey-blond hair

bounce against the tops of her shoulders. "She brought my C average up to a B+ in English, but she doesn't know jack about chemistry."

"No, chemistry's *my* area," Ron argued.

Carrie rolled her eyes. "Puh-lease. Just because you understand the elementary table and throwing together a few chemicals doesn't mean you get science as a whole."

"Speaking of," Michelle interrupted Ron's planned argument. "Did you hear about what happened last week in chem class with Sally Parker and Terrell Stuart? She found out he was cheating with Christie Permetter and threw some chemicals at him during a lab, and…" And with that, Michelle was off and running and nobody could get another word in for at least five minutes while she filled us in on more JHS gossip.

Until Dylan walked in.

"Aw, look, now there's a matching pair of them," he sneered as he walked past.

Tristan scowled and clenched his fists. But he didn't turn to look at Dylan, which made me proud of him. Maybe I was wrong to be so afraid of his losing control.

Michelle muttered, "I cannot believe he and Bethany Brookes are together. What can she possibly see in that jerk?"

"What?" I blurted out, leaning forward in my chair, sure I'd heard her wrong.

"Oh, yeah, for four months now," Michelle added, her eyes wide. "Talk about the last couple you'd ever think would get together. But she seems to like him for some reason."

So that was why she didn't want to welcome me back. She was dating my boyfriend's former best friend turned archnemesis now and was probably embarrassed about it or something.

But...Bethany Brookes and *Dylan Williams?* The idea just did not compute. She was so sweet and nice, and he was so... well, not. Was she dating him just to get back at Tristan for leading her on all last summer and this fall?

Tristan twisted in his chair and looked across the cafeteria. Sure enough, Dylan had just dragged a chair over by Bethany, turned it backward with a noisy dragging of metal legs across the linoleum floor, then straddled it. As we watched, he glanced our way, grinned, then leaned over and gave Bethany a kiss on the cheek that made her blush and lean toward him.

A single second of growling was all the warning I got. Next thing I knew, Tristan was gone. He reappeared across the cafeteria, where he held Dylan against the cylinder-shaped room's curved brown brick wall.

Oh, crap.

CHAPTER 6

I jumped to my feet and tried to remember to move human slow as I wove in between the tables to get to them.

"You son of a—" Tristan began.

Dylan laughed, or tried to. It came out as a wheeze past Tristan's forearm, which was pressing against Dylan's throat. "Jealous, Coleman?"

"I'm going to kill you, Williams," Tristan said, their faces only an inch away from each other. Tristan's irises had turned silver-white. Oh, so not good.

The thoughts of everyone around us slammed over me like a tidal wave....

Where the heck did he come from?

Whoa, looks like Coleman's still got the speed even after missing a whole season of practice! I didn't even see him move across the cafeteria. He's got to be juicing.

So Tristan isn't over Bethany after all! I knew he wouldn't get over the only girl who ever dumped him!

Oh, my God, look at how jealous Coleman is! He ran so fast over here I didn't even see him coming. He's going to try to steal Bethany back from Williams. But will she dump Williams for Coleman?

Oooh, look at poor Savannah's face. How devastating to have to see her boyfriend get so jealous over another girl! Any second now she's going to start bawling, and…

The descendants were thinking just as loudly. There was no way to shut out the ocean of voices. And way too many humans had noticed how fast Tristan had moved.

I risked closing the distance between us and grabbed Tristan's shoulder. "Tristan, let him go."

"He's—"

"I know. But you've got to let him go." *And you've got to calm down,* I added silently since we were surrounded by both descendants and humans who could easily hear even a whisper in the now dead-quiet cafeteria. *Everyone just saw you vamp blur over here. If you bite him, too, the council will have no choice but to go after you. Don't give the Clann what they want. If you do, Dylan wins.*

Tristan growled under his breath. Dylan's grin wasn't helping him regain control of his temper. But finally Tristan shoved himself away from Dylan and walked off.

Breathing out a sigh of relief, I followed him back across the cafeteria. My legs felt rubbery as I eased down into my chair again. Then I looked up and realized Tristan was still standing by his chair. I gave him a questioning look, then snuck a peek at his thoughts.

He was immersed in the thoughts of everyone around us.

I reached out and tugged at his hand. He blinked a few times, sank down into his chair, then slouched down in the seat with his arms crossed, lost in everyone else's thoughts.

Silence at our table, even though the noise level in the rest of the cafeteria had risen back to normal.

"I would have punched him in his stupid face," Anne said, then casually took a long chug of her soda.

"Anne, that wouldn't have helped the situation," Carrie said.

"No, he definitely should have hit him," Michelle said.

Tristan frowned, feeling like the rope in a game of tug-of-war between listening to my friends' opinions and everyone else's loud thoughts. He turned to me. *Sorry, Sav. I didn't even decide to go after him. One second I was here and the next…*

I sighed, reached over and patted his thigh. *It's okay.* I hoped.

But now everyone thinks I'm jealous about Bethany, and I'm not! I just hate that Dylan's using her to try to piss me off. She's a sweet girl. She deserves better than that.

This was definitely an awkward conversation to be having with my boyfriend, silently or otherwise. I tried not to squirm in my seat. *Let's just focus on getting through the rest of lunch without vamping out on anyone else, okay?*

One corner of his mouth tightened. *Go on and say it. You told me so.*

I shook my head, pressing my lips together. *Nope, not going to say it.*

Why not? You totally earned the right to this time. You warned me that coming here was going to push me too hard too soon, and just like you feared, I lost control.

I sighed. *Well, it could have been worse. At least you didn't actually bare your fangs or bite him.*

No, but I sure wanted to. His mouth slanted into a wry smile as our eyes met. He took my hand from his thigh and raised it to his lips for a kiss. *Have I told you lately how lucky I am to have you?*

I smiled. *Oh, you're just saying that to try to cover for the fact that you're jealous over your ex.*

He rolled his eyes at the joke. *You know that's not it.*

I nodded.

But did I *really* know that deep down?

I pushed the question away. Tristan loved me. He was just a good guy who hated to see Dylan hurt anyone, including one of his ex-girlfriends.

TRISTAN

Great. So much for proving I was in control all day long.

We stuck around in the cafeteria till ten minutes before the bell. Then Savannah and I cut out early, planning to grab a few minutes of alone time out on the catwalk.

Except it was already in use by Dylan and Bethany.

The rage rose up like a bonfire inside me, blistering across my skin, all but demanding I go after Dylan.

Then I felt the cool touch of Savannah's hand on my forearm, reminding me of all the reasons I shouldn't kill the punk descendant.

"I'm fine," I muttered to reassure her as we took the steps up to the ramp that led to the catwalk.

I planned on walking right past the couple without saying a word, just to prove I was in control again.

But then Dylan stopped kissing Bethany. Grinning, he clearly thought, *You always did have the best taste in women. Did she taste like honey to you, too?*

I stopped, my fists clenching at my sides.

"Dylan, shut up," Savannah hissed, stepping in front of me.

Dylan laughed. "Why, when it's so much fun to see him lose it over and over? You really should get a leash for that one. I don't think he's going to make it much longer if you don't."

Rumbling in my chest made me realize I was growling. I swallowed down the sound. *Control. Stay in control, Coleman. Don't give him what he wants.*

"Bethany, you should get out of here," Savannah muttered, glancing over her shoulder at me. She reached back to grab my forearm again, and this time her grip said she wasn't letting go for anything.

Bethany's eyes narrowed. "Why? We were here first."

"Don't be stupid, Bethany," Savannah hissed. "You could get hurt."

Bethany rolled her eyes. "I'm not some fragile flower, Savannah." She reached around and slid a hand across Dylan's chest with a smile. "Besides, Dyl will keep me safe, won't you?"

"You know it," Dylan murmured, turning his head to kiss her again.

"Bethany, can't you see he's just using you to tick me off?" I said.

They stopped kissing and Bethany smiled. "I don't think so. We started dating while you were gone, and we've been dating for months without you here to see it. If all he wanted was to make you jealous, why wouldn't he wait till you came back before asking me out?" Still smiling, she cupped Dylan's cheek. "I know my baby loves me. And for the record, if you're so worried about someone hurting me, maybe you should look in the mirror. Because Dylan has done nothing but treat me like a queen, which is more than I can say about you."

Dylan slid a hand around her waist and pulled her hard against him for another kiss. "That's right, baby. But don't be late for class because of me. See you after Charmers practice?"

Bethany nodded, threw me one last smirk, then walked down the catwalk with an extra swing in her blond ponytail, her thoughts full of confidence now that she believed she had two guys fighting over her.

Savannah glared at her fellow Charmer's back with one thought. *Ugh.*

Bethany stepped off the catwalk and headed down the sloping grounds' cement steps. The second she disappeared into the math hall on the sports and arts building's ground floor, I got in Dylan's face. "If you're leading her on, all the Clann abilities in the world aren't going to be enough to save you."

"Oh, yeah? And if I was, what are you going to do about it?"

My hands ached to grab handfuls of his shirt. Instead I clenched them down at my sides. "You really don't want to find out."

"Maybe I do," Dylan murmured. "Maybe that's exactly what I want, to see what the big bad Tristan can do now that he's turned. Why don't you prove how badass you are now, Coleman?"

"There's no audience around to save you now," I reminded him. Why was he pushing me so hard?

Savannah was right. Something was off. Dylan was obviously trying to push every button I had.

It smelled like a trap.

I took a step back, and his eyes flared then narrowed. Something bitter, like lemons, waved off him like a cloud. I checked his thoughts.

He was…afraid?

Told you, Savannah thought. *His dad's probably demanding he push us over the edge at school where everyone will see us lose control so either the council or the Clann will come after us. It's what he tried to do to me earlier this year.*

Yeah, but why? The Clann already kicked me out. What's the point of getting rid of me now? I'm not in his dad's way anymore.

"What's the matter?" Dylan said through gritted teeth. "Afraid to take me on now? I never knew you were a coward, Coleman. Did your daddy's death destroy you?"

Son of a… I breathed slowly, pushing the anger down again. "Shut up, Williams. You're not getting what you want here. I'm not going to give your dad the ammunition he needs to force the Clann to take us out."

Dylan's breathing sped up. He closed the distance between us, and this time it was his turn to grab my shirt and get in my face. "My father has nothing to do with this. This is all about you two freaks being where you don't belong…." He went on, spit flying in my face. But I didn't even hear him speaking anymore. It was all cover noise. The real truth was in his thoughts, in the memories of Mr. Williams's hand raised palm-out in the air, in the sounds of sizzling as spell after spell slammed into Dylan.

"Do it!" Dylan screamed in my face. "You freaking blood-sucker, you know you want to kill me. Just do it already!"

I grabbed his forearms, their bulging veins taunting me, calling to me. I pushed him away from me an inch at a time, watching as Dylan's eyes rounded and the muscles in his neck corded with the effort to fight me. But the physical difference between us was too much for Dylan to even have a prayer.

"What does he want, Dylan?" I asked. "He told you to tick us off, to push me over the edge. Why? I'm cast out. I can't be the leader anymore. So what does he want this time? What's the point of trying to get rid of me? Nothing I do will make my mother look bad now. She's washed her hands of me."

He'll kill me. The thought echoed over and over inside Dylan's thoughts as his chest heaved. He tucked his chin down, and I recognized that look.

As he ran at me, I whirled to the side and avoided the tackle. Dylan had always sucked at tackling. It was why he'd been so much better in the quarterback position.

Snarling, he turned around and came after me again. This time I grabbed the back of his neck as he missed me again. I pushed him against the metal railing, a *bong* vibrating down the entire length of the catwalk.

"Tristan," Savannah said.

I shook my head at her. *Still in control.*

Out loud I said to Dylan, "You know I can hear every thought inside that peanut-sized brain of yours. Why don't you just save us both time and tell me the truth?"

"Or what? You'll torture it out of me? Go on and try!" He whirled around, his fists flying through the air toward my face. I leaned to the left, then the right, neatly avoiding each blow.

"Tristan, the bell's about to ring," Savannah muttered.

Time was up. I grabbed him where his left shoulder met his neck, driving him back into the nearest pole. "Don't make me lose my patience."

Dylan closed his eyes. "Just do it already." *If you don't kill me, he will.*

"Why would he kill his own son, Dylan?" Savannah asked.

"Get out of my head, you b—" Dylan tried to scream.

Shaking my head, I tapped his left cheek with my open palm. I'd meant to barely slap him, but his pupils dilated and he started to slump. Cursing, I held him upright.

Turn me, Dylan thought as he fought to hold on to consciousness. *Just turn me or kill me.*

Whoa. Surprise almost made me let go of him. I regained my grip on his shoulder before he fell all the way to the cement. "What are you talking about?"

His eyes rolled as he blinked slowly. "I know she can do it. She pulled it off with you."

"You don't mean it," Savannah muttered. "You can't really want *this*."

But he did. He blinked hard, trying to clear his vision enough to stare at her. "You don't know him. I'm dead either way. At least if I were like you…"

Heat built in my chest, but this time the anger had a whole new target. Mr. Williams. "If your dad's using magic on you, tell the Clann. They'll put a stop to it—"

Dylan let his head drop back against the pole. "You don't get it. They don't care. Besides, it'd be my word against his. He's got too many friends on his side. The Clann will never stand against him."

"My mother would." The words slipped out of me as quickly as I thought them. Then I realized it was true. For all her faults and fears against vamps, she would never knowingly allow any Clann kid to be abused.

"She's not as powerful as she thinks," Dylan whispered. His pupils slowly contracted to their previous size.

What did he mean by that?

At first, I thought he was still trying to tick me off. But his tone was wrong, flat and unemotional now. Like he was just stating a fact.

"She's the Clann leader," I said. "Not even your dad would be stupid enough to mess with her."

He looked me in the eye, uncaring whether he got gaze dazed in the process. "Want to bet?" Before I could react, he looked away again. "Now either kill me or let me go, man."

Noise as other students drifted out of the cafeteria and headed in our direction.

"Tristan," Savannah murmured, her tone a warning.

I released Dylan and stepped back, lost in thought. He hesitated for a second then slunk off, shoulders hunched, hands shoved in his front pockets, his head hanging. He looked like a freshly beaten dog.

"Do you think he meant it?" Savannah asked just before the bell pealed, signaling the end of lunch. "About his dad threatening to kill him, I mean?"

I shook my head. "I don't know."

"Can't we do something to help him?"

I glanced at her in surprise. "Help the guy who's been bullying you for years? Are you serious?"

Her nose scrunched. "Yeah, I know. He's the world's biggest jerk. But that doesn't mean he deserves to have the crap magically kicked out of him all the time by his dad."

We slowly walked side by side toward the main building. I scowled at nothing, walking by sheer instinct, too lost in thought to notice the growing traffic around us as we neared the metal doors of the main building's back entrance.

Being furious at Dylan was a lot less complicated than whatever this new feeling was that was pushing around at my insides. If I didn't know better, I'd call it...pity.

Nah. Couldn't be.

"Maybe I'll shoot Em a text and see what she thinks." Dylan was never going to become a vamp, not if I had any say in it. But something about the whole situation didn't feel right.

What had Dylan meant about our mother not having as much power as she believed?

Yeah, I'd definitely have to talk to Emily about this. I doubted the Williamses had as much pull within the Clann as Dylan seemed to think. But it was better to give Emily a heads-up just in case something was going on within the ranks that she didn't know about. And while she was sniffing around, she could also tell our mother about Mr. Williams's abuse of his son.

CHAPTER 7

SAVANNAH

By the time Charmers practice wrapped up late that evening and Tristan and I drove home, I was exhausted.

"Want some help with your homework?" Tristan called out from his bedroom as I headed upstairs.

I hesitated. Since getting his memory back, Tristan's mind worked lightning-fast. He'd used the four-and-a-half-hour trip home from Arkansas yesterday to read all of our textbooks so he could get caught up on the five months' worth of homework I'd done for both of us during our absence. And not only did he read fast, but he also seemed to photographically memorize everything he read, as well. Getting good grades definitely wasn't going to be a problem for him from now on. Boredom while at school, on the other hand, was a real danger where he was concerned.

But it wasn't the smarter version of Tristan that made me hesitate. It was the idea of being in a room alone with him.

Every day since turning him last fall, we'd always had someone else around.

I was being ridiculous. I could handle the temptation.
Besides, Dad would be right downstairs, listening to every
sound we made.

"Sure," I answered him. "Let me change and I'll be right
over."

In my bedroom, I exchanged my school clothes for com-
fier pajama pants, thick wool socks and a hoodie. With no
humans around, I could finally put on some extra layers to
ward off the ever-present chill I felt in spite of the warm East
Texas weather. The bank signs all said it was 78°F today, but
to my frozen fingers and toes, it felt more like 28°F.

I padded over to Tristan's bedroom, next door to mine,
and knocked on the door.

"Come on in," he said, setting aside a textbook he had
been reading.

"Leave the door open, please," Dad called out from the
living room, making me roll my eyes.

We still weren't sure I could even have children if I wanted
to someday, since no female vampire ever had before. Their
bodies saw baby embryos as foreign infections that had to be
eradicated immediately. Then again, I wasn't exactly your
average female vamp, so...

Still, I left the door open to make Dad feel better, then
slowly walked around Tristan's bedroom.

Since returning to Jacksonville, we hadn't had time for
him to do much to his new room. So it was still mostly
bare, no pictures or posters on the dark green walls Dad had
painted, the old-fashioned rolltop desk's surface clean except
for Tristan's laptop, the bedside table beside him holding only

a brass lamp and his MP3 player, now plugged into the wall nearby and recharging. Then I spotted the photo of me taped to the wall above his carved oak headboard.

"Where'd you get that?" It looked like my school photo from last year, but I'd never given him one, at least not that I remembered. A closer look showed that it had been printed on thinner paper than photo stock.

Tristan continued to stare at me, watching me, his hands tucked behind his head. "There weren't many messages to run from the office during first period, and I got bored. I realized I didn't have any pictures of you. So I copied one from our yearbook. Too stalkerish?"

I smiled. "No. It's sweet. You know, you could even stick it in a frame if you want. Dad's okay with you decorating however you want in here. We both want you to feel at home."

When I glanced at him again, he caught and held my gaze. "Anywhere you are is my home, Savannah." He dropped his hand to the mattress beside him palm-up in invitation.

I slowly crossed the room to him and sat on the edge of the bed at his hip. His arm rose to make room for me then rested across my thighs, his hand curving around my hip.

Because my nerve endings screamed for me to get closer to him, I forced my mind to focus on other things. "Maybe you should call your mom tonight. You know, to let her know how your first day back at school went?"

I'd already texted my mother on the way home from school while Tristan had fun driving us in my car.

His mouth tightened. His eyelids dropped halfway, concealing his eyes from me. The memory of his mother casting him out of the Clann and her life right after I turned him flashed through his mind before he pushed it away. "Not a good idea."

"I know she screwed up that night. But she's still your mom, Tristan. And I know she's worried about you. Any mother would be."

"She's not worried about me. I'm dead to her now." His voice hitched on the word *dead*. He swallowed hard, the sound loud in the silence of the room.

"She can't really feel that way. She was just freaked out. She'd just lost her husband—"

"What about me? I lost my dad. Now it's like I've lost my mom, too. I feel like an orphan here, Savannah!"

I stared at him, shocked by the pain he was finally allowing himself to feel. I listened to his racing heart, waiting until it calmed down again. "Talk to her. Give her another chance. She just needed time to get used to all the changes."

"Whatever."

I blew out a long, slow breath through my lips. "Maybe the problem is you two are both being hardheaded. She made a mistake and said some things she shouldn't have. But she's your mother. You have to forgive her."

"Her first."

"What?

"Tell her to forgive me for becoming her worst nightmare. Then we can try to talk it out."

I sighed. There was no point in pushing Tristan about this any further tonight. It had been a tough day for both of us. We had plenty of time to talk about this later. "I should go, let you get to your homework or whatever. I don't really need help with mine."

"No, don't go yet. I already did my homework while you

were at Charmers practice. Which I notice you were awfully careful not to tell me about. Was Mrs. Daniels and everybody else happy to have you back?"

His anger and hurt and resentment, directed solely at his mother, was immediately packed away somewhere deep inside him. Now all I saw and sensed from him was love and loneliness.

It couldn't hurt to stay a little longer. "Yeah. Well, mostly." I let him see my memory of overhearing their thoughts and the rumors currently swirling around us.

He cringed. "We should come up with a story. One that doesn't involve eloping to Las Vegas or you getting knocked up."

"Why bother telling them a lie? They won't believe it anyway. You know how they are. They'll believe whatever story they choose."

I glanced at him, noticing the thick textbook at his other hip, still open and lying facedown. It must have been some pretty interesting reading. Even with his new speed-reading ability, he still wasn't much of a reader by choice.

I reached for the book. He shocked me by quickly laying his free hand over the cover.

"Oh, now I really need to know what you're reading." I tried reaching over him for the book again, losing my balance and falling across him. He just as quickly grabbed the book and used the advantage of his long arm to hold it beyond my reach.

"It's just a book from school," he said.

"Then why don't you want me to see what it is?"

Rolling his eyes, he sighed and turned the book so I could read the title on the front.

"Intro to Genetics?" I read aloud, my eyebrows as high as they would go. "Where did you get—"

"Mrs. Horne. Remember at lunch how I said I ran into her on the way to your chem class? Well, her youngest daughter's majoring in genetics at UT at Tyler and loaned this book to her. Mrs. Horne let me borrow it after I asked her about how to make that synthetic blood we all talked about"

"Have you told Emily about it yet?" He had mentioned that maybe Emily would be interested in blood pharming since she was destined to take over BioMed someday.

He looked away. "Nah. It was just a stupid idea I was kicking around for fun."

"Tristan, tell her."

"What's the point? It'll be years before she graduates from college and is ready to take over BioMed. By then, plenty of other companies will probably start making and selling the stuff for anyone who wants it."

"There doesn't have to be years of delay. Why wait till she can use the idea herself? Your mother's still on the board, right? Emily could pass it on to her, and then your mom could get BioMed to—"

At the mention of his mother, his eyes turned dark. "Get real, Sav. The BioMed board's all Clann. They're never going to take a vampire's idea and run with it, not even if it could make them a ton of money and give them leverage over the vamps."

Okay, now his hang-up with his mother was really starting to irritate me. He was making her out to be some kind of a radical anti-vamp racist. But she was still his mother. And from what I'd heard, she was also smart. Too smart to let a great idea like synthetic blood pass by the family company just because a vamp suggested it.

Before he could stop me, I grabbed his phone and took advantage of my vamp speed to shoot off a text to his sister.

He tried to grab the phone from me, but I managed to send it before he could stop me. "What do you think you're doing?"

"Making sure that fine mind of yours doesn't go to waste." Smiling smugly, I handed him back his phone.

Grumbling, he read my text message to Emily then huffed out a loud sigh. "All they're going to do is laugh at her."

"Not if she tells them the idea was hers to begin with. And I have a hunch she will. You always told me your sister was smart." At his reluctant nod, I added, "Then why don't you trust her to figure out a way to handle your mother? Maybe the board will still be stupid and shoot it down. But you'll never know unless you let her try."

He scowled but tossed the phone onto the mattress beside him in silent defeat. "As long as I get to tell you I told you so when nothing comes of it."

"Agreed. Now why don't you tell me what else you've been learning from this big ole book?" I scooted down to curl up beside him, draping an arm across his waist and resting my cheek on his shoulder.

Warmth began to radiate out from every point where our bodies made contact, and I sighed with relief as my always tense muscles finally began to relax. Why was it that I was only warm when touching Tristan? I didn't even have to be this close to him, either. Sometimes I could swear just our holding hands made my low body temp shoot up several degrees.

"I looked that up actually," Tristan murmured. "It's called vasocongestion, where blood flow is increased in localized areas. It's a physiological response to being, um, physically attracted to someone. It happens to humans, too."

I burst out laughing. "Good grief. Does that book cover everything?"

"No. I found that stuff on the internet. This is more focused on genetics."

I tilted my head back and grinned at him. "Have I ever told you how hot you are when you talk like that? Quick, say physio whatever again."

He laughed. "There's more where that came from." He slipped an arm around me then flipped open the textbook and began to read the introduction. I could tell from his thoughts that he meant it as a joke, but I didn't stop him.

After a page, he quit on his own, his mouth slanted in a wry smile. "Had enough of my nerdy hotness yet?"

"Nope. Keep reading."

"Huh. Could have sworn I heard you snoring there for a second."

"Ha-ha. I do not snore."

"You really want to hear this stuff?"

"Sure." If genetics was the thing that floated his boat now, why not learn about it? Not that I could really follow much of what he was reading. There were too many holes between my high school level science education and what his college textbook discussed. But clearly he was loving being the smartest one in the room for a change. Why not let him enjoy it for a while longer?

Besides, I really did love the deep rumble of his voice, and here was the perfect chance to hear it uninterrupted. And after such a long and stressful day, I couldn't think of a better way to soothe my ragged nerves. If I closed my eyes, I could almost pretend we were back in the cabin on that Arkansas mountaintop, far away from the rest of the world and all its problems with us. Just the two of us, where things were so much simpler...

I fell asleep four pages into the introduction and slept soundly without any nightmares for the first time in weeks, completely clueless as to what I'd just done and how it would change all our lives forever.

CHAPTER 8

TRISTAN

For the next few days, we tried to settle back into a normal life. Every time Savannah and I were together, I caught her trying not to wonder if my mother was actually considering my synthetic blood idea for BioMed. I knew she couldn't help the direction of her thoughts. But every time she slipped, so did I. Not that I needed her help.

Mom and the BioMed board would be idiots not to take the synthetic blood idea and run with it.

But when it came to vampires, Mom and the all-Clann BioMed board weren't usually all that rational, logical or reasonable. I could all too easily see them barely even considering any idea I came up with, much less one that would help their archenemies.

I should have asked Emily to claim the idea for her own before telling Mom about it so at least Mom would hear her out before rejecting the idea.

If only they could see the huge political benefits to the Clann, as well.

But I wasn't nearly as naive as Savannah. Neither BioMed nor any other Clann-held business would ever make anything that would help vampires, even if it meant curbing their bloodlust or need for real human blood.

So I let the idea go and tried not to care. I'd once dreamed of being free of all responsibility for the Clann or the family company. How could I complain now that I'd gotten that wish?

And once I let it go, I tried my best not to think about anything even remotely related to synthetic blood all week.

Until Emily texted me on Thursday at lunchtime just as I was sitting down in my new regular seat beside Savannah at her friends' table.

Mom liked the idea & presented it 2 the board this morning. They like!

Though reading the text only took me half a second, I had to blink a few times before I thought to show it to Savannah.

Just as she squealed and started to grab my hand with a grin, my phone buzzed with another incoming text from Emily.

Mom wants to do dinner at the house. U free 2morrow night at 8?

I stared at the words, their meaning barely registering.

Emily would never joke around like this, especially not about our mother with me.

Savannah either read the message or the thought in my mind. She froze then whispered, "You're going to say yes, right?"

Two yards behind us to our right, the cafeteria doors banged open then shut again as someone entered the building.

When I didn't immediately answer, she said, "Tristan, you have to go. It's your mother. She and BioMed liked your idea. She probably wants to celebrate with you."

"Or see for herself how different I am now."

Savannah groaned. "No, she doesn't. If she wanted to know that, she could just come over to our house for a quick visit."

A house full of three vamps? My mother? I thought, pointedly staring at her.

"Okay, point taken. But still, she wouldn't risk being alone with you if she were still afraid. So why else would your mother invite you over for dinner if not to celebrate and/or apologize?"

Sneakers squeaked to a stop on the linoleum floor behind me. I glanced over my shoulder and scowled, feeling my pulse take off. Dylan.

"Dinner with your mommy?" he said, and I didn't have to see his face to know he was sneering. It was all there in his tone. "You are the biggest idiot I've ever met, Coleman. Do you really think she's going to welcome you back into the Clann just because you had one idea?"

I growled deep in my chest as my blood heated with the need to grab and smash something. Preferably Dylan's face.

Stay in control, Savannah warned me. *You know he's just trying to get you to lose it again in front of everyone and prove you're dangerous.*

He should be thinking about how dangerous my fists are to his face, I thought. But I stayed in my seat.

"Get lost, Williams," Savannah muttered. "And you can tell your dad I said he can get lost, too. Neither of you are going to get what you want. Not here, not now. Not ever. We're not that stupid."

"We'll see." Dylan walked away whistling an unrecognizable tune.

When he was on the other side of the cafeteria, I let out a long breath and stole another glance at my phone. Emily was still waiting for a reply.

I slouched in my seat, my left knee beginning to bounce beneath the table. I had no idea how to feel about this dinner invite. Or maybe I did and was just afraid to admit it to myself. How stupid would I have to be to feel hopeful that my mother might be coming around and ready to talk? She hadn't called me, not once, or even sent one text message the entire five months I was in Arkansas trying to remember who and what I was.

And yet now I was supposed to jump just because she was finally ready to invite me over for dinner? A dinner she knew I couldn't even eat?

Something else was up.

Savannah groaned again. *Tristan, stop being so paranoid! This is your* mother *we're talking about. She wants you to come home for dinner. Maybe she wants to apologize for freaking out so badly about your being turned. Can you really blame her for reacting like that at first? Everyone knows how she feels about vamps. And then she was faced with her worst nightmare with no time to adjust to the idea, and the whole Clann was there breathing down her neck. She had just lost her husband and worked so hard to secure your lead-*

ership of the Clann, and then bam, her son switched sides and she did the only thing she could. She had to take over the Clann, which was no small thing all by itself. But on top of that she had all those descendants staring at her, waiting for her to make her first decision as Clann leader—

"Which was to kick me out!"

Everyone at and near our table stopped talking and turned to stare at us. I took a deep breath, crossed my arms over my chest, and made a point of clamping my mouth shut.

Sav, I get that she freaked out. But she went too far. She kicked me out of the Clann in front of everybody—

She was only doing what she knew they all expected her to. She had to prove her loyalty to the Clann first and you second—

Oh, and I guess that's why she never called or texted me afterward?

She was probably afraid the other descendants were watching her too closely and she'd get caught. Besides, I'm sure Emily kept her updated on your status.

If Mom is so sure she's being watched, why risk having me over for dinner tomorrow night?

Because for one thing, she can do spells to hide your presence at her house. And second, that would explain why she wants to meet with you in private instead of somewhere public. It would also explain why she had Emily send you the invite instead of sending it herself.

I scowled at nothing, making a girl walking by jump and scurry past a little faster. Savannah might have a point. But it still seemed pretty far-fetched.

You really think Mr. Williams would go that far?

It was Savannah's turn to frown and slouch down in her chair. *I wouldn't put anything past him and his ambition.* She sighed. *Look, just go have dinner with your mother already. Then you can find out what she wants. If I'm wrong about her wanting to apologize, then I'm wrong. But at least we'll know what this is all about.*

My phone buzzed again. I glanced at it then looked again, sure this time I was either dreaming or Emily was drunk texting.

She said u can bring Sav 2.

Savannah heard me read the text in my mind. She sat bolt upright in her chair. "Seriously? She said that?"

"Apparently. Em wouldn't joke about something like this." I smiled grimly and arched an eyebrow at her. "Now how do you feel about Mom's dinner invite? Still think it's a good idea to go?"

Eyes wide, Savannah opened her mouth, closed it, opened it again and cleared her throat. She reached for her purse, suddenly intent on checking her lip gloss in a tiny mirror inside. "Um, sure. I guess I could find something to wear." *Though why she wants me there...* she added silently.

I grinned, unable to resist the urge. *Who knows? Maybe she just wants to get to know you. It could be fun. Maybe you'll even become best friends by the time the night is over.*

Yeah, right, Savannah thought then cringed. *Sorry. It's just...* She took a deep breath. *I can see her wanting to reconcile with you. But me? The girl who turned her baby boy into a vampire?* She gave me a wry smile.

I reached for and held her hand, turning serious now. *Or maybe she just knows I would never go without you.*

Of course you would. She's your mother. You have to go, even if she hadn't included me.

If she can't accept you, then she can't accept me. I squeezed her hand while firing off a quick text with the thumb of my free hand to Emily.

We'll be there.

CHAPTER 9

SAVANNAH

Friday evening, Tristan and I rode to his house in silence. Thanks to Charmers practice running late, we, too, were running late, which I knew was driving Tristan nuts and making him even more nervous, though he didn't say anything.

He wasn't the only one nervous tonight.

What if I said something stupid and ticked off Mrs. Coleman? She already had plenty of reasons to hate my guts, since I'd basically taken her son from her and the Clann when I turned him.

I caught my thumbs drumming against the steering wheel and forced them to be still. Usually Tristan liked to drive my car, but tonight he had chosen to sit in the passenger seat instead. From the turmoil of his thoughts, I guessed he had too much to think about to want to pay attention to the road.

"It's going to be fine." I tried to reassure him yet again as we headed east toward his house.

He didn't say anything. Nor did he smile. He just sat there, staring ahead at nothing, his left knee bouncing so fast it was a blur.

I sighed. I couldn't wait to get tonight over with. Hopefully by the end of it, Tristan and his mother would have settled their differences, and we could all finally calm down and focus on the real challenge...getting through the daily life of being two hybrid vamps surrounded by humans and descendants in the heart of Clann territory. That was stressful enough without all this family angst thrown in on top of it.

I felt in my jacket pocket for my MP3 player, considering plugging it into the car's stereo. But then I spotted the entrance to the Coleman property a few yards ahead. Too late for music. Maybe we'd listen to it on the way home. With a sigh, I left the MP3 player in my pocket and focused on slowing down the car for the turn.

As soon as we turned onto the Coleman property, we felt it. Someone was using power, and lots of it. The wrought-iron gate was already open, the code box beside it smoking and charred.

Tristan hissed out a curse, the rapid-fire thudding of his heartbeat filling my ears. "Hurry!"

Oh, God.

I stomped on the gas, the car's back end fishtailing on the gravel before the tires caught and shoved us forward down the winding lane toward the Coleman mansion.

The two-story English Tudor quickly loomed into view. Once we reached it, I hadn't even shifted the car into Park yet when Tristan was out and at the house's front door, which, like the gate, someone had left wide-open.

I hurried to catch up in time to hear him calling out to his mother and sister as he entered the dark house.

The smoke hit me first, making me gag and my eyes burn and tear. From the stench of it, something seemed to be burning in the kitchen. Multiple smoke alarms pealed on both floors, forcing me to clap my hands over my ears to save my eardrums from rupturing. Tristan and I ran in a crouch through the foyer, tripping over stuff along the way, until we reached the kitchen. He grabbed something off the stove that was filled with flames and started to shove it into the sink.

I caught his wrist, stopping him just in time. "Use baking soda to put it out!" I had to shout over the screeching smoke alarms.

He left the saucepan in the sink to dart away somewhere and came back with a small box in one hand. When he poured it over the pan, the fire went out in a billow of powder.

Then we heard Emily scream upstairs.

"Emily!" Tristan yelled, running back toward the foyer while bent over to try to avoid some of the smoke. He disappeared up the stairs.

I grabbed the handrail to follow him. Suddenly a man dressed all in black appeared before me.

"Hello, freak," he said with a leer. "So glad you could join the party."

I glanced down at his hands. Each one held a stake.

So it was a staking party, huh?

My pulse took off, injecting my body from head to toe with adrenaline. The resulting rush was like nothing I'd felt before as time slowed to a crawl. Whole minutes seemed to pass between each of the man's heaving breaths, plenty of time for me to think. And to plan.

Even at the battle in the Circle between the vampires and Clann, I hadn't felt like this. I must have turned even more in the five months since then. Dad had warned that the evolution of my vamp side would increase every time I fed.

Was this how he saw the human world around him all the time, or only during moments of danger?

Upstairs I could hear small thuds, curses and explosions. Blue flashes of light like cameras going off lit up areas of the smoke overhead as, I assumed, Tristan and Emily fought their attackers.

I read my own attacker's mind then gasped.

He was Clann.

"Did Mrs. Coleman set this up?" I asked him.

His face scrunched in confusion. "I don't understand you, monster."

I snorted. Speaking molasses slow, I repeated myself so his human mind could make out every word I spoke.

He grinned then made a tsking sound. "Nancy would be so offended. That is, if she were still alive."

Oh, *no*.

I stepped in close to him, moving faster than he could blink. It wiped the smile off his face. "You'd better be lying, or I'll be the least of your problems tonight."

His right arm bent at the elbow, rising in slow motion. If not for the sinking horror filling my stomach with dread, I would have laughed at his stupid arrogance. He thought to stake a vampire?

I easily grabbed his arm and wrenched it behind his back, then caught his left wrist before he could move it, too. Leaning into his face, I said, "Better stick with your spells, descendant, if you want to take out a vamp like me."

Sleep, I thought, shoving my will into it. Energy burst out of my hands into him, and he crumpled to the floor, unconscious.

Then a second descendant tried to sneak up on me from behind.

Growling, I whirled to face him then darted forward and slammed my right palm into his chest, driving him backward into the entrance wall. The drywall cratered around him from the impact, and he was out. I let him drop to the floor.

I had to find Mrs. Coleman.

First, though, I reached out with my mind and found Tristan on the stairs. The distance made the volume of his thoughts quieter, but the open doors in between us still allowed me to barely reach him with concentrated effort. *I'm okay. Need any help up there?*

No, he thought back. *Emily and I've got them pinned. You okay?*

Yeah. I'm going to look for your mom. She didn't order this, by the way.

That's something at least, he thought back. *Be careful.*

Right.

I held my breath and ran, again in a crouch, keeping my hands out to warn me of walls before I could hit them. I found what felt like a hallway, judging by the two walls my hands found at either side of me. I slowed down and opened up my mind, searching for the telltale thoughts of anyone on the first floor. My left hand suddenly found empty space beyond it, and I stopped to mentally search the room. It was empty. Squinting, I continued forward down the hall, where the smoke seemed lighter and swirled away from me toward some kind of opening in the house. Open doors or windows maybe?

The room I entered was steadily clearing of smoke. My right hand found the coffee table just before I reached it, saving me from a bruised shin. But I wasn't crouched low enough for my hand to save me from tripping over something soft yet solid just to the side of the table.

I knelt there, half afraid to know, half sure I already knew. *Please don't let it be her.*

I waved my arms frantically through the air, creating a small breeze to help the remaining smoke clear. When that still wasn't enough to see, I put some willpower behind it and thought *wind blow.* A stronger breeze whipped up and gathered the smoke as it encircled the room once, twice then a third time before running back out the smashed, open patio doors.

I dared a glance down then closed my eyes as stomach acid rushed up to burn the back of my throat.

It was Tristan's mother.

She grabbed my ankle, opened her mouth as if to speak, but no sound came out. So I read her mind instead.

Mac...it's a lie...Mac's the key! Tell them...

She made a gurgling, choking sound, her eyes rolling wildly, her hands clawing at the air.

"Oh, my God. Mrs. Coleman—" I took her nearest hand in mine. "Tell me what hurts. Tell me how to help you!"

I raised my head, intending to scream for Tristan and Emily. But Nancy distracted me, her hand gripping mine as if to get my attention again so she could tell me something.

For a second her entire body convulsed, rocking and jerking as if she were having a seizure. She stiffened from head to toe then went limp, her eyes rolling to the side and staying there.

In total shock, I stared at her, mentally using all my senses to try to understand what was wrong with her and how to fix her. But even as I used my free hand to search her throat for a pulse, her eyes seemed to change, flattening and going dull.

I couldn't find a pulse with my fingertips, so I tried to read her mind again.

But there was nothing to listen to…no heartbeat, no thoughts, no answering squeeze or twitch when I patted the back of her hand I still held within mine.

Nancy Coleman, leader of the Clann and, more important, Tristan's mother, was dead.

CHAPTER 10

"What the…" Dylan muttered as he ran into the room then skidded to a stop on the hardwood floor. He stared down at Mrs. Coleman, then looked at me, his eyes going wide with shock. "You…you *killed* her?"

"What? No! I just got here. What are *you* doing here?"

Now his mouth snapped shut as he darted over to Mrs. Coleman's body and squatted down to check her pulse. But he didn't have to say anything. I could easily pick out the answer in his thoughts.

I gasped. "Your father did this? But why?"

He stared down at Mrs. Coleman. "Because it's time for new leadership." Silently he thought, *But this—killing Mrs. Coleman—this wasn't part of the plan. Was it?*

A rumble of footsteps warned us that we were about to be joined by several others just before Mr. Williams and three other descendants ran into the room.

"Vampire!" Mr. Williams roared and pointed.

I had just enough time to throw up a shield of energy around myself before the blue energy orbs hurtled my way, hitting my shield hard enough to force my calves and thighs to strain to keep me from falling backward.

"Savannah!" Tristan yelled, but it took a few seconds before he vamp blurred between Mr. Williams and Co. over to me while holding his sister tight against his side. As soon as he let her go, she wobbled then fell to her knees and threw up.

I increased my shield so it wrapped around both Tristan and Emily, as well. But the descendants had stopped throwing orbs at me as if waiting for something.

"You okay?" Tristan asked me, watching the descendants.

"Yeah. But your mom…"

"Why, Tristan, you fiend," Mr. Williams said with a slow smile that didn't reach his eyes. "You killed your mother!" He made a tsking sound and wagged an index finger. "You have been a very naughty boy this evening."

"What? I didn't…" Tristan glanced down at me with a frown. Then his gaze slid over to the body at my feet.

His eyes rounded, all color draining from his face. "No…"

Then he noticed Dylan still crouched over his mother's body with one hand at her neck, checking for a pulse.

"No!" Tristan roared, and the purely animalistic sound sent chills crashing through my body.

Then everything went really crazy, and even with the adrenaline-increased speed of my thoughts and reactions, I still had trouble following what happened next. To our left, more blue orbs exploded, forcing me to focus on holding the shield and returning fire against Mr. Williams and his crew.

"Emily, help!" I shouted. But when I glanced at her, she seemed too deep in shock over her mother's death. Emily had draped herself over her mother's body and was sobbing so hard her entire body rocked, though the sound was lost beneath the shouting and sizzling of flying orbs filling the room.

Then Tristan burst free of our shield and vamp blurred straight at Dylan.

"No, Tristan!" I yelled. "He didn't—"

But I couldn't speak fast enough to beat Tristan's speed as he tackled Dylan at a run, driving his former childhood friend backward.

"You killed my mother!" Tristan screamed into his face as he grabbed two handfuls of Dylan's shirt.

Then he picked up Dylan and threw him across the room with another animal-like roar.

Dylan hit the stone fireplace with a loud crack so hard the thick wooden mantle broke along its length and half of it clattered along with him onto the hearth. Air whooshed out of Dylan's lungs, and his eyes closed as he went limp.

Oh, my God.

Sirens wailed outside. I couldn't get a read on Mr. Williams's thoughts, so I searched one of his crew member's instead.

Police. And not only were they Clann, they were also very much on Mr. Williams's side and in on tonight's attack.

This whole thing was a setup to either kill the entire Coleman family or at least frame Tristan for his mother's death, leaving Mr. Williams as the clear choice to succeed Nancy Coleman as the next Clann leader.

"We have to go!" I grabbed Emily, dragging her with me over to Tristan even as Emily screamed and tried to reach for her mother again. She fought me so hard I was afraid I'd bruise or break her arms trying to hold her. "Tristan! We've got to go! The Clann police are coming for *you*."

He looked past me at his mother's body, taking a lurching step forward.

"She's gone," I said, risking letting go of Emily with one hand so I could grab his shoulder and shake him even as my heart ached for him. "We can't stay!"

His jaw clenched, his eyes turning white and narrowing as he looked at Mr. Williams.

Mr. Williams smiled back.

Tristan scooped up Emily in his arms. She didn't even have time to gasp before we took off with her out the patio doors and across the backyard west toward the woods and downtown Jacksonville.

I had run with Tristan before since turning him, but never as fast as this. Tonight the Tristan I had once known as a small boy was gone, replaced with a furious animal. Fangs extended and lips peeled back in a snarl, he ran on pure instinct with his sister, never looked down at her or around us as he vamp blurred through town toward my house. It was all I could do to keep up with him, and when we burst into the house through the front door, stopping only once we reached the living room, I had to bend over and catch my breath.

He set Emily on the leather couch then darted away to the front window to pace back and forth, his fists clenching and unclenching over and over. A quick peek at his thoughts actually made me flinch and stare in horror.

He wanted Mr. Williams and the rest of the Clann to follow him here. He wanted revenge. He wanted their deaths… and their blood.

"Tristan…" I whispered.

Dad vamp blurred into the room. "What has happened?"

Swallowing hard, I spoke as fast as I could, telling him what had happened at the Coleman house. With every word I spoke, his face grew darker and darker.

I looked down at Emily, expecting her to fill in the details of the fighting that had occurred upstairs. That's when I realized she wasn't breathing.

Oh, God. If Tristan lost her, too, he'd never survive it.

"Emily!" I whispered, checking her throat for a pulse. Nothing.

Tristan disappeared from the window, reappearing in a crouch at Emily's head. "Emily? Emily!" he shouted.

Dad grabbed Tristan's wrists before he could tap his sister's cheeks.

"Do not touch her," Dad said. "In your present state, you will kill her."

Tristan growled at him, chest heaving. "Let go of me. She is my *sister*."

"Tristan, please let him help," I said.

Tristan glared at Dad for several long seconds. Finally he nodded and took a step back.

"Was she awake before you picked her up?" Dad asked Tristan.

Tristan nodded, his eyes wild as his hands buried themselves in his hair and gripped the curls as if to tear them out.

"You ran too fast with her. The pressure of the movement prevented her from drawing a breath." Dad pinched her nose and opened her mouth as if to give her CPR, then hesitated and looked up at me. "I cannot. She is Clann. I..."

He was afraid he might give in to the temptation to bite her.

I took over, carefully giving Emily a deep breath, then another, and another.

Finally she started coughing.

Tristan dropped into a crouch beside her and took her hand, staring at his sister as if to make sure she really was okay.

Dad blurred out of the room then back with a glass of water, which he silently offered Emily. She took it with a grateful nod. After a few sips, she slapped Tristan's shoulder with a loud thwack.

"Don't you *ever* run that fast with me again, you idiot! You could have killed us both." Her free hand rested protectively over her tummy, which I now noticed was a huge round hill from chest to hips. She closed her eyes, her lips moving soundlessly. Finally her shoulders sagged and her eyes flew open. "It's still kicking. If you had hurt it—"

A screech of tires outside alerted us all to the arrival of guests. Great.

Tristan darted over to the window and snarled. "They're here. Good. We can finish this."

"No, Tristan," Dad said, and there was no room for argument in his tone. "We must get free and warn the council. If Mr. Williams has staged a coup, then war against the vampires is sure to follow."

A second war between the Clann and vamps. How many times had both my parents and Nanna expressed their fear of this very thing happening?

Our worst nightmares were about to come true.

For the second time that night, my skin broke out in goose bumps as the descendants both inside and outside the house ramped up their power in preparation. Obviously we'd have no time to pack.

Something pounded against the roof.

"What are they, navy SEALs?" I muttered in disbelief. They couldn't seriously be attempting to break into the house from the roof, could they?

Then we heard the crackling.

"They are setting the house on fire," Dad said, his face emotionless though his eyes were dark. "We must get out."

"That's exactly what they want," Tristan growled. "They're trying to smoke us out so they can take us."

I shook my head. "They don't have to smoke us out, Tristan. We can all die by fire right here inside. Remember?"

Dad disappeared then reappeared with a handful of papers, which he stuffed down inside his shirt, using the tucked-in top like a giant pocket for passports, cash and cards.

The crackling turned into a faint roar as tendrils of smoke began to form overhead, then quickly thickened into a cloud that drifted ever lower.

Great. More smoke.

"We must leave now," Dad said. "Through the side parlor windows, I think. We will stay within the cover of the woods and head west on foot. Emily, perhaps I should carry you this time to ensure you can still breathe?"

She hesitated then nodded. "Good idea."

Dad led us out the living room and across the foyer into the parlor. Suddenly the stained-glass window on the front door exploded inward, showering the foyer with a spray of colored glass. Tristan and I both dropped into a defensive crouch, our hands raised and ready to hit whoever came through with a spell.

Instead, fire burst through the foyer like a huge, fast-moving snake, twisting side to side almost as if it had a mind of its own and was searching for us.

Spell fire. It was the only explanation. But I'd never seen it used like this before.

"I will be right back!" Dad shouted then disappeared before I could argue that we shouldn't split up.

He reappeared three seconds later holding two plastic shopping bags full of something. Without explaining, he thrust the bags at me, then scooped up Emily.

"Tristan, the window," he said. "On three?"

Tristan nodded and we all got ready.

Tristan raised his hands, Dad counted, and on three the window exploded outward with Dad leaping out right behind the flying glass.

I took a deep breath then jumped after him and ran as fast as I could toward the surrounding woods that wound through Jacksonville, following as close to Dad as I could.

I glanced back to make sure Tristan was with us, just in time to see him leaping out of the house with a huge wall of flames at his back. At first I feared he was on fire, but once he was free of the house, I could see he was also clear of the fire, though the flames did their best to reach out through the window after us.

And then I saw the entire roof, covered in flames, collapse on my home.

Tristan grabbed my wrist and pulled me with him, jolting me out of my shock and horror. And then we were all running together too fast for me to think about anything but ducking and dodging low-hanging tree limbs thick with pine needles.

None of us slowed until we were deep in the woods that separated Jacksonville from the surrounding towns in an evergreen cocoon.

Finally, Dad stopped, easing Emily onto a nearby fallen tree so she could catch her breath. Tristan insisted on checking both of us for injuries. Seeing we weren't hurt, he moved away from all of us, turning his back to stare through the woods while Dad called my mother to ask her to come pick us up.

Tristan was too still, standing there with his fists clenched, his feet braced wide, his head unmoving. I tried to search his thoughts for some clue as to what was going on inside his head, but it was a raging roil of emotions way too mixed up and volatile for me to make out.

Emily walked over to him. He turned with a snarl. "What is *wrong* with you, Emily?"

"What?" she gasped.

"Why didn't you stop them before they killed her? They killed our mother, and you just hid in your room like a scared little kid. You let them kill her!"

Emily took a step back and gasped. Her hands clenched into fists at her side. "I tried—"

"Spare me. You and I both know you're capable of way more than that pathetic little display you put on back there. She wasn't perfect, but she was our mother. She deserved a real fight from you."

"I did the best I could!" Emily shouted. "I was upstairs dressing when they showed up. I fought them for forever all by myself. By the time you showed up, I didn't have anything left!"

His face contorted. "Since when have you run out of energy so—"

"Since this." She jabbed a finger in the direction of her rounded tummy. "This…thing is sucking up all my energy! I almost didn't have enough to even keep them off me tonight till you showed up. If you hadn't come when you did…" Her voice choked.

Tristan stared at her stomach as if seeing it for the first time, his eyes widening. We'd learned Emily was pregnant during the fight at the Circle where I'd turned Tristan, but with all that had happened, without seeing her, the reality hadn't hit until now.

Emily buried her face in her hands and sobbed.

Tristan took a halting step in her direction then another. And then he was there beside his sister, wrapping his arms around her and resting his cheek on the top of her head. "I'm sorry, sis. I shouldn't have said that stuff. I didn't know."

"Like I would really let our mother be killed?"

"I know. I was dumb. I shouldn't have said that."

"You shouldn't have even thought it!" She wrapped her arms around him, her crying muffled against his shirt.

"She's gone, Tris," Emily whispered. "She's really gone. They both are."

I wanted to go to Tristan, try to comfort him as I had in our connected dream the night his father died. But for the first time in a long time, I was on the outside. My dad and I might have lost our home tonight. But Tristan and his sister had lost their *mother*. And there was nothing I could say or do to lessen their pain.

My mother might not have been up for any mother of the year awards. But she'd always made sure I knew she loved me. And she was still alive. I could call or text her anytime I needed to, and I knew she would answer.

And now she was on the way to pick us up. But in doing so, Mom was putting herself in a huge amount of danger from multiple fronts. Mom had turned away from her Clann abilities and allowed them to atrophy years ago. She had no magic to call upon for even her own protection, much less mine or anyone else's if the Clann tracked us down.

And then there was the added problem of her being around Dad, Tristan and me. Just because she had been cast out of the Clann and never used her abilities didn't change the nature of her genetics. Her Clann blood would still be every bit as tempting to vampires as any other descendant's.

I swallowed hard and forced myself to turn to him. "You sure it's a good idea getting Mom involved in this?"

Dad sighed. "Believe me, I wish we did not have to. But she is your mother and therefore already involved. If she is not with us, the Clann could very well try to seek her out and use her as bait to lure us to them. Besides, her RV will be the best and most expedient way for all of us to get out of Clann territory and hide somewhere safe for a while."

I wished I could argue that the Clann would never do that. But after tonight and seeing how they had ruthlessly killed their own leader, I knew they were entirely capable of doing anything that would help them take over the Clann.

Not that all of them had known the full plan.

I remembered the shock and horror on Dylan's face when he'd discovered Mrs. Coleman's body, and how he'd assumed at first that I'd killed her. He definitely hadn't been fully in on his dad's plans for tonight.

I saw again how Tristan had grabbed and thrown him across the room even as Dylan tried to tell Tristan the truth.

Shuddering, I pushed that memory away for now as my stomach knotted painfully. I glanced at my feet and got a peek of the contents of the bags Dad had given me to carry. The shopping bags were filled with plastic bags of blood. "You risked getting killed for blood?"

"Of course," Dad said, his face blank. "We do not know when we will be able to restock. Especially once war breaks out. Blood suppliers have a habit of going into hiding during such times to avoid the Clann's retribution. If that happens again, we must be prepared."

Well, at least we had the comfort of knowing we wouldn't go hungry for a while.

"We must stay on the move until we meet up with your mother," Dad muttered, glancing around us uneasily. "The Clann will send the Keepers to search for us soon. When they do, these woods will not be safe."

The Keepers. Oh, crap. "Can I borrow your phone for a second?"

Dad frowned. "Now is not the time to engage in a long chat with your human friends."

"Not a chat, a warning. Ron's a Keeper, remember?"

He held out the phone. "Keep it brief."

With a nod, I dialed Anne's number by memory. Thankfully she picked up instead of her mother.

"Anne, listen to me because I don't have much time. Mr. Williams is staging a takeover of the Clann tonight. He killed Mrs. Coleman and tried to kill Emily and Tristan. He set it all up to look like Tristan and I killed her."

"Are you freaking kidding me?" Anne gasped.

"I wish. They burned down my house, too." Before she could ask, I added, "We're all okay, Emily and Dad, too. But we're going to be in hiding till we can find a way to set the Clann straight on what really happened. Dad says Mr. Williams is probably still going to become the new leader, though. And that means Ron and all the rest of the Keepers are going to have to obey his every order."

"Like h—"

"Don't start, Anne," I growled, needing her to listen to me for once. "Please don't encourage him to try to stand up to Mr. Williams. If they can kill Tristan's mother, their own leader, how hard do you think it'll be for them to take out one rebel Keeper?"

A second of silence, then she mumbled, "Okay. So what do you want us to do?"

"Tell Ron to be a good Keeper and do whatever he's told. Even if that means hunting for Tristan and me. Tell him I said he can't disobey them no matter what. These people aren't messing around." Remembering Dad's warning about my mom, I closed my eyes and said, "They could hurt Ron's family if he doesn't obey them."

She growled under her breath but thankfully didn't argue with me. "How will I know you guys are okay?"

"We'll get some disposable phones eventually, I guess. If Dad thinks it's safe to, I'll call or text you on one of them." Thinking fast, I said, "What if you call me Cousin Sally or something like that?"

"Good idea! You know I've got tons of cousins spread all over the country. In fact, I'll start calling and texting them all more. Then if the Clann checks my phone records, your long-distance calls will blend right in with everyone else's."

I couldn't help but smile. Trust Anne to find a way to get even a little excited about this situation. "That's a great plan. It might be a few days before I can call again. But I promise I will check in on you guys, okay? In the meantime, try really hard not to think about us."

"Oh, crap, I forgot, they can read our minds. How the heck am I—"

"They won't be able to hear your mind unless they're in the room with you or if you're outside. The danger zones will be when you're at school or around town. Which reminds me..."

"Yeah?"

"Promise me you won't go hunting for anything, in season or not, until I say it's okay? Dad says things are about to get really nasty between the Clann and the vamps. I don't want you in the woods if he's right."

"Okay," she grumbled. "Stay safe and keep your heads down."

"Will do."

I ended the call though I hated to have to do it. I wished there was some way to keep Anne and the others safe. But short of making some protection spells for them, which I couldn't do from a distance, they were on their own and at the mercy of the Clann.

Just like us if we didn't get out of here.

I snapped the phone closed and handed it to Dad. "Okay. Let's go." I turned to the Coleman siblings. "Um, guys?"

Emily sniffed and wiped her nose, stepping back from her brother. He turned away to drag his forearms over his face before turning to face us again, as if ashamed to be seen crying.

I told myself it was my father he was trying to hide his tears from. After all, I'd seen him cry before, like the night we dream-connected after his father's death. That time it had been me who had held him while he dealt with the shock and loss.

But a knot still managed to form in my throat, making it hard for me to say, "My mom's going to pick us up, but we've got to run awhile longer on foot and meet her halfway."

Tristan nodded, keeping his eyes lowered while Dad picked up Emily again.

Tristan? I asked silently this time. *Are you okay?*

"Let's go," Tristan said, his tone gruff.

Dad took off again, Tristan right behind him, leaving me to follow them with a sinking feeling deep inside the pit of my stomach.

CHAPTER 11

Five minutes later, we neared the highway. We ran parallel to it within the woods for a while, risking crossing roads when necessary, carefully skirting towns. I lost track of time, grateful for the chance to stop thinking about everything else and just focus on the job of putting one foot in front of the other and avoiding obstacles like trees, bushes and entangling weeds in the ditches and fields.

Then we saw Mom's truck and trailer waiting at the side of the highway up ahead.

We slowed down to a human jog, allowing Mom to see our approach in the headlights as we ran up the side of the road toward her. By the time we reached the trailer door, Mom was there to usher us all inside. In the kitchen area, she gave me a quick, hard hug, checking me over for injuries before turning to do the same with Dad.

His hard features softened for a moment. Finally he spoke up. "Joan, I told you we are all uninjured."

He stepped away from her to stow the blood bags in the fridge.

"Oh, please, Michael," Mom replied, rubbing at her eyes with a shaking, weather-roughened hand. "You and I both know you always say you're fine whether you really are or not."

From the main bedroom at the other end of the trailer came an endless, piercing yapping from Lucy, the Yorkshire terrier who was supposed to have been my birthday gift last November. At least until we'd discovered the dog hated vampires. From the frantic, fierce pitch of her barking, it was obvious she hadn't changed her opinion of our species yet.

"Stop it, Lucy!" Mom shouted with no success. The dog kept right on barking her little head off in an attempt to destroy both my supersensitive vampire hearing and my already frayed nerves.

"Tell me everything," Mom insisted once she was sure we were okay.

Dad told her the short version. She grabbed the edge of the nearby kitchen counter when he told her about the Clann's attack on the Coleman house. When he got to the part where they tried to burn us inside Dad's house, she had to sit down on the couch beside Emily.

"I can't believe the Williamses would do all of this," she murmured. "I grew up with Jim. He always hated vampires, but this..."

"Believe it," I said, trying to keep my focus on her so I wouldn't stare at Tristan, who still hadn't said a word. "Dad's right. This was way too coordinated not to have been planned ahead of time."

"He's taking over the Clann," Tristan said. "He'll declare war on the vamps next."

"Not until he's officially voted in as leader," Emily said.

"Which'll take, what, a couple of days to round everyone up for an emergency vote?" Mom said.

"We must warn the council." Dad stepped outside for a few seconds, reaching for his phone in his pocket even before his feet touched the ground. The door swung shut behind him, only to jerk open again ten seconds later. He reentered the trailer, shut the door behind him and cleared his throat. "They…have requested a meeting with us."

"Why?" The word squeaked out of me.

"They want to hear a firsthand account of what happened. They…"

I read the rest of it in his thoughts. "They think *we* started this? That we lost control or something? Didn't you tell them about Mr. Williams and his hit team of descendants?"

Dad nodded. "My words did not matter. They demanded to meet with both of you. Immediately. They are sending a jet to the nearest airport for us."

"Absolutely not!" Mom snapped. "Savannah had nothing to do with this."

"Neither did Tristan," I told her. At least, not the part where his mother died.

But he had lost control and killed Dylan.

He turned his head to look at me, his eyes narrowing. *I didn't lose control tonight.*

I swallowed hard and looked away. "We can't go right now. Tell them Mom and Emily need us here."

"They will not care," Dad said.

"Fine. Then we'll go with you—" Mom began.

"No," Dad said. "I will not take you or Emily into my kind's territory. You will be safer here in the States for now. You will hide together in this RV in some remote park far from the Clann until we return."

Emily moved behind me and grabbed her brother's arm. "Please. Please don't do this. Tristan." She looked at him with pleading eyes. "Please don't go. You're all the family I've got left. What if you get there and they keep you prisoner or...or..."

Tristan looked at my dad. "What if we refuse to meet with the council?"

"Then they will consider us as having sided with the Clann and will treat us accordingly."

We would become enemies of both the Clann and the council.

Just like my parents had been for years before Mom couldn't handle the stress of a life spent on the run.

Tristan read my mind. He turned to his sister and rested his hands on her trembling shoulders. "Sis, I've got to go." She opened her mouth to protest. "I've got to get everything cleared up with the council. We can't be enemies of both sides, especially if war breaks out."

Tears spilled down Emily's cheeks as she stared at him for a long moment. Finally she nodded and stepped away.

"I will drive us to the airport," Dad said as he exited the trailer.

TRISTAN

Sav's dad coordinated everything by phone while driving us to the nearest airport. I didn't know where we were or which airport we'd be flying out of, and I really didn't care.

All I could think about was the terrified look frozen by

death on my mother's face…the same look of terror that had twisted Dylan's face, too, just before I'd thrown him across the living room of what had once been my home…the sound his spine had made as he crashed into the fireplace.

We all stayed in the trailer in silence during the fast and bumpy ride to the airport, then waited in the RV until Michael came back to the trailer to tell us it was time to go. I gave my sister one last hug. Her growing tummy bumped into me, a silent reminder of how vulnerable she was now. I hoped I would return in a couple of days to look out for her. Her words about how I was the only family she had left kept echoing inside my head.

Savannah hugged her mother in silence. Her mother was sobbing loudly and making no effort to hide her fear.

"Joan, we must not delay any longer," Michael murmured, and she reluctantly released their daughter. "Get as far north as fast as you can then find a state park or RV park somewhere to hide in." He pressed a credit card into Joan's hand. She scowled and opened her mouth to protest. "No, no arguments this time. At least give me this one small reassurance that you will have enough funds for anything you need in my absence. Do not let that foolish Evans pride further endanger yourself or Emily and her unborn child."

He stared hard into her eyes until Joan finally nodded.

I followed Savannah out of the trailer, Michael right on my heels until we were all down the metal steps. Then he took the lead toward a jet on the runway. A man at a side gate frantically waved at us to hurry over to him, then he slid the gate open just enough for us to slip through before shutting and locking it behind us. We jogged at a human pace behind the man in gray coveralls, across the tarmac and up to the jet's long line of white metal stairs.

Savannah paused for just a second to wave to her mother, wishing she could take away her mother's fear, wishing she wasn't afraid, too.

Then we boarded the plane and braced ourselves for the trial to come.

The last time we had walked through the maze of underground tunnels that led to the council's headquarters beneath the famed City of Love, I had been handcuffed and blindfolded. So I was looking forward to finally getting to see exactly what we'd been led through. Unfortunately, the council was still cautious as always, insisting we wear black blindfolds from the time we were picked up in a black sedan at the airport and later while we were led through the winding maze of tunnels, until Mr. Colbert stopped us outside the council's meeting room. Only then were we allowed to remove the blindfolds, which was pretty disappointing but understandable.

Then we stepped inside the meeting room and I was even more confused.

The cement block walls had been painted red and covered with old-fashioned-looking tapestries in an apparent attempt to spruce up the joint. But not much else had been done to hide the fact that this room was built primarily for security from outside attack. I'd expected something a little more lavish and a lot less fortress.

Then I looked at the long table draped with a red cloth. Behind it sat a line of nine very old, very ticked-off vampires.

The air became tinged with a bitter flavor I could almost

taste on my tongue, like some kind of mixture of crushed herbs and weeds.

Fear, Savannah thought, her gaze unwavering from the council. *You are sensing their fear.*

Of what? I thought.

Fear that the peace treaty with the Clann has failed. Fear of what is to come. But most of all, probably fear of us.

Huh. So the council was afraid of us. That seemed a good bit of info to store away for possible use later.

"Tristan Coleman and Savannah Colbert," the vampire in the middle greeted us with a somber tone. "You stand before the council today in order to report what has recently transpired within the Clann."

I decided to take the lead, because Savannah's heart was hammering so loudly I was sure the council could hear it even if they couldn't hear our thoughts. "Yes. We came here of our own free will to tell you about the death of..." Suddenly my throat choked shut.

"Of Nancy Coleman," Savannah finished, reaching out to take and squeeze my hand.

Quickly she related how my mother had invited us to dinner at her house, how we'd showed up to find the security gate and front door open and the house filled with smoke and descendants already attacking my family, and how we'd battled them in order to save Emily, though my mother had been beyond saving.

I worked to keep my face impassive and my breathing steady. But it was a challenge, because as she told them what had happened, I could see it all again within my mind...how the smoke had clawed at my eyes and throat and lungs, making it hard to see the descendants. And yet the adrenaline rush had made everything seem to move in slow motion, giving me far too much time to think and fear.

And then Savannah's scream from downstairs, running down with Emily to find her and Mom there in the living room…

Realizing that Mom was dead, that we were too late to save her…

Dylan hunched over her…

The crack of his bones when he hit the fireplace…

Tristan! Savannah thought so loudly it was practically a shout, shaking me from the memories. *Did you hear them? They asked what happened to Dylan.*

I cleared my throat. "Yes, Dylan Williams. He helped his father and several other descendants attack my family. When I first saw him in my—that is, my family's house—he was bent over my mother's body."

"And then?" the vampire in the middle prompted. He looked familiar. Then I recognized him. Of course. He was Caravass, the leader of the council, the vampire who had come with his council members to the Circle last year because another council member, Gowin, had led them there with lies meant to create a war.

I'd expected Caravass to be wearing some kind of goofy robes like a monk or something that would show off his position as leader of all the vampires in the world. Instead, he wore a crisp black suit with clean modern lines to it, paired with a navy blue shirt and silver tie. If not for the pale, superthin skin and color-changing eyes, which kept shifting every few seconds from icy white-gray to blue and then green, I might have had trouble recognizing him as a vamp.

Savannah, remembering the last time she had faced the

vamp leader in this room, had no such trouble. She knew all too well exactly who he was and the power he wielded.

"And then I killed Dylan," Savannah blurted out.

I turned to stare at her. *What are you doing?*

You're my fledgling and my responsibility. I'll take the blame.

I silently cursed. Turning back to the council, I said, "No, *I* killed him."

"He's trying to take the blame for me, your...er, honors. But the truth is I lost control and killed him, and I'm really really sorry." Savannah had a death grip on my hand.

This was ridiculous. I opened my mouth to argue again.

Caravass raised a hand. "So what you are saying is that one of you two killed Dylan Williams after he and his father and their allies attacked your family and both of you, as well?"

"Yes, but it was me—" I started to say.

"I believe we have heard enough," Caravass said. "Please step outside while we deliberate."

"But—" I said.

"Outside now," Michael murmured, half turning and jerking his chin toward the door we'd come in through.

Savannah hesitated then tugged me toward the door, her dad's firm hand on my shoulder a second propeller pushing me to make my exit.

Growling under my breath, I stepped out into the tunnel, its curved walls and ceiling lit an eerie greenish hue by the fluorescent lights that ran along the ceiling for as far as the tunnel went until it turned at either end. The metal door to the council's chambers clanged shut behind Michael.

He turned to gape at it.

"What were you thinking in there?" I asked Savannah.

She rolled her eyes but didn't answer, either out loud or silently.

Women. Even when you could read their minds, they still managed to make no sense sometimes.

"Look, I don't care how much blood you gave me to turn me. That still doesn't make me or anything I do your responsibility."

I love you, she said silently, her chin poking out. *If I have to lie to the council to save you, then that's what I'm going to do. I won't see them hurt you.*

Oh, but it's okay for me to see them hurt you?

We were still glaring at each other when the door creaked open again and Caravass stepped out. He pulled the door shut behind him with a small smile.

"The council is in agreement. This Jim Williams has clearly staged a coup within the Clann. It was unfortunate that your human family was involved and you were forced to kill a descendant in self-defense. But you have been cleared of all wrongdoing against the Clann."

My family…involved? They were a heck of a lot more than just involved. My mother had been murdered! I crossed my arms and stared at him, my back teeth grinding together.

Easy, Tristan, Savannah thought, resting a hand on my upper arm. *He doesn't understand. He thinks you probably hated your family for casting you out of the Clann. Not to mention he's like two thousand years old and doesn't even remember what it's like to have a human family in the first place.*

I took a deep breath then let it out slow through my nose.

"Then we are free to go?" Michael asked.

"Soon. However, the council has asked for a…shall we say, show of good faith on your part?"

Michael froze.

I read the council leader's mind. "They want to know that we're on your side."

Caravass froze as well, losing all trace of humanity in the process. I'd seen wax figures at museums with more life to them. Finally he forced an attempt at a smile. "I forgot that you two are able to read all vampires' minds regardless of whether they are your elders." His Adam's apple worked as he swallowed. "I would prefer to discuss the council's…requests in a more comfortable venue, if you will permit."

We need to get back to Mom and Emily, Savannah thought, her fingers tightening on my arm.

I know. But Caravass and the council seem to be trying to play nice. For now. Let's see where he's going with these new demands. Maybe if they're not too bad and we can play along, we'll get out of here soon and keep the council off our backs. The last thing we need is to have both sides hunting us down in the middle of a war.

"Lead the way." I worked to make my tone and smile as diplomatic as I could, an accomplishment managed only by Dad's endless speeches and my brief stint as the Clann's leader.

"Wonderful! I promise you will not regret it." Caravass led us down the tunnel a few steps, then hesitated and turned back, his smile sheepish now. "Ah, I nearly neglected a bit of security measures. I deeply apologize, I realize this is completely inhospitable, but unfortunately it is also necessary to maintaining the secrecy of our humble chambers' location."

A nearby guard vamp blurred over to us with two blindfolds.

I held my smile in place. "Of course. Your caution is understandable now more than ever."

We allowed the older vamps to tie our blindfolds back into

place before leading us out of the tunnels through a different route than before and back up to the street level. We were guided into a car, which smelled and felt like the same one that had picked us up from the airport. But this time, Caravass got into the front seat with the driver, and Mr. Colbert sat in the back on the other side of Savannah.

Caravass gave directions to the driver. Twenty minutes later, the car stopped.

The front passenger door opened then shut. Mr. Colbert got out, as well. Then he and Caravass helped Savannah and me out of the car, four steps over what felt like cobblestone and through a glass revolving door into some sort of building, gauging by the way the air pressure changed around us. A hand at my elbow—Caravass's, according to his thoughts—guided me forward across soft carpeting and through a wide opening of some kind into a room I could instantly tell was cavernous because of how every sound seemed to echo on and on. Ahead, a bit of light filtered through the black cloth over my eyes, and I could hear music and the murmur of voices.

"You may remove your blindfolds," Caravass murmured.

I pulled the blindfold off, felt Savannah do the same at my side, and then heard her gasp of pure delight.

We were in some sort of theater or opera house. Row upon row of red velvet seats spanned in every direction. When I looked behind us, I discovered there were two tiers of private boxes surrounding three sides of the huge space, which was crowned with a highly detailed central molding design Savannah was silently squeeing over. Ahead of us stretched the biggest stage I'd ever seen, even bigger than the Broadway stages my mother had dragged our family to in New York year after year.

And Savannah was in love.

I looked at her, with her hands pressed together before her parted lips, her eyes wide and darting from side to side as she watched the dancers rehearsing on the stage, and I was nearly hypnotized by the light shining out of her. For just a moment, she was so bright she made me forget all the darkness surrounding us.

Caravass smiled and spread his arms wide with the stage behind him. "Welcome to our hidden gem of an opera house, where our very own dance troupe will be performing tonight to what is sure to be a packed house."

"There's a vampire dance company?" Savannah's eyes had widened and she spoke fast. Even without the ability to read her mind or hear her now racing heartbeat, we all would have recognized how excited she was.

Caravass nodded, his smile finally managing to warm up his icy silver eyes. "And I would very much like it if you three would do me the honor of joining me in my private box for it."

Savannah's breath caught in her chest. Her dazzling smile melted like a candle sputtering out as her shoulders slumped, and inside myself I felt that empty, black pit that had taken over the moment I'd seen my mother's body once again open up and try to suck me down.

"Ah, we have loved ones back in the States who require our assistance in hiding before this Jim Williams is officially voted in as the new Clann leader," her father explained for us. "It is our sincere worry that as soon as he does so, he will waste no time in declaring war against our kind."

Caravass's eyes flared wide then narrowed. "Is that so?"

Both Michael and I nodded.

"Mr. Williams is a real vamp hater," I added, fighting to separate Savannah's disappointment with my own feelings. "He'd love nothing more than to wipe every last one of us off the face of the planet if he can."

"Hmm." Caravass crossed one arm over his chest and tapped the index finger of his other hand against his mouth. "That is worrisome. But perhaps we could find some way to reach out to him and—"

I shook my head. "There's nothing anyone can say that's ever going to change his mind. He's what you'd call a hard-core racist against vamps."

Caravass sighed. "Then my worst fear has come true. After so many peaceful decades of working with your father and his father before him, I had so hoped we had managed to usher in a long-lasting era of peace. I will have to warn the council so that we can make preparations." He half turned, frowned at the stage then nodded. "Yes, I can see this evening's festivities must be cut short for everyone on our council. However, surely there is still enough time for you to at least meet the troupe before you go?" He addressed his question to Savannah.

She bit her lower lip and turned to her dad, and I could both feel and hear her yearning for his permission while also bracing for his denial due to lack of time. I had to forcibly stop myself from adding my own begging to hers as the mind connection once again blurred the lines between her feelings and mine.

Michael looked at her for two agonizing seconds, then nodded.

"Are you sure there's time?" she asked, her voice just above a whisper as hope shot her heartbeat into the stratosphere.

He nodded again.

She made a tiny, closed-mouthed squeal through her nose and vamp blurred down the aisle to the edge of the stage. Caravass followed at her heels to introduce her to the troupe.

Her blast of happiness was like four shots of espresso injected straight into my veins, rocking me back on my heels and making my eyes snap wide-open.

Enjoy, my daughter, Michael thought as we watched her jump up onto the stage to meet each of the dancers. *Enjoy while the world is still capable of allowing you to, for soon all dreaming will come to an end.*

Onstage, the troupe's director began to teach Savannah part of a routine. Although she was hesitant at first from the habit of hiding her abilities around humans, her face was still filled with a childlike wonder. She was like a little girl opening presents on Christmas morning.

"You are among friends, Savannah," the troupe's director said, resting a hand on her shoulder. "On this stage, no vamp ever has to hide her gifts."

Savannah took a deep breath then gave it her all, performing the short piece of choreography as it was meant to be danced. She whirled so fast human eyes couldn't have possibly followed her, her wild red curls flying out behind her and threatening to come loose from her ponytail holder in the process. Thinking of nothing but the choreography and ignoring her falling hair, she did some complicated little sequence of steps before launching herself into the air in a split leap that rose impossibly high. She seemed to hover there, almost making me believe vamps could fly after all, before landing so lightly her feet didn't make a sound on the stage's wooden floor.

In that instant I remembered the first time I'd caught her dancing in the Charmers dance room at our high school and how even then, not yet fully evolved as a vampire, she'd still moved with that same alien grace and lightness. It should have been my first hint that she wasn't completely human. But then, as now, she had only been my Savannah, so achingly beautiful that she literally robbed me of breath for a few seconds. God I loved her, and every time I thought I couldn't possibly love her more, she took my feelings for her to a whole new level.

I closed my eyes and immersed myself in her thoughts, forgetting who I was and concentrating only on what she thought and felt. As if her body were my own, I felt the way her blood rushed through her veins so fast that it seemed she really might be able to fly right up to the ceiling and beyond.

And finally I understood what dancing meant to her. It was indescribable for a reason. I had to experience it with her through her own senses, filtered through her emotions, in order to truly get it. I'd always thought dancing for her was like playing football used to be for me, but it was completely different. For me, football had always been a challenge to prove myself to my teammates, my coaches and even my parents. It was about beating all the obstacles and pushing myself to my limits and beyond over and over again.

For Savannah, dancing was the complete opposite of all that. Instead of having to push toward or through something, she was letting go of everything. As she moved, she set herself free, allowing her body to do what came naturally. When she danced was when she *stopped* fighting.

And in that short moment as I forgot who I was and simply enjoyed Savannah's experience up on that stage with her, I learned how to stop fighting, too.

And then my skin exploded with the stabbings of a million tiny unseen needles a second before the entire city was rocked by a series of rumblings, first in the distance, then closer and closer toward the opera house.

CHAPTER 12

Savannah gasped and froze for less than half a second. I was already running down the aisle toward her when she leaped off the stage and met me halfway. Caravass, Michael and the dancers joined us as we all ran up the aisle toward the exit then skidded to a stop in the foyer as the street beyond the glass doors erupted in a geyser of fire. Sirens began to wail throughout the city, and several of the dancers behind us hissed in alarm and took a few steps back.

"What is this?" Caravass asked Michael.

"The Clann," I muttered as Savannah's hand darted to the back of her neck and her gaze collided with mine. "I think they've found your headquarters."

Caravass turned round, icy white eyes toward me.

I held up my free hand in surrender. "No way. I swear we had nothing to do with this."

Savannah thrust out her wrist. "Take our blood as proof.

The blood memories will show you. We didn't lead them here or tell them anything about this place."

She was right. The council leader might not be able to read our minds, but he could still read the memories in our blood. I stuck my own wrist out beside hers.

Caravass hesitated, then faster than our eyes could even track, his hand darted out and reappeared at his mouth as two thin slices welled with blood across Savannah's and my wrists. Even as Caravass tasted our blood and read our most recent memories, the cuts began to heal. I had to tear my focus away from the amazing healing process in order to follow his thoughts.

He nodded, his eyes narrowing. "It is as you say."

"It's got to be Mr. Williams," I said. "He must have called an emergency vote already."

"But how could he have set this attack up so fast?" Savannah said, turning to look at the flames still roaring a good ten feet up into the air. Smoke was quickly filling the street and darkening the skies above. "And how did he know where the headquarters were?"

"He had to have already sent a team to get into position before the vote," Michael said.

"It is what I might have done if I were him," Caravass said.

"If the Clann's here, we need to leave," I told him, bracing for who knew what he might say in return. Would he demand we stay and fight at his side?

He stared at me with narrowed eyes then sighed. "I suppose it is too soon to ask you to join us in this war?"

War, Savannah gasped silently. *Oh, God. It's really happening.*

I shook my head. "I can't. If Williams has declared war,

then we've got to get back to the States to my sister and her mother. They'll be in danger, too."

Caravass scowled. "Fine. Michael, I trust you will remain at their sides at all times?" Silently he added, *To ensure they do not act against us at least?*

Michael nodded. "Of course. I will call you with any news I have. Will you flee the city?"

Caravass shook his head, his jawline hardening. "I must try to find any surviving council members so we can discuss our next move. If this Williams truly demands a war, then who are we to refuse him?"

We all pushed through the revolving doors, coughing as soon as we exited the building and the smoke slammed our faces and lungs with the smell of a thousand unknown things on fire. The sirens were a hundred times louder out here, forcing Savannah and me to let go of each other's hand so we could cover our too-sensitive ears before the sound could drive us to our knees.

Michael vamp blurred around the car still parked at the curb, getting into the front passenger seat while Savannah and I dived into the back. Caravass shouted directions to the driver as we slammed the doors shut.

Then we were careening on a madhouse ride through the city's streets, every one of them ablaze with shooting flames from both the streets' many access points into the maze of sewers and underground tunnels that seemed to match the city's layout of streets exactly. We didn't get too far, however, before traffic jams brought us to a halt.

"We must make a run for it from here," Michael shouted over the wailing sirens and shouting humans as he opened his door. To the driver he said, "Make sure the pilot knows we are on our way so he can ready for immediate takeoff."

The driver nodded.

Savannah gave me one last round-eyed look of terror, then we jumped out of the car on opposite sides and started running, struggling to keep her father in sight as we used every bit of vamp speed available to hide our passage through the city on foot. Mr. Williams's attack team had to still be in the city somewhere. The last thing we needed was for them to spot us before we could get out of Paris.

Finally Michael led us back to the airport and onto the jet. None of us dared sigh with relief until we were actually in the air, though, especially since both Michael and the pilot had to do some serious negotiating to get the locked-down airport to allow us to take off. We were lucky the vamp council apparently knew somebody working in the control tower today.

As the jet circled the city, all three of us stared out the nearest windows at the city below. The City of Lights and Love was filled with a whole new kind of light now, one that flickered and did its best to devour every building and body in its path.

And the States were probably next.

SAVANNAH

It was a really, really long flight back. And not just because we were worried about another war starting, or getting back to Mom and Emily and hopefully finding them as safe and sound as we'd left them.

It was because Tristan spent the entire return trip planning different ways to get close enough to Mr. Williams to make him pay for Mrs. Coleman's murder.

Worse, he didn't just want justice for his mother's death. He wanted to see Mr. Williams tortured slowly first, then kill him with his own bare hands. And possibly his fangs, too.

At first, I tried to remember that Tristan was still grieving for his mother, dealing with the shock from her death, and anger was probably part of that process. Anyone would be furious and heartbroken.

But when his fantasizing passed the five-hour mark and got downright bloodthirsty, I discovered I could only take so much. I dug into my pockets, found my trusty MP3 player and earbuds, and put on some music to drown him out inside my head.

When we finally reached our last airport stop, disembarked and headed over to a rental car Dad had arranged midflight to have waiting for us, I got into the backseat, assuming Tristan would join me there. Instead he took the front passenger seat by Dad.

Okay. Maybe Tristan needed a little space to work through his emotions.

I sat behind Dad, which gave me a view of Tristan's profile. *Are you okay?* I silently asked him.

Sure. And then came more of the same plotting to kill Mr. Williams.

Ugh. It was like being forced to listen to an all-day horror movie fest, whether you liked horror movies or not, and none of the movies were of your choosing. I stuck my earbuds back in and cranked up the music again until I fell asleep against the car door.

We stopped sometime later at a car rental place, where

we waited in the parking lot for another hour till Mom and Emily showed up with the truck and RV trailer. This time their tears were happy ones as they hugged us. Then they retired to the trailer to rest while Dad, Tristan and I all opted to ride in the truck for a few hours. Dad wanted to drive a little farther north.

This time I rode in the front seat of the truck with Dad, letting Tristan have the entire backseat to himself so he could stretch out his long legs. As we headed down the road again, Tristan threw a forearm over his eyes, and I thought he might finally rest. It had been too long since I'd seen him even grab a nap. Not since the attack at his family home, in fact.

But even then he didn't sleep, his thoughts swirling back and forth between his mother's death, Dylan's last words, everything Mr. Williams had said and done that night, and wondering where the new Clann leader might be holed up now with his battalion of descendant bodyguards.

Enough was enough. *Do you want to talk about it?* I silently asked, turning to look over the front seat at him.

What's there to talk about?

I swallowed, the raw pain and endless rage in his thoughts filling me with a horrible ache I hadn't felt since my own Nanna's death last spring. *Look, I know how you feel. When Nanna died—*

No, you don't *know how I feel, Savannah. You have no clue. You lost your grandma. But at least your parents are still right here. You can talk to them anytime you want.*

His words stung. They might have seemed true to him, but he was wrong. I'd only lived with my dad for about a year now. Before that, I'd lived with my mother and grandma, and with Mom always on the road for her sales rep job, Nanna had been my only constant parent for years. So while my parents might be alive, losing Nanna had still felt like losing a parent to me.

But Tristan was too wrapped up in his own thoughts to hear mine. *I'm never going to speak to my dad again, never know what Mom might have said…* But that line of thought was too painful for him to continue. The knot in his throat worked, his knuckles turning white as he gripped the tops of his thighs. *If I'd just been there a few minutes earlier…*

We had been late because Charmers practice ran over and I'd had to take a shower, fix my hair and makeup, and try to figure out what to wear that might make his mother hate me less.

He wasn't blaming his mother's death on me, I reminded myself.

Your parents' deaths aren't your fault, I told him. *You can't blame yourself.*

Silence. Finally, he thought very slowly and way too clearly to misunderstand, *I am going to track Mr. Williams down and kill him. If anyone's to blame, he is.*

I drew in a sharp breath through my nose, earning a curious glance from Dad before he returned his attention to the road. *There's a huge difference between fantasizing about killing someone, accidentally ending someone's life and actually setting out to intentionally hunt someone down like an animal. I know you didn't mean to kill Dylan. And I know you don't really mean to—*

I didn't accidentally *do anything to Dylan. I meant to kill him, just like I mean to kill his father as soon as I can find a way to get close enough to him.*

Tristan—

They killed my mother, would have killed Emily, too, if we hadn't gotten there in time! That whole family is poison, and the only way to stop that poison from spreading is to end them.

It had been a long time since I'd heard Tristan shout, and he'd only ever dared to yell at me once. Even if this time it was from inside his mind, it still startled me, and I had to fight my own rising emotions. He wasn't yelling at me. I couldn't take it personally.

I took a deep breath to steady myself. *Dylan didn't kill your mom. He didn't even know his dad was going to do that.*

He lied, he thought with zero hesitation or doubt.

I read his memories—

Memories can be faked. Remember the one I showed you of me and Bethany Brookes kissing under the bleachers? Never happened. I just imagined it to make you jealous.

I took a deep breath and tried to hold on to my patience, but it was starting to feel like a losing battle. *Dylan didn't fake this memory. He didn't have time to. Besides, he was too busy being scared of you.*

A memory, my own, flashed through my mind…the fear in Dylan's eyes as Tristan grabbed him, then Dylan's body soaring through the air, and the sickening thud and crack as his back slammed into the fireplace before he dropped into a lifeless heap on the hearth like a rag doll instead of someone I'd gone to school with, grown up with. Even though I'd seen Dylan's death with my own eyes, it still felt surreal. I'd never seen anyone my age die, much less someone I'd actually known.

He played you, Savannah, Tristan thought. *I can't believe you'd be dumb enough to fall for it.*

Okay, now he'd crossed the line. He did *not* just call me dumb. *Obviously you're upset about your mother, and I don't blame you. But I am not your punching bag, so quit taking it out on me. I'm on your side, remember? And how dare you call me dumb! Just because I think you should have tried to control yourself and figure out what really happened before losing it and killing someone doesn't make me an idiot.*

You are if you actually fell for Dylan's crap. And I already told you, I didn't lose control again! I knew exactly what I was doing.

I made one last attempt to stay calm. *Maybe we should talk about this later, after you've had more time to deal with everything.*

"I would calm down a lot faster if you weren't sitting there saying I don't know what I saw! I was there, Savannah! I could see with my own eyes what happened and exactly who was to blame! So stop telling me I'm wrong!" The roar of Tristan's words, shouted within the tiny space of the cab, punched at my ears over and over until I found myself actually leaning away from him.

Dad cleared his throat, but when he spoke, the words still came out in a growl. "That is my daughter you are speaking to. I will thank you to watch your tone, and do not shout at her again."

That was it. I was done trying to talk with Tristan. I faced front again, my whole body shaking with an explosion of fury. And this time, the anger was all mine. My stupid eyes burned then flooded with tears, which only made me angrier. Why couldn't I be more like a guy and punch something instead of bursting into waterworks? More than ever, I wished I could turn off the mind connection between us.

I also really wished I could get away from Tristan physically right now.

Finally I couldn't stand it anymore. "Dad, pull over."

The truck slowed and eased onto the shoulder of the highway.

As soon as we stopped, I muttered, "I'll be in the trailer."

I threw open my door, lurched out, slammed it shut without looking at either of them and stalked along the weed-broken asphalt to the trailer door.

Mom and Emily were sitting at the dinette eating something that smelled truly awful. The stench of it hit my nose like a slap, causing me to stumble just inside the doorway.

But then another scent wafted over to me. Something delicious that made my stomach slowly twist into what felt like one giant knot in my gut.

The ache in my upper gums and a glance at Emily's face were the final clues I needed. Oh, of course. Emily had gotten a small cut on her cheek last night, probably from either the broken window Dad had carried her through or maybe a tree branch in the woods. Mom had clearly cleaned up the wound and dabbed some antiseptic on it. But that didn't stop my nose from still picking up the slight scent of Clann blood.

"I'm going to sleep for a while," I pushed out through clenched teeth.

I ducked into the bunk room off the living room area, fighting my instinct to slam the sliding door shut behind me. Instead, I carefully closed it then stood there for a moment as my pulse pounded. It had been a long time since I'd felt the bloodlust, and it seemed even more intense now. Probably thanks to my anger.

Thankfully the bloodlust faded and I could breathe again. I turned to face the dark room. There were three beds, two upper bunk beds and one floor-level futon couch on the left side that could be folded down into a bed. Emily would probably need the floor-level futon since I doubted she'd want to try to climb a ladder all the time while pregnant.

I climbed the ladder up to the bunk bed over the futon, lay down on the mattress, and jammed my hands into the pockets of my jacket, only to find my right fingers tangled up in the wires to my MP3 player's earbuds. Lord, I hated earbuds. My ears were too small and the buds hurt the inside of my ears and fell out a lot. I'd only kept them in my pocket for emergency use. The soft headphones I infinitely preferred stayed in my Charmers bag, which was probably a melted pile of nothing in the wreckage of Dad's and my burned-down home now, along with everything else I'd once owned.

The Clann had probably even destroyed my car while they were there. All I had now were the clothes on my back, my MP3 player that was going to run out of battery life any second, and these stupid earbuds that didn't even fit my ears right.

I stuck the earbuds in anyway.

The bunk room door slid open, flooding the room with light.

I squinted, found Tristan standing there and closed my eyes. I so didn't want to hear another second of the Tristan Kills Mr. Williams channel. "Go away."

"I'm sorry I yelled at you and said you were dumb." His voice seeped right past the earbuds in my ears.

I rolled toward the window to hide my wet face then turned on my MP3 player and cranked up the volume to drown out his thoughts. "I don't want to talk to you right now."

Because if I did, I would say something nasty and mean to hurt him like I was hurting.

Except he'd just lost his mother and was already hurting. That didn't give him the right to take it out on me.

"Are you…crying?"

Now who was the idiot? "I'm a girl, Tristan. That's what some of us do when we get really ticked off."

Unlike some people who went on homicidal rages instead and killed their former best friends then screamed at their girlfriends.

"Wow." His flat tone thanked me for that thought.

Crap. I'd forgotten that just because my music drowned out his thoughts didn't mean he couldn't still hear mine.

"I told you now's not a good time to talk." I could control what I said to him, but not what I thought. Not right now. "Let's just…get some space from each other till we both cool down. Okay?"

"I said I was sorry. Can't you just get over it?"

That set off the fury all over again. "Tristan, *you* might be able to turn your feelings on and off like a switch and want to make up right now. But I don't work like that! You don't get to yell at me and call me names and then decide when *I* should no longer be ticked off at you about it!"

"Fine." The trailer rocked as he stepped out of the room. But still the door didn't slide shut. "Your dad said to remind you that we should feed. Want me to grab you a bag from the fridge?"

I shook my head. "I'm not hungry right now. Thanks."

"Sav, you need to eat—"

That was it. I rolled over to face him, propping myself up on one elbow. "You have been turned for all of five months.

Do you really want to stand there and try to tell *me* when I should eat?" I could feel my voice rising, but the anger was too far gone now to offer any hope of controlling my tone. Thankfully Mom hadn't had a chance to put a pillow on this bed or I might have been tempted to throw it at him.

His mouth opened. Then he snapped it shut and slid the door closed.

I flopped back on the mattress, closed my eyes and wrapped my arms around my cramping stomach.

In the kitchen, the refrigerator door popped open, slammed shut, followed by the creak and slam of the trailer door. Outside the trailer, a truck door snicked open then slammed shut, and a second later the trailer rocked as Dad drove us back onto the highway.

CHAPTER 13

I fell asleep, waking sometime around sunrise judging by the hint of light beyond the bunk bed's window, which was covered with pleated shades I didn't bother to pull up. My stomach was still cramping. Dad was right. I did need to eat or else risk feeling the bloodlust again.

So I forced myself to climb down the ladder, where I discovered Emily asleep on the futon couch. I noticed she'd opened the window by her bed. To help me ward off the bloodlust, or because she liked fresh air while she slept?

Her face and nose looked as puffy and red as mine felt, reminding me again of last night's horrors.

I shouldn't have let Tristan get to me last night. Yes, he shouldn't have yelled or said I was dumb. But he never talked to me like that, and he'd just lost his mother and killed his childhood friend who he believed had helped murder his mother. The least I could have done was accept Tristan's apology instead of letting his anger trigger my own so badly.

The next time we made a pit stop somewhere, I would go and talk to him.

I slipped out of the bedroom, easing the sliding door shut behind me. Mom was standing in the kitchen, her feet braced to compensate for the rocking of the trailer, while she washed dishes by hand in the sink.

"Hey, Mom," I said as I sighed, wrapping an arm around her waist and resting my chin on her shoulder. As always, the scent of her Wind Song perfume rose up to fill my nose. This time, though, I had to wrinkle my nose and fight a sneeze. Either Mom had poured the entire bottle over herself, or my sense of smell had gotten way stronger since the last time I'd seen her.

"Hey, sweetie." She tilted her head sideways to rest her cheek against the top of my head. "I'm glad to get to see you again, but this sure is a crappy way to have to do it."

"Yeah."

She hesitated then said, "I couldn't help but overhear some of what Tristan said to you in the bunk room. Did you two have a fight on top of everything else?"

I nodded. "He yelled at me and said I was dumb because I said he shouldn't have killed Dylan." My tongue stumbled over the word *killed*.

"Oh, my God. Not Jim Williams's kid? I thought they were friends."

"They used to be till..." Until Tristan and I had started dating. Guilt rose up to swamp me, making it hard to breathe. "Tristan thought Dylan killed his mom, so he threw him across the room. I think he broke his neck."

I couldn't talk about this anymore. I turned away, took two steps and sank down onto the edge of the U-shaped dinette bench, then propped my elbows on the table and my head in my hands.

I couldn't believe it had really happened. The whole thing seemed like a nightmare of a dream instead of something I'd really been a part of just a couple of days ago.

Could I have done something to stop Tristan? If I hadn't been in so much shock over his mother's death, if I had realized what Tristan might do...

I should have stepped in between them, or pushed Tristan away from Dylan before he ever grabbed him.

I should have done *something*. But instead I had stood there and watched as Tristan ended his ex–best friend's life.

Had I secretly wanted Dylan to pay for all those years of calling me names and picking on me at school?

Suddenly the trailer lurched forward a bit. I grabbed the edge of the table as the whole trailer rocked hard from side to side, then the vibration in the floor faded away.

"Must be time for more gas," Mom said as she dried her hands on a towel that hung from the oven door's handle. "That truck is such a gas guzzler when it's hauling this big rig behind it. I'd better go give your dad his card back. He can use mine instead now."

"Uh, Mom, I'm sure he'll be more than happy to cover the gas for us." I knew from past discussions with him that Dad used his mind-reading abilities to help him make a fortune. I hadn't had to worry about money since moving in with him last year.

She threw me a dark scowl. "Don't think I don't know how he gets his money. I didn't like it back when we were together, and I don't like it now. And I am not having my truck filled with gas paid for by his illegal activities. I work hard *the legal way* and make enough to pay for my own gas, thank you very much."

I started to argue that Dad wasn't exactly a mobster or getting his money from killing people as a paid hit man. He just read a few key minds to pick up insider trading secrets, then played the stock market accordingly.

Then I remembered how upset I used to be about Dad's insider tracing methods when I first found out about them. When had I gotten so used to the idea that it no longer bothered me?

It was just like Tristan and his need for revenge. It was a slippery slope. You started off not liking something, knowing it was wrong, but trying to either rationalize it or ignore it. And then the next thing you knew, you were almost ready to defend it to someone else, and maybe even do it yourself, in Tristan's case.

Mom stepped out of the trailer while I was still following that particularly twisty line of thought. I didn't realize she was gone until the trailer door banged shut.

I sighed and rubbed my pounding forehead. Tristan was probably still in the truck dealing with the blood memories from feeding last night. At least, I assumed he was the one who'd grabbed something from the fridge before leaving the trailer for the truck. I would have to wait awhile longer before speaking with him.

"Do not be ridiculous," Dad said outside the trailer, its thin metal walls doing little to muffle his voice. "I will of course cover all costs."

"Excuse me, but have you forgotten we're divorced?" Mom said. "I've paid for my own gas and snacks for years now."

"Joan, your pride is misplaced here. The Clann may be tracking your credit cards since I am sure they will assume you would want to come to your child's rescue."

"Oh, and yet they wouldn't be watching *your* cards?"

"Not these. They are under several aliases I keep for emergencies."

Silence as Mom absorbed that news. She sighed. "Why am I not surprised?"

A half minute later she came stomping back inside. "Unbelievable. Your father refuses to let me pay for anything!" She threw her hands up then looked around as if she didn't know what to do with herself.

"I'm sure he's just trying to play it safe."

"He could have at least asked me if I minded, instead of telling me this is how it's going to be. He treats me like an incompetent child."

Oh, boy. I cleared my throat. "Well, he is a vamp, and he's kind of used to making a decision and then following through on it. I'm not sure he's used to having to deal with a team other than the council."

Mom rolled her eyes and propped her hands on her hips. "Yeah, right. He can be diplomatic with his precious vamp council, but not with his wife?"

"Ex," I muttered, wondering how to get out of this conversation.

Her eyes flashed at me then narrowed. "Whatever. The point is, he obviously doesn't have the same respect for me because I'm just a measly human."

Okay, time to make a run for it. Nothing I said was going to help her cool off any quicker.

I stood up. "You know, I think I'm going to go walk around a little bit. Need anything from the gas station?"

Mom shook her head and returned to the sink, the dish in her hand banging against the sides of the metal sink with a swishy *bong* sound that vibrated right down into my teeth.

I tried not to run for the door. But once safely outside with the trailer door shut, I couldn't stop a sigh of relief.

Good grief. Now I knew where I got my temper.

"Hey," Tristan murmured, surprising me.

I spun to face him. "Oh! Hi. Um, I thought…" I waved a hand at the truck. "You know, that you'd still be out for the count from the blood memories."

He leaned against the side of the truck, his green eyes watching my every move. "I was for a few hours. But I didn't feed much. Wasn't hungry for some reason." One side of his mouth tightened in the semblance of a half smile. "So I thought I'd come man the gas pump while your dad checks the oil and tires."

I cleared my throat. "Listen, about last night. I'm sorry I got so mad."

He nodded, still watching me.

Okay, this was awkward. There was too much distance between us, both literally and figuratively.

I walked closer to him, stopping a couple of feet away to sit on the top of a cement cylinder in the island meant to keep vehicles from hitting the gas pumps. "Everybody says stuff they don't mean when they're upset. I know you didn't mean what you said last night."

"Which part?"

"The part where you said I was dumb."

"No, I didn't mean that."

I nodded. Then I frowned. "Wait. So you did mean it when you said you plan to kill Mr. Williams?"

Too late, I remembered to look around us. Thankfully we didn't have an audience.

Not that Tristan seemed to care. He shrugged. "Yeah, that part I meant."

Oh, great. I'd hoped he'd had time to cool off and come to his senses. "Tristan, you can't go after him."

His eyebrows shot up as if to say *oh, yeah?*

"How is getting revenge going to make anything better?"

"It'll sure make me feel better."

I shook my head. "But it won't bring your mom back any more than Emily's killing Gowin brought your dad back."

"I don't care. He has to pay for what he did."

I stared up at Tristan, and it was like looking at a stranger. Gone was the boy with the soft smile and even softer green eyes I'd first fallen in love with. He'd been replaced by someone so filled with hatred and anger that he couldn't even think straight, or see what killing yet another person might do to him.

I fought to find the right words to explain. "I know you're angry right now and that makes it hard to think clearly. But if you could find a way to push it aside, you'd see that wanting to kill Mr. Williams is only going to hurt you in the end. It's like that hunter in Arkansas. Remember how that felt so right at the moment, too? But if you'd killed him, how would you feel right now? And what about killing Dylan? Don't try to tell me there isn't a part of you deep down inside that's wrecked over his death."

Tristan stopped breathing, the muscles in his jaw forming knots along his jawline.

"Wanting revenge is a slippery slope." At his raised eyebrows, I tried to explain better. "You know, you take one wrong step that leads to another and then another, until suddenly you find yourself in a really dark place and you can't even figure out how you got there."

He stared at me. "So you're saying if I kill Mr. Williams, I'm going to turn into a serial killer?"

I rolled my eyes. "No, I mean…it's like a disease. Wanting to get revenge will eat away at your insides and take over your whole life if you let it. Look at how many hours you've already wasted obsessing over ways to kill Mr. Williams."

"You call it obsessing, I call it planning ahead."

"Does it really make you happy to spend all that time plotting ways to torture and kill him?"

"Yeah, it really does."

"Liar."

"What do *you* know about wanting revenge anyway?"

I stepped up to him. "You think I've never had a reason to want revenge? After dealing with Dylan and the Brat Twins calling me names in school for years? Should I have killed them for that? Or how about when your dad had Nanna kidnapped and tortured for information she didn't even have until she died? Should I have killed your father for that?"

Heat flared out of him. "Your grandma's abduction and death were a misunderstanding and an accident and you know it."

"Sure. And your mother's death could have been every bit as much an accident, too, for all we know."

I leaned against the side of the truck, all the will to fight draining out of me. "My point is that I've been wronged and dealt with loss, too. But I'm not letting it eat me up inside anymore because I can't afford to. Every time I let the anger take over, I'm not myself anymore. I lose control, and I prove they're right and I'm nothing more than a monster. And then they win. I don't want to live like that. So I chose to let it go a long time ago, to not let them have that power over me. Just because I'm a vampire doesn't mean I have to act like a monster. That's *my* choice, not theirs."

His eyes narrowed. "But that's what we really are, Savannah. Like it or not, we're supposed to be killers."

"You know perfectly well that we don't have to kill anyone to survive anymore. Nothing makes any of us monsters except the decisions we make and the actions we take."

Tristan's eyes blazed at me as he leaned forward and hissed, "He helped kill my mother. You think I'm supposed to just let that go?"

"I know, it hurts. But Nanna and your mom and dad, they're all gone, and nothing you or I or anyone else can do can bring them back. And I know for a fact that they wouldn't want us to destroy ourselves to try to avenge their deaths." I took a deep breath, pushing the ever-present anger back down inside. "I've been to the other side, Tristan. I've talked with Nanna. We're not supposed to waste our lives seeking justice. We're supposed to move on and let them go."

He shook his head. "I can't do that."

I looked deep into his eyes as my own burned and threatened to tear up again. I'd waited five long months for the Tristan I'd grown up with and loved to come back to me. And now I was losing him all over again. "Then they've already won."

"Jim Williams has to die, Savannah. There's no gray area here."

His jaw was set, his eyes and mouth hard. Even his feet were spread wide as if ready to take any physical blow. He was the perfect definition of the term *mulish*. There was nothing I could say to change his mind.

Still, I had to try one last time. "He's the Clann leader now. That means he'll have hundreds of descendants, not to mention the Keepers, protecting and helping him. If you try to go after him, he'll use that army to kill you. Is it worth that much to you? Are you willing to die to get your revenge?"

Tristan barked out a humorless laugh. "Thanks for the vote of confidence. But you're forgetting one thing. I'm their worst nightmare, remember? There's nothing they can do to stop me from getting to him."

It was like talking to an arrogant brick wall.

"How are we doing?" Dad asked as he returned from the gas station with a bright yellow plastic bottle of oil in his hand.

At first I thought he was asking about Tristan's and my relationship, and I nearly answered, *Lousy*. But then I realized he was talking about the truck's fuel tank.

"Nearly there," Tristan said. "This thing takes forever to fill up."

Dad nodded. "Yes, it does. I am going to add a bit more oil to the engine. Would you mind cleaning the windshield for us?"

"Sure." Tristan turned toward the island, reaching for a black squeegee sticking out of a matching colored plastic tub that hung from one of the awning's support poles.

"Hey, Dad?" I called out.

He stuck his head out from beneath the truck's open hood, black eyebrows raised in question.

"Mind if I go for a short walk over there?" I jerked my chin in the general direction behind me. I didn't even know what was off to the side of the station. All I knew was that I needed to get away for a few minutes, sort through my thoughts without anyone around me, and get some fresh air that didn't smell like gas fumes, human food or my mother's perfume.

He nodded, adding, "Do not go too far," then disappeared beneath the truck hood again.

I stuffed my hands in my jacket pockets as I walked off to the right of the station, unsure where I was going, desperate to shake the tightness that was now setting up camp in my chest.

The gas station was at the base of a tall hill covered in drought-yellowed weeds with a wooden fence line running along its ridge. Without really making a clear decision to, I headed up that hillside toward the fence through the weird predawn light.

Once at the fence, I stopped, gripped the weathered wood and looked down. On this side, the hill ran down about a hundred yards toward a tiny valley nestled between two more steep hillsides. On instinct, I climbed over the fence and walked down the slope toward that valley, welcoming the way the hillside's decline forced my thigh muscles to work to control my descent.

In the valley itself, I stood and looked around. How could wave after wave of weeds look so pretty and golden?

I dug the toe of my sneaker into the dirt, watching a tiny cloud of dust rise up as the fingers of my right hand played with the earbuds in my pocket. Finally I gave in to temptation, stuck them in my ears and turned on my MP3 player, ignoring its now red battery icon.

But even the music couldn't turn off the questions tormenting my mind.

How could I make Tristan see that his need to go after Mr. Williams was dangerous? That he was risking everything for his need for revenge?

The song changed from a fast one to a slow duet by Rihanna and Mikky Ekko. The pulsing piano notes coaxed me to close my eyes. I was pretty sure it was supposed to be a love song, but it had always hit me as more of a breakup song. Part of me yearned to dance to it, but I didn't.

Other than on that Paris stage with the vampire dance troupe, I couldn't remember the last time I'd danced. I'd been too busy, too focused on Tristan…saving him from death, saving him and every human around him from his vampire instincts, trying so hard to show him that just because we were vampires didn't mean we had to be monsters. I'd tried to show him a better way, a way to save the goodness inside us so our need for blood didn't erase who we were.

Now it all seemed like wasted effort, because he was determined to risk his life yet again for revenge.

How did you save someone who didn't want to be saved? Should you even try?

Or was I being selfish, holding on to something that wasn't meant to be, to someone who I seemed to need far more than he needed me?

CHAPTER 14

TRISTAN

"Has Savannah returned yet?" Mr. Coleman asked as he got behind the wheel of the truck.

"No. I'll go look for her." As long as Savannah wasn't inside a building, she would be easy enough to find. All I had to do was follow her thoughts.

Savannah? I thought, looking around and waiting for her reply.

No answer, but I thought I picked up something that felt like the warmth I always associated with her mind. It was in the direction of the nearby hillside. She must have taken a walk that way.

I headed up the hillside then stopped at the fence. It was like standing on the top row of seats in one of those ancient open-air amphitheaters. And there below in a tiny space just big enough for a stage was the star.

Except this one only stood around with her hands in her pockets and her head dropped forward.

The sun had finally risen enough to peek over the tops of the hills, but not enough to shred the shadows in the valley. Savannah stood within that darkness, her mind every bit as shadowed.

Because she was afraid for me.

Her lack of confidence was a real ego booster.

Why couldn't she understand my need to hunt Mr. Williams down and make him pay for what he'd done to my mother? She acted like I was about to commit some crime of my own. But I wasn't the bad guy here—Mr. Williams was. Seeking revenge wasn't wrong. It was a basic need to set things right, and the best way to do that was to make sure Mr. Williams could never hurt or kill anyone else ever again. Even the Bible had talked about an eye for an eye. So why couldn't Savannah see that? Why couldn't she understand that I would never be free of this fury burning me up inside until he was dead and buried in the cold, hard ground just like my mother soon would be?

Savannah and I had argued before. All couples did. But this time felt different, more dangerous somehow. Maybe because this time, instead of outside forces coming between us, it was our own beliefs and needs.

Savannah would come around, though. Eventually she had to. There was no way she could stay this blindly idealistic, especially now that Mr. Williams had declared war on the vamps. Couldn't she understand that he wouldn't stop until every last vampire was wiped off the face of this planet? Including Savannah, her father and myself.

It's different this time, she thought, her back still turned my direction. *That's why it hurts so much. Because it's different.*

Had she heard my thoughts in spite of the music still pumping into her ears from her MP3 player?

But she never turned to look up at me or showed any knowledge that I was there in the distance watching her.

It's up to him this time, isn't it? I can't save him from making this mistake. There's nothing more I can say or do… It's up to him to choose.

My hands gripped the top rail of the fence hard enough to make the wood creak in warning.

Her shoulders stopped moving as she held her breath. *I can't change his mind. And if he chooses revenge, I can't follow him down that road, either. If I do, we'll both be lost.*

I froze, forgetting to breathe, too. Had it really just come down to that? Choose between her or killing Mr. Williams?

She didn't know I was listening to her thoughts, hadn't consciously decided to put that choice before me. But the ultimatum was there all the same. She was really that hard-headed, that convinced that she was right and I was wrong, that I might die if I went after Mr. Williams, that even avenging my mother's death wasn't worth it.

I pushed back from the fence, anger rising up like a fever to burn my cheeks and eyes. Silently I turned and stalked back down the hill, past the gas station to the truck, threw myself into the passenger side of the front seat then slammed the door shut.

Fine. If that was how she wanted to see this situation, then that was her choice. But she was flat-out wrong, and I would prove it to her. When I took out Mr. Williams and was still the exact same guy she'd first fallen for, then she would understand.

"Where is—" Mr. Coleman said.

"She's coming."

A minute later Savannah appeared around the corner of the gas station. She got within twenty yards of the truck and hesitated. I could hear my heartbeat pounding in my ears like a clock ticking off the seconds.

Then she changed direction, opening the trailer's door and climbing the metal steps to rejoin the girls instead.

I shouldn't have been surprised. But after our talk this morning and my hope that we'd made up, it still felt like a slap in the face. And the sting didn't stop there. It traveled all the way down like a glowing ember to join the ache that had already set up camp in my chest hours ago, building the burn into a full-fledged fire.

The truck engine rumbled to life and the seat beneath me jerked forward as we continued our journey north in the complete opposite direction I should have been running toward.

I closed my eyes and concentrated on taking long, slow breaths past that fire in my lungs and throat.

The sooner I could go after Mr. Williams, the better for all of us.

SAVANNAH

It was during those long and seemingly endless days of driving north that Emily gasped.

I looked up from where I'd taken to lying on the couch. "What's wrong?"

She stabbed a finger at the screen of Mom's laptop, which

she'd been using along with one of the many disposable phones Dad had picked up to surf the internet. "Jacksonville made the national news."

I hopped up and moved to sit beside her so I could look, too. What I saw had me croaking out Mom's name.

Rubbing her eyes, Mom emerged from her bedroom.

"Look," I told her, my gaze glued to the screen as Emily clicked on a news video.

Mom slid onto the dinette bench at Emily's other side then gasped. "Is that downtown Jacksonville?"

I nodded. "It's on fire!"

The camera panned to show building after building on fire...including the hills in front of the Tomato Bowl. The fire was so high it blocked out parts of the stadium's brown stone walls so that only the second floor of the announcer's booth could be seen, and even that was hard to make out behind the rolling clouds of black smoke.

"The vamps set Jacksonville on fire as retaliation?" Emily whispered.

"That looks more like spell fire," Mom said. "See how it refuses to go out no matter how much water's thrown on it, and it twists around almost as if it's alive?"

"But that doesn't make any sense," Emily said. "Why would the Clann do that to their own headquarters?"

"How much do you want to bet the council sent some vamps to go after the Clann and things just got out of hand?" I pressed a shaky hand to my forehead. This was so much worse than I'd imagined. It was one thing to see Paris on fire as Mr. Williams's war declaration, and another to see bonfires blazing all over the town I'd grown up in. Paris had never seemed truly real to me. I'd never gotten to see much of it in the two times the council had summoned me there. What I knew of it was more from movies, and who knew how much of that was even the actual city itself instead of some Hollywood set in California?

But this…this was far too real to be any movie set. I'd gone to countless home football games with the Charmers at the Tomato Bowl, walked down those smoke-covered streets and sidewalks before and after the games and to shop. That antiques store was where Nanna used to sell her crocheted blankets and custom filet crochet names.

"That's the Jaycee building there," Emily murmured, reaching out to touch the screen as a pile of crumbled timbers and a partial wall collapsed across from the Tomato Bowl. "All those homecoming dances we organized there…" She meant the dances that the JHS cheerleaders organized every year. The Charmers dance team always held our fundraiser dances out at the Junior Livestock Barn at the edge of town.

I sat back on the bench, unable to watch anymore. Then I gasped.

Oh, no. Anne and Carrie and Michelle and Ron…

I grabbed another of the burner phones and dialed Anne's number from memory.

"Who are you calling?" Mom asked.

"Anne, to make sure everyone's okay. Can you call Dad and let him know what's happening?"

With a quick nod, Mom grabbed a phone.

"Hello?" Anne answered in a cautious tone.

"Anne!"

"Oh, my God, Sa—I mean, Cousin Sally!" she corrected herself just in time. "Did you hear the news about Jacksonville? The whole friggin town's on fire!"

"I know, we just heard. We're looking at the news videos online now. Is everyone okay? How's Ron? Was he hurt in the attacks?"

"Everyone's okay. He wasn't on patrol when the v—when the fighting broke out. He went on patrol afterward, of course, but by then they were long gone. Can you believe the news is blaming this on gang violence?" She snorted.

The trailer lurched and rocked as Dad slowed down and pulled over to the side of the road.

I sighed and rubbed my pounding forehead. "What about the high school? Did it get hit?"

"Not that I've heard. Oh, by the way, I thought you said T, uh, you know who killed Dylan."

"He did."

"Not unless Dylan's the next Jesus, because he was totally in school this week."

I froze, feeling the blood draining from my face. "Are you absolutely sure?"

"Yep." There was a beep. "I'm getting another call. It might be Ron checking in. He's been calling me every half hour to make sure I'm all right."

"Okay. Just save this number under, er, my name, and I'll call or text again soon. You can text or call me, too, if anything else happens. Stay safe, and hug Ron for me."

As we ended the call, Dad and Tristan entered the trailer. Tristan's and my gazes connected and held as I relayed everything Anne had said with one notable exception…the news about Dylan. But before my brain could figure out a way to deliver that tidbit of information in some gentler way, my stupid lips just blurted it out.

"Dylan's alive."

Tristan's pupils dilated and he went still.

"Anne was positive?" Dad asked. "She saw him with her own eyes?"

I nodded, still staring at Tristan, feeling the relief wash over him so hard his knees threatened to give out. "I don't know how. We all heard something in him crack when he hit the fireplace."

"Maybe it was other bones in his body, like his ribs?" Mom suggested.

"Mmm, I don't think so. I heard it, too. I definitely thought it was his spine," Emily said.

"Maybe his father used the old ways to heal him," Mom said.

"Mr. Williams? He's too selfish for that," Emily said.

Their ongoing debate faded into background noise as I watched Tristan grab the edge of the kitchen counter to steady himself. His reaction was everything I could have hoped for, and my vision blurred as emotion filled my chest. I stood up and walked over to him with a smile, stopping to rest my hands against his chest. There was the Tristan I knew and loved. I knew, in spite of all his claims otherwise, that he really had been torn up over Dylan's death. His overwhelming relief now was the proof.

See? I told him silently. No one else needed to hear this, just him. *I told you you're not a killer any more than I am. We're still the good guys, no matter how much blood we have to drink to stay alive.*

He stared down at me, too many emotions racing through his mind for me to follow at first. His hands slowly rose up to cover mine.

"I may not be a killer yet. But I will be as soon as I can

get close enough to Mr. Williams." His hands gently but firmly pulled mine down and away from him. "Mr. Colbert, we should get this rig back on the road before anyone notices us here."

My lips parted in shock as Tristan turned and exited the trailer without a backward glance. Out of the corner of my eye I could see Dad staring at me for a long moment before he left, too.

CHAPTER 15

TRISTAN
TWO MONTHS LATER

As much as I loved the great outdoors, a guy could only take so much of it before he started to miss a little technology in his life.

I found Ms. Evans and her dog outside taking an early-morning walk, got the okay to use her living room TV, then headed inside the trailer. Through the bunk room's closed door, I could hear Emily's loud snoring, and beneath it the tiny sounds of music. Savannah must be having to listen to her MP3 player all night long to cover Emily's log sawing.

Careful not to wake up either of the girls, I quietly searched through Ms. Evans's DVD collection, figuring the best I would find would be a chick flick. But at least it would be something to watch.

Huh. She had *The Eagle* on DVD, one of my favorites.

I popped the movie in, turned the TV's volume as low as it

would go, then kicked back on the sofa and sighed. Oh, yeah, this was way better than being cooped up inside the truck.

Five minutes later, the bedroom door slid open. I quickly grabbed the remote and paused the movie, worried I'd woken up Emily. She was a bear when she first woke up, and not even the sight of Channing Tatum in a leather skirt would make up for disrupting her sleep.

Instead, Savannah slid the door shut, turned in midyawn and stumbled to a stop. Blinking in confusion at me, she slowly tugged her earbuds from her ears. "Oh. Tristan. Hi."

"Hey." The word came out as raw as if I were talking around a mouth full of gravel. I cleared my throat. "Did I wake you?"

She shook her head, shutting off her MP3 player.

When had talking to the one person I loved more than anyone or anything else on earth become so awkward?

"Want to watch TV with me?"

She shifted her weight and glanced at the TV screen. "Um, sure. What are you watching?"

"The Eagle."

She blinked a couple of times. "What's it about?"

War, I started to say, then realized that would make her instantly hate the movie. "It's about a guy trying to recover the honor of his family's name."

She stared at me, and I could practically see her guard rising.

"It's a Channing Tatum movie," I added, remembering that she was a huge fan of his ever since seeing him dance in *Step Up.*

That did the trick. One corner of her mouth twitched as she took a step toward the couch.

I quickly sat up and swung my feet to the floor to make room for her.

She hesitated then sat at the other end of the couch closest to the TV, even though it meant she would have to crane her head back at an uncomfortable angle to see the movie.

Two months ago she would have sat right beside me, curled up against me with my arm around her. But not today. I swallowed my disappointment, not wanting her to read it in my thoughts.

I restarted the movie from the beginning so she could get caught up. A couple of minutes later, her gaze darted sideways in my direction.

"Um, Tristan, could you stop staring at me? It's kind of distracting."

"Right. Sorry." I forced myself to stare at the TV instead.

Halfway through the movie, Joan returned with her dog. As soon as they entered the trailer, Lucy started yapping and dived for my ankles.

What the… I yanked my legs up in the air out of the reach of its tiny snapping teeth, then stared at the dog in disbelief. It had to be the ugliest animal I'd ever seen, like some kind of deranged zombie dog with bald patches all over where its hair was falling out from mange or something. Yellow pee dribbled down its hind legs as it barked nonstop and leaped up in the air, doing its best to get at my feet. The smell of urine hit me so hard I nearly gagged and had to hold my breath.

"Lucy hates vampires," Savannah explained with a sigh, also levitating her legs in the air so the dog couldn't go after her ankles next. She stuck her left elbow on the couch's armrest then rested the side of her head against her fist.

I got the distinct feeling she'd had to deal with this a lot over the past two months.

I looked at Ms. Evans, waiting for her to grab her dog and lock it up in her room immediately. Instead, she cooed baby-talk gibberish in its general direction while she spent two minutes making herself a cup of instant coffee in the microwave and I stared at her in disbelief.

Finally the microwave dinged. Ms. Evans retrieved her mug, sighed loudly then picked up her dog and took both the barking hellhound and her drink to her room. Even once the door was shut, Lucy continued to yap.

I scrubbed a hand over my face. Holy hell. Maybe hanging out in the truck and outside was better. At least it was quieter and my ankles were safer.

Savannah got up, carefully stepping over the yellow puddle on the linoleum, and opened the cabinet doors under the sink. She stood up with an empty plastic spray bottle in her hand and a frown on her face. "Uh-oh. Out of bleach. I'll have to get some from the storage area. Be right back." Forcing a tired smile, she took the spray bottle with her outside.

Why was Savannah cleaning up after her mother's dog? And the way she automatically did it without hesitation made me think this must be a habit with them.

Something was off around here.

Then again, maybe this was some kind of arrangement they had worked out together?

If so, it wasn't right. But why was Savannah going along with it instead of saying something? There was no way she could like having to clean up something as pungent as this dog pee, especially when it came from a dog who seemed determined to kill every vamp it came within ten yards of if given the opportunity.

The whole thing seemed warped. But I wasn't exactly qualified to be the best judge of it, either. I didn't know too much about Savannah's relationship with her mother, other than that Ms. Evans had been gone on the road a lot even before Savannah had to move in with her dad after her grandmother's death. And since then, Savannah had only seen her mother every few months, though they had seemed to stay in fairly regular contact through text messaging and phone calls. Maybe they got along better at a distance, like Emily and our mother?

Women and their mothers. They made no sense.

I sighed and grabbed the remote. When Savannah returned, she might want to see the part of the movie we'd missed during Lucy's attempted attack.

I tried to rewind the movie to the point where Ms. Evans and her dog had interrupted. But I was unfamiliar with the remote's buttons and must have hit the chapter skip button instead, which rewound the movie too far. The floor cleanup was probably going to take a few minutes, so I let the movie play and turned up the volume to drown out the dog's continued yapping from the other end of the trailer, planning on hitting Pause once we got to the right spot again in the movie.

Two minutes later, Emily barged out of the guest bedroom, the wild blond curls around her head and the murderous glare on her face making her look like a vengeful fallen angel come to kill every last demon in her path. "Would you turn that down? I'm not deaf, and I know you sure as heck aren't, either!"

With one hand rubbing the top of her huge belly, which had seriously rounded out over the past couple of months, she waddled over to the kitchen and slammed things around while pouring herself a mug of milk from the fridge. More banging half drowned out the yapping dog while Emily searched for and retrieved a bag of graham crackers from the tiny slide-out pantry cabinet. Then, growling something unintelligible under her breath, Emily headed back through the kitchen in the direction of either the trailer's exit or the bunk room.

Wherever she was headed, though, she didn't reach it.

The trailer's main door opened and Savannah stepped inside. Glancing at her, Emily forgot to watch where she was walking and stepped barefooted into the puddle Lucy had left behind.

Shrieking, Emily hopped on her clean foot all the way to the bathroom.

"Oh, crap," Savannah muttered, vamp blurring from the trailer door to the kitchen where she grabbed a roll of paper towels. She vamp blurred again, reappearing in a crouch beside the urine puddle, which she began to clean up.

Great. Now she'll be yelling for hours, Savannah thought to herself as she scrubbed the linoleum.

Shouldn't her mother be cleaning up after her own dog? I thought to myself, forgetting Savannah could hear me. Two months of hanging out with her dad had spoiled me into being able to think anything I wanted without fear of Savannah's reaction.

Savannah's head popped up, her mouth open in surprise. She dropped her head again, refocusing on cleaning every last speck of mess. *Normally Mom cleans up after Lucy, but since Lucy does it constantly, sometimes Mom forgets to come back and clean it up for a while. Which of course drives Emily nuts and some-times even triggers her nausea from the smell. So it's easier for me to just go ahead and clean it up.*

But all I heard was how it upset Emily.

The shower turned on in the bathroom. Emily must have decided to clean her foot off in the shower stall. Seconds later, another shriek filled the trailer from the bathroom.

The dog's barking grew louder as Ms. Evans slid open her bedroom door and stuck her head out, using a foot to keep her dog from escaping past her. "What happened?"

Emily reemerged from the bathroom with a dripping hair-ball pinched between her thumb and index finger. "First I step in a puddle of pee left by your dog, and then when I go to wash my foot off in the shower, I find this!"

"Is it yours?" Ms. Evans asked, eyebrows raised over tired, I-couldn't-care-less eyes.

"Of course not!" Emily snapped. "My hair's blond."

"So is mine."

"No, yours is gray. Just like this hairball."

Whoa. Savannah and I both winced.

"Emily—" I muttered.

Ms. Evans's eyes narrowed as she pushed her dog back, slipped out of her bedroom doorway, shut the door so the dog couldn't get out, then grabbed the hairball from Emily. I could hear the older woman's teeth grinding as she threw the hairball into the trash can under the sink then slammed the cabinet door closed. "There. Happy?"

Emily's chin rose several inches as her arms crossed over her chest. "Actually, now that you asked, could we please try not to leave our dirty cups on the countertop with used

coffee bags and spoons inside them when the trash can and
the dishwasher are right there?"

"Emily," I said, this time letting my growling tone do the
warning. Emily was way out of line, no matter how frustrat-
ing the situation was for her.

Savannah stopped scrubbing and seemed to be focused on
taking slow, deep breaths. Probably to replace the pee smell
in her nose with the freshly applied bleach, though to me
the cleaner solution smelled equally as bad.

"Sure," Ms. Evans said. "And could we also try not to
leave our used milk cups on the countertop with an empty
cracker wrapper inside it when, as you pointed out, the trash
can and dishwasher are *right there?*"

Savannah's eyes rounded as she stood up. "Mom—"

"No problem," Emily said. "Oh, and by the way, could
you possibly start cleaning up after your dog instead of making your daughter do it for you all the time? She's not your
freaking Cinderella, you know."

"Emily, I don't mind—" Savannah tried to say.

"Oh, stay out of it, doormat," Emily said, her scowl darkening.

Savannah gasped.

"How dare you!" Ms. Evans said. "You ungrateful, spoiled
brat. You come into my home and think it's okay to insult
my daughter? Who do you think you are?"

"The only person around here who's bothering to speak
up for Savannah. Because obviously she's too scared to do it
herself." Emily threw an arm out wide in Savannah's direction without looking at her.

"I don't know how you used to do things with your

mother, but if my daughter has a problem with anything I do, she knows she can tell me about it."

"Really? Are you sure about that? Because what if she says something you don't like? Aren't you going to just run off and sulk for months?"

It was like watching a cross between a political debate and a tennis tournament.

"Wow, hello, Dr. Phil," Ms. Evans said. "I didn't know we had a licensed therapist in the house. And here I thought we were only having to put up with the Coleman princess of hypocrisy."

"Hypoc—" Emily started to say.

"That's right," Ms. Evans said. "You have the nerve to stand there criticizing everything I do, in my own home, I might add. But you can't even be bothered to remember to switch the wet clothes over to the dryer sometime this century!"

"Ex*cuse* me?" Emily said, dragging out the first word.

I looked at Savannah in confusion. *What are they talking about?*

Savannah's horrified gaze darted my way then went back to ping-ponging between her mother and my sister. *Emily offered to do the laundry, but she has a bad habit of forgetting to move the wet clothes over to the dryer.*

Which would explain the sour smell I'd picked up from Ms. Evans earlier. I'd thought it was her dog.

Why don't our clothes smell? I asked Savannah.

Her lips rolled in to press against each other. *Because I've been washing them for us so Emily wouldn't have a chance to let them sour.*

Huh. Then again, it was pretty amazing that Emily had

even offered to do laundry in the first place. At home, we'd had a housekeeper to do our laundry for us a couple of times a week.

I blew out a long breath and scrubbed a hand over my face. "Look, ladies, maybe we're all just getting a little stir-crazy around here. Emily, why don't we get a cabin for you—"

"Because they're all already booked up for the summer," Emily snapped, still glaring at Ms. Evans. "And quit trying to change the subject, Tristan."

Ms. Evans shook her head. "That's right, Tristan. Better do as the deposed queen says or she'll cut off your head! Oh, wait, that's right, she can't now that the Clann's probably kicked her out."

"They haven't—"

"That you know about," Ms. Evans said. "When's the last time you were in contact with anyone in the Clann?" In the wake of Emily's silence, she smiled smugly and nodded. "Uh-huh. That's what I thought. You could have been kicked out of the Clann by now and not even know it."

"They wouldn't do that."

"Why not? They kicked out your brother. Or do you think you're too good to be cast out? News flash. You're not."

"My mother only did what she thought was best for the Clann."

"By being the biggest hypocrite of them all?"

"She wasn't a hypocrite!" Emily said.

"She didn't cast you out. Just like a typical Coleman. A hypocrite to the end, punishing the Clann's rule breakers but only when it suits them." Ms. Evans shook her head. "All my childhood life, all I ever heard was how wonderful the Colemans were, how fair they were, how hard they worked for the good of the Clann and to keep the peace, and how Sam Coleman was the most progressive leader the Clann had ever known. Mr. Vampires-Aren't-Bad-Just-Misunderstood. So why did he marry your mother, who everyone knew was the biggest vamp hater of them all? And why was it okay to negotiate peace with the vamps, but it wasn't okay for me to marry one or have a baby with one? And now look at you. The Coleman princess, knocked up with a vamp's baby just like me. The perfect example of the biggest hypocritical family I've ever seen in the entire history of the Clann, and your mother still didn't kick you out before she died."

I stood up. This had gone way too far.

"You..." Emily's hand rose in the air from her hip and drew back openhanded over her shoulder.

CHAPTER 16

I vamp blurred over to grab her wrist just in time, working hard not to bruise her as I held her back.

"Take it back!" Emily shrieked, fighting to get loose.

I glanced over my shoulder at Savannah, expecting her to step in and help out. Instead she just stood there staring with huge eyes, her hands shaking as she gripped the roll of paper towels in one hand and the plastic bleach bottle in the other.

Ms. Evans reached back into her room and grabbed her dog. "I'm going outside."

I waited at least thirty seconds after the trailer door slammed before daring to release my sister. Then I vamp blurred back to the safety of the couch and braced myself for her wrath.

Emily surprised me, though, standing there silently for a moment, steaming behind the wall within her mind that hid all her thoughts.

Maybe getting pregnant and facing motherhood for the first time had matured her.

Then she huffed out a breath and crossed her arms over her chest. "Can you believe her?"

So much for the increased maturity.

Savannah's face shut down as she turned away from us to dispose of the used paper towels.

"She's unbelievable!" Emily continued. "Honestly, Savannah, I don't know how you managed to turn out so sane after growing up with her."

Savannah paused in the act of removing the trash bag from its metal container. *Oh, like your mother was perfect?* she thought but forced herself not to say out loud.

Hey, I thought before I could stop myself. *Don't bring my mother into this.*

Savannah's shoulders rose an inch. *Sorry. But your sister really needs to stop talking about my mother right now, okay? I know Mom's not perfect. But nobody's mother is. And Mom has sacrificed everything just so we could invade her home for months with no end in sight. The least your sister could do is show a little gratitude.*

Outside the trailer, footsteps crunched up the asphalt road. A second later, Ms. Evans's voice began to vent a stream of fury as she complained about Emily to Mr. Colbert.

Savannah sighed. *Great, now she's dragging Dad into this.* She tied the garbage bag shut, stuffed the bottle of bleach into the sink cabinet, then put a new trash bag into the can.

"Would you stop that?" Emily snapped, turning from the pantry with a frown at Savannah. "Your mother's dog made that mess. She should be the one to take it out."

"Emily, let it go," I said, watching how hard and straight Savannah's back had become. "Sav doesn't need you to fight her battles for her. If she has a problem with her mother, she can handle it herself."

"I don't have a problem with my mother," Savannah said, her voice so low Emily could barely hear her.

"Oh, please. Why wouldn't you?" Emily said, throwing her empty hands up in the air in frustration. "She shows that dog more love than she does her own daughter! It's ridiculous, the way she talks to it like it's her baby. And have you seen how she lets it lick her face? It licks its own butt!"

Okay, that was gross. But still, Emily needed to stop talking right now. Couldn't she see how upset Savannah was? It didn't take a mind reader to notice how quiet and still Savannah had become.

"And the way she leaves her dirty dishes on the counter all the time is just lazy," Emily continued, oblivious to her audience's reaction. "And then she has the nerve to complain about how I do the laundry? I wash her clothes, too, even when she can't be bothered to pick them up off her bedroom floor and stick them in the hamper. Even though the hamper is right outside her bedroom door!"

Lazy? Savannah thought. *My mother's one of the hardest-working women I know!* She turned toward Emily, her eyes blazing green.

"Emily," I said. "Shut up."

Emily turned her scowl on me. "What? I'm only saying the truth."

"Savannah doesn't want to hear it," I said, pointedly flicking a glance at Savannah, who was staring at Emily as if considering which body part to rip off her first.

Emily rolled her eyes. "Right. Because she's perfectly fine being the group doormat. Well, *I'm* not okay with it, and—"

The irises of Savannah's eyes turned white.

I jumped to my feet, not bothering to move human slow. "Emily, shut. Up. Just go away. Right now. Go away."

Gasping, Emily took a half step back out of pure instinct. Then her eyes narrowed. "Oh, so now you think you can scare me with your vamp speed, little brother? Well, I've got news for you—"

"Emily! Shut up or so help me God I will throw you into that bedroom myself!" I shouted.

"Fine!" Emily shouted back. "Side with the doormat and her mother and her demon dog!" She stomped past Savannah and me through the kitchen and to the bunk room, sliding its door shut behind her so hard it bounced open again in its track and she had to slap it closed again. The springs on her futon-style couch bed squeaked in protest as she flopped down on the mattress and burst into tears.

Holy hell on earth. I blew out a long breath. "You okay, Sav?"

She stood there shaking. Instinct told me I should hug her, rub her arms, do some kind of physical contact to help her shake off her emotions. But then I remembered how she'd chosen not to sit directly beside me on the couch earlier. With the way things were between us lately, she might not welcome any physical contact from me after all.

Finally she took a deep breath. "I'm fine." But she said it through gritted teeth as she grabbed the full trash bag from the kitchen floor and vamp blurred out through the trailer doorway.

I took a long, slow breath in then out. There was no way this argument had come out of nowhere. It must have been brewing for months. And if I'd come around the ladies more often than just to space out in the bunk room for a few hours a week after feeding, I probably would have sensed it and been able to prevent it.

Instead, I'd been trying to give Savannah space and time to think and hopefully miss me enough to change her mind about taking out Mr. Williams. And all I'd really done was left her to get caught between the two princesses of the RV park.

I stepped outside and looked around for her, finding her on the trail past the nearest metal trash barrel. Judging by the jut of her chin and the determined, steady pace of her walking, she looked ready to escape this park on foot if need be.

"Sav, wait up," I called out to warn her of my approach as I caught up with her at a human pace for the benefit of any fellow campers who might be looking.

Her shoulders hitched up another inch. But she didn't tell me to go away at least.

"I'm sorry about what Em said," I muttered, shortening my stride to match Savannah's as I shoved my hands into my pockets. "She was way out of line."

"Yeah, she was." She snapped her mouth shut, refusing to vent the hundred and one heated thoughts thrashing around inside her head. "So was Mom, though. They're both being ridiculous."

I don't know how much more of it I can take! she thought, and I didn't know if she was just thinking to herself or had meant for me to hear that part.

"I didn't realize it was getting that bad."

She glared at nothing ahead of us. "You wouldn't believe how much complaining I have to listen to. And not just from Mom. Every time one of them's not around, the other one takes the opportunity to vent to me. It is *constant*. I've tried mediating. I've tried to explain why they're doing the stuff they're doing. They're both so used to living on their own and doing what they want."

"And they're both too stubborn to want to change their ways for someone else's sake."

"Exactly. And they're both completely blind to how they're so much alike!"

I tried not to smile. I could see the humor because I hadn't had to live in the middle of it all for two months. "So what are we going to do about it?"

She looked at me then. "We? Uh-uh. You. You can talk to your sister and tell her to clean up her crappy attitude and stop criticizing every single thing my mother does wrong."

"Oh, come on, Sav. That's not fair and you know it. Your mother's just as much to blame for this situation as Emily is. She was way out of line back there, talking about my family."

"Really? Because I thought she was just pointing out the facts. Your father did claim to be all 'equal opportunity' for the vamps and yet still strangely chose to marry a vamp hater. Why is that, Tristan?"

I took a deep breath to push back the anger so I could answer her in a steady tone. "I don't know. And to be honest, I don't care because it doesn't really matter now, does it? They're both dead."

She flinched and looked away. "Right. So I guess we'll never get to find out why your mother kicked you out of the Clann but not your sister."

"I can tell you why. Because Emily never told her who the baby's father was."

"Because no one can read her mind unless she lets them?"

I nodded.

"That is so weird. How can she do that?"

I shrugged. "I don't know. She's always had the best mental shield of anyone in the Clann. How do you think she always got away with so much crap without getting caught?" I'd told Savannah about several escapades my sister and I had gotten into as little kids.

She sighed and looked away. "Whatever. The point is—"

"The point is, they're both in the wrong, and they could both act a lot better for the sake of the team."

"The team?" Now a hint of a smile kicked up the corners of her mouth.

"Yeah. Well, you know, it's like sports. We're all in this together, right?" At her reluctant nod, I added, "So if we all want to keep from killing each other, then we all have to compromise for the sake of others."

"Which neither of them wants to do, if you couldn't tell from that fight back there."

"Right." I sighed. "I'll talk to Emily, and you talk to your mother. We'll make them see that they've got to ease up on each other and stop focusing on every little thing the other does wrong."

Savannah hummed a grouchy note deep in her breath. "Maybe you should talk to both of them." At my pointed stare, she said, "You don't understand. She's my mother. I can't just walk up to her and tell her what to do!"

"Not tell her what to do, but make suggestions."

Silence.

"Sav, she's your mother. She loves you. She'll listen to you."

"Or ground me for sassing her."

I couldn't stop a smile this time. "Ground you from what? Ever leaving the trailer?"

She smiled down at the gravel road beneath our feet.

"So you'll talk to her?" I pushed a little. "Today?"

She chewed the inner corner of her mouth, vertical lines forming between her eyes.

"Sav…" I coaxed. "You need to talk to her. I can't do it. I'm not her kid."

"Maybe I can get Dad to talk to her."

"Sav!" I said with a half laugh of disbelief. "You're a vamp now. I don't think she's going to throw you over her knees and spank you."

She looked at me with eyebrows raised. "Want to bet?"

I was starting to lose my patience. I took another deep breath. "Okay, out with it. What's the real reason you don't—"

"Because our relationship's not like that anymore, okay? Used to be, I could talk to her. Now, it's like there's all this distance between us. She's always so polite with me. It's like being around a stranger. And…maybe Emily's right about some stuff. Let's face it, Mom doesn't have to be here with us. She could just go get a new car and take off. The only reason she's stuck around is probably to make sure I'm safe."

"Have you talked to her about this?"

She shook her head. "I can't."

"You need to, or it's going to keep bugging you."

Her chin stuck out as she shook her head again. "I'll be fine. Trust me, sometimes it's way better to just keep your opinions and feelings and issues to yourself."

A memory of Emily and her mother arguing flashed through her mind.

"Yeah, for those two. But not for you. You never tell anyone when they're upsetting you or irritating you. You just keep it all bottled up inside."

"It's called keeping the peace," she muttered through gritted teeth.

"Yeah, well, when you're the only one who's trying to do that, it's never going to work. All it does is make you miserable. How do you expect anything to change if you don't talk it out?" Not to mention how eating down all her anger instead of letting it out had nearly made her vamp out today.

Oh, like telling you my feelings worked out so well for us last time? she thought, then looked away, hating that I could read her every thought.

"Just because we had one argument doesn't mean you should be afraid to say how you feel. Especially to me."

She sighed. "Don't you get it? It's all this sharing of opinions and feelings that's gotten everyone into this mess right now. Mom, Emily, you and me. Everyone is mad at everyone else because nobody can agree on anything. I just want everyone to stop fighting and get along already!"

And then she burst into tears.

Whoa. I turned and took the risk of gathering her to me. She surprised me by not fighting me and instead burrowed into me. I bent my head, resting my chin on her soft hair, its familiar lavender scent filling my nose.

Oh, yeah, the situation had definitely gone way, way too far. But at least it had finally gotten my girl back into my arms.

Silver linings.

Now if I could just find a way to keep her here…

I stroked her back until her sobs calmed down. "Sav,

you've got to stop doing this to yourself. It's not your fault that Emily and your mom aren't trying harder to get along. And you and I are going to be fine, even if we argue sometimes."

"I don't want to fight with you anymore," she said, her voice thick and muffled against my shirt. "I miss the way things used to be between us."

I turned my head, resting my cheek against her hair and smiled. She'd finally come around. "I missed you, too."

But she was listening to my thoughts instead of what I said. She stepped out of my arms with a frown. "I didn't say I'd changed my mind about killing Mr. Williams."

I scrambled to play mental catch-up. What had I missed? "I thought you said you missed me and don't want to fight anymore—"

"I do miss you. And I don't want to fight with you anymore. But that doesn't mean I agree with you." She quickly dragged her wrists over her cheeks to dry them as her frown deepened into a scowl.

Great. So we were still at square one on this. "Look, Sav, I told you killing him's the only way out of all of this. Sick of Emily and your mom's fighting? Tired of being stuck in a trailer with them in some RV park somewhere? The answer's obvious. We have to kill Mr. Williams. It's the only way."

Growling, she turned around and started walking back up the hill toward the trailer, muttering things under her breath about how stubborn and reckless and suicidal I was. Not that the muttering kept me from hearing every word.

At the top of the hill, I said, "Look, disagree with me all you want about Mr. Williams. But you can't disagree that we have to talk to those two women in there—" I nodded at the RV up ahead "—and fast, before they kill each other."

She stopped walking and stared at the RV, silently debating. But at least she was still listening to me.

"Just talk to her about the dog for starters," I said. "She doesn't have to get rid of it completely. We could board it at a kennel or something. Think short-term solutions here."

"She'll never agree to it. She'd hate the idea of sticking that dog with a bunch of strangers who might mistreat it or starve it and never pet it or give it any exercise."

"Well, what about somewhere else, like a foster family?"

She frowned. "It would have to be someone Mom knew and trusted."

"What about one of your friends?"

"Maybe. I could call Anne and see what she thinks. I'm still not sure Mom would go for it, though, even if one of my friends could take Lucy. That dog is all she has now."

I touched her chin, lifting it until she looked me in the eyes. "That's not true, Savannah. She still has you, and if she loves you, then that's what should matter the most."

Everything inside me went still, leaving me confused and thrown off track by my own words.

Savannah's soft half smile further derailed me. "I'm not sure she'll see it quite that way." She sighed. "But I do have to agree, life would be a whole lot better for everyone, including Lucy, if she went on a doggy vacay for a while." Her glance flicked down the hill and across the creek, where her mother and the dog were strolling together. Something that felt an awful lot like dread drifted from her through the air between us. "Okay. I'll see what I can do about the dog."

"Thanks, Sav."

Still frowning, she turned and dug her phone out of her pocket. Dialing Anne's number, she shot me a wish-me-good-luck smile over her shoulder. Then Anne answered.

I stood there for a moment, watching Savannah fall into her usual habit of pacing around the campsite while listening to Anne rattle on and on about everything Savannah had missed in Jacksonville since their last conversation. I didn't try to listen to either end of their discussion, though. I was too lost in my own thoughts.

I'd meant what I said about how having Savannah should be more important than anything else.

So why was I still holding on to my need to avenge my mother's death?

Was I acting like Savannah's mother and that dog, holding on to something even when it hurt everyone else around me?

Confused, I walked away, needing space to think. But even after I walked all the way down the hill to the bridge, across the creek and along its bank, I still hadn't cleared the mess inside my head.

The trail distracted me for a moment as I hiked over rocks and in between towering boulders the creek cut through when its winter waters flooded a wider path. Now dry from the summer drought, part of the trail branched off and up-ward, and I followed it, climbing over rocks until I reached the top of one of the dark gray boulders and could look down at the creek below me.

I sat there for a while, listening to the gurgling flow of the water below, thinking about my mother and all the argu-ments we'd had over the years about football and Savannah and leading the Clann. I had loved my mother, of course.

Who didn't love their mother, even when she drove us nuts? And mine had definitely done her best to drive me crazy. Especially with that dream-blocking charm she had insisted on hiding in my bedroom somewhere so I couldn't dream connect with Savannah for years.

But I'd also always known all of Mom's arguments had come from one place…her love for me and her desire to protect me, however misguided she might have been. Maybe Savannah was right and even Mom's casting me out of the Clann had been a way to protect me as well, though at the time it sure hadn't felt like it.

Again, the questions haunted my mind…. What had Mom wanted to tell me at that dinner before she died? Had she planned to apologize? To tell me she still loved me in spite of what I'd become?

Because of Mr. Williams, I would never know.

And again, the anger rose within me. But now its heat felt more like a poison inside me, burning instead of warming me.

Was Savannah right? Was I letting my desire for revenge destroy me from the inside out?

At the very least, it was keeping me apart from Savannah.

I kept trying to tell myself that she would come around. That once Mr. Williams was dead and she saw I was still the same, she would understand. But what if I never found a way to get close enough to kill him? Already it had been months since my mother's death. Two months of distance from Savannah, of not holding her hand or kissing her. Two months of not getting to listen to her laughter or her voice whispering through my mind. These two months without her had been pure hell, taking me right back to last year when we were broken up.

I had vowed back then that if I ever found a way for us to be together again, I would never allow anything to come between us.

But wasn't that exactly what I was doing now by holding on to my need for revenge?

If I could ask my mother for advice, I knew what she would say. She would say that I had to go after Mr. Williams and never stop, no matter how much it might cost me, until he paid for what he'd done. Because that was how she had felt about the vampires who had killed her family when she was little. She had let that loss fill her with anger and fear and a need for revenge that had darkened every day of her life until its end.

And I was doing the exact same thing.

I was turning into my mother.

I buried my face in my hands and groaned. Savannah was right. I had felt an incredible amount of relief after learning Dylan was still alive after all, though at the time that relief had seemed shameful.

She was also right that for two months, I'd thought of nothing but ways to kill Mr. Williams. And in the process, I'd risked losing the one person who mattered the most in my life, even as she begged me to let go of all that darkness inside me and come back to her. I'd held on to my anger, thinking it somehow made me noble or more of a man, that only the weak would allow their family to be killed and not seek retribution for that crime. I had thought I would be like Maximus in that *Gladiator* movie, or Mad Max, the hero who would stop at nothing until the deaths of his loved ones were avenged.

But even after getting their revenge, what had those guys ended up with? Nothing but more death and loss and loneliness.

Did my need for revenge really matter more than my love for Savannah?

CHAPTER 17

SAVANNAH

I walked along the gravel road that wound through Palisades State Park. The summer sun's heat was nice on my skin, warming me as nothing else did lately. But even the bright sun and gurgling creek—which to me seemed plenty big enough to be called a small river—weren't enough to erase the dread growing inside me with every step I took.

How would Mom react when I told her we needed to find Lucy a new home for a while? Anne had called Michelle, and both Michelle and her mom were happy to take Lucy. And Mom had always liked Michelle.

But this was Mom's dog we were talking about here. Lucy really was like a human child to her, and she never went anywhere without her.

Would Mom hate me for even suggesting this? Would she start to blame me for losing her job and the privacy of her home and her dog?

I really did not want to have this talk with my mother.

At the end of the hill, I had to turn right and cross an old-fashioned but well-maintained wood-and-metal bridge spanning the creek, which would lead me down to the flatter side of the brownish-green water's shoreline where Mom and Lucy were hanging out.

Halfway across the bridge, I had to stop and admire the view. I could imagine a lot of couples taking their informal wedding photos here overlooking the dark gray boulders that rose up several hundred feet above the creek, carved from the cliff sides by the flowing water and shaded by shallow woods. Unlike East Texas, however, these woods were made up of mostly hardwoods. So even here in the outdoors I was reminded of how far from home the Clann had forced us.

Sighing, I finished crossing the bridge, following the road again till it led me down past an open and flat rocky area, and past that to a grassy, shaded area with several picnic tables and fire pits where fishermen liked to sit sometimes. Today I found only Mom and Lucy at the edge of the creek, watching mallard ducks that had flown in to swim in the smoother parts of the creek.

I couldn't believe Dad had been comfortable letting Mom go this far from our RV alone. Then I sensed his emotions, annoyance mixed with determination and that ever-present wariness, downwind somewhere nearby. I glanced around at the small wooded area to the right of the creek and spotted a slight shift in the shadows among the trees. Ah, there he was. I knew he'd never let her get so far out of his sight.

Repressing a smile at his protectiveness, I pretended I didn't see him and instead called out to Mom to warn her of my approach so I wouldn't scare her.

Unfortunately, I was also upwind to Lucy, so the dog immediately started barking before I even reached them.

Mom saw me, smiled and raised her hand, waving her entire forearm side to side in greeting.

"Hey!" Mom said as I joined her, and the dog went wild at the end of her leash. "Isn't this weather wonderful?"

"Yeah." I cleared my throat, bracing myself for what had to be said. *It's for the good of the team,* I reminded myself. "You know, Lucy's not looking too good lately."

Mom frowned at her. "I know. Her hair's starting to fall out. Poor thing. She's not eating much, either. That's why I've been taking her out for all these walks, to give her more exercise so she'll start eating again."

I couldn't help but wince this time. "Um, I don't think it's the lack of exercise that's the problem. I think it's me and Tristan and Emily's baby. We're freaking Lucy out."

Mom sighed. "I was hoping she'd get used to you guys."

"Mom, it's been weeks. She's getting worse, not better."

So was the situation inside the trailer.

Thank heavens Mom couldn't read my thoughts.

She stared at Lucy, who was peeing down her own legs, the dog's entire body shaking as she fought to get at my ankles with her teeth. More tufts of hair floated out from Lucy into the air, caught a breeze and were carried over the broad greenish-brown creek.

"I think we need to find her a place to stay. Just for a little while," I added, already hating how my words would hurt my mother. But this had to be done, for Lucy's sake as much as everyone else's.

Mom's face fell, her lower lip sticking out, and I had a

glimpse of what she must have looked like as a little girl. "But she's my baby! Normally she's so sweet and cuddly...."

"I know. But she's just so stressed out right now. And it would be temporary, like a vacation from the vamps for her. She could be somewhere she felt safe again, like Michelle's house. I know she'd love to dog-sit, and I'm sure her mother wouldn't mind."

Mom bent down and scooped up her dog, cradling Lucy against her chest near her face.

"Mom," I murmured, hating this whole situation. "The stress is making her sick. I don't know how much longer she can take it."

Mom closed her eyes, rubbed her cheek against the top of Lucy's quivering head, then whispered, "Fine."

I swallowed down the lump in my throat, my eyes stinging. Today I was one of the worst daughters on the planet. What kind of person took away their parent's cherished pet?

We walked back to the RV in silence, Dad following at such a long distance that I could barely make out his emotions. We took our time, none of us eager to return to the confines of our prison on wheels. A prison that had once been Mom's home. I wanted to reach out to my mother, put an arm around her, comfort her in some way. But Lucy was there and would have bit me if I got too close to her owner. And there wasn't anything I could think of to say to make Mom feel better. The fact of the matter was this whole situation sucked.

When we returned to the RV, Tristan was nowhere to be seen. Emily was on the couch with a bag of Harvest Cheddar-flavored Sun Chips, my favorite kind before my vamp side had developed too much for me to be able to keep human food down. She stiffened but didn't look at us as we entered the trailer.

Mom froze, scowled, then muttered "Good night" to me and shambled off to her own room with her dog, her door softly clicking shut behind them.

I started to go to bed. But the room was too empty and quiet, and it was still early.

Emily noticed me wavering in the bunk room's doorway. "Want to watch a movie with me?"

"What are you watching?" Too late, I realized it was the same thing I'd asked her brother earlier today.

"*P.S. I Love You.* It's awful. Her soul mate dies."

A snort escaped me. "Sounds great." I flopped down on the dinette bench, twisting around to look over its curved back where it attached to the couch so I could see the movie, while Emily cranked up the volume to cover the barking from Mom's bedroom.

Emily restarted the movie at the beginning, reminding me again of her brother. Thinking about him hurt too much, though. I forced myself to focus on the movie instead, grateful for the distraction from the distance still keeping Tristan and me apart. And within minutes, I was sucked in.

The movie's beginning reminded me of Tristan and me... the couple's initial fight, the way they loved each other so much, how the heroine feared losing the hero.

And then the hero died, just like I was scared Tristan would. But unlike Tristan and me, the movie's heroine had no ability to turn him and save him, so he was just gone forever.

Like Tristan would be if Mr. Williams or one of his people managed to stake Tristan or set him on fire with a spell or decapitate him. Which the Keepers were more than power-ful enough to do with one swipe of their huge clawed paws when they were shifted into panther form.

How could Tristan not be afraid of dying? Did he really think vampires were invincible, despite all Dad's and my warnings and even seeing several vamps, including Gowin, die at the Clann's hands? Even Tristan's combination of Clann and vamp abilities wouldn't be enough to protect him against an entire army of descendants and Keepers.

I could hardly stand to watch the movie's heroine as she struggled to deal with the loss of her soul mate. That would be me, if Tristan went after Mr. Williams.

For the second time today, tears poured down my cheeks. I swiped at them and tried to blink fast to keep more from forming. Then I realized I wasn't the only one crying.

Emily was hunched over on the couch as much as her huge belly would allow, her face buried in her hands as her shoulders heaved in time with her sobbing, which was get-ting more intense by the second.

"Emily?" I reached out for her shoulder, hesitated, then went ahead and gave in to the urge to comfort her and risk scaring her. She was crying too hard. It couldn't be healthy for the baby.

"Emily, it's okay, it's just a movie," I tried again when her sobbing only grew louder.

"No, you don't understand," she said in between hic-cups. "I…"

She couldn't breathe enough to get the words out.

I patted her back awkwardly, feeling completely out of my depth. My friends were all way too proud of their tough jock status to ever break down and cry in front of each other.

Even the loss of Nanna hadn't caused my mother to break out in near-hysterical sobbing like this. What should I do to help Emily? Surely the movie couldn't have made her this sad. Unless it was the pregnancy hormones?

"Shh," I whispered, getting up and grabbing a roll of toilet paper from the bathroom. I was back with it in less than a second. I held out a wad of the paper to her, which she took and pressed to her face.

I tried to read her mind, but as always it was like trying to pry a metal bear trap open with nothing but human strength to help me. I sighed. "Emily, I can't read your mind enough to help you. You'll have to talk to me."

Silently I sent up a prayer. *Please don't let this be about my mother again!*

Her hands dropped to her lap as she turned incredulous eyes toward me. "What's wrong? What isn't wrong right now? My mom's dead. My dad's dead. My brother's being accused of killing our mother. I'm nineteen, single and knocked up with the baby of my dad's murderer. And I can't even go home!"

She pressed the toilet paper wad to her face again, her wails muffled within its softness.

Suddenly the trailer door burst open.

"What happened?" Tristan demanded, his eyes wild as he searched the trailer for attackers.

"We're fine," I said. "Just…watching a sad movie, is all. You know, it's girly stuff."

His eyes rounded in horror. Then he frowned, his gaze caressing my face. "Are you sure you're okay?"

Oh, yeah. I'd forgotten my own tears from a few minutes

ago. I hastily dragged the backs of my hands over my still damp cheeks and forced a smile. "Yeah, I'm sure."

Frowning, he slowly turned and walked back down the metal steps. With one last backward glance at me, he eased the door shut.

Instantly I felt the renewed loss of his presence, which pricked more tears into life in my eyes. Jeez, what was it about tears that, once you started crying, you couldn't seem to stop?

I rolled off more toilet paper, this time for my own face. "You're right. This sucks. All of it."

Emily sniffed. "I can't believe I got myself into this." She waved her hands at her stomach. "I was such an unbelievable idiot."

The pain in her words reached out through the air and joined with my own. "Oh, Emily. Everyone screws up sometimes."

A humorless laugh huffed out of her. "Not like this! If not for me, Gowin never would have been able to get close enough to kill my dad. And now I'm going to have Gowin's *baby*." She clenched the wet paper in one fist and pressed it to her mouth as if afraid to say more, her green eyes round with fear as she looked at me, silently pleading with me to say something reassuring.

"It's going to be okay," I lied for both of us, praying my lack of a poker face wouldn't ruin the lie.

"How? How can this possibly be okay? I mean, I don't even know what I'm doing! I don't know anything about babies or how to have one or raise it. Especially a half—" She stopped, her eyes widening still further.

"Go on and say it. A half breed like me." And there was

that old familiar heat in the pit of my stomach just waiting for its chance to take over again. As usual, I pushed it back down and did my best to ignore it. I'd already nearly lost control earlier today. I couldn't afford to let the anger drive me to vamp out again.

"I'm sorry. I keep saying crap I really don't mean, and I hear myself saying it and know how awful I sound. I know you and your mom must think I'm the most ungrateful, world's biggest bi—"

"It's fine. You're pregnant," I said, lying like crazy now. It wasn't okay. But saying so when she was already miserable wouldn't help the situation, either.

"No, that's no excuse. I know better. I just can't seem to make myself stop once I get going. It's like, if I can focus on the clogged bathroom drain or the dog pee then I won't be thinking about *this*." She held her hands out palms-up in front of her belly. "Or what I'm going to do once it comes *out* of me."

She whispered the last words, and her fear filled the trailer around us, turning the air too thick for me to breathe or get any oxygen out of.

Oh, crap. Not good. Her fear was filling the air with adrenaline-laced pheromones that were doing their best to trigger my predatory instincts. And somehow I was pretty sure that Tristan would not be able to forgive me if I bit his sister.

I hopped up to my feet and tried to casually open the window over the dinette.

"I'm due any day now, you know," she murmured, staring at me.

Carefully I took a small breath then nearly sighed with relief. The fresh air would soon clear the trailer of any blood-lust inducing scents.

"Have you decided…whether to keep your baby?" I asked, hesitating now over the words, unsure whether I should even say them. It wasn't my place to be nosy about her decisions or her life. But maybe Tristan was right about everyone's need to vent their emotions and Emily would feel better if she talked about hers with someone.

She nodded, wincing. "I can't give it up for adoption. I know it's an option, but it doesn't feel right to me. I mean, it's not this kid's fault that I was stupid and fell for all of Gowin's lies. Besides, it's half Clann and half vamp. If I don't raise it, who will? The Clann would probably just kill it. And the vamps…" She didn't finish that thought, darting a glance at me and then away again.

"You know, my mom could probably give you a lot of advice," I said slowly. "After all, she has been there and done that."

She cringed and stared down at her hands clasped now over the top of her tummy. "You're right. I should have thought of that." She looked up at me with big eyes full of hope. "Do you think, if I apologized…"

"She'll forgive you," I said, and this time I didn't need to lie. For all her faults, my mom also had a really big heart. If Emily sincerely apologized, Mom would forgive her immediately.

She sighed. "I shouldn't have said all that stuff to her today. It's just, every time I see you two together I keep thinking about how Tristan said she practically abandoned you the past couple of years when you needed her most—" She clapped a hand over her mouth. "I'm sorry. See? I don't know where it comes from and it just spews out of me—"

I sighed. "It comes from what you see as the truth." I stared down at my own handful of wadded-up paper in my lap. "You're half-right. She did sort of leave me with my grandma when all my Clann and vamp abilities started showing up and I needed her most. But she was doing what she thought was best. And she wouldn't have been able to help me anyways. She can't do magic." At Emily's raised eyebrows, I explained. "She never wanted to be in the Clann and chose to let her skills fade away instead of strengthening them. So when I started turning…"

"She was afraid of you?"

"Not so much that she was afraid I would hurt her, but that her being around would make it harder on me. She knew that at least Nanna had the strength to control me if I ever lost it and vamped out at home."

"And what was your grandma supposed to do then? Set you on fire? Stake you?"

A short laugh escaped me. "No, of course not. Nanna knew how to use the old ways of magic to dampen the bloodlust around our house."

"Really? How? Because we could totally use a spell like that for your parents." At my sharp look, she said, "Oh, come on. Any idiot can see that they're still in love and fighting it. I'm assuming because of the bloodlust and the energy draining effects if they kiss?"

I shrugged. "Mostly. But I don't think they got along all that well even when they were married and had Nanna's bloodlust dampening spells to help them."

Emily stared at her stomach. "Even if your mom can help

me with some things, I highly doubt she'll know what I should say when this kid asks me what happened to its dad someday."

I winced. "You're right, that discussion is going to be hard. But maybe if you just stay honest with your child..." I thought about the day my parents had told me what I really was. Dealing with that discovery had been rough. But it had been made even worse by the fact that my family had lied to me and kept secrets from me for fourteen years before finally telling me the truth. "Just don't wait too long to tell your kid the truth. Trust me, it only makes things worse for them."

"What if this kid learns how bad its dad was and decides to follow in Gowin's footsteps someday?"

I frowned. "Then that'll be its decision, not yours. As long as you do your best to show it a better path, that's all you can do. It's up to each of us to decide who and what we want to become."

Like Tristan.

Emily sighed and dropped her head back on the sofa. "Being pregnant really, really stinks."

I made the most sympathetic face I could. "I'm sure it doesn't help that this is your first time and you have no idea what to do. If only there were some kind of manual...hang on. Maybe there is!"

I jumped up and vamp blurred into the bunk room to dig through my jeans until I found it...the credit card Dad had given me the other day to buy stuff from the local gas station outside the park. He'd said the Clann shouldn't be able to trace it because it was under one of his aliases that nobody else knew about, and that it was safe for us to use for whatever we needed.

I found my phone, pulled up the internet and found an ebookstore website. A long series of fast screen taps, and two minutes later we had an account all set up and ready for use.

"Here." I tilted the phone so Emily could see the screen, too. "They've got tons of ebooks on pregnancy and motherhood. *What to Expect When You're Expecting. The Complete Single Mother. The Complete Idiot's Guide to Motherhood.*"

"Seriously?" Emily laughed. "Let me see that." She took the phone and peered more closely at it. "Wow. I had no clue they'd have so many guidebooks for mothers." She glanced up at me, her smile turning wry. "I guess I'm not exactly the first female to ever get pregnant."

I returned her smile, glad her mood was lightening up. "Or the first girl to get freaked out about it."

Before she could protest, I went ahead and bought several ebooks for her, then happily handed her my phone to read them on. Anything to keep her happy and off Mom's back!

"Just as long as you give it back every now and then so I can talk to my friends back home."

"Right." She started to read one of the ebooks, then hesitated and looked up at me. "Thanks, Sav. For the ebooks and for listening. I didn't realize how hard it was just keeping all of that to myself."

I smiled. "Vent anytime. Just as long as it doesn't include calling my mother names."

She laughed. "Okay. And for the record, you handled yourself way better than I would have if someone were talking about my mama."

It was my turn to make a wry face. "I don't know. For a minute or two there, it felt like a pretty close call. If Tristan hadn't been here…"

She heaved herself up off the couch, then dug her knuckles into the small of her back and stretched. "Yeah, speaking of, when are you two going to work out your issues already?"

I stood up, taking my time throwing away my wad of paper in the trash beneath the kitchen sink before answering. "That's kind of up to him. He and I don't agree on some things right now."

"And what, you can't compromise and meet him halfway?"

I shrugged, not wanting to talk about Tristan's and my problems with his sister. Besides, it wasn't really the kind of issue you could compromise on. "Hey, listen, I'm really tired, so I think I'm going to turn in for the night."

One blond eyebrow arched knowingly, but thankfully she didn't push the issue. "Sounds like a good idea. All this bawling has wiped me out, too."

The bunk room was a small space even for one person to undress in, much less two. So I let Emily get ready for bed in there first while I took a shower.

When I stepped out of the bathroom, I caught myself pausing in the kitchen, looking and listening. Hoping Tristan had felt…something after our talk together this afternoon and decided to come back to me.

But the living room and kitchen were empty, the rest of the trailer silent as well except for Emily's snoring from the bunk room. Even Lucy had worn herself out for once and given up barking.

There were people within reach of me. But even still, I was alone.

And I couldn't stand it.

I slipped on some shoes and snuck outside. Dad was right where I expected to find him, sitting in the front seat of the truck's cab, the windows rolled down to let a cross breeze through while he read some book he'd found who knew where. Tristan wasn't stretched out in the backseat as usual. He must be taking a walk along the creek. Good. I didn't want to have to ask him for a private moment with my dad.

Dad looked up and smiled as I climbed into the passenger side of the front seat.

"You seem rather deep in thought," he murmured, closing his book. "A penny for your thoughts?"

I started to tell him no one said that phrase anymore, then gave up. "I was wondering about you and Mom. About... how you two always fight all the time."

"A difference in personalities, I suppose." He frowned. "You do know our arguments have nothing to do with you and that we both love you?"

I waved off the parental reassurance. "Yeah, I know. It's just..." I took a deep breath as my throat tightened. "How do you know when the disagreements are too much? When it's time to just give up and let go?"

His head rocked back an inch. "Ah. That is a deep question to be thinking about. The answer is not at all simple, because it varies for everyone. For instance, part of being a vampire for many years is that it teaches us how to have a lot of patience. After all, if you cannot die and no longer have a natural lifespan, then your perception of the passage of time is quite different from a human's. So for one of our kind, forever would not be too long to disagree with someone we loved enough."

I looked down at my hands as my fingers twisted together in my lap. "What if the other person doesn't feel that way? What if..." I swallowed hard and tried again. "What if they feel too strongly about the path they're on, and it's a path you can't or don't want to follow them down?"

Dad sighed. "You mean like your mother getting tired of being on the run with me and insisting on our divorce?"

"Yeah. Something like that."

He turned his head to stare through the windshield at the hills that rolled down to the creek in the moonlight. After a moment of silence, he said, "I agreed to divorce your mother because it was what she wanted. She needed to feel safe again, and she felt like I could not give her or you that safety. She wanted you to have a chance to grow up with a normal life for as long as possible. She also wanted freedom and independence. What can you do when the person you love no longer wants to be with you, other than to release them and allow them to live the life they choose, even though that life is not with you?"

"But couldn't you have maybe found a way to change her mind eventually if you just kept trying to talk to her about it?"

His smile was sad. "It is both human and apparently vampire nature to want to hold on to that which you love with every ounce of strength that you possess. But if you truly love someone, that is the only real way to love them. To love loosely is the hardest love to learn. But it is also the strongest and most selfless form of love you can give another."

Learn to love loosely. There was a clear ring of truth in his words. Maybe that was why they hurt so much. Because I knew it was what I had to learn how to do.

I had to learn to love Tristan loosely, to let him go instead of trying to hold on to him or change his mind.

"Thanks, Dad. Good night." The words came out rough past my hoarse throat as I climbed out of the truck.

Back inside the trailer, I slipped into the dark bunk room and climbed into my bed as quietly as possible so as not to wake Emily on the futon below. Across from me, the third bunk bed where Tristan always rested while lost to the blood memories after each weekly feeding now stretched out empty and silent, waiting for his return. I stared at it until the lump in my throat hurt too much. Then I plugged my MP3 player into the wall charger Dad had bought for me at a store, put my earbuds in my ears, turned on my MP3 player and tried to lose myself in the music.

CHAPTER 18

The next morning, I asked everyone to gather in the kitchen area for a meeting.

I took a deep breath, pushing aside the guilt for the moment. This was for the best, for everyone. "Yesterday Mom and I talked about Lucy, and she agreed we need to take Lucy somewhere away from vampires for a while. I think we can all agree that Lucy's health doesn't look too good."

Murmurs of agreement from the group. Mom stared down at Lucy, who was yapping out a hoarse cough from her arms.

"Mom?" I asked.

She nodded. "I know. Lucy needs a break."

"Right. So I talked to Anne, and she talked to Michelle and Michelle's mom, and they agreed to keep Lucy for us so she can get better."

Mom's mouth tightened as her lower lip trembled. But she didn't argue.

She didn't have to say a thing. I still felt like crap.

"So we need to plan a trip back to Texas," I finished, feeling like the world's worst daughter.

Hang in there, Sav. Tristan squeezed my hand, his eyes soft with understanding. *I know this is hard. But it really is the right thing to do. Your mom will see that, too, eventually.*

Before or after she cries buckets of tears from losing her dog and her job and her home to our invasion? I stared at a spot of spilled coffee that was quickly turning into a stain on the tan countertop where Mom must have set her spoon earlier.

"Good," Dad said, leaning a hip against the edge of the kitchen counter. "This will give me a chance to restock our blood supply."

All of us looked at him with frowns of surprise and confusion.

His eyebrows shot up. "Surely you have noticed the rapidly dwindling supply?"

I hadn't really. I'd been too caught up in trying to play peacemaker between Emily and Mom and upset about Tristan and the distance between us.

Dad sighed. "At any rate, we are nearly out of blood and must restock very soon. So a return trip to East Texas will allow me to meet with my supplier there and pick up a large enough quantity to hold us over for a while longer."

Mom's frown deepened into an all-out scowl. "Why can't you get blood from somebody around here? Don't you have suppliers all over the U.S.?"

"I used to. But I have already attempted to contact them without success. They may have gone into hiding now that war has broken out. My East Texas supplier is the only one whose number is even still working."

"Okay, so then why don't you have him ship the stuff to us here?"

"Because," Dad said in a tone that showed he was struggling for patience. "The mere fact that my East Texas supplier is the only one still willing to speak to me makes me question whether he has been compromised by the Clann. If he has been, then I have no desire for him to know where we are currently hiding, in case he tips them off."

"Then have him do a blind drop instead."

"If he has been compromised, that will not afford any additional protection for us. The Clann could still be there waiting for us to pick up the supplies. Plus, meeting with my supplier face-to-face will allow me to directly and immediately ascertain whether he has been compromised. Since he is human, he is particularly vulnerable. However, a quick read of his mind when we meet will either reassure me or inform me that I need to find a new supplier should we ever desire to permanently take up residence in East Texas again someday."

Oh, of course. He needed to meet with his supplier in person because none of us could read minds, human or otherwise, over the phone.

I wondered if all blood suppliers for the vamps were human. Maybe that made it easier for them to work around lots of donated blood in health care jobs without losing control and going on a bender like a vamp might?

Mom's eyes flared wide then narrowed. "That is really dumb, Michael. If your supplier has been compromised, then meeting with him in person is the *worst* thing you could do!"

At the angry tone of her owner's voice, Lucy began to bark in earnest, her entire body jerking with the effort.

Dad glanced at me then cleared his throat. "Perhaps we

should discuss this further outside without an audience. Or the dog present."

Mom rolled her eyes. "Oh, please. Like Savannah hasn't heard us argue before? She's a big girl and she knows we don't get along. She can handle the truth."

"Actually, I really don't mind being left out of this," I said, rubbing my forehead, which was starting to pound. I couldn't tell if the growing headache was coming from having to sit in on yet another argument or the dog's barking.

Mom huffed. "Fine!" She threw open her bedroom door, shut Lucy into the room, then whirled around to face Dad. "Please, by all means, lead the way." She threw an arm out wide toward the trailer door.

Dad's face darkened into a scowl. Silently he exited the trailer with Mom hot on his heels.

The door had barely banged back into its frame before Mom started yelling.

"Would you at least attempt to keep your voice down?" Dad hissed, his voice carrying right through the trailer's thin metal walls and windows. "We do have neighbors who might not want to have to endure this discussion with us."

I slouched down on the dinette seat until the back of my head met the top of the seat back. I used to be so lucky that my parents were divorced and never saw each other. I really missed those days.

"Do I look like I care?" Mom said, but at least her voice dropped to a harsh whisper. "Look, all I'm saying is we need to stick together and avoid any kind of traps the Clann might have set up for us. You have no idea what they're capable of. Did you know Mr. Williams has buddies in the CIA? They have access to all kinds of technology now…satellites, drones, you name it! They could easily be listening for any mention of you anywhere in East Texas right now!"

"Or even listening to us right here right now," Dad muttered.

Mom must have missed his attempt at humor, because her voice dropped to a whisper. "In a state park in South Dakota? You must be joking."

"Actually I was—"

Mom railroaded right over him. "My point is, what if you call your supplier and their satellites or whatever overhear your conversation? They don't even have to mess with your supplier directly in order to compromise him. They could just listen to you two plan to meet and then lie right there in wait for you to show up. And then where would I—I mean, our daughter be? She needs her father, now more than ever. None of us can afford to be stupid and risk getting caught."

"I know that, Joan. Please do give me some credit. My supplier and I always speak in code. The conversation would not contain any words likely to alert any eavesdroppers as to our real identities or intentions."

Mom growled under her breath, clearly not mollified in the least.

So Dad dropped the ultimate bomb of reason on her. "I understand this is frightening for you. But do try to remember the blood is not just for me and Tristan. Our daughter also needs this to survive."

"Oh, he's good," Tristan muttered.

I flashed him a tired smile. "He learned from the best in the guilt-trip business. He lived with my mother for three years."

One side of Tristan's mouth tilted up in a half smile, making my heart lurch.

Mom must have conceded defeat during Tristan's and my short exchange, because the trailer door opened and my parents came back in.

"Kids, buckle up. We're headed to Texas," Mom muttered. "Sav, honey, you'll need to call Anne and get her to arrange a meeting for you with Michelle. Have your dad figure out what time we'll arrive and a good meeting place."

From the couch with her eyebrows raised, Emily silently handed me my phone, which showed one of her new pregnancy ebooks on the screen. I closed the ebook reader program then searched through my contacts list for Anne.

"For safety, I believe we should split into two groups once we arrive in East Texas," Dad said.

I looked up in surprise.

"If there is any risk of the Clann showing up at my meeting with my supplier, then it would be foolish to hand every member of our group over to them at once."

"If they do show up, you're going to need help," I said.

"Which is why Tristan will come with me and you ladies will continue on to do the dog exchange," Dad said.

Now my heart was really racing. I opened my mouth to argue, but Tristan was faster.

"He's right, Sav," Tristan said. "Like you said, your dad shouldn't go alone. And it's too high-risk for all of us to be there together."

"Whoa, hang on a second," Emily protested. "I don't want you there either, little brother. Remember, they want you even more than him."

"Yeah, but he's got to have some kind of magical backup,"

Tristan said. "We have no idea what kind of spells they could try to use on him."

My stomach twisted and rolled. I didn't like this at all.

Tristan stared at me. "It's the safest way."

"Why don't we get blood from somewhere else?" I said. "There's got to be all kinds of blood banks around. Couldn't we just break into one and—"

"And risk tipping off the Clann as to our whereabouts?" Dad said.

I let out a long, slow breath through my nose. I saw their logic. But it didn't make me like the plan any more.

"We need this, Sav," Tristan murmured. "You, me, your dad. We all need this."

Suddenly I sort of understood my mother's less-than-mature reaction of a few minutes ago, because part of me really wanted to stomp and yell and argue at the top of my lungs.

Instead I pressed my lips together hard, letting the small bit of pain distract me, and nodded.

Logically I could see that this was probably the only good plan we could come up with right now. But that didn't mean I had to like it.

CHAPTER 19

It took a few hours to figure out what time we needed to leave at as well as schedule a meeting place and time with my friends. The guys handled the breakdown of all the hoses and lines that tethered the trailer to the park's RV pad hookup, while we females worked within the trailer to clean up the last of the dirty dishes, finish the laundry and secure everything in the cabinets and fridge.

By ten o'clock that night, we were on our way.

As usual, Dad insisted on driving the truck. Once again, Mom was annoyed by his seemingly chauvinistic attitude, and I braced myself for yet another of her venting sessions about it. But this time she surprised me by staying quiet and holed up in her room with her dog, probably to eke out every last moment she could spend with Lucy. Emily was pretty unsteady on her feet while we were on the move, so she tried to sleep through most of the trip. Tristan and I opted to watch movies together in the living room.

And though we still couldn't agree on Tristan's need to go after Mr. Williams, when Tristan reached out and covered my hand on the seat between us with one of his hands, I couldn't help but turn my hand over and lace our fingers together.

Thanks to the terrible gas mileage that Mom's truck got while hauling the heavy trailer, plus Emily's desperation for drive-through food once she woke up—which she hadn't gotten to have in two months—the fourteen-plus-hour trip took closer to eighteen. Even without using the GPS app on my phone, I could tell we were close to Texas the next afternoon when the flat landscape turned into open rolling hills, many of them now dotted with black and brown cows. The southern states also showed their recent sufferings from drought with pastures covered in mostly dead brown grass, which made a sharply contrasting background for the green pine trees that began to show up the closer we got to East Texas.

Then the sporadic pines turned into long stretches of woods, and I was reminded again of why East Texas was called the Pine Belt. While up north, I'd gotten used to seeing mostly hardwoods and only a few evergreens here and there. The sight of all those pines both welcomed me with their familiarity and surprised me with the realization of just how much I had missed them.

I was home again.

Except that feeling didn't make any sense to me. I'd always planned to leave East Texas and the Clann's stranglehold over that area as soon as I graduated from high school, and once gone, I had never expected to look back. Yet here I was, feeling a strange pain of what could only be called homesickness. Shouldn't I be horrified to be back and anxious to leave as soon as possible?

Ignoring the current movie on TV, I stared out the window behind the couch at the familiar landscape zooming by and tried to make some sense of my mixed emotions. But it wasn't easy like it should have been. Because, while I was afraid of the Clann and being back within the heart of their territory, there was also this undeniable excitement buzzing in my stomach and tingling in my hands and feet, as if my body had a mind of its own and yearned to jump out of this trailer and run through the woods on either side of the highway.

The roller coaster of emotions only grew worse when we stopped in Mineola at the car rental place to drop off Dad and Tristan.

"Can I just go on record one more time and say how much I hate this plan?" I muttered while standing in the parking lot with Tristan. Dad had gone inside the agency to pick up the car.

"I know. I don't like it either, but—"

"Yeah, I know. We need this." I looked up at him. "I know I don't have to say it but…please promise me you'll be careful."

Tristan smiled. "I will. I'll look after your old man, too, while I'm at it."

I sighed.

Then Tristan kissed me. After two months of suffering through the distance between us, the shock of that kiss slammed every one of my senses almost to the point of overwhelming me. I'd nearly forgotten just how right it felt to kiss him, like coming home and discovering my biggest purpose in life all in one blinding flash of joy. I wound my arms around his neck, desperate to be closer to him, wishing I never had to let him go. We'd had only a couple of days back together. And now this.

"It'll only be a few hours," he murmured against my lips.

"Didn't Tom Hanks say something like that to his fiancée right before getting on a plane that crashed and left him missing on an island for five years?"

Tristan chuckled. "Yeah, well, he wasn't half vamp and half Clann either, now was he?" He sighed, his strong arms looped around my waist. "I would do a spell to give myself wings and fly back to you if I had to."

I let my face show my doubt on that one. "I thought we couldn't do magic like that."

He shrugged and grinned. "Where there's a will, there's always some way."

Yeah, that was exactly what I was most worried about... Mr. Williams's will to kill Tristan if he ever got the chance.

"Sav, honey, we've gotta go," Mom called from behind the wheel of the truck.

I rose up on tiptoe to kiss Tristan one last time, our lips pressing together hard enough to bruise. Then I stepped away from him and walked around the front end of the truck, refusing to look back as I got into the passenger-side seat. This wasn't a Kodak moment. I would see him again in just a few hours. Their plan was potentially dangerous, but between Tristan and my dad's combined skills and experience, they would be fine. I would see both of them again before the sun even had time to set.

"Lie to yourself some more, Savannah," I muttered, pressing a shaking hand to my knotted stomach.

Still, try as I might I couldn't help but stare at Tristan's shrinking reflection in the side mirror as we pulled out of the parking lot and back onto the highway, or stop the lump from forming in my throat.

Anne had warned me that the perimeter of Jacksonville was too heavily guarded with Keepers both night and day for us to risk going there. But meeting in Tyler meant the girls wouldn't have to travel very far, since it was only a half-hour's drive from Jacksonville. So I had arranged with Anne to meet them in the Barnes & Noble parking lot. The lot had the added advantage of being right across from the mall where we all used to shop together, so it wouldn't be hard for any of us to find. Plus it was plenty big enough to admit Mom's truck and trailer.

The only concern was maintaining the invisibility spell on both the truck and trailer during the meet-up to keep us hidden from any Clann who might pass by. Because Emily's advanced pregnancy was sapping most of her strength, it had been up to Tristan and me to create the spell. And it would be all on me to maintain that spell for two hours, which was the minimum amount of time Dad said he would need to travel to his meeting with his supplier.

It was hard not to constantly check my phone for messages or calls from Dad during the half-hour drive between Mineola and Tyler. The silence in the truck's cab didn't offer any distraction, either. I had thought Mom would at least be happy about finally getting to drive her own truck again. Instead, all she could think about was the impending loss of her dog, whom we had resorted to giving the doggy equivalent of a Valium from a vet Mom had visited up in South Dakota before the start of this trip. She was so worried Lucy would remember being left with strangers and blame her for it later that she wanted to keep her sedated for the handoff.

Emily cleared her throat from the backseat, where she had stretched out. "So, um, I'm reading this ebook about what to expect when you're pregnant, and it says I should be seeing an ob-gyn every month and taking folic acid and stuff. Do...you guys think maybe we could find me a doctor to see up north once we get back?"

Mom's hands tightened on the steering wheel. "I'm sorry. I thought your mother might have already explained this to you. You can't see a normal doctor. Not for this baby. Any human doctor will do an ultrasound on your baby and say it's stillborn. Damphirs don't have a heartbeat till well after they're born, at least from what I experienced with Savannah."

I forgot to breathe for several seconds. Wow. It was one thing to know I was different, and another to picture myself as a newborn without a heartbeat. "How'd you know I was still alive?"

"Because you moved around and blinked your eyes and stuff."

Huh.

"Is there anything else I should know about this baby before I pop it out?"

This started a long question-and-answer session between them that continued right up until the moment we pulled into the bookstore parking lot and found my friends already waiting for us there.

I shoved my phone into my jeans pocket, then jumped out of the truck as soon as Mom had finished parking, surprised

yet again by my reaction as my eyes welled up with tears. I
hadn't realized just how much I missed seeing my friends.

Michelle leaped out of her car with a loud squeal and ran
over to give me a big hug, making me laugh. Good thing
we'd planned on talking inside the trailer instead of the bookstore, or we definitely would have attracted a lot of attention.

"Wow, I didn't realize anyone would actually miss me," I
said with a grin as I returned her hug, concentrating not to
squeeze her too hard and crack her ribs.

"Of *course* we miss you!" She glanced around. "Didn't
Tristan come with you?"

"Oh, um, no," I said. "He had something to do with my
dad."

The other doors of Michelle's car opened. Grinning, I
waved at Carrie and Anne to hurry up and join us.

"Is everything okay between you two?" Michelle frowned,
distracting me while Carrie and Anne walked over to join
us. Carrie, never much for physical displays of any kind, also
surprised me by leaning in for a hug.

"Yes, we're fine," I told Michelle, looking at her and almost missing Anne's swoop in for her own ferocious version
of a hug. "Whoa. Anne, are you feeling okay? Since when
did you turn into a hugger?"

She leaned back and scowled at me with the darkest look
I'd ever seen on her face. "Oh, I don't know, maybe when
my best friend ran out of town without even stopping to say
goodbye?"

"I know. I'm sorry," I said. Thankfully Anne knew the
entire story already. It would have killed me to have to lie to
her. She'd also said she would come up with a cover story for

me for Carrie and Michelle, since they didn't know anything about the existence of vampires or what the Clann really was.

Not that her story seemed to have stopped Michelle's ever curious mind from running wild with questions, which it was doing right now. Michelle's constant stream of thought was a little distracting, and I was doing my best to block it out.

Anne stepped back and propped her hands on her hips, looking me over. "You're skinnier. Paler, too. Isn't Tristan feeding you anything?"

The twinkle in her eye told me she was only joking. Vampire humor. Lovely.

I sighed and smiled back at her. "Thanks. Always good to hear how great I look. Speaking of…" I blinked a couple of times, wondering if I was seeing things. "Did you get…highlights?" Anne's thick chestnut hair was no longer a single shade of brown but now sported wide chunks of honey-blond. She was also wearing it down instead of in her trademark ponytail.

One corner of her mouth hitched up. "Yeah. Ron talked me into it. I told him it was a dumb idea but…" She wrinkled her tanned nose.

"No, I like it." I studied the new look and nodded. "It makes you look…I dunno, more girly?"

She swatted at my upper arm. "Gee. Thanks."

"Hey, why don't we go hang out inside the trailer so we can sit and talk?" I suggested, remembering the plan. Once we were inside the trailer, the invisibility spell would kick in and keep any Clann who might be searching for Mom's truck from noticing us. We wouldn't be totally invisible, just not worth noticing for some reason. Mom had opted to stay in the truck with her dog, but Emily had already gotten out and gone into the trailer, probably to pee yet again. She seemed to have to go every twenty minutes or so.

We all went inside and I gave them a quick tour. Emily reemerged from the bathroom just as we were settling into the dinette.

"Hi," she said with a tired smile.

My friends' eyes widened as they saw how pregnant Emily was.

"Everyone, this is Emily Coleman. Em, this is Anne, Carrie and Michelle," I said.

"Nice to meet you," Emily murmured. Then she made a face and touched her stomach. "Whoa. Big kick there. Listen, I hate to be rude but I didn't get much sleep last night with all the moving and shaking. So I hope y'all don't mind if I take a nap and leave you guys to get caught up?"

My friends and I all made murmurs of agreement and waved her on to the bunk room. As soon as the door slid shut, Michelle leaned forward.

"I can't believe the rumors are really true about her being pregnant!"

I cleared my throat, knowing Emily could probably still hear us. "Um, yeah. It's kind of a touchy subject though, so…"

"Oh, right. Of course," Michelle said, her cheeks turning pink. "So tell us about you and Tristan being on the road together. Tons of fun in the sun and hot romantic moonlit walks on the beach?"

A snort slipped out of me. "Uh, not really. We've been… having some issues." Feeling the surge in Michelle's curiosity, I quickly added, "We'll work them out eventually, though." Hopefully. Quickly I tried to change the subject. ' I'd really rather hear about you guys. So tell me, Anne said you two have boyfriends now?"

Michelle turned pink again. Carrie waved her hand in the air and said, "Oh, you know, they're just fun to double date with."

But the warmth emanating from both of them said their feelings for their new guys were developing into something a lot more than just "fun."

"I brought pictures!" Michelle said, whipping out a small photo album from her back pocket that looked stuffed full of images.

For the next hour, my friends told me about everything I'd missed the past two months…the strange "gang violence" that had briefly but so devastatingly destroyed a huge part of Jacksonville and the town's recovery afterward, the two brothers Carrie and Michelle were now dating who were Christian rock band members they'd met on the same night at some church function, all three girls' successful tryouts for the JHS varsity Maidens volleyball team.

The photos of the junior prom and their group date dinner before it at a popular Asian grill in Tyler were the hardest to look at, though.

"You guys looked great," I murmured, tracing a finger over a picture of them laughing around the grill as flames apparently shot up from their food. They looked really happy.

Tristan and I should have been in the picture with them. Would I never get to go to prom with Tristan?

Michelle launched into a long story detailing their grand shopping expedition for dresses for two weeks before prom, with occasional jokes and laughter added by Carrie and Anne. I tried to laugh with them around the tightness in my throat, but it took some effort and I was pretty sure my lack of a poker face threatened to give away my true feelings.

Finally Anne bumped her shoulder against mine. "You're awful quiet. Spill."

I swallowed and shook my head, holding on to my smile for all it was worth. "Oh, you know. I'm just jealous. I wish Tristan and I could have been there with you guys."

I was missing so much, first during the five months spent away in Arkansas, and now another two months on the run from the Clann. It seemed that, no matter how hard I tried, I just couldn't have a normal life. I wanted to be one of them, a regular human with normal worries like what dress to wear to prom and whether I'd make the varsity volleyball team. I missed our monthly slumber parties at Anne's house, the way her mother always made us take off our shoes before entering their house and her homemade veggie pizzas, even though the smell of the human food turned my stomach. I missed getting to listen to Michelle's rambling gossip at lunch every day, and Carrie teasing Anne about fumbling some dive for the volleyball at practice or a game. I missed listening to Ron's and Anne's thoughts about each other that they worked so hard to hide from themselves and everyone else because they were crazy in love and trying to keep it under control.

I missed it all. And even though I tried to tell myself that I'd never really been one of them due to my hybrid genes, it didn't make me feel any better. In fact, knowing I might live forever and my human friends wouldn't made every moment I missed experiencing with them even worse. I'd never realized before just how limited my time with them would be. I'd thought at least we would have our junior and senior years together before we graduated and went off to separate colleges. Now I didn't even have that much time with them.

"Oh!" Anne said. "I nearly forgot. To honor this lovely reunion, I got us all a little something." She dug into her jeans pocket, then pulled out a wad of what looked like black cord. After a minute of untangling, she proudly held up four cords with odd little metal charms dangling from each. "They're friendship necklaces, or you can wear them as bracelets if you want."

She passed them out so we each had one, then explained, "I've actually had them for a while but wanted to wait till we could all put them on at the same time."

I held up mine and studied the charm. It looked like a metal puzzle piece.

"I looked everywhere for a four-piece friendship bracelet charm, but they're impossible to find," Anne said. "Then I found this guy in Mexico who cuts apart Mexican change to create four pieces. I asked him if he could do it with a U.S. quarter, which he could. So I found a quarter from our birth year, sent it to him, and tada! See? They all fit together."

We held our charms together, twisting and turning them until sure enough, they fit together again into a U.S. quarter. Then I noticed the four hearts that formed the cuts so each of our charms had one heart-shaped edge and one heart-shaped hole along the other cut edge.

"Wow, Anne, this is really awesome!" Michelle said.

I had to admit I was completely impressed. I'd never realized how thoughtful Anne could be. I'd always thought of her more as a spur-of-the-moment, fly-by-the-seat-of-her-pants girl. But this had obviously taken some true planning.

"Thank you," we took turns saying, making her all but glow.

Carrie and Michelle chose to wear theirs as necklaces, while Anne and I wore ours in multiple loops around our right wrists.

I stared at my friendship charm, at the heart-shaped edge and the missing heart from its other edge. A glance at my watch showed my time with my friends was already almost over. I had thought the two hours would pass by slowly, filled with dread and worry about Tristan. But the reassurance of my silent phone in my pocket had allowed me to completely forget the time. Soon I would have to say good-bye to Anne, Michelle and Carrie. They would go back to living their human lives. And while I would be with Tristan, I would once again return to my new life of running from the Clann. And all I would have would be the occasional text or phone call and my new friendship bracelet to keep me connected to them.

My eyes stung, and I discovered I couldn't breathe well.

While my friends continued talking about the friendship charms, I focused on regaining control over my wayward emotions, telling myself that I was being ridiculous, that Tristan and I wouldn't have to be on the run forever, that someday we would return to Jacksonville and the life we'd hoped to have together there. That I would see my friends again, and I wasn't really missing out on that much.

But it all felt like lies. Because I really had no idea when the war between the Clann and the vamps might end, if ever. Soon my friends would be going their separate ways to college, and then it would be even harder for us all to stay in touch. They would start careers somewhere, get married, have families. And our brief time together as a circle of friends would be gone, just nice memories from the past that could never be repeated or recaptured.

Every day that the Clann forced Tristan and me to stay on the run was another day I missed spending with my friends, creating those precious memories.

Mom opened the trailer door and poked her head in. "Sav? I'm sorry, hon, but we need to go."

It was time.

I felt physically ill as I walked my friends to Michelle's car. Mom followed us so she could carefully lay the still drugged Lucy in the backseat. Mom also transferred all of Lucy's tiny dresses and collars and leashes, Lucy's doggy bed, her food and water bowls, and a huge bag of her favorite dog food into the trunk of Michelle's car.

"I think the bumper just dropped a good six inches," Carrie muttered, making me laugh despite my tight throat.

Michelle looked a little wide-eyed and slightly overwhelmed as Mom gave her a written list of instructions on how much to feed Lucy and when and how often to walk her. But she only smiled and promised to take the best care of Mom's dog, and even thanked my mother for trusting her with her baby. Clearly Michelle was a dog owner and understood the whole dog ownership thing, which seemed to slightly reassure Mom.

Once Mom had given Lucy the last of many kisses and returned to the truck sobbing, my friends and I all took turns hugging goodbye. The entire time, Carrie's and Michelle's minds nearly blasted me with a thousand questions they somehow forced themselves not to ask out loud. I wished so badly that I could tell them everything, that I could explain why I had to be gone for who knew how long. But they would never believe me, and even if they did, just knowing about vamps and the truth behind the Clann would endanger them. It was better for them not to know, even if that meant putting a little emotional distance between us.

Then I hugged Anne, and the reminder that she did know everything and still chose to be such a loyal friend was nearly my undoing.

"Stay in touch so I don't worry too much, okay?" she muttered near my ear.

I nodded, the huge knot in my throat too tight for me to speak. A rebellious tear slid down my cheek as I stepped back from the car and watched them all pile inside. And then, with the music cranked up and their windows rolled down, they all waved madly and drove away.

Taking a few shaky breaths, I forced myself to focus on Tristan and Dad. Better to worry about the guys than to have a pity party and bawl over what I couldn't control.

Which reminded me…

I checked my phone again and frowned. Still no updates. What was going on at the blood supply pickup?

I hopped into the front passenger side of the truck.

"Any word from our guys?" Mom asked as she started the engine.

Silently I shook my head as a growing sense of unease crept over me.

Something must be wrong. They should have completed the pickup by now.

Maybe the supplier was running late?

"I'm sure they're fine," Mom muttered. But I didn't need to read her mind to know she was getting worried, too. It was all there in her tone and the pinched lines between her eyes.

"Let's go back to the rental place and wait for them," I said, working hard to keep my voice even. Maybe if I tried to stay calm, Mom would, too.

"Right. Good idea." Mom forced a smile for my sake as she steered the truck and trailer into traffic. "Don't worry, hon. Your dad didn't survive this long by being stupid. He's got amazing instincts. In fact I used to tease him about being part Clann because he always seemed to smell a trap a mile away."

I forced a smile of my own. "Right. Plus he's got Tristan with him. So between the two of them..."

"Exactly."

I looked out the window and, for the first time ever, silently begged my notorious speed demon of a mother to drive faster.

TRISTAN

We drove east on Interstate 20 for an hour, passing by Kilgore and several billboards advertising the world-famous Kilgore College Rangerettes dance/drill team, which made me smile. If Savannah were with us, she probably would have begged us to stop by the Rangerettes Museum on the way back. Along with nearly every other Charmer, she was a huge Rangerettes fan. Savannah had even convinced me to agree to take her to the Rangerettes' annual Revels show last spring. But before we could go, the vamp council had dragged us to Paris for her "test" and then everything blew up with the Clann's abduction of her Nanna, followed by our breakup for months.

Maybe we could stop by the museum on our way back. That ought to earn at least a smile from her.

Once we passed Kilgore, Mr. Colbert took an exit off the highway, made a quick, sharp turn back on a side road, then a hundred yards later the asphalt abruptly ended and turned into a single-lane dirt road. We stayed on the dirt road for another ten minutes as it wound through acres of thick pines occasionally broken by open pastures where cattle grazed.

Finally we crossed a single-lane cement bridge over the local creek and entered a huge square field that appeared to have been recently clear-cut, judging by the number of dead pines now lying on the ground.

"Interesting choice of location," I muttered as Mr. Colbert parked in the road at the edge of the clearing.

He hummed an agreement, dark eyebrows pinched and shadowing his eyes, which stayed on the move as he visually scanned the area. Finally he nodded, and we opened our doors to get out.

Mr. Colbert froze, sniffed the air. "Something's wrong."

Then I felt it…an explosion of pinpricks all over my neck and arms.

Acting on pure instinct, I dived over the hood of the car, grabbing Mr. Colbert on my way down in a tackle. Immediately we rolled, and not a second too soon, as a reddish-orange orb flew toward us from the south and our car exploded into a huge fireball.

We jumped to our feet and took off running in the direction we'd originally come in from.

"This way!" Mr. Colbert shouted, grabbing my shoulder and pulling me more west when I tried to go north.

Then I smelled it and understood. The northern breeze carried a strange, musky scent that was half human and half something exotic.

Keepers.

The Clann had called in help for this ambush.

I reached out with my mind and found a small group of Clann coming our way from the southwest, downwind where we couldn't smell their approach. They were trying to box us in. We'd have to circle around them.

"More Clann ahead, eleven o'clock," I called out over the roar of the air rushing between us as we ran through pines and pastures, weaving around cattle and over barbed-wire fences.

Mr. Colbert nodded. We turned more north.

But not soon enough.

Fifty yards to our left, a group of Clann spotted us from the road where they were waiting in the back of a camouflage-painted pickup truck. At the same time, more pinpricks of pain stabbed at my skin in warning just before a blue orb hurtled toward us at chest height. It was going to hit Mr. Colbert.

I reached back, grabbed his nearest arm with both my hands, and threw him ahead of me while I ducked to avoid taking the hit myself. But I missed seeing the second orb trailing a split second behind the first.

I stood up too soon, and it slammed right into me.

Air whooshed out of my lungs from the impact. It felt like a car had just nailed me. The orb hit me hard enough to knock me off my feet. Air whistled in my ears as the world rotated clockwise ninety degrees then soared past me.

"Tristan!" Mr. Colbert yelled.

The world went black and silent.

CHAPTER 20

SAVANNAH

Ten minutes later as we reached the Tyler city limits, pain suddenly exploded in the back of my neck.

"Ow!" I cried, reaching up to rub it. What the heck? I glanced at Emily in the backseat. "Did you just hit me?"

Her eyebrows shot up. "What are you talking about?"

And then the strangest sensation of emptiness formed inside me, robbing me of breath.

Something was wrong.

Mom hissed out a curse, distracting me.

"What is it?" I asked.

Then I noticed the red-and-blue lights flashing behind us. Oh, no. We were being pulled over by a state highway patrol.

Emily twisted around to look behind us and muttered her own curse.

My heartbeat revved into overdrive as I remembered the time when one of the Jacksonville cops had pulled me over for a ticket. That police officer had been a descendant, and I'd spent the entire fifteen-minute ordeal hearing his every thought as he'd debated whether to follow the law or handcuff me and take me out to the woods somewhere to get rid of the town's half-breed menace. Thankfully he'd opted to only give me a ticket, but it had been a close call I never wanted to repeat.

If this state trooper was Clann, too, I doubted any of us would be seeing the inside of a jail cell unless it was one specially built by the Clann.

But wait. He couldn't be Clann. If he had been, he wouldn't have seen us in the first place, right?

The air hissed out of my lungs as I remembered.

"What?" Emily said.

"The invisibility spell. I forgot to maintain it. It was only supposed to last a short while. If we needed it to last longer, I was supposed to give it another boost of energy."

Which meant this cop could be Clann after all.

"What should we do?" I said.

"Pull over," Emily told Mom.

"Are you crazy? He could be a descendant!" Mom said, her knuckles turning white on the steering wheel.

"She's right. We'll never outrun him," I said, thinking fast. "And if he is Clann, we can't risk leading him to the guys. We have to pull over."

Mom hesitated then slowed the truck and eased it over to the side of the road. She parked then looked at me, her eyes wild, her thoughts panicked. *I won't let them take my daughter!*

"Easy, Mom," I said. "He might not be a descendant. Maybe we were just going too fast or something."

But then the cop's door opened and I felt that low-level

prickle of needles racing over the back of my neck and down my arms.

Since Emily and Joan couldn't use their abilities, they both looked at me, eyebrows raised in question.

I shook my head in silent answer. It wasn't me using power.

"He's Clann!" Mom hissed, her hand darting out as if to grab the gearshift.

"No!" I put my hand over hers to stop her. "We're too heavy and slow in this thing. We'll have to try something else."

But what? I was the only one who could use power right now. And the only spells I knew were defensive ones.

I could throw energy orbs at the guy, maybe enough to knock him out. But I had no idea how long the effect would keep him unconscious while we tried to get away. And once he woke up and alerted the Clann, we wouldn't get far.

Unless he'd already called someone in the Clann as soon as he pulled us over...

Outside, the patrolman's door thumped shut before he slowly walked toward us, his khaki uniform pressed and starched to within an inch of the fabric's life.

"Roll down your window, Mom," I muttered. "I can't hear his thoughts."

She did, slowly, as the officer approached the truck. The closer he got, the better I could pick up his thoughts.

The plates are wrong, he thought while studying Mom's license plate. *I'd better not call this in yet till I'm sure, though.*

"He hasn't called the Clann yet," I whispered. "There's still time."

The cop stopped at Mom's door, only inches away from my mother.

"License and registration, please," he said to Mom, his tone almost bored as he looked at her then me. No blip of recognition on his face or in his thoughts.

Then he looked at Emily in the backseat. He froze, and I knew we were busted. He must have recognized her from a Clann meeting or something.

"Ah, one moment, please," he muttered. "I forgot to grab a pen."

He headed back to his car, trying to act as if nothing was wrong and he had all the time in the world.

"He recognized you, Em," I said without looking away from the cop as he opened his car door, sat in the driver's seat, and reached for something.

His cell phone gleamed silver and black as he dialed a number then held the phone to his ear and stared at us.

Emily cursed loudly. "He's calling the Clann!"

My mind went absolutely blank with panic. The next thing I knew, I was twisting over the front seat back, pushing Emily to the side out of the way, and raising both my hands.

A burst of energy exploded out of me, passed through the back glass of Mom's truck, and slammed into the officer, knocking his head backward. His head rebounded forward, then his whole upper body slumped over toward the passenger seat.

Mom shrieked.

"Oh, my God," Emily whispered. "Savannah, what did you do?"

Breathing hard, I stared at the man in shock, waiting for him to sit up and retaliate with an energy orb of his own. But he didn't move.

I opened my door and slid out, never looking away from

the cop. As I walked toward his car, I heard two of the truck doors open as Mom and Emily got out to follow me. I could hear their steps crunching out of sync with mine on the shoulder of the highway beneath the low roar of the cars whipping by us.

What had I done?

I risked a glance at the traffic. Had anyone noticed the unconscious trooper in his car? No one seemed to be slowing down.

At the open door of the trooper's car, I edged closer to the man, visually searching his body for some signs of life.

Then I saw the rise and fall of his breathing and my knees turned wobbly with relief. Good. He was still alive.

"He's still breathing," I said. "But I don't know how long he'll stay out. When he wakes up…"

As if on cue, the man groaned and twitched.

"Do a memory confusion spell on him," Emily hissed.

"What?" I asked.

"You know, tell him to forget he ever saw us and push your willpower out with the thought at the same time. Hurry up! He's going to wake up any second."

"I can't—"

"Yes, you can. They're easy."

Gritting my teeth, I raised both my hands palms-out toward the cop. "You will forget you ever saw us."

Emily snorted. "Puh-lease. That didn't even raise a single hair for me. You forgot the willpower part. It's everything. Without it, you're just saying words."

Taking a deep breath in through my nose, I held it and tried again. "You will forget you ever saw us." This time, I imagined the cop doing just that…waking up in his car on the side of the road with no memory of how he got there or why he'd fallen asleep.

I thought about how much we needed this to happen, and what would happen if it didn't work.

"Now, Savannah!" she shouted as the man slowly eased himself upright in the seat. "Do it before it's too late!"

The man turned to look at us, reached for his phone with one hand, and threw his other palm out toward us.

Time was up.

Taking a deep breath, I bent down, grabbed the man's chin and forced him to look at me. Then I stared into his eyes. They were brown with a thick fringe of eyelashes. He was younger than he'd first appeared, maybe his middle or late twenties.

Fear flashed within those eyes for a second.

Freeze! I thought, panicking.

Energy burst down my arms and hands, flowing like invisible hot water along my skin and off my fingertips.

And incredibly he did just that, his entire upper body freezing yet still pliant.

"Thatta girl." Mom sighed and rubbed her forearms. "You've got the willpower flowing. Now just tell him not to remember anything."

"No, just this one stop," Emily said. "You don't want him to have total amnesia, do you?"

They started to argue. But their voices were fading away now, just background noise.

Another sound rose up to drown them out, a low throbbing like a drumbeat that filled my ears at first and then my mind, calling to me. Out of the corner of my eye, I saw my free hand reach down to touch the man's shoulder. Then it glided up to caress the side of his neck above his starched collar.

There. The drumbeat was in his throat, pulsing beneath my fingertips, his skin so soft and fragile that it was like holding tissue paper.

I felt a strange sensation in my mouth, one I hadn't felt in many months, a sort of aching in my upper gums. And then two pricks against my lower lip as my fangs descended.

My mouth and throat were so dry that it actually hurt to try to swallow. I leaned closer to the state trooper, or maybe I pulled him to me. At that moment, I wasn't sure and didn't care. All I knew was that only inches separated us now.

A curse from behind me, then hands grabbed at my shoulders and tried to pull me back. But the hands were like the weight of a jacket draped over my shoulders, so slight I could easily ignore them.

Just a taste. That was all I wanted. Just a little taste of this descendant before me. Dad had said to only go after evildoers, right? And this descendant definitely qualified as an evildoer. He was going to use his power as a police officer for bad, to turn us over to the Clann. He was abusing his power as an officer of the law. And for that, he deserved to die.

Just a little taste...

"Savannah, no!" a familiar voice shouted in my ear.

I wanted to ignore that voice. Every vampire instinct within me said to, or better yet, to simply swat its owner away from me.

But a tiny part of me deep inside said not to, that I knew that person and would never want to hurt her. Because...

I frowned and tried to remember, though the drumbeat inside my head made it so hard.

I didn't want to hurt her because…she was my mother. Not my vampire mother, Lillith, the mother of all the race of vampires who slept beneath the desert. But my birth mother, my human mother.

My Clann mother.

I turned to her, and now it was a faster heartbeat that pounded in my ears. It was still Clann blood that called to me. But as I slowly drew closer to her, the scent of her perfume was like a smack to my face, forcing me to back up and wrinkle my nose.

That perfume was not at all what I was craving.

And yet something about that perfume was also familiar, reminding me of warm hugs and soft hair tickling my face, of gentle hands rocking me to sleep or handing me a mug of hot soup when I was sick.

That perfume reminded me of being loved and protected.

Slowly the drumbeat in my ears faded into the background. I blinked once, twice and again then looked around me and frowned. I felt like I was slowly waking up from a vivid dream, one that kept trying to claw me back under.

Or maybe it had been a nightmare.

"Savannah, snap out of it!" a different female voice shouted.

Then a hand slapped my cheek. It didn't move me, but the faint sting was enough to push that sleepy feeling away a little more.

I blinked again. "What… Where am—"

"She's coming back to us," Mom said.

"Oh, no she doesn't," the other one said. Emily, I remembered now. "She's not finished making him forget. Savannah, look him in the eyes. But this time, ignore the blood."

She said the last words slowly, as if I were a child, making me frown.

"No, it's too dangerous!" Mom said. "Can't you see what being so close to him is doing to—"

Emily ignored her. "The cop, Savannah. You've got to make him forget he ever saw us."

And now I remembered. The state trooper. He was a descendant. And he was going to tell the Clann where we were.

"Hurry up, he's coming out of it!" Emily said.

I leaned back into the car, this time touching only the man's chin with a single fingertip to direct his focus back to me again. He looked up, and again I could feel his heartbeat trying to reach out to me.

I swallowed. "I can hear it. His blood…it's calling to me."

"You have to fight it," Emily insisted. "Don't listen to it. Only think about the magic and using it to make him forget."

But that drumbeat, slow and steady, was pulsating in my ears, its hypnotic music trying to rob me of all thought. So much power. He could be an endless supply of Clann blood for Tristan and me to feed on….

The thought of Tristan was like another slap, this one deep within my mind. I blinked hard a few times, then refocused.

I looked into the man's eyes one last time. "You've never seen me or anyone with me. Is that clear?"

Slowly he nodded.

"You will forget us," I ordered, the command rolling up from somewhere deep within me, and more of that liquid rush of energy poured along my skin and out my fingertips. "Go to sleep now. And when you wake up, you will have forgotten all about this stop."

His eyes drifted closed and he sat back against the seat,

his head slowly rolling forward until his chin rested against his chest.

"Whoa," Emily whispered. "He's like her puppet. Are you sure Clann can't be gaze dazed?"

"Don't be ridiculous," Mom snapped. "Of course they can't. It's like the mental shields the two species developed over time. It's a protective mechanism. Besides, you felt her use of the power, too. She just threw in a ton of compulsion spell along with the memory confusion part."

Once more, I could hear the man's heartbeat, even slower now as he slept deeply. It begged me to lean in closer. *Just a taste…* it whispered.

I stumbled back and slammed the door shut, muffling the sound. It wasn't much, but it was enough.

"Let's go," I said, forcing my feet to turn and take me back to the truck. Then I sat there, waiting, staring out the window at the sunlight glinting off row after row of trucks and cars and SUVs at a nearby dealership. Seeing again the sunlight glaring on the hood of that state patrol car…

I had almost bitten that cop. I could have drained him dry, and nobody would have been able to stop me.

Mom and Emily followed a few seconds later, still discussing the mixture of spells I'd probably just used on my victim, both of them trying but failing not to feel afraid.

But this time their fear didn't come from being pulled over by a cop who was in the Clann. This time they were afraid of *me,* and not because of the magic I'd just used.

Tristan. Dad. They would understand what I had almost done, how hard it had been to resist. Especially Tristan. He'd lost control to both the anger and the bloodlust before.

But could he forgive me for almost losing control after I

had spent so long telling him not to do the same thing? After I had spent the past two months preaching at him over and over that we weren't monsters just because we were vampires?

I was such a hypocrite.

I grabbed my phone from my pocket, too fast apparently because both Mom and Emily gasped and flinched. I froze, staring at the phone's screen, willing myself not to show any emotion. Human-slow this time, I tried to call Dad's phone again.

It went straight into voice mail.

I pulled up the app menu and tapped the one that had two green circles on it.

"What are you doing?" Emily asked from the backseat.

"It's a locator app. If Dad's phone is on, it'll find him. He set it up for emergencies so we can find each other."

The screen said: Phone cannot be located.

Emily read the message over my shoulder, though I noticed she did so from a distance. "What does that mean? Are they out of range?"

"No. It means his phone's turned off."

Or had been destroyed.

Now I understood why Dad never told me the location of the meeting. He didn't want us to try to save them if the Clann was waiting for them. He might have even turned off his phone on purpose after they attacked just so I couldn't try to track him down with the locator app....

No. I couldn't think like that.

It might not be a Clann ambush, I told myself. It could be plain old car trouble and no cell tower coverage wherever they were at.

"Let's stick with the plan," I said, trying to keep my voice from shaking. "We'll wait for them at the car rental place."

None of us said it out loud, though we were all thinking it...

What will we do next if Dad and Tristan don't come back?

CHAPTER 21

By the time we pulled into the car rental agency's parking lot, they had closed for business. Dad and Tristan had planned ahead for this and arranged to leave the car in the parking lot and the keys in the agency's overnight drop box.

But when we pulled into the parking lot, the guys' car wasn't there.

Mom and I shared an uneasy glance.

Emily sighed. "They probably stopped to do some human grocery shopping for us or something. I'm sure they'll be back any minute now. Until then, my back is killing me, so I'm going to go lie down in the trailer." She got out of the truck then hesitated. "Anyone need anything while I'm up?"

Mom and I both shook our heads, and I gave her a faint smile of thanks for the gesture. She smiled back tiredly then headed for the trailer.

And then we waited.

And waited.

And waited.

When they finally showed up, it wasn't at all as we'd expected.

For one thing, Dad was on foot.

And Tristan was draped over his right shoulder, fireman-lift style.

I leaped out of the truck and ran over to him, asking him what happened, opening the trailer door for him so he could take Tristan inside.

He dropped Tristan on the couch. Tristan was so tall his long legs hung off the side.

"What happened?" Mom asked.

"We were ambushed," Dad muttered. "Tristan was able to fire off enough spells to take out the Clann nearby and clear the way for us. But he missed seeing one last stray orb that one of them launched, and it hit him hard enough to send him flying into a tree. I grabbed him and ran out of there before the Keepers in the area could catch up."

I ran a shaking hand over Tristan's forehead. Then I realized...

"He's not breathing. He's not breathing!" I tapped Tristan's cheek, calling his name repeatedly in a rising shriek I couldn't seem to stop. His head lolled with the most awful crunchy sound popping from his neck, which made my stomach flip over and bile rise to the back of my throat. "Dad, what's wrong with his neck?"

"I believe he may have broken it when he hit the tree trunk."

A broken neck. Just like Dylan, we'd thought. Karma? Or... "Was Dylan there?"

"He may have been. We were in too great a hurry to escape to notice our attackers' specific features. Mr. Williams himself could have been there for all we were able to ascertain."

Emily came running out of the bedroom. She saw Tristan and dropped to her knees beside him, grabbing his limp hand and tugging it as she called out her brother's name.

Dad grabbed my shoulders, pulled me up to my feet and gave me a little shake. "Savannah, listen to me! He is not dead. At least, not permanently."

I wrenched myself free of Dad's grip and crouched beside Tristan again, using my every sense to try to pick up any sign of life from him.

But there was nothing. No heartbeat, no thoughts within his mind. Nothing but a cold and utterly lifeless shell of a body.

My father was obviously lying to me.

I stroked the hard planes of Tristan's face, felt the rasp of whiskers against my palm, traced a fingertip over that full lower lip that had only hours ago kissed me goodbye.

"Dad..." I whispered, unable to look away from Tristan in case his eyelids moved.

"I promise you, he *will* come back. You must give him time for his body to heal first."

We were vampires. I'd turned him. Other than fire, decapitation or a stake to the heart, he should be indestructible. Nobody had told me our bodies actually took time to heal. "But...when we get cut, it heals immediately."

"Superficial wounds do. What his body is now doing is actually knitting the broken bones together and cleaning the blood of any marrow released into it from the breaks."

I took a deep breath then held it as I realized Emily's and Mom's fears were releasing pheromones into the air.

"How long has he…" Mom couldn't finish the question.

"Less than an hour."

"And how long will it take until…" Mom began.

A thump sounded, so faint even my vampire hearing could barely pick it up. Then a double thump followed.

Afraid to speak, I laid my cheek against his chest.

Another double thump came from within him.

"He is returning to us," Dad said.

I sat up and froze, staring at Tristan's face, watching and waiting, scared to even breathe.

The double thump continued, evening out into a solid heartbeat. Then his chest slowly rose and fell as Tristan took his first breath again.

Emily squeaked. "His fingers…they moved!"

And then his eyes fluttered and opened. He saw me and smiled. "Hey. Told you I'd come back."

"Don't ever do that to me again," I whispered, cupping his face so I could lean over and kiss his forehead, his cheeks, then the tip of his nose in gratitude.

"Welcome back, Sleeping Beauty," Emily joked through her tears. "And thanks for scaring the ever-living crap out of us!"

Sighing, Tristan eased upright, wincing as he tilted his head first to one side then the other with another, more slight crunching noise.

I cringed as my stomach rolled over again. "Could you maybe not do that so much? Dad said you broke your neck, and I really don't want to barf all over you now that you're breathing again and all."

"Mmm, feels like I broke it," Tristan muttered. He rubbed the back of his neck with a scowl. Then the words truly registered with him. He looked up at Dad with wide eyes. "Wait. I did *what?*"

"You took a direct hit that threw you into a tree," Dad said. "Then I picked you up and carried you back."

"Huh." He blinked a few times. "So you're saying I died again?"

Dad nodded.

My stomach lurched, and my body felt incredibly tired. I sat back on the floor, holding Tristan's hand. Now I knew what he must have felt like during our stay in Arkansas. Holding his hand, with its steady pulse in the wrist, was like holding on to my last shred of sanity.

"Wait a minute," Mom said. "What about the blood?"

Dad scowled at her in silent answer.

Mom rolled her eyes. "Great. No blood. Then what are you guys supposed to live on?"

"I will have to think of an alternate plan."

"Like what?" Mom pushed, earning an even darker scowl from her ex.

"I do not know yet. I will figure something out after we are safely far away from East Texas. For now, we must focus on that. This rig is far too slow to outrun the Keepers if they find us still sitting here."

"Fine," Mom said. "The keys are in the ignition. I've had all the excitement I can stand for one day. I'm going to take a nice long nap." She walked on stiff legs back to her room, eased the door shut, and then the bed springs creaked as she apparently flopped into bed still fully clothed.

"I will have to stop and purchase more disposable phones

soon," Dad said. "When we stop, everyone please stay in the trailer so you will not be seen."

We all nodded, and he left the trailer. A second later the truck's engine started and the trailer rocked and swayed as we headed down the road.

I didn't care where we went, where he stopped for phones or how long it took to get there. We'd figure out a solution to the blood supply issue later, too. For now, as long as Tristan had a pulse and was breathing, that was all that mattered to me.

Emily rubbed her forehead, carefully got to her feet and walked over to ease herself down backward onto the dinette bench. "Oh, man, this day sucks."

"So now that you heard about my day, how did yours go?" Tristan asked with a wry grin as he tugged me up off the floor and onto the couch beside him.

Ugh. I didn't even want to remember that whole scene with the Clann cop. Unfortunately, my memory was too rebellious to be stopped and it all played out lightning-fast within my mind.

"Son of a…" Tristan hissed, his hand tightening on mine. "Are you all okay?"

I nodded.

"Yep, thanks to your girlfriend," Emily said. "She hit him with several spells one right after the other to freeze him, then make him forget he ever saw us, and then she put him to sleep."

And in the process I also vamped out and nearly bit my mother and your sister, I confessed silently, because saying the words out loud would have compounded the humiliation to a level I wouldn't be able to live with.

Tristan stared at me. Finally he blinked again. *But you didn't lose control obviously.*

I shook my head, pressing my lips together to hold back a flood of tears. *But the point is I almost did lose control. I could have killed them, all of them!*

But you didn't. He stroked my cheek, staring into my eyes. *Everyone got away safely because of you.*

I looked away, unable to maintain eye contact with him any longer.

TRISTAN

I stood up then held out a hand to Savannah. She hesitated then took it, letting me tug her to her feet and over to the dinette to join my sister. After we sat down beside each other, I kept a hold on her hand, unwilling to let go of that small contact between us. It had been too long since we'd even held hands, and I was blown away by how much my skin seemed to crave hers.

Maybe we couldn't get past the whole Mr. Williams issue yet. But at least we still had this.

We sat in silence, each of us sort of savoring the relief and trying not to remember the terror of the past couple of hours.

When her father stopped for burner phones at a Walmart, I looked at Savannah.

"Hey, you okay over there?" I said with a half smile, trying to coax a return smile out of her. Maybe she was just tired.

She sighed. "I'm grateful you're alive. But I'm so tired of this. All of it. The fighting, the running and hiding, the constant fear and feeling so out of control. And then when I think it can't get any worse for us, you die on me. And this is just what *we're* going through. What about everyone else?

There are people out there getting caught in the cross fire who are dying, and they're not lucky enough to be able to come back. They're losing loved ones. And many of them are innocent humans who don't even understand what's going on or why their lives are being destroyed."

Savannah shook her head and stared out the dinette window. But I knew from her thoughts that she wasn't seeing the sun setting behind the traffic whizzing by on the interstate.

Strangely, the emotion coming off her in wave after wave wasn't anger like I expected, or even fear. It was…guilt. Which made zero sense.

I had to say something. "Sav, I know we've got it a little easier being on the run than some people who've been hit the hardest by the war. But you do know this war isn't our fault. Right? Mr. Williams started it, not us."

Those big eyes, now a slate-gray, flashed at me. "If it's not completely our fault, then we sure as heck at least helped him start it. Think about it. He never would have been in a position to kill your mother, take over the Clann and declare the war if not for Gowin's killing your dad and then forcing me to turn you."

Emily's mouth dropped open as red bloomed in her cheeks.

Savannah held up a hand and turned toward my sister. "I know you didn't know Gowin would do all of that, and I'm not blaming you. Honest. I'm blaming myself."

Emily frowned. "How are you at fault for my stupid choice to sneak around with Gowin?"

"Are you always in the habit of breaking the rules and dating vampires behind your parents' backs?" Savannah asked.

"No, not really."

"And what made you decide to give in to the temptation to date him in the first place?"

Emily scrunched her nose. "It might have been inspired just a tiny bit by my little brother's whole Romeo and Juliet thing with you. It just seemed so romantic and tragic and forbidden."

Savannah nodded. "That's exactly my point. Tristan and I didn't realize what we were doing when we started dating. But I see now that it was like knocking over a domino. We started sneaking around, then you started dating Gowin, and one thing led to another and then another. Our choices gave others the opportunities they needed, and now we're in the middle of a second war that's killing thousands everywhere... vamps, Clann *and* humans."

I flopped back against the upholstered bench with a soft thud. I hated to admit it, but I kind of saw Savannah's point. The three of us hadn't intended to help Mr. Williams and Gowin play their parts in the start of this war, but ultimately that's what we'd done.

I looked at Savannah. "I still can't regret falling for you."

Her smile was a little wobbly, but it was still a smile. "I know, I can't, either. But I do regret what it's caused. And I hate the fact that we're running and hiding from it all instead of doing something about it. I think..." She took a deep breath. "I think we should figure out a way to take him down. Not kill him, but get him removed from the Clann leadership position and then turn him over to the Clann so they can decide together how to punish him."

"If they ever come to their senses, you mean," Emily muttered. "Right now he's got them so afraid of the big bad vamps that they'll take any kind of leadership at all as long as it promises to keep them safe."

"But he's *not* keeping them safe!" Savannah said, her voice rising a bit. She stopped, regained control over her emotions and added, "Why can't someone wake the descendants up and make them see how Mr. Williams is actually endangering them all by insisting on this stupid war? There's got to be some other way to stop him. Couldn't we find some way to make the Clann see that he's a horrible leader so they'll replace him?"

Savannah and I looked at Emily.

She returned our looks with raised eyebrows. "What?"

"Uh, sis, if any of us here know how to play the political game, it'd be you. You and I both know you're using that whole blonde cheerleader stereotype like a mask to hide that diabolical mastermind genius of yours. Remember all those pranks you came up with when we were little kids, not to mention how you always found a way to talk me into helping you pull them off?"

Emily's mouth hitched into a wry grin. "Yeah, good times, good times."

"Let's face it, if Dad could have gotten over his old-fashioned ideas, I think we both know which one of us should have really been next in line to lead the Clann."

Emily's throat worked as she looked down at her hands, clasped loosely on the table. After a moment, she sighed. "We can't change the past. But maybe we could find a way to change the currently crappy future. If killing Mr. W is off the table..."

"It is," Savannah growled.

Emily looked at me. I shrugged one shoulder.

She sighed. "Then I guess all that leaves us with is to ruin him politically somehow, like you said."

"Why can't you two just tell the Clann who really killed your mom?" Savannah said.

Emily scowled. "For one thing, memories can be planted or made up, and they know I'm biased toward protecting my brother whatever it takes. For another, I was upstairs when Mom died, so I can't actually show them a firsthand memory of her death and who exactly killed her."

Savannah and Emily tossed around a few more options, but I'd stopped listening for a minute, distracted by the way my sister kept making this weird twisty expression with her mouth every time she said Mr. Williams's name.

"Sis, what are you really thinking?" At her raised eyebrows, I added, "You keep making this weird face like something's bugging you."

"It's just something about the night Mom died that keeps nagging at me. But I can't figure out what it means or even if it means anything at all."

"Walk us through it," Savannah said.

"It was when I was upstairs fighting Mr. Williams and a couple of his apes outside my bedroom. Remember, Tristan? And you came roaring up the stairs?"

I nodded, and she continued. "Before you showed up, I kept trying to read his thoughts to see what his strategy was and if there was a way for Mom and me to escape. Of course, I guess she was already gone downstairs...." She cleared her throat. "But his thoughts were shielded even better than my own. I couldn't get a single thought out of him, until you came up the stairs and suddenly he had to fight us both. And then his shield slipped, just a little, and for a second I picked up this image of a kid in his mind. There was something about the kid that he was afraid of. But before I could get more than a picture of the kid's face and a sense of Mr. Williams's fear, he clammed up again."

She shrugged. "Like I said, not sure if it means anything or nothing at all."

Savannah leaned forward, her eyebrows pinched. "If Mr. Williams is afraid of it, then it's got to be a weak spot for him. Maybe this kid knows something that could help us."

"Did you get the kid's name?" I asked.

Emily shook her head. "I didn't have to. I recognized him. His name's Mac Griffin. I remember Mom talking about him and showing me his family photo back when we were prepping for your big leadership run against Mr. Williams."

Savannah gasped. "Did you say his first name's *Mac?*" At Emily's nod, Savannah said, "Your mom…when she was dying and I was trying to figure out what was wrong with her, she said or thought something about Mac and how it was the key to the lies, or something like that. I thought she was referring to a computer or maybe just talking nonsense because she was in so much pain and kind of out of it. But…"

I rubbed a hand over my mouth. "Was this Mac kid at the voting?" I'd talked to so many people that afternoon at Dad's wake and funeral.

"No, he was too young. He's only fourteen, I think. But I remember Mom talking about him because of what happened to his parents. They were victims of one of Gowin's hits on the Clann. Mac was the only survivor. Dad had Dr. Faulkner looking into all those descendants' deaths. And then after Dad died, Dr. Faulkner kept looking into them. He kept telling Mom there was something off about Mac's memories of the night his parents died. The week of her death, she even went to see Mac in person. When she came back, I noticed she was mentally shielding even harder than usual, and she wouldn't tell me anything about her trip other than that Mr. Williams had some explaining to do."

"How in the world did this kid survive a vamp attack?" Savannah asked.

"Mom said apparently he wasn't home when the vamps hit. By the time he returned, they were long gone and his parents were already dead."

"I think we should talk to him," I blurted out, surprising us all, including myself. At the girls' questioning looks, I added, "Like Sav said. Anything, or anyone that makes Mr. Williams afraid has to be worth looking into. And besides, if Mom's last words were about this kid, then he's got to be pretty important. Maybe she was trying to tell us to look into it."

Emily frowned. "Just one problem. I have no clue which Clann couple he was placed with."

"Who would know?" I asked.

"Dr. Faulkner does. But I don't know if we can trust him."

"Who else?" I said.

"Well, Mom had their names and addresses in her Black-Berry. You know how anal she was about using that thing for everything she did. She always kept a record on it of every trip she made and important conversations she wanted to remember for later."

I looked at Savannah, reading the same cautious hope on her face that I could feel trying to take root in me. "If we could get that BlackBerry, we might be able to track this kid down and see just what it is about him that's making Mr. Williams so antsy."

"Oh, no, little brother." Emily leaned back on the seat. "I know you're not that crazy. That BlackBerry's in our house. You know, the one right by the Circle that was just hit by the vamp council a few weeks ago? That whole area is going to be crawling with Clann guards now. You'd have to be absolutely stupid to even think about getting anywhere near that place!"

I looked to Savannah again. *How about it? Feel like getting a little stupid with me?*

CHAPTER 22

One corner of her mouth twitched as she fought a grin. She sighed instead. *Tristan, you nearly died today.*

If we don't find a way to stop him, you and I both know today might not be the last of it.

Her hint of a smile evaporated. *I don't know. It sounds pretty dangerous. It would have to be seriously worth the risk.*

I looked at my sister, searching her eyes since I couldn't read her thoughts. "On a scale of one to ten, just how scared would you say Mr. Williams was about this kid?"

She scowled so hard it looked like she was sucking on a mouth full of fresh-cut lemon. "Eleven. But I only got a read on his thoughts for less than a second. And you just barely escaped the Clann an hour ago! Don't you think that's plenty enough excitement for one lifetime?"

"I'm not looking for excitement, sis. In fact, it's the total opposite I'm hoping for. I want peace. I want to get on with living my life instead of running from it." I stared at my sister.

"Come on. Don't lie to me and say you haven't been wondering how you're going to have and raise a baby on the run."

Emily's eyes narrowed. "That is a low blow."

"But the truth. Right?"

She growled out a long breath, then raised her hands. "Fine. Get yourselves killed. See if I care!"

I smiled, but it felt a little dark around its edges. "And if we don't die and get the phone?"

"*If* you manage to survive, and *if* you actually manage to get ahold of the BlackBerry, I'll help you wade through Mom's notes and contact list," Emily muttered.

A hum suddenly filled our end of the trailer.

Emily's eyes rounded. "What the…"

I glanced under the table and offered up an apologetic smile. "Sorry. That's my knees." My old habit of bouncing my knees, and the resulting soft tap of my heels against the floor, sounded like a steady, low vibration once you threw in vamp speed.

I turned to grin at Savannah, expecting to see her as excited as me.

Instead, she was cringing. "Um, just one small problem. We'll have to convince my parents first."

Even without vamp speed of thought, it would have only taken me half a second to decide which parent to approach first. "Let's get your dad onboard. Then he can help convince your mom."

"Agreed." She added a short but emphatic nod, realizing just as quickly as me that her father was way more pragmatic and strategic than her mother.

We waited till her dad returned from the store with new disposable phones to replace his and my old ones that were destroyed during the Clann's ambush. He popped his head through the trailer doorway, intending to have us activate the phones and take one of ours in the meantime so we could call him while he drove in case of an emergency.

Savannah waved him all the way inside the trailer then quickly told him everything we'd just discussed.

"Hmm, I understand your line of reasoning," he said, rubbing a finger over his lips in thought.

Hearing his voice, Ms. Evans stumbled out of her bedroom with a series of huge yawns.

"Time for a pit stop already?" she murmured. "I swear it feels like it's only been an hour or two."

"That is because it has been only an hour or two," Mr. Colbert said.

She frowned at him. "Is something wrong?"

"Now, Joan, I want you to stay calm and hear these kids out," Mr. Colbert said, which was probably exactly the wrong thing to say.

Ms. Evans's face shut down. "Whatever it is, the answer's no."

"Mom," Savannah groaned. "You haven't even heard our plan yet."

"I don't need to. I can already tell I'm going to hate it."

"Maybe," Savannah said. "But you might also see the logic in it. Please just listen first?"

Quickly Emily and I took turns explaining what Emily had seen in Mr. Williams's mind, our mother's dying words that Savannah had overheard and why we all felt we should track this kid down. Then Savannah carefully described how we would need to find Mac using the Clann contact list on my mother's BlackBerry.

"Which you now have?" Ms. Evans asked Emily.

Emily shook her head. "It's at my house."

Ms. Evans's eyes flared wide then narrowed and she crossed her arms over her chest. "Absolutely not."

"Joan—" Mr. Colbert began.

She turned on him. "Don't. Don't even start. How can you even think of standing there and siding with them on this crappy idea? You and Tristan could have died today. Oh, wait, I nearly forgot, Tristan actually did die today!"

Savannah tensed beside me. I rubbed a thumb over her knuckles to try to help her relax again.

"That's right, I did," I said. "And yet I'm still willing to put it all on the line and go for it. You grew up with Mr. Williams, didn't you?" At Ms. Evans's hesitant nod, I continued, "Then I think you know better than any of us here that he's never going to stop destroying everything his power can reach until someone makes him stop."

Ms. Evans drew in a long breath, held it, then let it out fast and loud. "Fine. But I'm going with you to make sure Savannah is safe."

"No way," Savannah said at the same time as her father shook his head and said, "Absolutely not, Joan."

Ms. Evans's eyes went as round as I'd ever seen them, and I actually found myself leaning back a few inches on the bench seat. "First off, Savannah, you're my daughter. I tell *you* what to do, young lady, not the other way around. And as for *you...*" She jabbed a finger at Mr. Colbert's chest. "You aren't allowed to tell me what to do anymore, either! We're divorced, remember?"

That shut up Mr. Colbert, but not Savannah.

"Mom, please try to be reasonable about this." She hesitated, winced but forged on. "You can't do magic, remember? If you come with us, I'd have to worry about protecting you and myself and helping Tristan all at the same time. You wouldn't want me to be distracted and end up getting hurt because of it, would you?"

Ooh, low blow, using the guilt trip on your mother! I thought with a silent laugh.

Savannah glanced sideways at me, trying not to grin. *Hush. Now* you're *distracting me!*

Ms. Evans's anger deflated, pulling some of the heat out of the air as it faded. Her face crumpled. "I guess I see your point. But if I can't go, then neither can Emily, right? She can't do magic, either."

And I really don't want to be the only one left out of this! Ms. Evans thought to herself, forgetting almost everyone present could read her mind.

"Excuse me?" Emily said. "I'm the only one who probably remembers what my mother's phone even looks like or where it might be in our house. If I don't go, how will anyone find it?"

"I'm sure Savannah and Tristan can look it up on the internet to see what it looks like," Ms. Evans said, her tone just a tad smug now. "And you can always give them ideas of where to search ahead of time."

I cleared my throat. "Uh, sis, she kind of has a point. You can't do magic. And the baby's too far along. You've got to stay safe and think about protecting it." I nodded at her stomach.

Her hands darted up to rest over her stomach as her mouth dropped open then snapped shut. She flopped back against the seat with a huff and a scowl. "Fine. So we'll both stay in the RV somewhere."

Savannah squirmed then finally spoke up again. "Um, yeah, about that. The Clann's probably got the Keepers searching all over East Texas right now for us. I don't like the idea of leaving you two alone like sitting ducks while we're gone." She looked to her dad with raised eyebrows.

He hesitated, his face darkening and freezing like a rock. Finally he sighed. "Agreed. I will stay with them and protect them during your mission."

"Are you insane?" Ms. Evans hissed. "I don't care if we're sitting ducks! Michael, you can't be serious about allowing those two to go running right into the heart of Clann territory alone."

Mr. Colbert's chin lifted an inch. "I am and I will. Like it or not, with their combined Clann abilities and vamp speed, reflexes, strength, and the ability to both smell and hear any Clann or Keepers even thinking around them, they are far more capable than us now, Joan."

"But there are only two of them up against who knows how many guards!" Ms. Evans whispered, her eyes shimmering with fear and tears.

Savannah froze and stopped breathing, feeling her mother's fear as it flooded the air. *No, not now!* she thought, the words almost a scream within her mind. Then I noticed her jaw muscles clenching as she fought to keep her fangs from extending.

Savannah, I thought, squeezing her hand out of pure instinct.

Don't breathe, she thought, even as a strange, fast drumbeat filled my ears. *Tristan, look at me.* She shifted just the tiniest bit toward me so I could make full eye contact with her. *Just look at me and don't breathe.*

Twin points pricked the inside edge of my lower lip as my fangs tried to distend and my pulse raced. Oh, hell. The bloodlust.

"Emily..." I muttered, gaining my sister's attention while Mr. Colbert murmured soft but steady arguments and reassurances to his ex-wife about the mission.

Emily glanced at us, did a double take, then casually slung her arm up along the edge of the dinette seat below the window. A second later, she flicked her wrist and slid open the window. A fresh burst of air blew in on the evening breeze, clearing the small space of Ms. Evans's fear-based pheromones that were triggering Savannah's and my bloodlust.

Still, I waited a minute before daring to take another breath. *It's okay, Sav.*

She hesitated, then took a half breath. Immediately her shoulders sagged and her gaze dropped to the table. But she couldn't hide her horror and guilt from me.

Sav, look at me.

She hesitated again before looking at me. Her irises were slowly turning from white to light gray again.

It's only instinct, I reminded her. *Didn't you tell me the only thing that makes us monsters is the choices we actually make?*

She looked at the tabletop again. After a few seconds, she dipped her head once in agreement.

"Good," Mr. Colbert said. "Then it is settled."

At first, I thought he was agreeing with Savannah and me until I remembered we'd kept our conversation silent and he couldn't read our minds. He must have finally gotten Ms. Evans onboard with the plan.

He walked toward the trailer door. "Let us get this rig turned around, then, shall we?" Flashing us a dark smile, Mr. Colbert exited the trailer. A second later, our truck's engine restarted and we felt the trailer being pulled out of the parking lot back in the direction we'd just come from.

"Jacksonville, here we come," Emily murmured in an ominous singsong voice, her smile tight and forced as she massaged the small of her back.

CHAPTER 23

SAVANNAH

We didn't drive all the way back to Jacksonville. Instead, Dad found an RV park in Mineola to camp out at. Then we said our goodbyes.

Mom was openly sobbing as I hugged her. It was awful, and I thought I'd have to use a little of my vamp strength just to pry her arms loose.

"Joan, you are distracting her," Dad muttered.

"Right." Mom sniffed loudly and let me go. "You just be careful and get back here in one piece, okay? With or without the darn phone, I don't care. Just get back safely."

"I will."

I hesitated before Dad then went ahead and hugged him, too. He wasn't always big on physical displays of affection. But I could have lost him earlier today. And in case anything did go wrong tonight, I just couldn't leave without saying a proper goodbye. The gesture surprised him, making him freeze up. Then he relaxed and returned the hug, even reach-ing up to pat my back twice before I stepped away.

"Drama, drama, drama," Emily muttered. But then she reached out and grabbed her brother and only remaining family for a sideways, one-armed hug. "You heard her. Get your butts back here safely, even if you can't find the phone."

"Yes, ma'am," Tristan said, flashing a grin at her. He used his height advantage to reach down and mess up her hair, then grabbed my hand and we stepped out of the trailer.

As soon as we had our bearings, we took off at a run. Both of us tried not to think, focusing on staying in the right gen-eral direction but within the cover of the woods as much as possible. The air was still muggy with the heat and moisture of the day, making it feel like we were running through a jungle instead of our home state. But the heat felt good on my perpetually cold skin and helped my muscles loosen up. So did the rare opportunity to stretch my legs and run free.

If not for the destination and needing to check the sur-roundings flashing past us for warnings of nearby Keepers or Clann, I almost could have enjoyed the journey.

Then we hit Jacksonville, and I saw in person all the wreckage of its downtown buildings, including my last home near the Tomato Bowl, which itself still bore the black-soot scars and scorch marks of the recent battles waged on its grounds. There were signs everywhere that Jacksonville was trying to rebuild…large rectangular metal bins heaped full of burned wood and other debris, orange-and-white-striped barricades to keep people from parking close to the burned-out shells of the buildings hardest hit by the fires, even sev-eral small trailers bearing various construction company logos on their sides parked along the main street's curb to provide headquarters for the construction crews.

We stopped there for a few seconds, both of us struggling to absorb the impact of what the war had done to our hometown.

It was Tristan who shook himself free of the paralysis first. "Come on. Let's go find a way to make sure this never happens again."

I swallowed the lump in my throat, nodded, and we began running through the shadows again, fugitives in our own hometown.

Heat stirred to life again in my stomach. I had spent months pressing it down. But this time, I let the burn build and spread, fueling me as we ran through block after block of homes and more pine trees, leaping chain-link fences, only to come out two minutes later at the most familiar landmark of all...Jacksonville High School. Again my feet stumbled as instinct demanded I stop and stare at the place where I'd spent so much of the past three years of my life. At least the campus buildings seemed to have come through the war untouched so far. Maybe because of the magic crawling all over the place, which was making my skin feel like it was under attack from an entire mound of fire ants. I couldn't stop myself from rubbing my forearms to try to get rid of the sensation.

A part of me yearned to take a look around and see if any of the outer buildings, like the sports and arts building containing the Charmers' dance room and the theater where we practiced so much for Spring Show, had been affected by the war. But there was no time to look around or feel nostalgic. We had to keep moving fast.

I pushed aside my personal feelings and picked up speed

again, Tristan having slowed so I could catch up. We circled around the south side of the campus and turned straight west, the trees patchy and offering far less cover as we crossed the last seven hundred meters until we came to a stumbling halt in the woods at the edge of the Coleman property.

As soon as we stopped, I could feel it…magic in use, and a heck of a lot of it, judging by how my entire body was covered with a million tiny stabbing pinpricks. Just the sensation of that much power in use in one place was a major distraction and might become a problem all its own if we had to stay here for long.

Sense anyone? Tristan thought, sniffing the air with his head cocked at a slight angle as if listening, as well.

But we were both using many more senses than just our ears and noses. The entire night seemed filled with things trying to distract us…insects in the grass, a breeze that kept shifting directions and making it hard to figure out how to stay downwind of anything that might be sharing the night with us. Even the clouds racing through the sky were another movement I had to mentally ignore as I searched the area.

There, beyond the house about three hundred yards away, I thought. *Keepers?*

He looked that way, drawing in a long breath through his nose. *Yeah, I've got them now. They're upwind of us.*

For now. With this shifting wind…

Yeah. Probably a spell to help the Keepers.

I frowned. The Clann sure weren't messing around with their protection of their sacred Circle now. *Think we can get to the house without their smelling us?*

If we move fast.

But what about when we reach it? Won't the doors and windows all be locked? How will we get in without making any noise?

A silencing spell?

I frowned. *Won't they feel that?*

With all this power in use? Nah. Any spells we use will blend right in. He reached out and covered my hand with his, stopping me from scratching at my arms.

I glanced down at myself. Wow. I hadn't even realized I was clawing at my own skin. I looked at him. *How can you stand it?*

He shrugged one shoulder, still scanning the grounds with all of his senses and his mind. *Used to it, I guess. Comes with the territory of living beside the Circle all your life. That and growing up with the Clann leader.*

So which way in?

He looked at his house. *See that second-floor window above the back patio doors? That's my room. It might have the least amount of spells and locks on it, since it's on the second floor. And there shouldn't be any furniture in front of it. Think you can climb those timbers?*

I studied the sprawling mansion's English Tudor exterior. *I think so.*

He drew in a deep breath and took my hand again. *Okay. Ready?*

More power seeped over my skin, and I realized this time it was coming from him. I raised my eyebrows.

Invisibility spell, he thought, one corner of his mouth lifting. I nodded.

And then we ran as fast as we could across the open ground of the backyard, reaching the house in less than a second. The timbers extended from the stucco by about an inch, giving my fingertips and the toes of my shoes just enough of an edge to grip so we could climb up the back wall.

Watch the shingles, he thought. *They might be noisy.*

We angled sideways as we climbed over the wall above the patio roof.

Tristan tried the window, cursed silently, and a little more power arced over my skin. The window latch popped free, making my muscles twitch with panic. He raised the window and crawled inside, then reached out a hand to pull me in after him.

Welcome to my room, he thought as he crept on silent feet between a king-size bed and a desk.

But I didn't need to look around. I'd already seen it.

At the door now, Tristan picked up my thought and glanced back at me in surprise. *You did? When?*

The night you were turned. Emily and I came up here to pack a few things for you. I could feel my face burning. *Um, sorry for the invasion of privacy.*

He opened the door. *I don't have any secrets from you anyways. Though I've gotta admit, I always had a much better idea of how you'd see this room for the first time....*

Tristan! I almost whapped his shoulder then stopped myself, remembering that even a small noise would risk alerting the nearby Keepers to our presence. *Okay, refocus. The phone. Emily said it would probably be in the office?*

Tristan nodded. *This way. Down the stairs and to the left.* He led the way across the second-floor landing's thick carpet to the quarter-spiral staircase. *Watch the second step. It creaks in the middle.*

I concentrated on placing my feet exactly where he had on each step, and we made it down the staircase in silence.

As we moved past the kitchen and down a short hall, flashes of memory from the last time I'd been in Tristan's family home came back to me. I couldn't tell whose memories they were, though. I could almost swear I still smelled smoke. Another memory from that horrible night, or an actual lingering smell?

Tristan hesitated halfway down the hall, staring straight ahead of us, his shoulders tight as a muscle worked in his jaw.

Up ahead, moonlight flooded the hall from the den...the room where we'd found his mother's body.

My chest ached with renewed pain for his loss. Needing to comfort him or maybe myself, I reached out and rested a palm against his shoulder blade, wishing I could take away the pain of that night from him.

Tristan flinched as if startled by my touch then drew in a slow breath and let it out.

The office is this way. He turned to the left, easing open a heavy, paneled door stained a light shade that gleamed in the moonlight. Where was all the light coming from? Oh, yeah. Must be from the French patio doors.

A drawer slid open, thumped shut, then another rolled open as Tristan searched the desk that took up the center of the room. There wasn't enough room for both of us to try to search it at the same time, so I hung back closer to the door to stay out of his way and simply looked around.

I could imagine his dad sitting in the bigger leather chair behind the desk, an indoor throne from which to rule the Clann. Had Tristan ever come in here to talk to his father, maybe while sitting in one of these chairs? I ran a hand over the top of one of the two leather wing-backs closest to me.

Silence made me look up before Tristan silently replied,

Yeah, I did. More than a few times. They liked to make me sit there while Mom yelled at me for screwing up yet again or told me for the thousandth time why I should be more focused on preparing to become the next great Clann leader instead of playing football. His jaw hardened as he returned to searching the drawers.

I wanted to say something that would help make this moment less painful. But no words came to me. Maybe getting out of here as quickly as possible was better.

I walked around the room, checking the many shelves filled with leather books that lined every wall in case the phone could have been left on one of them for some reason.

It's not here, Tristan thought.

I turned to face him with a frown. *Where else could it be?*

Maybe their bedroom? Or the kitchen? She could have set it down anywhere before... He didn't finish that thought.

If it was her main phone, wouldn't she have had it on her instead?

We stared at each other as a horrible feeling crept over me. If the phone had been in her pocket when the Clann took her body away, we might have risked coming here tonight for nothing.

Wait, I thought. *What about the den?*

I stepped out of the office, turned left down the hall and entered the room where it had all come to a horrible end. If the phone had been in Mrs. Coleman's pocket that night, it could have fallen out. I searched the leather couch, checking under the throw pillows and beneath the cushions, then under the couch itself.

A small creak in the den's doorway made me look up fast. Tristan stood there, his fists opening and closing, his breathing fast. I hadn't expected him to follow me in here.

Then I glanced down and saw it…something small, black and rectangular under the coffee table. I grabbed it. *Is this it?*

No response.

Tristan? I tried again.

His eyes darted side to side. I peeked at his thoughts. They were filled with images of that night…his mother's body lying where I was now crouched on the floor, the stone fireplace where he'd thrown Dylan in a mindless rage. A long black crack ran at an angle between its stones now, probably from the impact of Dylan's body against it.

We needed to get out of here. Just being in this room had to be torture for him.

Come on, let's go, I thought, standing up. *We've got what we need.*

I crossed the room to him, but he didn't move. Only when I reached out and cupped his cheek did he flinch and make eye contact with me, his eyes dark and tortured and desperate with pain.

He reached up to grab my hand.

This time I was the one who took the lead, tugging him after me through the den, around the couch toward the patio doors. I unlocked the doors, eased the handle down and opened one.

An animal's roar erupted in the distance to our left from the direction of the woods that concealed the Circle. The Keepers on guard…we must have triggered a spell or made a noise that alerted them.

Go! Tristan thought, and we ran to the right across the yard, trying to reach the cover of the trees in the same direction as we'd arrived.

As we ran, I glanced over my shoulder. Four sleek black

panthers, each one at least six feet long from head to butt, were closing in on us. I'd never seen just how fast they were. *They're catching up!*

We'd never be able to outrun them. Not like this.

CHAPTER 24

Tristan twisted as he ran, throwing a blue energy orb over his shoulder. A snarl of pain rang out as it slammed into one of the Keepers, knocking it off its feet.

I threw an energy orb of my own behind us, hoping to take out another. But I didn't take enough time to aim well, and the shot went between two of the panthers.

The woods became thicker, and we had to focus to avoid running into trees. The Keepers had the advantage…by following us, they only had to swerve when we did, and because they were lower to the ground, they weren't continually slapped and scratched by as many branches as we were.

As a result, we were only two steps ahead of them no matter how fast we ran, dodging and weaving among the trees, hurdling fallen trees and large branches. We headed almost straight northwest this time right toward Bullard, attempting to leap off the sides of the larger trees along the way in the hopes that this would make the Keepers lose track of us. But we couldn't pull this move often. The pines usually had branches thick with needles set too low on their trunks to allow it. And even when we did manage it, the Keepers never lost sight of us, their yellow-green eyes following our every move without hesitation.

Tristan threw another energy orb, and a screech that sounded like a screaming woman made the hairs on the back of my neck stand up.

Got another one! Tristan thought.

We circled around Jacksonville's northern side, still keeping to the woods as much as possible, occasionally having to dart through traffic at one intersection and again on the highway when they couldn't be avoided. Horns blared and brakes screeched each time, making my eardrums whine in protest.

We ducked back into the woods, aiming deeper within them, away from the highway now. Long after we'd left the Coleman property behind, we heard an *oomph*. I risked a glance back. One of the Keepers had tripped over a log, apparently not leaping high enough to clear it, and in rolling had tripped the other Keeper, as well.

Christopher, are you all right? I heard one of the Keepers think to the other.

His voice was familiar. Ron!

I slowed just a bit so I could keep glancing behind us.

I think I broke my ankle, the one who must have been Christopher replied. *Go! Don't lose them, or the Clann—*

Yeah, I know, Ron said, then he took off after us again in a burst of renewed speed.

Confused, I nearly stopped completely. But Ron was barreling straight for us, his long black body and powerful legs and paws eating up the distance between us.

Is that Ron? Tristan had also slowed down.

Yeah, but something's wrong. Just go!

We added a burst of speed. But now we had a problem. We were getting closer to the truck and trailer. Ron was a good friend, but the Keepers could read his mind and learn anything he knew. We couldn't lead him back to the others.

But I couldn't use magic on him, either.

Logic told me to keep running.

But something far more powerful than that made me stop and turn to face him.

When he was only six feet away, he looked behind him then skidded to a stop. *Good, they're gone,* he thought. *Finally we can talk!*

Relief rushed through me, making me light-headed. "You scared the crap out of me, growling like that!" I wanted to walk over and pat his head or scratch his ear, but somehow I didn't think he'd appreciate it.

Tristan grinned. "She wasn't the only one."

Hey, I had to keep up a good front for Christopher, he said, sitting down on his haunches and checking his left paw. *They know we used to be friends. They've been watching my family non-stop ever since you guys left.*

I sighed. "I was afraid they'd do that," I murmured, my heart aching that he and his family were being put through all of this for us. "Thank you for tripping your partner."

How else was I going to get to say goodbye? His teeth, pointy like fangs, shone white in what little moonlight managed to get through the trees as he panted.

"How's your, er, paw?" I asked.

Wrist, Ron corrected in a grumble. *And it's fine. Christopher just stepped on it when I tripped him.*

"They're going to be even more suspicious if you lose us," Tristan said.

Hmm. Not good.

"Tell them we beat you up," Tristan suggested with a grin.

Ron snorted. *Yeah, right.*

"What if you tell them you caught us but we managed to get away?" Tristan said.

They'll know it's a lie. They'll be able to smell the lack of blood that would have been shed in the fight.

"Then let's give them something to smell." Before Tristan or my survival instincts could stop me, I reached over and raked my fingernails across my left forearm, opening four gashes. Blood instantly welled up and spilled down my arm and onto the ground as I walked over to Ron.

Tristan cursed and reached for my wounded arm.

"I'm fine," I told him. "Now let's hurry up before it heals and all this blood's wasted."

I tried not to flinch from the pain as I dragged my wounded arm over Ron's face and down his right shoulder. "Okay, let's dance so this looks right." At both boys' confused frowns, I explained. "The Keepers will probably want to come here and double check your story, right? So we should create a fight scene just to be extra safe. You don't have to use the claws on me for real. Just stand up like you're going to bite my head or something."

Ron blinked his yellow eyes twice then leaped up in a powerful, fluid movement. I caught his huge, furry shoulders with both my hands. His paws landed on my shoulders, each one the size of my face, and we stumbled back and forth a bit. It was the weirdest couples dance ever. But at least it would make the blood splattering over the area more realistic.

A few seconds later, Ron fell back to the ground on all fours again.

Tristan immediately grabbed my left forearm with gentle but determined hands as if he planned to bandage the wound. But he was worried for nothing. Already, the gashes in my arm were healing. Bending over, I dragged my forearm across my thigh, letting my favorite jeans soak up the leftover blood. There. Done and done.

I stood up, hating what had to come next. "Well, I guess we'd better go before more Keepers show up."

You know you didn't have to do all that, Ron said.

"And you didn't have to help us escape." I swallowed hard. "I'm glad I got to say goodbye to you. Please be careful, for Anne's sake as well as your family's. Okay?"

I wished I could hug him. Then I couldn't resist it anymore. I wrapped my arms around his furry neck and squeezed, mindful not to choke him or break any of his bones.

Aw, we miss you two, Sav, he thought.

He and Tristan nodded at each other in some unspoken guy language that probably meant "thanks" or "see you later" or something.

"Sav," Tristan said. "I can hear a Keeper headed our way."

Bye, Ron, I thought. Then I turned and ran away with Tristan back toward the only home we had left.

TRISTAN

Emily was smart, moving the SIM card from our mother's phone to another before going through the Clann contact list just in case Mr. Williams was using his CIA contacts to watch all our old family phones.

"Got it!" she crowed a few minutes later. "Mac Griffin's living with a Clann couple in Natchitoches, Louisiana."

"That's only a couple of hours from here," Mom said. "I go there all the time to meet with clients."

"Would you like to drive?" Dad said. "I am sure you know the quickest way."

Savannah's jaw dropped.

Ms. Evans blinked a couple of times in surprise. "Uh, sure." She turned toward the trailer's exit then hesitated. "Want to ride with me and keep me company?"

We all couldn't help but stare as Savannah's parents exited the trailer together. A minute later the truck engine started and we were off.

"Did that really just happen?" Savannah muttered, making me grin.

Emily shook her head in disbelief. "Okay, let's stay focused. We need a plan for how to get to this kid. Though I guess we can't really call him a kid since he's only a few years younger than us."

"Not to mention it sounds like he's had just as rough a time of it as us," Savannah murmured.

"We'll try to go as easy on him with the questioning as we can," Emily said.

"What's with this 'we' business?" I said.

Emily glared at me. "I am going. Don't even bother arguing about it."

"But you're pregnant—"

"Yeah, I'm pregnant, not dead!"

Savannah laid a hand on my forearm. "Tristan, we could use her help with the questioning. Your spells have always been way stronger than mine, and she could tell you which ones to use on him to get him to talk without hurting him."

Grumbling, I gave in. "Fine. But if I say we have to leave in a hurry, you run without arguing. All right?"

Emily nodded.

We worked out the details of a rough plan for how to approach the foster family's apartment, which was on the second floor of a three-story building on Front Street near the Cane river in the heart of Natchitoches's downtown area. The directions were a little confusing until we found an actual map of the town, because several of the streets began as one name then suddenly turned into a different name for no apparent reason. This included Front Street, which was called Jefferson Street until you actually reached the downtown section of it, where it switched names.

The biggest problem, however, was parking…there was nowhere nearby large enough to park the truck and trailer without drawing a lot of notice. So we opted to leave the vehicles in a shopping center's parking lot across the river on Keyser Avenue then vamp blur across the bridge and the remaining eight blocks while partially carrying Emily between us so she wouldn't get worn out. And just in case the descendants would be using vamp wards, which we fully expected them to be, Savannah and I spent the rest of the two-hour drive energizing charms to block them.

A fan and frequent visitor of Natchitoches, Ms. Evans was sad that we wouldn't be able to see the town's famous Christmas light display and December weekend fireworks show, which drew a ton of tourists every year. The rest of us were more disappointed that we wouldn't have the tourist rush to hide in. But we planned around the less than optimal summer timing. Savannah's parents decided to walk in separately and pretend to be tourists shopping in the area so that they would be close enough to help if needed but our group wouldn't be so large that it would attract notice. We took advantage of our monthly unlimited talk time phone cards and kept a call going between our two groups' phones so they could hear everything we said once we split up in the shopping plaza's parking lot.

Then we were off. To Savannah and me, the summer night felt pretty good, but as soon as we exited the trailer, Emily started muttering about the heat and humidity. The heat of her unborn baby, which already kept her temperature higher than normal, made the heat almost stifling.

"Hold your breath, sis," I said.

Emily took a deep breath.

With a quick nod to Savannah, I wrapped an arm at Emily's back, Savannah took her other side, then we vamp blurred across the cement bridge, took a right at the intersection and continued without stopping past block after block of colonial and Victorian homes. Along the way, crepe myrtles scented the air with their nearly overpowering floral perfume.

We knew the instant we reached the downtown area because of the sudden wall of orange-ish-brown brick that rose up on our left side, at which point the map had said Jefferson Street turned into Front Street. Now the residential homes were replaced with brick buildings that housed shops and restaurants both historical and relatively new. Roughly half the buildings were two and three stories tall, and most of these featured balconies with intricate black wrought-iron railings, which reminded me of pictures and movies I'd seen of New Orleans.

We didn't slow down until we turned left down Trudeau Street, which gave access to the parking lot and private court-yard for the apartments Mac's foster family lived in. Though the parking lot had a nice wrought-iron and brick fence, it wasn't gated. So we had no trouble entering the premises and slipping right up to the back of the L-shaped building.

When we paused, Emily let out her breath, grabbed the small of her back and winced.

"Are you okay?" I whispered.

She nodded.

I scouted out and found the staircase that led us to the second-floor balcony. From there, it was a simple matter of finding the right apartment.

I wished we could read minds through walls and doors. It would make this a lot safer. But without that ability, we were forced to take the old-fashioned route and use our eyes and ears, sneaking peeks through the window and listening for any sign of people inside.

Sounds like a TV's on in one of the back rooms, Savannah thought.

I glanced at Emily to make sure she was in place. She stood with her back against the building's brick exterior. The plan was for her to stay there until we'd secured the apartment, then we'd call for her to join us inside. Her scowl indicated how much she loved this part of the plan, but I'd refused to back down on this point. Without the ability to do magic, this was the only way I was comfortable letting her come along.

Okay, let's make this as fast as possible, I told Savannah. *I'll bust the door open and take the lead. You stay behind me in case—*

Excuse me, but I'm perfectly capable of taking the lead. Savannah arched an eyebrow.

She had a point. *Fine. Would you like to go in first?*

She hesitated. *Nah, that's okay, you can go first.*

Grinning, I thought, *Okay, so like I said. I'll bust the door in and you stay right behind me. Any descendants, hit them with a sleep spell. We should minimize actual damage to anyone as much as possible. Once we find the kid and are done questioning him, we'll erase everyone else's memories. Hopefully there won't be a trail to lead back to us.*

She nodded then reached out and squeezed my hand. *Love you. Now let's get her done.*

Appreciating her attempt to use humor to keep herself loose, I grinned then softly grabbed the apartment's door handle and checked my watch. The entire silent conversation had taken all of two seconds thanks to the speed of vamp thought. Nice. Any descendants inside probably hadn't had time to sense our presence.

Tapping Emily's shoulder to get her attention, I held up one finger human slow, two fingers, three fingers, then shouldered the black wooden door open. The wood frame gave way like softened butter smearing across toast.

At the same time, Savannah raised her hands and put out a silencing spell to cover the entire apartment so the neighbors wouldn't hear anything.

I scanned the living room and adjoining bar area. Clear. Savannah entered the room behind me, trailing me as I moved down the hall, checking a bathroom and master bedroom suite on the way. The video game noises grew louder as we vamp blurred to the end of the hall to the last door and opened it.

A boy, sitting on his bed playing an XBox, slowly peered up through a sideswept mass of dark brown hair. Or maybe it was the adrenaline rush combined with the vamp reflexes that made his reaction seem so slow. His eyes widened. He dropped his game controller in his lap, both hands rising through the air as if to throw a spell at us.

I was faster, hitting him with a freezing spell as Emily had coached me to do on the way to Louisiana.

He froze, then his shoulders slumped and his facial muscles went slack.

"Are you Mac Griffin?" I asked.

He nodded.

"Savannah, tell Emily she can come in. The apartment's clear."

Savannah disappeared then reappeared three seconds later. Emily joined us several seconds after that, muttering a string of curses and complaints as she rammed her shins into objects in the dark along the way.

"This him?" she asked when she finally found the bedroom.

"Yep. What should we ask him?" I said, maintaining eye contact with Mac.

"Let's start with the night of his parents' deaths," Emily said.

"Mac, tell us about the night your parents died," I repeated. Emily had warned us that only the person performing the truth spell could make the commands. Anyone else's directions would simply be ignored.

"I went out with some friends to a movie. It was a Quentin Tarantino movie, lots of blood and stuff. Mom would have killed me if she had known I was seeing it. We had to bribe the ticket guy an extra thirty bucks to let us in since it was rated R. He's such a pr—"

"Tell him to get to the point," Emily grumbled. "I don't want to still be here when his foster parents get back."

"Skip to the part where you return home," I told Mac.

"Jason was our driver that night. He lived three houses down from us, so I walked home. On the way, I felt…" He hesitated, frowning. One hand drifted up to slowly rub the center of his chest. "I don't know, weird. Something made me stop by the cars parked at the curb. And then… And then…"

"What happened then?" I said.

His face screwed up into a frown. "I…can't remember. Something. Something important. Something bad…"

"Push him harder," Emily said.

I stared into the kid's eyes. "Try to remember." I pushed out some willpower with the words.

"I…I can't remember."

Pinpricks erupted over my skin. Clann power. Someone else was using nearby.

CHAPTER 25

"I'll check the entrance," Savannah whispered before disappearing.

Rubbing her forearms, Emily asked, "Are they back already? We should get out of here."

"Still clear," Savannah called out in a stage whisper from
the living room.

Emily and I frowned at each other. "Maybe a spell on the
apartment somewhere?" I suggested.

Emily looked at the kid, crossing her arms above her
rounded tummy and rubbing a finger across her lips. "Why
can't he remember?"

I saw her line of thought. "A memory spell. It's got to be."

"Mmm-hmm. But where?" I glanced around the room. It
was pretty Spartan in here, just a desk with some papers and
pens, the small flat screen on the wall and the XBox console
with a short stack of games beside it.

"If someone doesn't want him to remember that night,

they'd have to put the spell directly on something he'd keep close to him at all times."

I looked the kid over, then froze. His left wrist sported a round watch on a black leather band. It had to be charmed. He wasn't wearing anything else except clothes, which I doubted anyone would charm since he'd change them daily.

I unfastened the watch and lifted one of the bands. On the tan underside of the leather was stamped a Celtic braid design.

"Looks like a vamp ward," Emily said. "Could be double charmed as a memory confuser, too, though."

Remembering how one of Emily's vamp wards had knocked Savannah out and nearly killed her, I cringed. Good thing we'd made those vamp ward blockers before coming here. But it was another reason we'd have to hurry this interrogation along before the vamp ward wore out the blockers or vice versa. If this vamp ward was anything like the ones my mother once made for me and Emily, it would trigger a silent alarm to its maker to signal that the ward had just been taken off.

"Mac, you need to be quick now. Can you remember what happened when you got home?"

He shook his head.

I looked at Emily.

"Try taking it farther away from him."

I whispered Savannah's name. She appeared at my side, took the watch and disappeared back to the living room.

"How about now?" she questioned.

"Mac, now can you remember?"

The frown melted from Mac's face. "Whoa. Yeah, now I can. I was walking up the street toward my house, and I saw two guys leave my house and cross the street. They stopped by a big black SUV to talk. Something about them looked wrong. That weird feeling got stronger." His heartbeat sped up, its thumping filling the room. I swallowed hard and tried not to pay attention to it. "I crouched down on the sidewalk and snuck closer to them, using the parked cars to hide me, so I could hear what they were saying."

Emily and I both leaned in closer. "What were they saying? Did you recognize any of them?"

Savannah reappeared in the room without the watch, which she must have left in the living room. But instead of joining us by the bed, she circled it and opened the window. *Don't listen to his heartbeat,* she told me silently. *It'll trigger the bloodlust in you if the fear pheromones haven't already. He's afraid of the vamps he's describing. One of them must have been Gowin.*

"Go on," I said, working not to inhale through my nose as Mac's heartbeat seemed to grow still louder.

"They were talking about 'the next hit' and how it was all too easy. One of them wanted to try to find me, but the other two said something about blood trees and how they needed to go somewhere safe for a while first."

"Blood trees?" Emily said.

"Blood memories," Savannah said. "He probably just heard them wrong."

"What did they look like?" I asked him.

"One of them was short with light hair, pale skin, red lips and teeth, and white eyes like yours. He was kind of blurry around the edges, like he had some kind of spell on him that was trying to hide him but it wasn't strong enough or something. The other guy I recognized. He's Mr. Williams."

I froze. "Are you sure, Mac?"

Mac slowly nodded. "He came back later to pick me up

from the police station after I found my parents and called 911 for help and the police took me there. I didn't want to go with him, but he grabbed my wrist and then...and then..." He frowned. "And then I woke up here with you guys. Right?"

Whoa. That must have been one heck of a memory confusion spell Mr. Williams had put on Mac's watch to make him lose whole months of time.

"How could it have lasted this long without wearing out?" I asked, focusing on the memory confusion charm because the thought of Mr. Williams teaming up with a vampire was just too much for my mind to accept.

"The foster parents," Savannah whispered. "They must be reenergizing it to keep it going. Which means..."

"They're in on it," Emily finished for her. "Or at least partially."

"Mac, let me make sure I understand," I said, forcing myself to speak human slow as the second rush of adrenaline made me feel like I was trapped inside a slow motion movie. "Are you saying Mr. Williams and a vampire murdered your parents? And then Mr. Williams took you from the police station afterward and you don't remember anything that's happened since?"

He nodded, his frown returning. "Why? Has it been a long time? What month is it?"

Emily waved an impatient hand at him. "Relax. We'll get you caught up later. We don't have time for that now." She sighed and turned to me. "Well, this explains how Mr. Williams knew where to hit the vampire council headquarters. Gowin must have told him its location."

"But why would Gowin team up with him?" Savannah

said. "I read Gowin's mind that last night in the Circle. He didn't need Mr. Williams to tell him where the descendants were. He found that information himself when he broke into the Keepers' records on the Clann genealogy. And once he was filled up on Clann blood and learned how to do simple Clann spells, he would have been able to attack descendants without help."

"Unless he needed help for the first hit," Emily said. "Weren't the Griffins the first victims?"

I nodded. "So Mr. Williams helped him get close enough to kill them, and he took it from there."

"But why would Mr. Williams help him?" Savannah asked, pinpointing the part I was having the most trouble under-standing. "And why would Gowin tell him where the council headquarters were when that would endanger Gowin, too?"

Gowin's half of the equation was easy to figure out. "Gowin had to trade something for Mr. Williams's help," I thought out loud. "Maybe he figured Mr. Williams could take out the council if Gowin couldn't manage to do it on his own at the Circle."

"And Mr. Williams teamed up with Gowin to help get rid of Dad, and he was supposed to kill you, too," Emily said. "He thought that would clear his path to becoming Clann leader. But he forgot about the rule allowing Mom to take over in Tristan's place."

"But Mr. Williams hates our kind," I said. "He'd never voluntarily speak to a vampire, much less help a vamp kill his own people."

"Not unless it was the only strategy he could come up with to become Clann leader," Emily said. "Think about it. How else would he be able to take out both you and Dad? Neither of you trusted him enough to let him get close enough somewhere alone to do it himself. He had to have help from a totally unexpected angle. Maybe he even figured he'd kill Gowin once Gowin was no longer useful to him."

"But to murder fellow descendants…" I murmured.

"Tristan, ask him if his parents were anti-vamp," Savannah asked, her voice soft.

I repeated the question for Mac.

"No. And that was the worst part of it. Seeing their necks ripped out like that after they spent years supporting your father's peace treaty with the vampires… They believed peace was safer for everyone in the Clann than another war."

Savannah's and my eyes met as the final piece clicked into place. Mr. Williams saw the chance to temporarily cross enemy lines and make an alliance that helped him not only remove what he believed to be all competition to Clann leadership, but to also take out a few vamp sympathizers in the process. And then he'd suppressed his only surviving victim's memory, killed my mother and framed Savannah and me for her death to help cover his tracks and ensure the vote for him as Clann leader. He'd probably been banking on the fact that his reputation as a vamp hater would clear him of any suspicion in helping Gowin behind the scenes to take out his own people.

If not for that one mental slip around Emily, he might have gotten away with it.

Outside the apartment, car doors slammed. Savannah disappeared. A second later she whispered in the living room, "Two people are headed toward the stairs."

"Mac, you are freed of my hold," I muttered, putting some willpower into it to end all my spells on him.

"What are you doing?" Emily protested. "Are you crazy? What happened to making him forget we were ever here?"

"We can't leave him here, Em. He's just as much a victim in all of this as we are."

Mac blinked. His eyes widened as he sucked in a sharp breath of air.

I stepped back and held up my hands palms-out. "We're not here to hurt you, I swear. All we want is to help. Do you remember what happened to your parents?"

His eyes narrowed. "Yeah. Yeah, I do." He cursed under his breath.

"We'll leave right now. You can pretend you never saw us," I said even as my ears picked up the sound of footsteps thudding along the cement balcony toward us. "Or you can come with us, tell everyone in the Clann what you saw and help us take him down and make him pay for what he did to both our parents. Your choice."

"Tristan," Savannah hissed, her voice barely a sound at all as she reappeared in the bedroom doorway.

Silence on the balcony as the descendants discovered the broken door. Needles of pain ramped up over my skin in warning as they gathered power.

"Time's up. Decide." I looked at the girls and jerked my head at the window. "Back exit?"

Emily flinched but followed Savannah over to the window, where Savannah put her hands on the edges of the screen and looked to me for a sign.

"I'll help," Mac said, rolling across his bed and jumping up to stand with us. When I held out a hand, though, he hesitated. "No offense, but if you're planning on carrying me, could she do it instead?" He smiled shyly at Savannah, his cheeks turning pink.

Jealousy, quick and pointless, flooded me.

"Sure," Savannah said with a smile. "Wrap an arm around my waist like this." She put her arm around him and he followed suit.

Whatever it takes to get him on our side, she thought, throwing a meaningful glare over the kid's head at me.

Sure. Within reason. I grabbed my sister and nodded at Savannah to push out the screen. Then Emily stepped on my foot and I jumped with the other out the window and down two stories to the cement below, making my free leg absorb all of the impact from both our bodies.

"The baby okay?" I muttered while Savannah brought Mac through the window and down to the ground beside us.

Emily frowned, touched her stomach with one hand and the small of her back with the other. "I think so. But I must have landed wrong, because my back is killing me. I'll be okay, though."

"Hold your breath. This is going to be fast."

"Mac, hold your breath, okay?" Savannah warned.

Shouting overhead, then blue orbs erupted from the window in our direction. I fired one back with my free hand to create some cover fire while Savannah took off in a vamp blur with the kid.

"Mr. Colbert, we're headed back fast. Meet us there," I said for the benefit of our listeners on the other end of the cell phone call, which a quick glance showed was still connected.

With one last energy orb fired over my shoulder at the descendants leaning out the second-story window, I vamp blurred up the side street then down Front Street, taking the bridge a second later and arriving at the trailer a second after that.

Savannah's parents were there seconds later, Ms. Evans joining in on the gasps of the other two humans even as Mr. Colbert jumped into the truck and got us back on the road.

When the humans had caught their breaths again and everyone had settled down around the dinette table, I looked at Emily and said, "Where to next?"

Her mouth thinned into a tight line. "Now we call every descendant on that list and see how fast they can get to the Circle for a little Clann hearing."

"We—I mean, they—have those?" I said.

"Sure. Dad talked about them once or twice. The Clann can hold emergency meetings, or hearings, to decide how to punish a descendant for breaking Clann law. The morning Ms. Evans died was an informal one." Her tone drifted off as she gave Savannah a sympathetic grimace.

"So we just hide out with Mac until all the descendants can travel to the Circle?" Savannah frowned. "I don't like it. It'll take too long for everyone to get there, maybe even days. In the meantime, Mac's foster parents will have already warned Mr. Williams that we have him. We'll lose the element of surprise."

Emily blew out a long sigh. "Well, how else are we supposed to get a lot of descendant witnesses there to hear Mac's story? We have no idea who's on Mr. Williams's side, so we've got to get as many descendants as possible to hear him all at once before Mr. Williams can have him silenced again."

"What about doing it online?" Mac suggested, speaking for the first time since we'd reached the trailer.

We all looked at him in surprise. His cheeks turned bright red, making the zits on his cheeks appear purple in contrast.

"Good idea," Savannah said. "We could record him telling his story then send it to all the descendants. Then we could keep him safely hidden and Mr. Williams couldn't do anything to stop us from spreading the word."

"Yeah, but video doesn't let anyone read his mind and verify he's telling the truth," Emily said.

"I thought you said memory can be faked," I said.

"Yeah, if you're good like me. Mac's fourteen—"

"Fifteen in two months," Mac said.

"Whatever. He's not that good." Emily waved a hand in the air as if scrubbing a dry-erase board clean. "We need at least some witnesses in person to hear Mac."

"What if we do both?" Savannah said. "We could gather a bunch of witnesses and record both his story and their verifying that he's telling the truth."

"Better yet, what if we do it live?" Emily muttered, her fingers drumming the table. "When Mom had to take over leading the Clann, I talked her into trying out some twenty-first-century technology. Namely, online conferencing tools, which I set up on her laptop."

"We don't have her lap—" I started to stay.

"No, but I can set up any laptop with the same program," Emily said. "All I do is set it up, call all the descendants ahead of time and tell them to watch their email boxes for some huge breaking Clann news of an emergency type, then when we start the meeting I'll send out an email blast to invite them all to join the online conference so they can watch everything live."

"I'll get mine." Ms. Evans jumped up and hurried into

her bedroom, bracing her hands along the pantry door then the wall opposite it, followed by the bathroom door to keep from falling as the trailer swayed on the road.

Emily winced and rubbed at the small of her back again.

"Hey, sis, are you all right?" That was the third or fourth time I'd seen her reacting to back pain.

She froze, her eyes going wide, then her whole body sort of melted into relaxation again. "You know, I think I just might be having false labor pains."

All I heard was "labor pains." "The baby's coming? *Now?*"

She quickly shook her head, her blond curls bouncing wildly around her face. "No, I said false labor pains. I read about them. They're pretty common. It's too soon to be real labor, and besides, my water hasn't broken. Don't worry about it, the books all said they'd go away. Let's stay focused on getting this conference call set up."

Ms. Evans returned a few seconds later with her laptop and set it on the dinette table.

"So has anyone decided where I should be driving us to?" Mr. Colbert's voice said from my pocket.

I'd forgotten about the still-open line of communication.

Grabbing the phone, I held it up and said, "Yeah. Looks like we're headed back to Jacksonville."

Ms. Evans sank down onto the dinette bench, propped her elbows on the table, and dropped her head into her hands. "Oh, good Lord, not again."

I looked at Emily. "Tell everyone who is close enough to Jacksonville to go to the Circle for an emergency meeting. Then call Mr. Williams last and tell him we'll meet him there in a couple of hours. Tell him we're tired of running and ready to turn ourselves in. But tell him we'll only show up if he's there in person. We won't answer to anyone but the Clann leader himself."

CHAPTER 26

SAVANNAH

"Hey, Sav, you still got the phone with Mom's SIM card in it?" Emily asked.

I nodded, pulled the phone from my pocket and handed it to her.

She tried to press the keys then had to hold down the power button to turn it on. Immediately it buzzed and beeped as a flood of missed calls and messages hit it one after the other.

"What in the world?" I muttered as Emily handed it back to her.

The only people who had this number were my parents, Tristan and...Anne.

Twenty-two missed calls from Anne, plus eleven missed text messages. I checked the first missed text.

Ron says the Clann and Keepers nearly caught S&T. WTF is going on?

Okay, so she'd heard about our little return trip to Jack-sonville. No big deal. Ron also would have told her we es-caped safely. So what was with all the rest of the missed calls and texts?

I read the next one and froze.

Michelle & Carrie missing, Clann took them! Ron says Keep-ers sent to kidnap them.

"Oh, my God." I held the phone so Tristan could read it aloud. He had to take the phone from me because my hand was shaking it too badly to let him see the words.

I stared at the dinette table's mottled tan-and-brown lami-nate surface, the colors blurring as my eyes stung. It was my worst nightmare playing out all over again. Only this time the Clann had taken two of my best friends instead of my grandmother.

And this time, it was Mr. Williams in charge instead of Mr. Coleman.

"But why—" Emily began.

"Lucy." The word rolled out of my mouth like a church bell tolling. "The Keepers must have tracked our smell to Michelle's house. I need to call Anne."

Tristan held out the phone to me.

Anne picked up already shrieking. It took me a long time to get her to stop cursing and calm down enough to tell me the whole story. But it was still faster than trying to wade through the missed calls and text messages.

"Ron says after you guys escaped, the Keepers reported back to Mr. Williams and he went ballistic," Anne said so loudly I had to hold the phone away from my ear. At least this let everyone else listen in, too, though. "He ordered all the Keepers to go on patrol and try to track your scents. Two Keepers said they picked up your scents at Michelle's house. But Michelle was sleeping over at Carrie's. I was supposed to go over, too, but I was grounded." She didn't go into a lengthy explanation of why she was grounded. "Then Carrie's parents saw the girls were gone and called me thinking we'd all snuck out somewhere together, since they'd left their cars and keys and everything. I called Ron, and he checked with the Keepers, and…"

I pressed my fingertips to my pounding temple. "But they don't know anything! What's the point of taking them, even if Michelle has my mother's dog and it smells like us?"

Tristan scowled and reached out to hold my hand. "I've got a feeling Mr. Williams was looking for any excuse to take your friends in for interrogation."

Interrogation.

An image of Nanna, held in the air by a spell, her mouth stretched open in a silent scream, filled my mind. Oh, God. If the Clann were doing that to Carrie and Michelle…

"We have to get them," I whispered. "Does Ron know where they're holding them?"

"Yeah—" Anne said.

"No, we can't, not yet," Emily said. "Not now that we have the proof we need to take Mr. Williams down!"

I rose as far as the dinette table's edge would let me and leaned over the table toward her. "They've got my friends! Who knows what they're doing to them right now. We have to rescue them."

I was wrong about Mr. Williams. He really was that evil. This was all my fault.

Emily glared back at me. "I'm sorry they got caught up in this. I really am. But if you rescue your friends before we take care of Mr. Williams, he'll only put a target on them and their families. They'll be in even more danger than they already are. Do you want your friends and their families to have to go on the run just like us?"

Crap. She had a point. Growling, I forced myself to sit down.

"Sav?" Anne called out from the phone's speaker. "What are we going to do?"

"She's right," I said through gritted teeth. "We've got proof that'll get Mr. Williams removed as Clann leader. Once he's out, we'll free Carrie and Michelle."

"But—" Anne said.

"I'm not forcing them and their families to go on the run," I said.

"I can't believe you! You're going to let them be tortured, maybe even *killed?*" Anne yelled.

I set the phone down on the table, turned my head and buried my face against Tristan's shoulders. God help me, but that was exactly what we had to do. *Please let them be okay,* I prayed.

Tristan picked up the phone and spoke to Anne in a rapid murmur just slow enough for her to follow, outlining our plan against Mr. Williams. But from her loud cursing, I gathered she wasn't any more appeased. She wanted a rescue mission *now,* and she didn't care about the consequences as long as Carrie and Michelle were freed. Everything else could wait.

"You tell that redheaded witch that if anything happens to our friends, it'll be her fault!" Anne said.

The line went dead.

Clearing his throat, Tristan ended the call and handed it to Emily. *You know she didn't mean that,* he thought to me.

I propped my elbows on the table and buried my face in my hands, scrubbing at my burning eyes. I had no clue whether Anne meant that last part or not. Either way, she was right. Our friends were enduring who knew what at the hands of Mr. Williams and his buddies within the Clann because they were my friends and had tried to help me and my mom. And now they would have to endure the Clann's torture even longer, again because of me.

A tiny ember of heat glowed to life in the pit of my stomach, then exploded into a virtual bonfire, heating every part of me from the inside out.

Tristan was right. Mr. Williams needed to die.

"You don't mean that," Tristan said, startling me and making me jump.

I stared at him. "Oh, yes I do. He needs to be stopped permanently. What human prison would hold him, though? None, and the Clann doesn't have a prison for descendants, either. So the only way to ensure he never hurts anyone ever again is to kill him."

"Fine. But let me be the one to do it. You're ticked off enough to do the deed yourself, but you and I both know later on you'd regret it."

I scowled at him. Was he serious? "So it's okay for you to have his death on your conscience but not mine? Why?"

He blinked several times. "Because you have me to do it for you."

"So you're saying I'm not capable of doing the dirty work

myself?" I could hear my voice rising, not in volume, but in tone.

He rolled his eyes and scowled. "Look, I'm not trying to be sexist here. I know you're perfectly capable of doing it yourself. All I'm saying is, why should you have to when I can do it for you? It's like...like taking out the trash. You have the ability to do it, you've probably done it a bunch of times, too. But why should you have to if I'm around to take care of it for you? That's a guy's job, to do the dirty jobs so you ladies can keep your hands, or in this case your consciences, clean."

I looked at Emily. Her eyes were wide with disbelief, too.

She shook her head. "It's got to be something Dad taught him. That's all I can figure."

Tristan sighed and crossed his arms. "Dad always said real men look after the women they love and protect them from the dirty parts of life wherever they can. Maybe it's not politically correct or whatever, but that's how I was raised." *And I'm not apologizing for it,* he finished silently.

I sighed. Another battle for another day. Besides, while his old-fashioned belief in this area was wrong, it also came from a place of love and pure intentions. "Look, Tristan, all I'm saying is if this comes down to a battle and any of us have a clear shot at Mr. Williams, none of us should hesitate to take it. Okay?"

Tristan frowned. "Sis, make your calls to the Clann quick." Then he dialed Dad's number. "Better step on it. The sooner we get this hearing over with and Mr. Williams removed as leader, the faster we can get her friends released."

Hopefully before any permanent damage is done to them, he

thought to himself then cringed as he remembered I could hear his every thought. *Sorry.*

I didn't reply. What was the point? My head was filled with the exact same thoughts and fears.

CHAPTER 27

TRISTAN

She was trying to hide it with a brave face, but our mental connection let me know just how much of a seething, guilt-ridden wreck Savannah was inside.

I wished I could reassure her that Anne's report might be wrong, that Ron had heard it all wrong, or maybe even that the whole rumor was a lie designed to lure us close enough for the Clann to capture us.

But knowing Mr. Williams's history, all the worse now that we knew he'd helped Gowin kill his own people, told me otherwise. Carrie and Michelle were the latest humans caught in this stupid war. And we had no promise of any kind that they would survive it. By kidnapping and torturing them, Mr. Williams could take out two goals in one move... inflict fear and possibly even pain on our friends while also possibly pulling us into a trap.

I froze as I realized what I'd thought. It was true. I did

consider Savannah's friends my own, as well. They'd accepted me into their circle despite plenty of reasons not to.

For their sakes as well as Savannah's and mine, I hoped they would make it till we could get them out of wherever the Keepers had put them. Best-case scenario, maybe the Keepers were still holding them somewhere and Mr. Williams hadn't had time to interrogate them yet.

Worst-case scenario...

Knowing Savannah could hear my thoughts, I didn't follow that line of thinking.

We would get them out of there. Just as soon as we got rid of Mr. Williams, one way or another.

Emily burned up every cell tower we passed, calling countless Clann. Many tried to ask her questions, but to her credit, she handled every conversation smoothly, telling them the emergency didn't give her enough time to answer their questions by phone. But she promised all would be answered in the email she'd be sending out to everyone tonight if they couldn't hear it all in person at the hearing in the Circle. Most descendants lived too far away to make the hearing. But there were at least twenty or more who said they would be there.

Then she called Mr. Williams. I was surprised when he actually picked up.

"Emily," he greeted her warmly. "I hear you're planning a surprise for the Clann this evening. I've received many a call over the past hour saying that you're inviting everyone to the Circle, and asking whether I know what you're up to."

"What I'm up to has to do with those two innocent girls you're currently holding for questioning," Emily said, her eyes blazing but her voice amazingly even.

"Ah, so you heard about Savannah Coleman's unfortunate two friends. Yes, well, that is what happens when you help a traitor and a murderer of a Clann leader."

You'd know about that, wouldn't you! Savannah silently screamed. But she managed to keep her lips clamped shut.

"We want them released," Emily said, following the plan step by step.

"I'm sorry, but I really can't do that. We have good reason to believe these girls know the whereabouts of Savannah and your brother, Tristan."

"Yeah, well maybe you should just stop interrogating them and ask me that instead, because I'm sitting right across from my brother and his girlfriend."

"Hello, Mr. Williams," I said.

Savannah leaned in, a thousand things she'd like to shout flooding her mind. I laid a hand on her forearm in silent reminder to stick with the plan.

She swallowed hard. "You'd better not hurt my friends, or so help me…"

Mr. Williams made a tsking noise, sounding so much like his son that it managed to actually creep me out a little. "Threatening the new Clann leader after murdering the previous one? My, my, but your list of crimes is adding up. Why don't you two simply turn yourselves in and save us all a lot of time and grief."

"Sure, if you agree to release Sav's friends," I said.

Silence as Mr. Williams absorbed the offer. "You would turn yourselves in willingly without a fight in exchange for them?"

"Yes," Savannah said. At least this time she had no problem speaking.

"Hmm. I suppose they would be useless to me if I no longer needed them to reveal your whereabouts. However, if this were some sort of attempt to trick me and you two did not keep your end of the bargain, I might be forced to question them even more…strongly in order to find you."

There was a ripping sound and a low scream, then Carrie yelled, "Don't do it, Sav! He can't get anything out of us anyways, so just—"

Her words turned into a scream.

I twisted and grabbed Savannah's shoulders as she tried to lunge for the phone, which Emily grabbed and held out of her reach. "I'll kill you! Do you hear me? If you hurt them any more, I will kill you and all the Clann spells in the world won't be able to save you!"

I had to struggle to hold her while Emily told Mr. Williams to meet us in an hour at the Circle. When Emily ended the phone call, Savannah collapsed against me, her hands fisting around my shirt as she fought the rage. Over her head, I jerked a chin at the dinette window, and Emily leaned over to open it, letting out precious cool conditioned air but also giving us some fresh air so Savannah wouldn't have any lingering human fear pheromones to trigger her bloodlust except her rage.

She tilted her head up to look at me, her eyes round and white, her fangs fully extended and biting into her lower lip. She didn't even seem to feel the pain as two drops of blood welled up. "We have to stop him, Tristan."

"We will." I stroked her back as she buried her face against my neck, drew in long breaths, and struggled to rein in her fury.

Emily cleared her throat and suggested Mac come with

her to watch some TV. Watching Savannah the entire time, he slowly slid around the dinette and then sat with Emily on the couch behind us.

An hour later, I held Savannah's shaking hand as our entire group slowly walked around my family's home and across its backyard. At the edge of the woods, we hesitated. I looked at Emily, making sure she was ready. Sweat beaded her upper lip and forehead as she winced. Then she realized I was watching her and waiting for her signal. At her nod, I took a deep breath and looked at Savannah. *Ready?*

Teeth clenched, she nodded and took the first step into the woods.

A ripple of pinpricks erupted across my skin, signaling that either we'd triggered a spell or someone in the Circle was gathering power. Whatever the cause, it took real effort not to stop and touch the ground to gather even more power of my own in turn.

Not yet. First we would try Emily's plan and go the politically strategic route.

Mac stayed one step behind and in between Emily and me. The combination of heartbeats and fear-induced pheromones from him, Emily and Ms. Evans was a tough distraction to ignore and made me grateful we weren't in an enclosed area. I wasn't sure even holding our breaths would have prevented the bloodlust from kicking in otherwise.

Light glimmered through the thick pine branches ahead, signaling we were getting closer to the Circle. Not that I needed the guidance. I'd grown up in these woods and knew every inch of them by memory. The light did let us know that we were expected, though.

When we reached the edge of the Circle, I didn't know

whether to feel relief or worry. The Circle was only about a third as full as it had been the night the Clann had met to vote me in as leader. Had these thirty descendants shown up because of Emily's call, or at Mr. Williams's request? Did we have any shot at having even one unbiased and fair judge present to hear us? Or was this plan doomed from the start?

Mr. Williams, seated in the stone chair that had once seated my father, and his father, and his father before him, stared at Mac as the scared but furious kid entered the Circle with us. Then he pasted on his trademark smile, the one that said so many things… "trust me, I will steer you right," "isn't this a sad night to have to take part in," "don't you wish everyone could just follow the rules and get along."

For that smile alone, he deserved to die. There was nothing about this man that spoke the truth, from his perfectly tailored suit to his salt-and-pepper hair so carefully trimmed and styled. And though Savannah, her dad and I were the vampires here, Mr. Williams's eyes were the creepiest in the clearing. Why couldn't everyone see those were the eyes of a cold and calculating serial killer?

Soon they would know the truth.

"I see your group has grown," Mr. Williams called across the Circle as, at either side of him, several descendants tightened their ranks and drew in closer to the stone chair.

I had to do a double take. His buddies all had white hair. As some kind of sign of their obedience and loyalty to their new leader?

Then Dylan stepped forward, tilted his head hard from left to right with a popping sound, and rolled his shoulders to loosen them up. And I understood.

That was how Dylan had survived the night of my mother's

death. Mr. Williams must have made his closest followers use the old ways—sacrificial magic—to heal his son's spine. Judging by the unchanged color of Mr. Williams's hair, though, it appeared he was only willing to make his followers give up part of their life force.

They must not have given enough of their life force. Dylan looked like crap, with sunken-in cheeks, colorless skin except for the dark circles under his eyes, which peered out from beneath greasy, dull hair that was months past due for a cut.

"Where are my friends?" Savannah demanded, her hand tightening on mine.

Mr. Williams stared at her with that same cold smile. "Emily, do you think that recording this moment for YouTube is really the wisest way to show your loyalty to the Clann and its secrets?" He nodded at the laptop she held open and turned toward him.

"Oh, I'm loyal to the Clann, all right," she said. "Just not to those who would destroy it or its members with—as you put it—secrets. Speaking of which..." She turned to address everyone else in the Circle. "Thank you everyone for coming here on such short notice. I know how this must look to you right now. But I promise if you hear us out, you're going to understand the truth very soon."

"You mean like the truth of whose baby you carry?" Mr. Williams said.

Emily flinched and froze. She swallowed so hard it made an audible click in the silence. "Yes. The same person whom you apparently got quite close to, as well. Mac, why don't you tell everyone how your parents, the Griffins, really died last year?"

Mac hesitated then took a tiny step forward and cleared

his throat. He hesitated, scanning the crowd of frowning and confused faces.

"Mac..." Emily muttered. "Any day now please."

He cleared his throat again. "Right. Um, so...the night my parents died, I was out with some friends at the movies. When I came back, I saw a vampire..."

"Gowin," Emily supplied.

"Right, Gowin, and this man, Mr. Williams, leaving my house." Gasps rose up from several descendants. Mac paused then continued. "I heard him telling the vamp—Gowin—that they needed to find me. But Gowin said he needed to rest first. Then they left, and I went inside and found my parents' bodies."

Emily slung an arm around his shoulders for comfort. "And after you called the police and they came and got you, what happened next?"

"They took me to the police station, and then Mr. Williams showed up and grabbed my wrist, and I didn't remember anything until tonight when you guys showed up."

"Lies!" one of Mr. Williams' white-haired friends shouted. "This kid is obviously in league with the traitors."

Mr. Williams made a show of gently gesturing for everyone to quiet down. "Let's not jump to conclusions. This poor boy has been through a lot. He could be simply confused or perhaps even under a spell—"

"You mean like that memory confusion spell you put on me for months?" Mac shouted, ignoring the plan now. "Or how about the spells you must have used against my parents to help that bloodsucker get close enough to kill them?"

I put an arm out to block him as he tried to step forward in fury.

"Test his memories," Emily said in a quiet voice. "That's why he agreed to come here tonight, so every one of you could see for yourself that his memories are true."

Mac clenched his fists at his side as fear poured out from him. But he nodded and lifted his chin, waiting for the invasion into his mind.

The crowd went silent then began to murmur.

"It is simply a planted memory," Mr. Williams said. "Why on earth would I ever ally myself with one of their kind?" He nodded at Savannah, her father and me. "It is obvious they have come here to foolishly spread lies and doubt among us so that we will become divided and weakened before another vamp attack."

"We also came here to free my friends," Savannah said, her entire body shaking with anger now. She was having trouble keeping the fury in check.

"What friends?" Mr. Williams's eyebrows rose.

Everything inside both Savannah and me sank. Oh, God. Had he already killed them?

He'd never planned to release them at all. Though why I was surprised by his latest treachery, I had no idea.

"The humans you had your Keepers take from their homes tonight," I said. "Don't play dumb, we know you have them."

"I have no idea what you are talking—" Mr. Williams began.

"Here they are," a Keeper called out as he and another man dragged Carrie and Michelle into the clearing. Both girls' mouths were duct-taped shut and their hands bound behind their backs. "We brought them just as you said." The Keeper hesitated, searching the Clann leader's furious face. "You did say to bring them here, right?"

"I never—" Mr. Williams began.

"No, I did," Ron said, resting his hands on his hips. "When I heard you had them kidnapped, I called the guards and told them to bring our prisoners to the Circle tonight so everyone else could see exactly what you've been using the Keepers for."

And then a third Keeper led Anne forward to join Carrie and Michelle. Like her friends, Anne was also bound. Unlike them, her eyes were filled with more fury than fear.

"We caught this one with these—" the third Keeper tossed down a black compound bow and quiver full of arrows "—trying to rescue her friends."

CHAPTER 28

Ron and Savannah both gasped out Anne's name. Clearly Ron hadn't realized his girlfriend would try to rescue Carrie and Michelle on her own and get caught in the process.

"I have no idea what these Keepers are talking about," Mr. Williams said. "I never told them to kidnap any humans. Perhaps they misunderstood me in an overeagerness to help the Clann—"

"Why are you lying about the Clann's allies now?" Ron shouted as he stepped into the light of the clearing where other Keepers, both in human and panther form, stood gathered together. They'd arrived so silently that I hadn't even seen or heard them. Too bad most of them were on the wrong side, because they definitely had some impressive skills.

I hoped I wouldn't have to kill any of them tonight.

Ron continued. "Keepers, search each others' minds. Who of you received his orders to go after these innocent humans and interrogate them for knowledge of Tristan and Savannah's location?"

Several Keepers in human form raised their hands, including the three guarding the girls.

"Descendants, check our minds for yourselves," Ron said. "See the truth. Your leader is lying to all of you about so many things."

"Why should we listen to you, a traitor to your own people? Haven't you broken your own Keeper laws by helping these bloodsuckers escape earlier tonight?" Mr. Williams's eyes narrowed.

Ron's parents gasped and stepped forward to look past the other Keepers at their son. "Ron, you didn't!" his mother whispered. "Sweetie, you know the oath and its consequences if it is broken. You'll lose your shifter abilities."

Ron's chin rose. "I haven't forgotten my oath…to help defend and protect the Clann against outside enemies." He stressed the last two words. "But obviously the law doesn't consider Tristan or Savannah to be outsiders of the Clann, or I couldn't still do this." Scraps of clothing exploded outward as he rapidly shifted into panther form.

Mr. Abernathy took a deep breath then turned to face the Keepers. "Ron's right. We never agreed to help the Clann wage a civil war against its own members. And I for one am sick of being used to hunt down and terrorize innocent people, human or otherwise." He turned toward the Circle. "I will keep my oath to protect the Clann against outsiders. But that is all."

Mrs. Abernathy took her husband's hand and they walked along the edge of the Circle back toward the Coleman house. As they passed their son, Mrs. Abernathy paused.

"Son, please come home with us now. This is no longer the Keepers' fight."

I can't, Mom, he thought. *My friends need me here.*

Mr. Abernathy hesitated, glancing from his son to the human prisoners to us and finally to his wife. "He's right again, hon. We can't leave these innocents to who knows what fate. We Keepers are more *honorable* than that."

Murmurs rose within the Keepers' ranks. The Keepers standing on either side of Carrie, Michelle and Anne let go of the girls and stepped back.

Then all the Keepers, human and panther, turned and stared at Mr. Williams.

Emily cleared her throat. "I know none of you have any reason to believe me. But I have one more thing to show you that will reveal just what kind of leader you've got running the show around here lately. This is what really happened the night of my mother's murder...."

She closed her eyes, took a deep breath, and then sent her mental shield crashing so everyone present could read everything within her mind.

I was so shocked that it took me a few seconds to believe I was really seeing it. My sister, the queen of the mental shield, had purposely allowed everyone here total and complete access to every thought and memory within her mind. This from a girl who wouldn't even allow her little brother to read her thoughts. Ever.

I saw what others saw...Mom's plans for dinner that night, telling Emily she was going to apologize to me and admit she'd acted too hastily in casting me out of the Clann.

Mom had been planning to invite me to rejoin the Clann. She'd believed that, by sharing my idea for creating synthetic blood to sell to vampires and thus give the Clann an enormous amount of leverage over vamps worldwide, I'd proven I was still her son deep inside.

"Oh, Tristan," Savannah whispered, squeezing my hand.

Everyone else saw what I'd witnessed for myself later that night. I didn't need to read Emily's thoughts or memories any further. She'd already answered the one question that had haunted me for over half a year now.

My mother had still loved me, regardless of what I'd turned into.

Everyone else present finished reading Emily's memories. Including Mr. Williams. "You've twisted that memory! Your mother called me for help when Tristan and Savannah showed up at your house and attacked her. My friends and I tried to save her, even at the near cost of my own son's life— at *his* hands." He pointed a finger at me, then turned back to Emily. "Everyone knows now that you are a vamp lover and a traitor to the Clann. You would say and do anything to save your brother, despite the fact that he killed your mother."

"I show the truth," Emily murmured, her voice shaky as a bead of sweat trickled down one side of her face. "I only wish I had been downstairs so that I could also show them that *you* killed my mother, not Tristan or Savannah."

Mr. Williams slowly smiled. "As you say, you did not see her actual death so…" He spread his hands out palms up in open question.

"I'd suggest they read your memories, but we all know what a liar you are now," Emily said.

"Read Dylan's." The words blurted out of me, completely unplanned.

Dylan froze and Mr. Williams went pale. "Leave my son out of this—"

"Like you said, he was there," I said.

"But he didn't see who killed Nancy Coleman, either," Mr. Williams said, and I could tell from his wide smile that this was the very fact he had been counting on.

And why he probably hadn't bothered to alter his son's memories.

"No, but he can verify whether my mother actually called you for help," I said.

Everyone in the Circle slowly turned to stare at Dylan.

I didn't have to join them in reading his mind. I knew what they would find.

A ripple of movement and low-level noise spread across the descendants as they read the truth then turned to stare at their leader, murmuring to themselves or their neighbors in growing distrust and anger.

"He's lying to us," someone muttered within the crowd. "It's right there in his own son's mind. He planned to attack the Coleman house that night. Nancy never called him for help at all!"

Growing murmurs spread like tiny spots of wildfire within the Clann's ranks and were echoed on the laptop Emily held out.

"I call for a vote to remove Jim Williams as Clann leader!" someone on the conference call shouted from the laptop and was echoed by several others, both online and in person, who seconded the vote.

But I remembered the rules. Clann law stated that leaders couldn't be voted in or out unless all the adult descendants took part in the vote and a majority were in agreement. There was no way to legally do this over a conference call.

Thankfully Emily remembered this. "I recommend that we meet here in one week's time to hold an official vote to remove Jim Williams as our leader. Does anyone second this recommendation?"

Hands shot up throughout the Circle, prompting Mr. Williams to leap to his feet.

"No!" he shouted. "We have to stick together against the vampires or we'll be too weak to survive them."

"The only threat the Clann really has to fear is you," Emily said.

Mr. Williams didn't even raise his hands, yet two blue orbs shot out from them, knocking the laptop out of Emily's hands.

And then chaos erupted as his white-haired line of friends joined in, shooting energy orbs at the Keepers.

"Dylan, take him out!" Mr. Williams screamed at his son.

I didn't need to read anyone's mind to figure out who he was referring to.

But I was too busy blocking spells from Mr. Williams's friends to worry about Dylan for now. If he wanted me, he'd have to get through an entire clearing full of fighting first.

CHAPTER 29

SAVANNAH

When the fighting broke out, I discovered for the first time that I was paralyzed. Everything about this moment was like my nightmares brought to life, and all I could think was *not again*.

I couldn't lose Tristan again.

The last time I'd been in this Circle, fighting had also broken out. And I'd seen Gowin almost rip Tristan's heart right out of his chest. If not for my hybrid blood and Emily's quick fire spell to kill Gowin, Tristan would have been gone forever.

Even though we were vamps, I could still lose him tonight. The only difference was, this time it would be permanent. I knew now that we would both survive if his neck were broken, because his body could heal from that.

But he wouldn't heal from a stick shoved through his chest, or fire, or if a descendant managed to take off his head with a spell. And now that every descendant alive had spent the past two months in fear of being attacked by rogue vamps, everyone present would be armed and fully capable of killing us in less than a second with one well-aimed spell.

Thankfully most of them simply wanted to get clear of the Circle with their own lives intact. Several of them ran in a crouch, trying to duck the spells flying through the air. Some weren't so lucky and were hit in the back with energy orbs from Mr. Williams or his allies. The unlucky descendants slammed to the ground and didn't get up again.

With the reassurance of Tristan fighting at my back, I was able to at least turn my head and look for the rest of my group. Mom, Dad, Emily and Mac were hunkered down at the edge of the clearing behind a tight grouping of pines, the younger boy bravely shielding them all from flying spells. From the rapid movement of Emily's lips and the frequent pointing of her fingers, it seemed she was telling him what to do and where to aim it.

I turned to check on Tristan and see if he needed any help taking down one of Mr. Williams's guys.

That's when I discovered I was standing alone in the middle of a sea of fighting descendants and Tristan was nowhere in sight.

TRISTAN

"Tristan Coleman!" Mr. Williams's scream managed to rise above the roar of the fight.

I twisted and turned until I found him standing by the stone chair with his son.

Time to finish this.

I wove through the crowd, dodging spells and energy orbs

and flying bodies. But when I got to the stone chair, I found only Dylan waiting for me.

"Where is he?" I asked.

Dylan slowly raised his hands palm out.

I stared at him. "Don't do this."

Blue light gathered like a condensing fog before both of his hands.

Cursing, I raised my own hands. The shield took the hit of the two orbs easily. I wasn't even rocked on my feet.

Dylan threw another orb, then a fourth. Each thudded against my shield. But it was like he wasn't even trying.

Impatient now, I closed the distance between us and grabbed him by his shirt. "Where is he?"

Dylan swung a fist at me. I leaned to the side to avoid it. He threw his other fist at me, and this time I caught it.

I pushed him back and down until he was kneeling on the ground. "Don't make me kill you. Just tell me where he is."

Dylan closed his eyes, his throat working beneath my grip as he tried to swallow. "Do it. Just finish it already."

The old anger rose up within me. I dropped his fist then raised my own, prepared to answer his death wish.

But something stopped me. Maybe it was the memory of how I'd felt two months ago when I thought I'd killed Dylan, or the relief that had blasted me when I'd learned he was alive after all. Or maybe it was some stray memory of when we were kids playing football together. Whatever it was, I hesitated. And then I reached out with my mind and read his thoughts.

His mind was filled with memory after memory of his father yelling at him, telling him he was a loser and probably not even his own son, of his father hitting him with orb after orb of energy while threatening to kill him.

"I swear I didn't know he was going to kill your mother," Dylan croaked. "You were right. I should have stood up to him. Now finish it. Please. I can't...can't take it anymore."

Dylan wanted to be free of his father, even if it took dying to do it.

Bile rose up to burn the back of my throat. I let go of him and stood up. "You don't have to die to be free."

He slowly opened his eyes and looked at me in confusion.

I held out a hand, praying everything Savannah had told me over and over was right and that I wasn't making a huge mistake here. "If you really want to be free of him, help me end this."

Dylan hesitated, his hand rising almost as if it had a mind of its own. His fingers wrapped around the base of my thumb, and I pulled him up to his feet. We both froze, remembering countless times over the years when I'd pulled him upright after a sack on the field during practices or games.

He took a deep breath then made eye contact with me. "Okay. Let's finish it."

We worked side by side, systematically searching for and knocking out each of his father's devoted followers, and it was almost like the old days. Only this time Dylan didn't carry a ball, and we weren't just blocking tackles.

Then I got drawn off in a separate battle, helping one of the descendants fight back against one of Mr. Williams's loyalists. When I turned back around, Dylan had found his dad. And judging by the steady stream of blue light pouring out of Mr. Williams's hands at his son's head, now inches from the ground, his father had figured out Dylan had switched sides.

"You think you can betray me and get away with it?" Mr. Williams screamed. "My own *son?* I'll kill you for this. I'll kill you!"

Mr. Williams's elbows bent, his hands drawing back toward his chest for a second. Then they thrust forward and twice the blue light came pouring out at Dylan, pinning him on his back to the ground.

SAVANNAH

I heard Tristan's name yelled out, but not from where. And no matter how much I looked, I couldn't see over the crowd enough to find him.

I spotted Anne, Carrie and Michelle all huddling at the base of a tree. Carrie and Michelle looked terrified. Anne just looked furious.

I ran over to them, keeping low to avoid the spells in the air. "I can't believe you tried to rescue them on your own!" I yelled at Anne as I bent over and bit through the plastic zip tie around her wrist.

As soon as her hands were free, she ripped the duct tape from her mouth and shouted back. "Well, you obviously weren't going to do it!"

"I was, too! I just had to make sure Mr. Williams wouldn't have them tracked down and killed the second I freed them, or worse, that he'd go after their families." I bit through Carrie's and Michelle's zip ties next.

Carrie tore off her own duct tape with one hand then reached for Michelle's. But instead of ripping it off, she yelled, "Can't we leave hers on?"

I grinned as Michelle slapped her hand away then removed the duct tape from her face with a startled howl of pain.

"Crap, that hurts!" She turned to me with wide eyes. "Savannah, would you please explain what is going on around here?"

"Well duh, Michelle." Carrie leaned over and shouted in Michelle's ear. "Isn't it obvious? The rumors about the Clann being a bunch of witches are true. And they're apparently at war with vampires."

"But which one are you and Tristan?" Michelle said.

"Uh, both actually." Seeing her open her mouth to pelt me with questions, I threw up a hand. "Not now. I'll explain later."

A scream, even higher-pitched than all the other screams and shouts filling the Circle, made me twist and look around. Emily, there by my parents and Mac. Something was wrong with her. She was seated on the ground, her upper body braced against a tree trunk, both her arms curved around her stomach. Had she been hit by a spell?

Her round eyes widened still further, then narrowed into slits as she cried out again then pursed her lips. Her cheeks curved out like a chipmunk's out then sucked in repeatedly, almost as if she were blowing up a balloon.

Or doing Lamaze breathing.

Oh, no. The baby. She must be in real labor after all.

I visually searched the Circle, spotted the descendant I was looking for, then vamp blurred across the fifty yards of embattled descendants until I reached him. "Dr. Faulkner!"

He whirled and almost zapped me with an energy orb before recognizing me. "Savannah!"

"It's Emily. Her baby's coming and it's...it's like me. She needs your help delivering it. Quick, hold your breath."

He barely had time to suck in a breath, his thoughts startled and trying to figure out why he should be holding his breath at all now. Then I wrapped an arm around his waist, lifted him a few inches off the ground, and vamp blurred with him over to Emily.

As soon as we stopped, he gasped, grabbed the tree trunk with one hand for support, and bent over in an effort not to fall down. When he found his balance again, he crouched down at Emily's feet and checked her pulse then felt around her tummy.

"The baby is definitely ready to come now," he said, his words almost lost within the sound of all the fighting around us. "We need to get you out of here, somewhere safe—"

"Not a hospital!" Emily managed between hard puffs of air out through her lips.

"The house," Dad suggested. "I will carry her. Savannah, you bring the doctor."

"I should—" Mom began, meaning to go with Emily and help her.

I read the answer in Dad's thoughts even before he shook his head. Dad might be forced to rely on Dr. Faulkner's medical experience as far as helping Emily deliver this baby, because the doctor was the only descendant here capable of helping her. But that didn't mean Dad would risk putting Mom's safety into the Clann doctor's hands, too. Not if there was even a slim chance that Dr. Faulkner was on Mr. Williams's side.

"Stay here with Mac behind the tree out of sight," Dad told her. "I will be right back."

He didn't wait for our agreement before scooping Emily up into his arms then disappearing.

"Hold your breath," I warned the doctor again, waiting

just until he'd had a chance to suck in a deep breath before grabbing him once more and vamp blurring him through the woods, across the backyard and into the now open patio doors into the Coleman house.

Dad was laying Emily on the couch when we arrived.

I set the doctor on his feet. "I'd better get back. Good luck, Emily. You're going to do great."

She didn't even look up, her face red and scrunched as she started Lamaze breathing again.

I turned and vamp blurred back the way I'd come, returning to my human friends in the Circle in less than a second to find Anne deep in argument with Ron, apparently over whether it was safe for her to use her beloved compound bow and arrows on anyone in the fight. Thank goodness it looked like Ron was going to win the argument against that idea.

A blue orb zinged through the air toward me, passing so close that I actually felt its sizzle and passing heat on my nose and cheeks. I reared back just in time to miss the second one on its tail then looked for its source. There, a white-haired man crouched against a tree to the northeast. He sneered as he threw two more orbs my way.

"Stay here while I draw him away," I shouted to my friends then vamp blurred several yards away from them.

The plan worked, at least to draw his focus away from them. But when I dropped down into a crouch to throw some orbs back at him, I realized just what kind of descendant I was trying to outgun this time. I didn't even have enough time to throw up a full shield. This guy was fast, fast enough to make me think maybe speed was his specialty. I went for the next best solution, forming small shields around my hands, then knocked away the orbs before they could hit me.

A third one flew at me while I was still blocking the one before it. I held my hands palms-out in front of me just in time for the miniature shields to take the brunt of the hit. But the force was still enough to push me back onto my butt.

Crap. Not a good defensive position. I needed to be able to move and dodge his shots.

I jumped to my feet and ran with bent knees away from my still far-too-vulnerable human friends. A glance back at them showed Anne was actually in the process of drawing back an arrow, its lethal tip aimed in the loyalist's direction. Great. Here I was trying to protect them by purposely drawing fire in the direction opposite of them, and she was still crazy enough to think she could shoot someone.

I ran again without looking where I was going, seeing only an opening in the fighting from my peripheral vision, thinking only to make the loyalist look at me instead of Anne. His shots trailed me, each one a half second behind my movements, as if this guy had practiced hunting moving targets and knew how to lead his shots.

Another orb nearly hit me, and I was forced to stop in a crouch and block the barrage of orbs with my miniature shields. If I could just get a long enough break between shots, I could expand the shield to cover my entire body. Then I'd be free to use my hands for more than just blocking.

I was so over the defensive position in this battle. This guy needed a taste of what he was way too happy to dish out nonstop at me.

The hits pushed me backward, threatening to topple me again. Instead, I fell forward onto my knees and dug into the ground to brace myself.

"Savannah!" Mom screamed from somewhere at my left.

I looked her way, instinctively throwing up my hands to shield any additional orbs from my attacker.

But he'd discovered a better target.

Two blue orbs flew through the air straight for my mother as she tried to run to me.

"No!" The word roared out of me as I threw every ounce of willpower I had into forming a shield around her.

But even with my vamp reflexes and speed, she was too far away. My shield reached her a half second too late.

Her face twisted into a silent scream as the orbs exploded like mini fireworks over her entire body. Her back arched, her face going pale.

Then she crumpled to the ground.

A sizzling sound warned of another orb, this one headed my way. But I couldn't look away from my mother, not even to save myself.

Just like Nanna, my mind echoed over and over as I ran to her and dropped to the ground at her side.

I heard a strange *thunk* from the direction of my human friends and a man's scream from behind me.

"Mom," I whispered, stroking her face.

But my mother's open eyes refused to blink. And when I checked her neck, I couldn't find a pulse.

CHAPTER 30

TRISTAN

I closed the distance between the Williamses and myself, doing what I should have done years ago for my old friend.

Crouching beside him, I threw a shield over him with one hand then held a palm up in warning against his father. "No more. He's not an animal. He's your son."

"He's mine to kill if I choose," Mr. Williams hissed, and finally his face showed his true inner self, his eyes dark and squinting beneath thick eyebrows, his mouth twisted into a snarl. Gone was the polished politician.

I wished I had a camera so everyone else could see him like this.

"No, he's not," I said. "He's had enough of you. And so have I. You've lost. Quit while you're ahead."

Snarling, Mr. Williams tried to hit us with more energy orbs.

But this time he'd bitten off more than he could chew. As

I shielded both of us, Dylan sat up halfway and threw orbs back at his father, knocking him off his feet.

Dylan rolled the rest of the way up and threw a hail of orbs at his father now, a roar of anger and fear and heartache clawing out of his throat the entire time.

Mr. Williams tried to hit his son again with energy, but he couldn't get through my shield.

Then I switched to throwing my own set of orbs at the man. When they hit, he let out an *oomph*. Then his head fell back to the ground and his eyes closed.

I hesitated then walked over and checked for a pulse.

Savannah would be proud. Mr. Williams would live to see an official Clann hearing.

Even as I crouched over him, his eyelids flicked up, his eyes rolling around as if to reorient himself.

When those eyes found my face, they locked onto mine, and in their hatred-filled depths I saw again all the reasons why this man should die. I saw the way he'd smiled at my mother's empty shell of a body lying on the floor. And how he'd smiled tonight at me even while holding Savannah's best friends hostage for no reason other than that he could.

If ever a man deserved to die, it was this one.

My hand reached out to close around his throat, squeezing tighter and tighter until I could feel his pulse leaping in desperation beneath my grip. It would be so easy to simply twist my wrist and end him forever. No one would ever need to fear him again.

"Do it," he croaked, his eyes narrowing as he smiled up at me. "Do what you were made to do, killer."

I deserved this right to end him. He'd killed my mother, helped the vampire who'd killed my father, nearly succeeded in killing my sister. Killing him would be justice for all that I had lost.

"Do it, Tristan," Dylan muttered, reminding me that I wasn't alone here. "Make him pay for everyone he's ever hurt."

Dylan deserved justice, too, for all the years of abuse he'd endured at this monster's hands.

I looked around us at the Circle, still filled with Mr. Williams's loyal followers, each white-haired descendant just as bent on killing anyone who stood in their way as their leader had been. Mr. Williams had created this scene of destruction and death with his hatred and desperate need for power. How many lives had he hurt or ended indirectly by starting this war?

I wasn't the only one who deserved the right to end Mr. Williams's life. We'd all lost because of him. Was any one of our losses greater or more valuable than another's?

"You monster!" Mr. Williams snarled, his voice stronger now that my hand had relaxed slightly at his throat. "You can't even manage to do this right, can you? This is why the Colemans never deserved to lead. You don't have the guts to do what has to be done."

Be still, I thought, pushing out the willpower with it, staring at him until the spell hit him and he froze.

"You're right, Mr. Williams. I am a Coleman. And I may be a vampire, too. But that doesn't make me a monster." I stared down at the worthless waste of a life now lying helpless at my feet, hearing again everything Savannah had tried so hard to tell me, and finally, truly understanding. "What makes us monsters are the choices we make. And that makes *you* the monster, not me. I'm a Coleman, and there's a reason my family's led this Clann for four generations. We're not more powerful than you. We're just better people because we have the guts to make the right choices, even if they're not the easy ones. Killing you right now would be easy, and it might feel good for a while. But it would also be something *you* would do, because you're so messed up by hatred and fear that you can't even think or see straight anymore. I choose not to let hatred and fear twist me into something I'm not. I'm not going to kill you and let you turn me into someone like you."

"Tristan, he deserves to die," Mac said. At some point he'd found his way across the clearing to join us. "For my parents. For yours. For everyone he's hurt."

"Yeah, he does deserve to die." I stood up. "But not at my hands, or Dylan's, or even yours. Everyone in the Clann has been hurt by his hatred. Everyone has equal right to decide his punishment."

I looked around at the Circle. There were a few of Mr. Williams's diehard loyalists gathered at the base of a large pine at the edge of the clearing trying to fight their way out. But the descendants and Keepers surrounding them looked equally determined not to allow their freedom. Speaking of people who could handle themselves...

I looked around for Savannah, shocked to realize I hadn't been worried about her at all for a change. After everything she'd been through without me around to protect her, apparently I'd learned to trust her skills. She was every bit as strong and smart and fast as me, maybe even smarter since she'd figured out the whole slippery slope of choice thing way before I did. Knowing her, she'd probably taken out half the loyalists here plus already freed her friends and—

"Tristan, look out!" Dylan shouted from behind me.

I turned in time to see Mr. Williams sit up and thrust his hands, palms-out, in my direction...and a huge red orb burst out of Mac's hands. The orb slammed into Mr. Williams's chest, knocking him back to the ground so hard his body actually bounced twice.

"He was going to kill you!" Mac whispered, his eyes round with horror as he stared at Mr. Williams. "His mind was wide-open. He didn't even care if I heard him think it."

I checked Mr. Williams's mind. But this time there was no invisible wall shielding his thoughts from the world around him. There was no thought at all, in fact.

He was dead.

Just to be sure, I checked his neck for a pulse. Nothing, not even a faint stutter out of rhythm.

I stood up, walked over to Mac and stared at him. When we'd found him earlier tonight, I'd thought of him as a kid. But I was wrong. It wasn't our age that determined whether we were kids or adults. It was what each of us went through, the terrors and trials we faced and survived, that made us grow up slower or, in Mac's and my cases, faster.

And Mac had definitely become a man tonight. A man who had just saved my life.

I held out my hand.

He glanced at it with a frown, not understanding at first. Finally his eyes widened and he reached out to shake it.

"Thanks, Griffin," I said. "Thanks for having my back."

He nodded.

Then I heard Savannah's scream.

A blur of red hair caught my eye. Then Savannah reappeared hunched over a body on the ground.

Her mother.

Cursing, I ran to her, kneeling at her side.

"Mom!" she kept crying out over and over, cradling her mother's head, rocking back and forth. Her face was dry, her eyes wild and round but slate-gray, her fangs nowhere to be seen.

A memory of seeing her like this before, with her Nanna, hit me hard enough to knock me to my knees. I reached past her, trying to find her mother's pulse. Nothing. I reached out with my mind, blocking out the world around us, seeking her mother's thoughts. Though I'd never had trouble hearing Ms. Evans's every thought before, this time I couldn't hear her at all.

Mr. Colbert appeared at the edge of the clearing, maybe having heard his daughter's scream. He saw us gathered on the ground, blurred over, then froze before crumpling to his knees at his ex-wife's other side, grabbing her arm and gently tapping her cheek. "Joan, honey. Do not do this to me. Joan!"

The scent of blood hit me hard and fast, swamping my nose as Savannah ripped into her own wrist with her teeth then thrust that wrist against her mother's mouth. "Come on, Mom. You've got to drink."

But the blood only spilled out of the corners of Ms. Evans's mouth.

"It's too late," I whispered.

"No!" Savannah pressed her palms to the ground.

I grabbed one wrist. "What are you doing?"

"I'm going to over-ground so I can cross to the other side and bring her back."

"Are you insane?" I stared at her, hoping to see some hint of reality return to Savannah's eyes.

"I know what I'm doing. I've crossed over before and come back."

"You're talking about killing yourself!" I wouldn't let her do it. I didn't care how much it hurt her to lose her mother. I couldn't let her do this.

"I'll be fine. Let me go."

"No." I looked at Mr. Colbert, hoping he'd supply some backup against his daughter and help me make her see reason. But he only sobbed and rocked his dead ex-wife, his mind shut down to anything beyond the breaking of his heart.

"You've got to let her go," I told Savannah.

She jerked her wrist free. "I'm doing this, Tristan. Whether you like it or not."

I stared at her, thinking fast. Short of knocking her out, I had no idea how to stop her, magical or otherwise. "I can't stop you, can I?"

She shook her head, her mouth a thin line. "Just hold me till I get back." She pressed her palms to the ground, hesitated, then reached up with one hand and grabbed the back of my neck, pulling me to her for a fierce kiss that ended too soon. "I will come back to you. I promise."

Her hand dropped to press against the ground one more time. Then she closed her eyes and a shock wave of energy burst out of her and into the ground so hard it actually rolled the earth in a wave that rippled out to knock everyone still standing off their feet.

The life fled out of Savannah, and her empty shell of a body began to fall.

I caught her, letting her weight take us both to the ground, where I sat and held her against me, making sure her palms kept touching the ground so she could draw enough energy to come back.

And then I prayed like I never had before to a God I wasn't even sure still heard vamps.

CHAPTER 31

SAVANNAH

The sounds of descendants and Keepers battling Mr. Williams's loyalists faded away, only to be replaced by the voices of two angry women deep into an argument.

My soul rose out of the shell of my body, the two parts that made me who I was staying tethered by a thin silver cord that stretched between my soul's navel and my body's. Here in the between world, the Circle was peaceful and quiet, the sounds of all the living muffled as if heard underwater.

I looked around and spotted my mother's soul hovering several yards away from her body, the silver cord that connected them thinned out almost to the point of breaking.

The only thing apparently stopping her from continuing on to the other side was Nanna's spirit, who had gotten right into her daughter's soul's face and was jabbing a finger at her. Mom's soul flinched every time the tip of Nanna's finger poked through her.

"Mom!" I cried out as I pushed my soul to float over to them. Since my soul had no real physical presence, my feet had nothing to make contact with in order to make walking effective. It must have been the will that counted toward actually moving around.

"I am trying to talk some sense into my daughter," Nanna hissed.

"Mom, you can't go yet."

"That's what I've been trying to tell her. Joan, stop being so hardheaded and listen to me for a change. I'm not kidding around here. Take two more steps and that thing's gonna break." She waved a hand at the overstretched cord between Mom's body and her soul. "Once it breaks, there's no going back."

Mom scowled. "That's what I'm trying to tell you. I don't want to go back!"

"Mom, you can't mean that," I whispered as too much emotion filled my chest. If I had been in my physical body, it would have been hard to breathe.

Mom turned to me with a sad smile. "I do, honey. I'm tired of living."

Nanna growled out a sigh. "Everyone gets tired of living at some point. But I did not raise you to be a quitter. And that's exactly what you're trying to do here...you're trying to give up on life just because it's a little hard right now."

"A *little* hard?" Mom turned to her mother with wide eyes that quickly narrowed. "I've lost everything! My job, my dog, my home. My life's a freaking country song."

"You're going to get your life back now," I said. "The war's over. We won."

"So what if we won for now? The Clann and the vamps

hate each other too much for peace to really last. Vampires and descendants will never be able to safely live together for long."

"Oh, so that's what this is about," Nanna said, her chin lifting. "You're giving up because of a little heartbreak and lost love."

Mom closed her eyes and shook her head, her shoulders slumping as if the weight of the world had just been dropped onto her back. "I'm so tired, Mom. I just want to be done with it all. Can't you see? It is time for me to go. What do I have to go back for? A failed marriage? My stellar parenting of my daughter?"

"Mom, we all make mistakes," I said. "Look at how my sneaking around with Tristan ended up costing Nanna her life."

"Oh, child," Nanna murmured, her eyes soft with love. "You know I forgave you for that a long time ago."

I shrugged one shoulder. "Still, it was a choice with some huge consequences for others, consequences I didn't even take the time to consider, and I should have. And I'm sorry."

Mom's eyebrows pinched together as she looked from me to Nanna and back. "That was one mistake, Savannah. I've made hundreds as your mother. I've been a horrible parent, and everyone knows it. I practically walked out on my own daughter just when you needed me the most."

"No, you tried to save me," I said. "If you'd been around, it might have triggered the bloodlust—"

"That's a copout and we all know it. You were fine around your Nanna, weren't you?" Mom took a deep breath. "The truth is, I was running away from my past, from my thousand and one screw-ups. I've been a coward, and you deserve a lot better. If not for your father—"

"He helped me with the vamp stuff, sure," I said. "But what does he know about being a girl or a teen or dating or boys? You were the one who helped me with all of that."

"From a hundred miles away while constantly on the road?"

"Sure. I always knew you were only a phone call away. And besides, when you left, you didn't just walk away. You made sure to leave me with the best person who could help me at the time." I smiled at Nanna, who gave me a small smile in return. "I always knew you loved me, Mom. And that's way more than a lot of people can say about even parents who are around all the time. What's more important... having a parent be physically there but who never bothers to say 'I love you' to their kid? Or one who always takes time to listen, really listen, and always makes sure I know I'm loved?"

Mom slowly shook her head. "Even still, no child should have to call or text her mother just to talk to her every day. I should have been there for you, but I wasn't."

"Fine, so you ran away," Nanna snapped. "So why don't you do something new and try *not* running away for a change? Or are you so selfish that you don't even care about the heartbreak you'd be leaving behind?"

Mom winced and looked away. "It's too late. I can't change anything I've done. I deserve to lose everything."

I had to speak up on that one. "Mom, what are you talking about? You haven't lost me."

"Yes, I have. You've got your dad and Tristan now. Neither will ever get sick or old and die on you. What more do you need? Certainly not a pathetic excuse for a mother like me who's never around and can't even help you learn to do magic."

"I don't want you around to help me with the magic," I said. "I can figure that out on my own, and Tristan can help. I want you there to be my mom, because I love you."

"I don't think you've quite lost your love, either." Nanna pointedly looked past us at something.

We all turned and looked at Dad as he continued to rock Mom's body, his eyes closed, tears slipping down his cheeks. He'd never looked less like a vampire or more like a regular guy.

Mom's eyes rounded. "But…how could he possibly still love me when I drive him nuts all the time? We fight constantly. And there's the whole bloodlust problem. Not to mention the tiny fact that I'm getting older and more wrinkly and gray-haired by the second. Pretty soon I'll look old enough to be his grandmother. And look at *him*. He could have anyone!"

"You two only argue so much because of that infernal pride of yours," Nanna said. "Girl, how many times do I have to tell you you've got to let it go? What does it matter who pays for what as long as you're together?"

Mom sighed. "Well, maybe I could ease up about some of that stuff. But he just drives me so insane all the time! Why can't he ever, just once, let me pay for something?"

I thought about what Tristan said earlier tonight. "You know, maybe he can't help it. Maybe it was just how he was raised. Maybe somebody taught him that being a real man meant taking care of the woman he loved in every way possible, including financially."

One of Mom's eyebrows arched. "That is so incredibly old-fashioned."

"True." I fought a smile. "But it also comes from a place of love."

"Hmm."

I couldn't tell whether the sound she made was a thoughtful one or an irritated, dismissive one. She kept staring and frowning at Dad, rocking her empty body, and on this side of the afterlife I had no ability to read her mind.

She also wasn't making any move to get back into her body and return to life.

I blew out a long, slow breath. Maybe Dad was right. Was I being selfish by begging my mother to live when she didn't want to? "You know what? If you really don't want to come back, then—" I took a deep breath and made myself say it "—then maybe you shouldn't."

"What?" Nanna croaked.

"No. We're being selfish, Nanna. Mom should make up her own mind. It's her life and her choice to make, not ours. If Dad and I aren't good enough reasons for her to want to live, if she'll be happier here than back there, then we should love her enough to let her go."

Mom's eyes widened as she stared at me.

I walked over to my mother. "I wish I could at least hug you goodbye." I thought of all the things I would miss about her...the smell of her Wind Song perfume and her frizzy blond curls tickling my face when we hugged, the sound of her voice as she rambled on about her day, the way she could make me laugh just by telling me some workplace gossip. "You do what you think is right for you, and I'll love you either way, okay?"

Then I made myself turn and walk back to my body, carefully sitting down into it.

Just as I started to lie back, Mom sighed. "When did she get so dang grown up on us?"

Nanna just chuckled.

"All right, I'm coming back with you." Mom started to hug her mother goodbye, but her arms passed right through her. She gave Nanna a rueful smile. "See you later?"

"In your dreams, kiddo."

I smiled, knowing Nanna meant that literally since she'd shown up in Mom's dreams before to boss her around.

Mom walked over to her body. "So I just sit down in it?"

"Yep," I said. "It's easy. Just sit down in your body, then lay back and relax and when you wake up you'll be alive again."

"As easy as dying," Nanna joked.

Mom sat down in her body and frowned. "It feels weird. Kind of...tingly." She started to lie back, then hesitated and her face lit up with a huge grin. "Hey, at least I get my dog and my job and my house back to myself now, right? It'll be like playing a country song backward!"

"Right," I said with a laugh that came from more than a little relief. Everything would be fine now. Maybe even better than fine.

Mom lay back in her body. Then her real eyes fluttered open on the other side. Dad froze, whispered her name, then hugged her even harder.

And that's when I remembered what I'd forgotten to warn Mom about. "Uh-oh."

"You didn't tell her you gave her your blood, did you?" Nanna snickered. "Well, there's more than one way to die as a vampire."

I sighed. "She's going to stake me."

"Maybe when she gets her memory back. But that'll be months from now. In the meantime, why don't you leave that to me and your dad?"

"Thanks, Nanna." When it came to dealing with the Evans women's temper, I could use all the help I could get.

Then I lay back in my body and closed my eyes.

When I woke up, Tristan was holding me so hard he would have crushed me if I'd been human. As it was, I still couldn't move my arms enough to touch his face. So I settled for whispering his name, not wanting to startle him.

Those long golden-tipped eyelashes rose. He looked down at me with the most haunted eyes I'd ever seen. Then he stared at me as if afraid to blink. "You're back?"

I nodded.

"Thank God."

"Don't forget Nanna, too."

"Huh?" He shook his head. "Never mind. Just swear to me you will never do that to me again." Then he pulled me up to him for a lip-crushing kiss that was more about sharing our relief to be together and alive than for the joy of the actual kiss itself. It was only minutes later when he finally relaxed and his lips softened against mine that I truly forgot everything else.

Till Dad cleared his throat. "Ah, Savannah? You did not give your mother your blood, did you? She...smells and sounds and feels decidedly...not human."

His voice was more than a little strained.

I sat up and twisted around to look at him and Mom. She was looking all around her with the bright-eyed wonder of a small child. Oh, boy. I knew that empty-eyed look all too well.

I cleared my throat. "I, um, might have tried to turn her in order to save her."

Dad groaned. "You could not have picked a worse fledgling to make. She will be all but impossible to train. Just look at her. She is already feeling the beginnings of the bloodlust. We will be lucky if we do not wind up on that Arkansas mountain for another year!" Then he looked at his ex-wife and a slow smile spread across his face.

I didn't have to read his mind to know what he was thinking. "I don't suppose you'd be willing to train her for me? You know, so I could maybe actually finish high school sometime this century?"

Tristan nudged me. *She doesn't remember all the fights they've had.*

Nope, I told him, watching as my mother turned to look at Dad and her eyes lit up even more with the beginnings of a shy smile.

But you know her memory will eventually come back. And when it does…

I sighed. "When she gets her memory back, she's going to kill both of us."

Dad's smile instantly became an openmouthed look of shock. "I would never take advantage of your mother in the absence of her memory. I would simply endeavor to keep her safe and away from all humans and train her just as I helped you train Tristan. I am sure by the time her memory returns, she will feel nothing but love and gratitude toward both of us."

Oh, yeah. He was headed for heartbreak city. "Fine. But

no romantic stuff at all until she gets her memory back. Or else."

"Agreed." He murmured the word as he stared into Mom's eyes.

I couldn't stand it. I had to warn him. "Dad, when she does get her memory back...what if she breaks your heart again? What if you two just aren't meant to be together, and it has nothing to do with your being from enemy races?"

Dad smiled, and I'd never seen his face light up like that. "Have you not figured it out yet? Love is always worth the risk."

Suddenly the Circle's relative quiet was pierced by the distant wailing of a baby.

"What the..." Tristan jumped and pressed his hands to the ground as if ready to leap to his feet.

I grabbed his wrist to stop him and smiled. "That would be your nephew."

His eyes widened even further. "Emily went into labor? I thought she said it was false labor pains earlier."

"Apparently not," Dad murmured with a smile. "We took her to the house for the delivery. Dr. Faulkner has been assisting her."

We all sat very still, listening, waiting to hear if Emily was okay, as well.

Finally she made a strange sound that was half sobbing and half laughter, followed by the strangest sound of all coming from her...soft cooing to her newborn child.

CHAPTER 32

ONE MONTH LATER

Emily stood by the throne, Samuel Tristan Coleman happily gurgling in one arm as she used her free hand to drop her vote into the stone chalice Dr. Faulkner was holding. He smiled at her and then at the gathering of Clann who had filled the Circle. Thanks to a few well-placed spells, what would have been a stifling meeting impossible for most humans to withstand in the heat of East Texas in August was made bearable by the artificial breeze that blew continually over us.

Tristan and I stood at the edge of the clearing along with the Keepers and Anne. Our presence would have been unusual even for a normal Clann gathering. But for this event, Emily would not hear of our being left out. And as Tristan liked to say, she got her way as usual.

I just wished Carrie and Michelle could have been here. But after the dust had settled a month ago from all the fighting in the Circle, they had both decided they'd rather not know a thing about vamps or what the Clann really did. Carrie's decision I sort of understood. She liked her world to be orderly and tidy and easy for her to categorize. Vampires and witches at war in her own hometown was anything but neat and tidy. But Michelle's decision completely surprised me. I'd always thought she lived for the latest gossip, and this was the biggest secret she'd ever heard.

"It's too big to keep is the problem!" she'd said, her big eyes full of fear. "I just know I'll blurt it out at school someday, and then my butt'll be toast for sure."

So Tristan and I had reluctantly abided by their decisions, and with Emily's guidance, we'd carefully erased their memories of the entire night in the Circle using a combination of the gaze daze and a little Clann spelling for added measure. Which left only Anne and Ron to hang out with this evening, since Mac was still too young to vote. At least he was happy with the new Clann couple Emily had found for him to live with.

Tapping on the stone chalice made me jump a little.

You nodding off over there? Tristan teased.

I threw him a wry smile. *No. Just mentally drifting off a bit. Well, wake up, because this is the good part!*

While holding the voting chalice, Dr. Faulkner muttered something, and a wave of goose bumps and pinpricks broke out over my bare arms and neck. Then he raised the chalice in the air.

"It is official. Emily Coleman, you are our new—and, I have the pleasure of adding, our first officially elected female—Clann leader!"

Tristan and I joined the crowd's cheers and clapping as

Emily slowly nodded her head in acceptance. Then she turned to smile at the most unusual knot of guests gathered directly before the throne...Caravass and his circle of bodyguards, whom she had personally invited and insisted on having present today. Caravass had reportedly been thrilled with the suggestion and only too happy to show his support, which was further evidenced by his joyous smile and clapping now.

From his thoughts, I gathered that a good part of his happiness came from relief that the war was truly over and he and the surviving council members could finally breathe easier again.

I tried not to laugh at how his every move made nearby descendants jump a little before they reminded themselves of all the descendants surrounding him. Apparently the new peace treaty wasn't quite enough reassurance against renewed violence yet. That would come only with time and healing and many years of peace.

Emily stepped around the side of the stone throne then took her new seat, and all the descendants present bowed down to one knee before her. Anne bowed, too, though I had to grab her hand and tug her down with us. As for Caravass and his bodyguards, they were momentarily stymied as to what was the right strategy. If they bowed down on one knee, would it look as if the leader of the vampires was making himself subordinate to the leader of the Clann?

They settled for deeply bowing their heads in respect.

After everyone rose again, Emily said, "Thank you. I will endeavor to follow in my father's footsteps and lead this Clann to the best of my abilities. And now, as my first act as Clann leader..."

She works fast, Tristan thought with a tiny eye roll.

I struggled not to laugh out loud.

"I hereby request that a vote be taken to reinstate Tristan Coleman, Savannah Colbert and her mother, Joan Evans, if she wishes, back into the Clann as full descendants with all rights and privileges."

I turned and stared at Tristan. *Did you know she was going to—*

No, I had no clue.

Do we get a vote in this?

Tristan's mouth twitched. *Since we're not actually members of the Clann, I don't think we get a say.*

"All in favor, please raise your hand." Emily scowled at the descendants before her as if daring anyone to be so stupid as to thwart their new ruler on her very first day as leader by not raising their hand.

It took a few seconds, but eventually every adult descendant present raised a hand.

Emily smiled again. "Great! And now that our first order of business is out of the way, we can move on to the second."

"Are we going to be here all night?" Anne muttered.

Ron shushed her.

"I hereby nominate, in full conjunction with Caravass, council leader of the vampires…"

Caravass turned to smile at us.

Emily continued. "…that Tristan Coleman and Savannah Colbert from this day forward faithfully serve both the Clann and the council equally as peace ambassadors. As such, they will use their unique abilities to ensure good and honest communication between our peoples at all times so that we may attempt to avoid any repeats of the mistakes of our past."

Murmurs rose up within the ranks. Tristan and I froze

and gripped each other's hands so hard it was a wonder our fingers didn't break off.

Emily held out her hands palms-down in a calming gesture. "I understand that it is going to take time for all of us to move past the horrors of our history. Many wrongs have been committed on both sides. But if we do not take active steps toward helping ourselves heal, how are we to move forward together? Tristan and Savannah, you both represent the best of both our worlds, vampire and Clann united. With your abilities to read both Clann and vampire minds, as well as your vampire speed and strength and Clann abilities to spell-cast, I can't think of any two people more perfectly suited to keeping the peace between our worlds. Will you accept this honorary role?"

She stared at us, letting her mental shield slip enough so we could clearly hear her think, *Don't you two dare make me look like an idiot up here on my first day on the job! Just say yes and thank you. If you find out later you hate the job, we'll work something out. Okay?*

Caravass's smile slipped a little where it met his eyes. He slowly mouthed one word, "Please."

I looked up at Tristan. *This wasn't exactly what we had planned. You're helping Emily rebuild and retool BioMed to make synthetic blood....*

And you're going to be performing with the vamp dance troupe on holidays and after you graduate, Tristan thought.

Then again, it would be a good way to ensure the peace lasts a little longer this time.

One corner of Tristan's mouth tightened. *True. And if you're going to be in Paris so often anyway, wouldn't be too hard to*

stop by a council meeting or two just to check in and make sure ev-
erything's going smoothly.

I nodded. *You'll have to rein in your sister, though. You know*
she'll keep coming up with more duties for us if we let her.

Right. And the last thing I want is for us to become her minions.

I barely managed to swallow down a snort of laughter at
that one. *So we're agreed?*

Yep, I think so.

We turned to face the two leaders and all the hopeful descendants and the human staring at us.

"We accept," we said at the same time.

She smiled, mouthed "Thank you" then stood up. "Well,
then! Now that all the business has been taken care of, who's
ready for a party?"

"Oh, thank the lord," Anne muttered. "I want out of
these shoes ASAP."

"Aw, but they make your ankles look sexy," Ron said.

Anne's cheeks turned pink. She opened her mouth to fire
off some smart-aleck retort, then hesitated and gave him a
quick kiss on the cheek instead.

Ron grinned. "Just for that, I'll take you home to change
right now if you want."

"Home? Who said anything about going home? I left some
sneakers in the truck. I'll be right back." Anne took off
through the woods.

"Wait up, I'll go with you." Ron loped off after her, his
thoughts focused on trying to get another kiss out of her
once they reached her truck, parked in front of the Coleman mansion.

"Not just the *Coleman* mansion anymore," Tristan murmured, slipping an arm around my waist.

I ducked my head and smiled. "Right."

Since Dad was still a little busy in Arkansas with Mom's training, Tristan and I had opted to move into his family home with Emily and baby Samuel. I'd worried that memories of the deaths of his parents and my Nanna would make this place a bad option for us to stay in. But thanks to the years of our dream connecting together, we also had made many good memories there. Emily preferred to stay closer to the Circle now that she was in charge of keeping it safe, which would be harder to do if we all lived in Nanna's old house instead. And by rooming with Emily for a while, at least until graduation, we could help her out with raising little Samuel.

A familiar head of shaggy blond hair moved through the crowd toward the edge of the clearing nearby.

"Dylan!" Tristan called out.

The blond head paused then changed direction as Dylan came over to join us.

"Where you off to in such a rush?" Tristan said. "You're usually the last to leave a party."

Dylan grinned, a hint of pink coloring his cheeks. "Well, I…uh, to tell the truth, I've got a date with Bethany and I don't want to keep her waiting."

"So you really do like her then?" I asked, silently adding for Tristan's benefit, *I told you so.*

Dylan shrugged and ducked his head. "She just really gets me, you know? Anyways, I've got to run. She only seems like a perfect sweetheart till I show up late."

I laughed as he waved over his shoulder at us then took off at a jog.

As the crowd mingled and nibbled at the refreshments

Emily had brought in personally from a catering company, Emily eventually made her way over to us, her baby boy seemingly a permanent attachment to the crook of one arm.

"Thanks for the heads-up on the membership reinstatement and peace ambassadorships," Tristan muttered, leaning sideways to nudge his sister's free side with an elbow.

She laughed. "I knew you'd never say yes otherwise." At his raised eyebrows, she explained. "Dad always said it's the Clann leader's job to know my people's preferences as much as possible. He also said my job is to try to help you grow. You two need this ambassadorship to make you stay a part of things. Otherwise it'd be way too easy for you to sneak off and never be seen or heard from again."

Mmm, the idea of sneaking off is rather tempting, I thought. *Dylan might have had the right idea today, you know.*

Tristan ducked his head to try to hide his grin.

"The thing is, we do have plans of our own that are going to take up some time, as well," I said as gently as I could. If Emily the pregnant mom-to-be could be a total pain, I had no desire to see what a fit Emily the Clann Leader could pull off.

"I know, I know," Emily said. "Which is why I promise I won't make you do any traveling for your job for at least the first two years."

"No traveling at all?" Tristan asked, both eyebrows raised sky-high.

"Well, maybe a teensy bit. But only during the summer or spring break, or you know, when it fits in with your school and dance schedules…"

Told you so, I thought to Tristan without looking at him. If I dared look at him right now, I might burst out laughing.

Emily paused. "Are you two even listening to me?"

Tristan grinned. "Of course! In fact, we're already doing our jobs and keeping the peace. See? Here's how it works. We love you, sis. Now go away. Your power trip is starting to wear us out. We've got plenty of time to go over all your awesome plans for the Clann, and a newer, stronger peace treaty with the vamps, and whatever else that busy mind of yours comes up with later. For now, why don't you go and enjoy your coming-out party?"

"Are you trying to shoo me away?" Emily gasped. "You can't speak to the Clann leader that way!"

"No, but I sure as heck can talk to my annoying sister like that." His grin stretched wider. "By the way, the whole mother thing looks good on you."

She tilted her head to look down at the baby in her arms. A soft smile slowly spread across her face. "I can't believe it's not way harder. But he's so easy to love! And to think I was scared to death I couldn't do this." Sighing happily, she wandered off to mingle with her guests and was quickly enveloped in descendants who wanted to wish her well or put in their first requests for help from their new leader.

"See? Dealing with her will be no sweat. As for your mother, however..." Tristan gave a pointed look over my head in warning.

I turned around to see Mom and Dad walking toward us, holding hands. Mom looked different. Her once weathered and tanned skin looked smooth, and her usually frizzy blond hair gleamed like a gilded picture frame around eyes that, once a mix of green and brown like the East Texas forests, now shone silver like Dad's eyes. Like mine and Tristan's.

My mouth dropped open. "Dad, Mom! What are you two doing back already? We figured it would be months—"

"I know. And it is a bit of a risk. But your mother seems to be doing so well that I thought we would stop by for just a tiny test to see how she handles it."

I leaned in and muttered, "A tiny test? Are you crazy? This clearing is filled with descendants!"

I know, but I could almost swear she's already got her memory back! He looked at me and clearly thought.

Squinting, I studied Mom as she rattled on about the beauty of the Arkansas mountains to Tristan. There was something a bit...off about her, and not just because she was a vamp now. "Hmm, I see your point." In a normal volume, I said, "So are you two enjoying your vacation getaway?"

"Oh, it's been wonderful!" Mom gushed to me, and there was nothing odd about the light in her eyes now. "Your father has been spoiling me rotten. We feed anytime I get the least bit hungry, and whenever I get bored hanging out at the cabin practicing tai chi, he takes me to some of the local shops to look around."

I glanced at Dad, my eyebrows shooting up. He was already taking her around humans, too?

He shrugged his shoulders. "She handles it all very well for a fledgling. And besides, I had to come to this momentous occasion today to tell Emily congratulations on securing the Clann leadership position. Joan, will you be okay here with our daughter while I speak with the Clann's new leader?"

Mom laughed and waved a hand. "Of course, darling!"

She watched him walk away then sighed. "Poor man. He doesn't know what to think, does he?"

I turned to look at my mother in shock. "You already have your memory back, don't you?"

She nodded with a huge, naughty grin. "Turns out I'm a thousand times better as a vamp than a descendant! My memory returned a couple of weeks ago. Personally I figure it's because I wasn't very Clann to start with, so it wasn't like the vamp blood had a whole lot to turn in the first place."

I gasped. "Mother! Why don't you tell him?"

"Because he's finally letting me pay for my own things now! But since *I* can read his mind and finally make some sense out of the things he does, I know he's only doing it to try to keep me happy. The second he learns I have my memory back, we'll be right back to arguing over who picks up the tab for everything. And I am so enjoying having both my husband and my own financial freedom at the same time."

Ugh. I looked at Tristan for help. His eyes widened as he gave a tiny shake of his head. *Nuh-uh,* he thought. *I'm staying way out of this one.*

Thanks a lot, I told him silently.

Smart choice, Mom thought with a dark grin.

Tristan and I both froze. Oh, crap. She could read our minds now.

Her grin stretched as wide as the Cheshire Cat's.

I sighed. "Mom, you have to tell him you have your memory back."

She blew out a noisy breath through pursed lips. "I know. And I will. I promise. Just one more month? It's been so nice just to be with him without the constant arguments. And keeping your lips zipped about it for one more itty bitty month would be the least you could do to make up for *turn-*

ing me without asking me first." She sharply enunciated the last six words, making me flinch.

"But you're lying to him," I said through gritted teeth. "And you can't sustain a relationship built on lies."

Dad was headed back our way.

Mom stared at me through squinted eyes. "And just when the heck did you get so grown up on me again?"

It was hard not to smile at that one, but I gave it my best try. "Promise me you'll tell him within one month, or else I'll tell him myself."

"Fine. I promise. Besides, I'm running out of funds on all my credit cards anyway." When Dad returned, Mom looped her arm through his and rested her cheek against his shoulder. "This party's getting a little boring, hon. How about we go find somewhere to shop? It'll be my treat. I think I have a little more left on that purple card of mine."

Dad opened his mouth to argue then sighed and smiled at her. "Anything you wish, dear. It is your money, after all." He threw me a helpless look. "I suppose we will see you two soon for a visit?"

I looked Mom in the eye. "Oh, yeah. We'll be checking in on you two real soon. No more than a month from now, tops."

Remember, you promised, I thought to her.

I know, I know, she answered just as silently. *Party pooper.*

"That sounds good," Dad said. Then he and Mom walked away through the woods, slowly picking their way over mounds of fallen pine needles.

When I thought they were far enough away that they couldn't hear us, I groaned and turned toward Tristan. "Those two are unbelievable."

"Mmm, well, at least they seem happy. And if dealing with your parents is the toughest thing we face, I think we're going to be just fine."

"*We?* What's this we? Five seconds ago you were all 'they're your parents, not mine!'" I laughed, rising up on tiptoe and wrapping my arms around his neck as he slipped his around my waist.

Tristan grinned. "Just promise me we won't be like them, and I can happily live out eternity with you."

Feeling silly, I held up a pinky like we used to do when we were little kids. "Pinky swear?"

Chuckling, he hooked his pinky with mine. "Always."

And then we sealed the deal with a kiss.

★ ★ ★ ★ ★

ACKNOWLEDGMENTS

A huge thank-you goes out to everyone who made this series possible:

First and foremost to Natashya Wilson. Your editing is absolutely spot-on. You've caught a thousand things I would have missed, and offered a million and one ways to make my writing read so much better. You've made this series what it is, and I can't thank you enough for your tireless work and belief in this series and these characters. Thank you for loving Tristan and Savannah even more than I do!

Last but definitely not least, I want to thank everyone at Harlequin who has contributed their wonderful skills, talents and energy toward making this series as beautiful and error-free as possible:

Art...Erin Craig (art director for *Crave* and *Covet*), Gigi Lau (art director for *Consume*), Amy Wetton (designer for The Clann eries), Margie Miller (creative director for TEEN), Nikki Omerod (photographer for *Consume*).

Managing editors Kristin Errico and Ingrid Dolan.

Production controller Jean Delaney.

Marketing…Amy Jones, Mary Sheldon, Midya Tsoy, Subeena Ishaq Nigro, Shana Mongroo.

Digital Marketing Team…Larissa Walker, Fiona Cunningham, Nicki Kommit, Jayne Hoogenberk, Amy Wilkins, Siobhan Clayton.

Publicity…Lisa Wray, Tiffany Shiu, Michelle Renaud.

And a big thanks to all the copy editors, typesetters and proofreaders who touched the series and made it perfect!

The CONSUME Playlist

CHAPTER 1
"Safe and Sound" by Taylor Swift and The Civil Wars

CHAPTERS 2 & 3
"Radioactive" by Imagine Dragons

CHAPTER 4
"Demons" by Imagine Dragons

CHAPTER 5
"Catch My Breath" by Alex Goot and Against the Current

CHAPTER 6
"Famous Last Words" by My Chemical Romance

CHAPTER 7
"Make You Feel My Love" by Trisha Yearwood

CHAPTERS 8 & 9
"I Don't Care" by Adam Gontier and Apocalyptica

CHAPTER 10
"No One Moves, No One Gets Hurt" by Bedouin Soundclash
"The Son Never Shines (On Closed Doors)"
by Flogging Molly

CHAPTER 11
"Say (All I Need)" by OneRepublic

CHAPTER 12
"Hurricane" by 30 Seconds to Mars

CHAPTER 13
"Stay" by Rihanna and Mikky Ekko

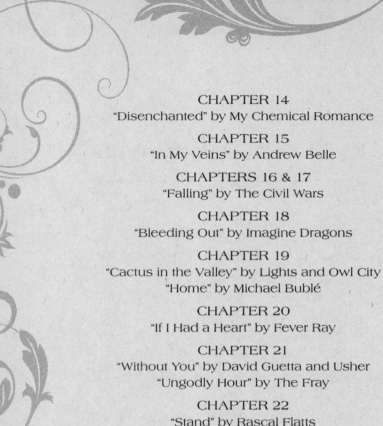

CHAPTER 31
"When You Come Back to Me Again" by Garth Brooks

CHAPTER 32
"Kings and Queens" by 30 Seconds to Mars
"Feel Again" by OneRepublic

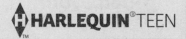

THE GODDESS TEST NOVELS

Be sure to look for the Boxed Set coming Oct 2013!

Available wherever books are sold!

A modern saga inspired by the Persephone myth.

Kate Winters's life hasn't been easy. She's battling with the upcoming death of her mother, and only a mysterious stranger called Henry is giving her hope. But he must be crazy, right? Because there is no way the god of the Underworld—Hades himself—is going to choose Kate to take the seven tests that might make her an immortal...and his wife. And even if she passes the tests, is there any hope for happiness with a war brewing between the gods?

Also available:
THE GODDESS HUNT, a digital-only novella.

From one of Harlequin TEEN's edgiest authors,

Katie McGarry

Coming
December 2013!

Available wherever books are sold!

Praise for PUSHING THE LIMITS

"A riveting and emotional ride!"
–*New York Times* bestselling author Simone Elkeles

**"McGarry details the sexy highs,
the devastating lows and the real work it
takes to build true love."**
–Jennifer Echols, author of *Love Story*